The time has come . . .

"You're thinking about going your own way, aren't you," someone else said.

"*Our* way," the Cloudman responded. "I have made it clear many, many times that I don't like my fate being in the hands of . . . others. This is the best opportunity humankind has had in two hundred years. We've got to try sometime. I think now is the time."

Dr. DeGroot stood up once again. "I can see why you didn't want the Ainge here, Mr. Cleddman," he said heatedly. "Without the Engines, the Ainge would have no authority on a human vessel, now, would they?"

"Dr. DeGroot, this isn't about the Ainge," Cleddman said firmly. "This is about powering our own vessels with our own engines, doing our own technical checks to see that all systems are working the way they should be working—and if they *do* blow up in trans-space, then we can examine the engines themselves, if anything's left, to see for ourselves what went wrong."

Holcombe thought he could hear a page of history turning over a massive leaf. Cleddman had suggested nothing less than an act of absolute liberation, an act many human beings—billions of them, in fact—might not want.

Also by Paul Cook

FORTRESS ON THE SUN

THE ENGINES OF DAWN

PAUL COOK

A ROC BOOK

ROC
Published by the Penguin Group
Penguin Putnam Inc., 375 Hudson Street, New York, New York 10014, U.S.A.
Penguin Books Ltd, 27 Wrights Lane, London W8 5TZ, England
Penguin Books Australia Ltd, Ringwood, Victoria, Australia
Penguin Books Canada Ltd, 10 Alcorn Avenue, Toronto, Ontario, Canada M4V 3B2
Penguin Books (N.Z.) Ltd, 182–190 Wairau Road, Auckland 10, New Zealand

Penguin Books Ltd, Registered Offices:
Harmondsworth, Middlesex, England

First published by Roc, an imprint of Dutton NAL,
a member of Penguin Putnam Inc.

Cover art by: Chris Moore

ISBN 0-7394-0170-X

Printed in the United States of America

—For Tom Smith

*and the best years of our lives
at Northern Arizona University
1968–1972*

"Solitudinum factunt et pacem appellant."

—Tacitus,
speaking through a British chieftain
regarding the Pax Romana

1

Twenty-seven-year-old Benjamin Bennett rolled over in his dormitory bed in the middle of the interstellar night thoroughly disgusted with himself. His Bombardier friends had often taunted him about his relationships with various members of the female population at Eos University. "One-Minute Bennett," they called him. No relationship he had ever seemed to last long enough to be memorable, let alone meaningful. Maybe they were right.

"It's not you," Ben told his date, throwing his left arm across his eyes, sunken in despair. "At least I don't *think* it's you. Ix! Who knows what it is?"

"Well, it's something," his date, Jeannie Borland, said.

Ms. Borland was a twenty-five-year-old, platinum blond graduate student in atmospheric chemistry whom Ben had met about a month earlier when Eos University had made its last planetfall. He and his dorm mates—Eos dropouts called the Bombardiers—had gone kiting in the incredibly blue skies of Ala Tule 4 while the other students of the spacegoing university went about their various field trips down on the planet's surface. Ben had met Ms. Borland when he and the Bombardiers rested their wings in the AtChem gondola, lofting in the thermals of a placid mountain range. Ben thought he'd pursue her more aggressively when the university returned to its circuit through the known stars of the Sagittarius Alley.

And *this* was what happened.

Young men might reach their sexual peak at the age of nineteen or so, but it rarely tapered off so quickly. Moreover, Ben was in the best physical condition he had ever known. Though only five feet, ten inches tall, he was broad-shouldered and muscled enough to have won several wrestling scholarships when he was an undergraduate back on Earth. He worked out almost daily and theoretically *should* have been able to rise to the task.

In the semidarkness of the room, Jeannie Borland's illicit cigarette glowed dully. Her unaugmented breasts had that still-youthful pear shape to them, and her deliciously long legs should have inspired him to do *something*. But they didn't.

He sat up, sweeping his long black hair back into a ponytail, which he banded swiftly.

"Maybe it's the Ennui," Borland said, blowing a ghost of smoke to the ceiling.

"*I* think they put saltpeter in the food," Ben said.

Borland tapped an ash to the ashtray on Ben's nightstand. "Saltpeter? What's that?"

"Something they used to put in food to keep horny young boys from . . . getting frisky. Back in the old days."

"I don't believe it," Borland said. "That's barbaric. No one would do that here. Not on Eos."

"The Grays would," Ben remarked. "And they've got the Ainge behind them. After all, we can't have Mom and Dad worrying that Sally and Suzie will come home pregnant."

"No chance of that," Borland said listlessly, the tobacco calming her.

Ben eased out of bed, stepping into the gelatinous puddle his clothing made on the floor. Its response circuits activated at the familiar signature of his feet and his rugby jersey and shorts began flowing up his legs. When they found themselves back in their default configurations, they solidified. Ben's jersey said: RUGBY PLAYERS EAT THEIR DEAD. But only, Ben thought, if their testosterone levels were high. He moved his uncooperative "boys" around to help his underwear settle in.

"Look, this is the first time this has happened to me," Ben said. "You've got to believe me."

"Mmm," Borland said, tugging at her cigarette.

Actually, it had already happened—two weeks ago, with Christine Jensen, a biology student, and two days later, with Lisa Holdaway, an urban-dynamics sociology major who had been a student in one of the science classes he taught.

"It's the Ennui," Ms. Borland said with certainty.

She sat up and crushed out her cigarette. Sensing that the heat had gone out of the cigarette, the nightstand swallowed the ashtray. The room, meanwhile, quickly cleared the air.

Ben thought about the so-called Ennui, said to plague the spread of humanity across the stars. "That's a fairy tale. It's natural for civilization to slow down as it moves out among the stars. The Alley's a big place and we've only been traveling it for two hundred years."

"The pace of life in the Alley *has* slowed down," Borland said, stepping away from the bed. "They've got statistics and actuarial charts that prove it."

Ben refused to believe that the fabled Ennui was responsible for anything, let alone the apparent lack of technological advancements in the last two hundred years. It most certainly was *not* responsible for his temporary impotence. If, indeed, that's what it was.

Ms. Borland stepped into her clothing puddle and Ben watched as her panties and bra slithered to their default configurations. He swallowed hopelessly.

When humans left the confines of the Sol system, in 2098 C.E., to colonize nearby star systems, the sky seemed to be the proverbial limit for scientific advancements of all kinds. Peace had been secured on Earth; the Human Community formed. Faster-than-light technology was around the corner, and there was even the real possibility of medical science extending the life of the average human indefinitely. But sometime early in the twenty-third century, either just before or just after the Enamorati appeared, technological and cultural advancements seemed to lose steam; there seemed to be fewer of them.

But then the Enamorati appeared, and savants everywhere forgot about the Ennui.

Humans had known that alien civilizations had existed since the early twenty-first century, when undecipherable signals came from a civilization in the Magellanic Clouds. These were quite accidental transmissions from a culture, now probably extinct, that was more than 200,000 light-years away. A few years later, a series of small, very intense gamma-ray explosions near Beta Lyra were picked up. Some were patterned, intense, and directional, as if weapons were being used. This was the so-called Beta Lyra Space War, but at 12,000 light-years the H.C. was a mere bystander. When the Enamorati arrived, humans suddenly found themselves involved in very real space travel with very real alien allies.

The Enamorati were a spacegoing culture from a world located 2,300 light-years toward the galactic center of the Milky Way Galaxy, deep inside the Sagittarius Alley. The Enamorati were missionaries from a culture whose planet had been destroyed in an unimaginable ecological disaster. The name "Enamorati" was the Italian equivalent of the attitude the aliens doctrinally shared toward all beings, sentient or otherwise, whom they happened to meet in their travels. The Enamorati had no interference clause, no Prime Directive that kept them out of planetary affairs not their own. Theirs was a mission of a religious bent, obliging them to offer the Human Community two things that it needed desperately: the location of habitable worlds *and* the transportation it took to get them there in a reasonable amount of time.

If the Enamorati had something like a Prime Directive, it came in the form of their staunch refusal to give humans the technical details of their giant Onesci Engines. The mathematics that led to the development of their FTL technology had been given to them ten thousand years ago by their greatest Avatar, a physicist named Onesci Lorii. Humans could use the Onesci Engines as freely as they wished, but they had to allow the Enamorati to handle the technology. This was a matter of deep seriousness for the Enamorati, and humans had to respect it if they wanted to ply the spaces between the stars.

Ben checked the time. "It isn't even fourteen hundred yet. Want to see what's going on in the student commons? Catch an Experience? They're showing *Mayberry Agonistes* tonight. Andy and Barney against the aliens?"

The romantic mood, however, had dissipated along with Ms. Borland's cigarette smoke.

"I don't think so, Ben," Jeannie Borland said, adjusting the chevrons of her collar. "Maybe some other time."

"They say it's the greatest science-fiction movie ever made," Ben said. "Wild Bill Kelso and George Reeves as Superman?"

"Sorry, Ben," Borland said.

At that moment, a gentle knocking came at the door to Ben's room.

"Are you expecting someone?" Borland asked, checking to see if her clothing had cohered properly.

For a moment Ben thought that his room's AI circuits had smelled Jeannie Borland's cigarettes and subsequently tattled to campus security. Tobacco was making a comeback on some of the worlds of the H.C., particularly among young people eager to leave their youth behind and to experience the world of mature grown-ups. Someone unaligned with the Grays—the university administration—or the Ainge religious faction on board the ship had apparently smuggled several different brands of cigarettes onto Eos a few planet stops ago and was now selling them to just about anyone who would buy them. They weren't quite illegal, but their use was definitely frowned upon.

"Not really," Ben said. "Stand back. Open," he then commanded the door.

"Oh!" Jeannie Borland said, gasping.

Standing in the doorway was an Enamorati. He stood there in his gray-green environment suit and had a sad expression on his face—routine for an Enamorati.

This Enamorati was different, however, for cradled in his frail, birdlike arms was the body of a little white polar bear.

"Please forgive me," the being said in slightly inflected English from inside his mist-filled helmet. "I found your pet. It was right here before your door. I am so sorry."

This just wasn't Ben's day.

2

Eos University had a contingent of about a hundred Enamorati—all castes, their mates and progeny included. But beyond the often-seen Kuulo Kuumottoomaa—*kuulo* meant "steward" in their language—the other Enamorati usually remained in their chambers at the aft end of the four-thousand-foot-long ship, where they tended their enormous Engine. The lone Enamorati who stood before Ben's door, however, was not of the Kuulo caste. He was an Avatka, an engineer. And this engineer had a dead bear in his arms.

"It's not mine," Ben said to the Avatka. "I don't have a pet. Sorry."

The Avatka seemed puzzled, but there was no direct way to confirm this from the being's expressionless face. "Forgive me. I assumed that it was yours. It was lying before your door."

Ben looked off to his right. The hall was otherwise empty. "I don't think anyone on this floor has a pet. At least not a polar bear."

Jeannie Borland hovered behind Ben. "I've seen it before. It belongs to a girl in Cowden Hall."

"What's it doing here?" Ben asked.

Jeannie Borland shrugged.

Enamorati generally were no taller than five feet. But bolstered by their environment suits and with servomechanisms amplifying their shoulders and hips, they often seemed bigger than they actually were, and far more intimidating. The Enamorati were aware of this impression on human beings, and they often sought to avoid making it. This Enamorati seemed all too conscious of his sudden impact upon the young humans and tried to modulate his voice.

"I apologize for the disruption then. Could you help me return it to that person?" he asked of Ms. Borland.

She backed away. "I don't really know who owns it. Ben will help you though." She turned quickly to Ben. "Find me at the Museum Club at twenty-one hundred hours tonight, if . . . things change."

She edged past Ben, pulling a specter of tobacco behind her. She fairly raced to the nearest transit portal. A second later, she was gone.

The alien, oblivious to the nuances of human speech and social intercourse, hadn't a clue as to what had just passed between Ben and his erstwhile date. Instead, he gave the small animal to Ben. "If you could do this for me, I would be deeply in your debt," the alien said. "I do not wish to be of further discomfort."

Ben gently took the little bear from the alien's spindly arms, brushing the e-suit as he did. Ben thought he could detect a goblin of the air the Avatka breathed, but this, he knew, was impossible. A leak in the alien's e-suit would mean suffocation for the alien and severe nausea, perhaps even death, for any human nearby.

Though the little bear was definitely dead, there were no signs of blood on the animal's pelt. Moreover, no bones seemed crushed or broken. Strangulation did not seem the cause of the animal's passing, either.

For a fleeting moment Ben thought that the Avatka might have been responsible for killing the little bear, but that, too, seemed unlikely. The Enamorati claimed to have ended their species-wide violent stage about ten thousand years ago. They did not kill; they did not steal; they did not even lie. They lived entirely in the shadow of the religious vision of Onesci Lorii and had been doing so for thousands of years.

A yellowish mist swirled inside the alien's helmet. Pale and desiccated, the Enamorati looked like a race of mummified corpses with very sad eyes.

"Okay," Ben told the alien. "I'll do what I can."

"Thank you," the being said. "And should the animal's owner wish to speak with me about this, they may summon me at any time. I am the Avatka Viroo. Summon me directly or consult the *kuulo* first. I am at your disposal."

The frail being walked down the hallway, passing the transmission portal that Jeannie Borland had taken, and stepped into the connecting passageway. The being apparently wanted to walk back to the Enamorati compound rather than be teleported directly. Some Enamorati were odd that way.

Ben looked around. It was 2:00 P.M. on a Friday afternoon and most of Babbitt Hall was deserted—the students elsewhere in the ship. Most would be either in the field house or at the cinemas or in the Museum Club, starting their weekend early. The students who came from deeply religious Ainge families were probably still in their dorms studying. The polygamous Ainge, descendants from a splinter Mormon colony on the Isle of Ainge on Tau Ceti 4, still kept to clean, drug- and stimulant-free living. With any luck, Ben thought, the young woman who owned the bear would be a daughter of the Ainge and would be in her dorm studying with her suite mates before Friday-night services.

Ben stepped over to the wall. He pressed it with his hand and a luminescent menu for the ship's directory appeared. Any wall in any part of the ship had this feature. Ben tapped the wall menu command for FIND. But find who?

He tapped out the letters for the word PETS, then pressed ENTER. Pets were certainly allowed among the students, support staff, and faculty. But they were also registered with the university.

The word PETS appeared with a listing of two dozen kinds of animals as pets kept on board Eos University.

"A horse?" he said. "Someone has *horse* on the ship?" He would have to look up CYNTHIA JENEY later, just to satisfy his curiosity.

But someone did have a bear, so Ben pressed the glowing word BEAR.

The name that appeared on the wall register read: JULIA WAXWING—COWDEN HALL—ROOM 220. Cowden Hall was the exclusively female dorm in Eos University and it was in the next wing over.

Ben toggled the com/pager at his belt and spoke into the pin at his collar. "ShipCom, open. Ben Bennett paging Julia Waxwing, please," he said. As he recalled, the nearby wing of Cowden Hall was filled with young women mostly studying the physical sciences. Whether Julia Waxwing was an undergraduate or a graduate, he didn't know and the wall menu didn't say.

The automated voice from ShipCom's computer said, *"Sorry. There is no response. There is no forward paging. Do you wish to leave a message?"*

"No," he said. "Com, close."

At that time of the afternoon, Julia Waxwing could be just about anywhere on the ship. University classes were never held on Fridays, but the labs were open, as was the library. Some professors even held office hours on Fridays.

On the other hand, the fact that there was no forward paging meant that regardless of where she was, Julia Waxwing didn't want to be disturbed.

"Now what?" he wondered aloud. He could just leave the bear in front of her dorm room, where she would find it whenever she got back from wherever she was. But that wouldn't do. Just because he'd had a dismal day didn't mean that he had to make it dismal for someone else.

But he *had* to do something.

To Ben's left, just a few yards away, the transit portal suddenly came alive with bluish light. Almost instantly, two figures fell from the portal's assembly ring and came crashing to the floor, sputtering with laughter.

These were friends of his, students he'd bonded with when they met at the beginning of the university's tour three years ago. One was George Clock, a gregarious ash-blond young man who used to be a geography major, specializing in satellite mapping techniques. The other boy was Jim Vees. Vees, a black American, had been an astronomy student until the Ennui—or something—got to him and he dropped out of his studies. He slept a lot, now. These were the Bombardiers. Only Tommy Rosales was missing at the moment.

Since George and Jim had bombed out of their programs, all they seemed to do was play as much as possible. Transit-hopping was one such form of recreation on the ship. Students often transit-hopped in an attempt to get high off the strange euphoric tingle that occurred when a person's molecules were stripped for transport over the ship's network of optical cables, then reassembled again. That's what these two had been doing. Hopping.

Ben stood above the two laughing Bombardiers with the dead bear in his arms. Clock pointed to the animal. "I'll bet this comes with a real *good* story," he said. He hadn't yet seen that the animal was lifeless.

"Believe it or not," Ben said, "an Avatka gave this to me a few moments ago. He found it right here, in front of my door."

"An Avatka? Here in Babbitt Hall?" Clock asked, climbing to his feet.

"Say, that animal looks dead," Jim Vees said. He was slower getting to his feet.

"It is dead," Ben said.

"Did the Avatka kill it?" Vees asked.

"I don't know," Ben said. "He said it was dead when he found it."

"Whose animal is it?" Vees asked, softly caressing its fur.

"It belongs to someone named Julia Waxwing, over in Cowden Hall. She's not answering her com and she's blocked all forward paging. Ever hear of her?"

The two dropouts shrugged and shook their heads.

Clock then said, "You know, she could be in the student commons, in the student media lounge with everybody else."

"Let's transit there," Vees said, always looking for an excuse to transit.

"What's going on at the commons?" Ben asked.

Vees smirked. "President Porter is going to release the contents of the last data bullet we snagged, the one we got right before we jumped into trans-space a couple of weeks ago."

"What's so important about that bullet?" Ben asked.

"Inside sources say that another ship exploded," Clock said. "A really big one this time. The bullet has all the information on it, but the administration's been debating whether to share the fully decompressed data with the rest of us. Maybe they think we'll riot if we get the whole story."

"What ship was it?" Ben asked.

"The *Annette Haven,* outward bound to Ross 154," Clock said. "At least that's the rumor. It's got the Grays worried."

Ben wasn't familiar with the *Annette Haven*. There were so many Engine-driven ships now in service that it was impossible to keep track of them all—freighters, people carriers, cargo vessels of all shapes and sizes, to say nothing of H.C. exploratory craft looking for new worlds to add to the Alley.

However, space travel had always been hazardous and ships every now and then still succumbed to systems failures, or even the unseen microparticle that would core a spaceship in a heartbeat. Disasters in space happened to humans and Enamorati alike.

"Someone at the student newspaper checked the H.C. manifest of ships in our data banks," Clock went on. "The *Haven* was a passenger liner. Big. It could transport at least nine hundred humans at a time. It had an Enamorati crew of twenty. If the Engine blew, there'd be nothing left but a trans-space ripple."

Both the Ainge and the Enamorati happened to believe that trans-space was the actual body of God, and that their duty was to lead pilgrims through it. Most of the H.C. didn't see it that way, but used the Engine-run ships anyway. Trans-space, however, did act like the Old Testament Jehovah and saw fit to remind humans and Enamorati alike of the dangers of space travel. Fiction had made space travel seem effortless, even safe. But the truth was that faster-than-light travel was just as hazardous as slower-than-light travel, and many thousands of lives had been lost in the last two and a half centuries of space travel. Many more would be lost in the future.

"How many Ainge Auditors were on the ship?" Ben asked.

Clock laughed. "The *Haven* probably didn't have more than one or two. It was just a liner."

"Darn the luck," Jim Vees said soberly, his transit high having worn off. "*Our* Auditors should be so lucky."

There was no love lost between Jim Vees and the Ainge. Though Jim had come from Earth, part of his family had converted to the Ainge religion and had spent much of their efforts trying to get the rest of the family to join. The Ainge, because of their relationship to the Enamorati, represented the fastest-growing religion in the H.C. But fifty million followers of Ixion Smith were not enough reason for Jim Vees to check his brain at the door.

"But get this," George Clock continued. "The student newspa-

per says that one of our archaeology professors had a clone-son on
the *Annette Haven.* Somebody famous, but they won't say who.
Maybe Porter is going to tell us."

"An archaeology professor?" Ben asked.

"That's what they're saying," Clock affirmed.

Ben stepped back to the wall and called up the student directory
once again. He came up with JULIA WAXWING, then asked for any
kind of declared MAJOR.

On the screen appeared the word ARCHAEOLOGY.

"Figures," Ben said.

3

Confirmation of the space death of the *Annette Haven* spread quickly through the halls of Eos University. There were no specifics. The data bullet had to travel light—the lighter, the faster. Undoubtedly, when Eos arrived at their next port of call, specifics regarding the passenger manifest and details of the cause of the ship's destruction would be much better known.

To Albert Holcombe, Regents Professor and chair of the archaeology department, the news was particularly devastating. As he had already shared with his colleagues, the clone of his second son, Joshua, a boy named Seth, had been on the *Annette Haven*.

Not that progeny mattered much to Albert Holcombe. The human race now numbered around ten billion, and a billion of those were clones, or the clones of clones. But Seth, at least as Holcombe remembered him, seemed to be the only Holcombe to have any life left in him, any *esprit, joie de vivre*. Even when Seth was a youngster on Tau Ceti 4, he would run circles around the fuddy-duddies of the Holcombe camp. It was no surprise to Holcombe when the boy became a StratoCaster, one of the BronzeAngel sky-runners, in fact. Holcombe always glowed with pride, thinking that a member of his family had pursued a disreputable career and actually made something of himself. But now the boy was dead—nothing more than blasted atoms in the indescribable vacuities of trans-space.

Unfortunately, Eos University was more than one hundred light-years from the Sol system at its farthest point on its four-year Alley tour. Holcombe didn't imagine that either Alex Cleddman—Eos's pilot—or any of the Grays would turn the university around just to

accommodate his grief. In fact, the first thing that Captain Cleddman had announced at the hastily convened University Council
meeting was that the ship would be continuing on its course to its
next port of call. Holcombe merely nodded, accepting the grim
ways of fate.

Cleddman, sometimes called the Cloudman by the students, was
a stocky tree stump of a human being with massive arms, muscular legs, and no neck. He had played Australian-rules football in
college, and the rough and tumble of the game had seemingly
driven his head into his shoulders by several inches. He stood five
feet five, compact and solid like a BennettCorp data bullet.

Cleddman placed a hand on Holcombe's shoulder, meaning to
be sympathetic. "I never thought the *Haven* would go up. I've rid-
den her myself. I thought she was invincible."

"We all think we're invincible every now and then."

"I'll make sure you get the full report on the accident as soon as
it's decompressed at the next port," the Cloudman said.

"I appreciate it," Holcombe said. "Thanks."

A junior member of the mathematics department in the back of
the Council hall stood up and looked around. "Excuse me, Captain. Shouldn't one of the Auditors be present at this meeting? It's
written in the faculty bylaws. It's part of our charter."

"I notified them," Cleddman said, turning. "But they're preparing for Friday-night services."

"Then perhaps we can wait until tomorrow or Monday," said the
faculty member. Like the Ainge priests and the university administration personnel, this young man wore a gray tunic. Holcombe
despised gray. . . .

Captain Cleddman cut off the faculty member a with slight ges-
ture. "I understand your concern, Dr. DeGroot, but we are letting
the Kuulo stand in for High Auditor Nethercott. Will you allow
that?"

Off to the left of the podium stood a hologram projection stage.
A 3D image hovered there, that of the ranking Enamorati, the
Kuulo Kuumottoomaa. The Kuulo was actually somewhere deep
inside the Enamorati compound at the far end of the giant ship. It
was easier for him to be present this way and to speak without
being locked in his e-suit.

The alien looked in the direction of Dr. DeGroot. His Standard English was flawless as he spoke. "I will advise Mr. Nethercott on the content of the meeting as soon as he is available. Our Ainge brothers will be fully informed."

"That's acceptable," Dr. DeGroot said.

Holcombe thought he could detect a note of disappointment in DeGroot's acquiescence. Everybody knew there were factions on the ship that were itching to catch their pilot, who was not of the Ainge religion, in a lapse of protocol. But Cleddman would never give them the chance. Hooray for Cleddman.

The alien's next words, surprisingly, were for him. "Albert Holcombe, we, too, share your loss. Many of our own perished on the HCSV *Annette Haven.* The loss is no less meaningful to us. I can assure you that our engineers will do what they can to make certain that a similar accident doesn't happen to us."

The pilot cleared his throat. "That's why I called this meeting. This is as good a time as any to bring the matter up, but in light of what's just happened to the *Haven,* I think it's time we took up the proposal Physics and Mechanical Engineering made last year when the *Aurora Lee* was lost in transit to Beta Draconis 5."

The Council hall fell absolutely silent. Even Holcombe hadn't expected something like this.

"No offense, Kuulo," the Cloudman said, "but humans feel better if they're working on their own problems instead of waiting around for someone else to deal with them."

"What are you saying, Mr. Cleddman?" someone asked in the rear.

"Physics and Engineering have three different stardrive systems in development that could rival the capacities of an Onesci Engine. The math is there and I've seen the schematics. I think we should consider shifting all of our technical resources over to Physics and Engineering to see if we can get one of the stardrive systems up and running. For real."

The forty-member Council started rumbling and shifting about in their seats. Holcombe noticed that the 3D image of the Kuulo Kuumottoomaa remained impassive.

"You're thinking about going your own way, aren't you," someone else said.

"*Our* way," the Cloudman responded. "I have made it clear many, many times that I don't like my fate being in the hands of . . . others. Sorry, Kuulo. This is the best opportunity humankind has had in two hundred years. We've got to try sometime. I think now is the time."

Dr. DeGroot stood up once again. "I can see why you didn't want the Ainge here, Mr. Cleddman," he said heatedly. "Without the Engines, the Ainge would have no authority on a human vessel, now, would they?"

"Dr. DeGroot, this isn't about the Ainge," Cleddman said firmly. "This is about powering our own vessels with our own engines, doing our own technical checks to see that all systems are working the way they should be working—and if they *do* blow up in transspace, then we can examine the engines themselves, if anything's left, to see for ourselves what went wrong."

Holcombe though he could hear a page of history turning over a massive leaf. Cleddman had suggested nothing less than an act of absolute liberation, an act many human beings—billions of them, in fact—might not want. Those people, members of the vast Ainge Church, would have the most to lose, at least in terms of political influence.

The Enamorati Compact was signed on Tau Ceti 4 in 2205 C.E. by Ixion Smith, president of the Ainge, acting on behalf of the Human Community. It formally bound humans to respect the religious aspects of the Onesci Engines. No ship using Onesci Engines could engage in war; acts of piracy or unprovoked violence were forbidden. But along with the Enamorati engineers, several humans, high priests of the Ainge religion called Auditors, would always accompany the Enamorati. Their relationship to the Enamorati was special and inviolate. Cleddman had just suggested an end to all that.

Humans *did* have a form of trans-light travel, but it was limited, employing molecular compression based on nearly ancient fractal mathematics. So-called bullets of compressed matter, the biggest a millimeter in diameter, could be shot through trans-space to allow for a decent system of real-time communications between worlds light-years apart. The mysteries of trans-space, let alone Engines efficient enough to move people through it, still eluded the best minds of the Human Community.

The Kuulo Kuumottoomaa held up his hand, pleading. "Mr. Cleddman, we believe that our Engines are the best that can be made, especially for a ship this size. And I hope you understand that we have no desire to die in space, either. When we know more of what happened to the *Annette Haven*, we will do everything we can to make certain this great ship will not suffer the same fate."

"I'm sure you will," Cleddman said. "But I would much rather have a greater say over how I live and die than I have now. If the problem *is* with the Engines, then *I* want to know exactly why. But you're never going to share that information with us, and that we can no longer tolerate."

"Speak for yourself, Alex," said Dr. DeGroot.

"I'm speaking for myself and every human being who has died in-transit in the last hundred years. I'm also speaking for you, too. I'm an equal-opportunity pilot. I fly anybody. I just want to arrive in one piece."

"The odds of perishing in-transit are still ten million to one," Dr. DeGroot said. "And I trust the Enamorati *and* their Engines."

A female faculty member from Biochemistry stood up. "Captain, you can't possibly do this without the approval of the university administration and faculty. We're a university first, a spaceship second."

"The Eos University charter allows me to take control of the ship if or when the *vessel* is threatened. I'm not invoking that charter now. But, I *will* if I have to. And if I have to, I want to be ready. This shouldn't disturb the functions of the university. And, yes, I will consult the administration if or when the time comes for us to break away."

"Are we close?" a voice asked from the rear.

"Not yet," Cleddman admitted.

"Then isn't this a little hasty?" someone else asked. "We don't know what happened to the *Annette Haven*. It may have had nothing to do with its Engine."

"This has been brewing for quite some time now," Cleddman told them. "I'm not the only pilot in the H.C. who feels this way.

But as far as I know, we're the only ones in a position to test the advances we've made so far. And, I might add, if we pull this off, Eos University will be unsurpassed in excellence and fame."

"You're doing this because you don't like the Enamorati," Professor DeGroot said.

"No, I'm doing this because I don't like to be blown up," Cleddman said. "And I don't think you do, either. In any event, when the time comes I will run this through all the proper channels and nobody on the Council will be left out of the debate. But as I said earlier, it's my job to maintain our safety. This is definitely *not* a political matter."

"Not yet, it isn't," grumbled Professor DeGroot.

With that, the 3D image of the Kuulo winked out. Evidently, the Kuulo had heard all he wanted to hear; so had a number of others.

The impromptu meeting seemed to be at an end.

4

In the oval arena of Eos University's ShipCom center, Cutter Rausch shook his head at the information on the large monitor screen in front of his subordinates. Rausch was a slender, quiet man in his mid-thirties, and calmness had served him well over the years. Chaos and confusion could be everywhere around him, but rarely was the communications chief moved by outside calamities. However, the news of the *Annette Haven*'s demise had unsettled him deeply. His staff wasn't taking it well either.

Their computer, the greatest in the H.C., had massive databases; every book, every journal known to humankind was in storage, and this included all current information on businesses and corporations that was in the public domain. Rausch had found the most up-to-date crew manifest for the *Haven*.

"Look at that, Cutter," observed his second-in-command, Lisa Benn, a fortyish blonde who was frowning at the screen. "The crew all have Ainge names. Turley, Romney, Mullin . . ."

Rausch's third-in-command, dark-haired Maree Zolezzi, saw something else important. "I don't see any known members of the KMA on the crew. If it's all Ainge, somebody's bound to think the KMA blew the ship up."

Rausch rubbed his chin as he pondered the list of the ill-fated ship's crew. "Maybe," he said. "Maybe not. There are other political factions in the H.C."

"But none are as outspoken as the KMA," Benn said.

Rausch shook his head. "Even the most radical factions of the KMA would never be this brutal. Even if Jack Killian were still alive, he would never have sanctioned something like this, no matter how many Enamorati might have been on board. He'd lose most of his supporters, including me. We're just going to have to wait until the final reports come in. In the meantime, let's just hope the Police Council doesn't go on a witch-hunt."

Maree Zolezzi steepled her fingers before her as she thought at her console. "A ship is going down now about once a year. It just *can't* be mechanical."

Rausch nodded. "Unfortunately, the energies of trans-space absorb unprotected matter, so there's no way to know."

The other members of Rausch's crew included three junior officers and an intern from the university. This intern, Clare Kronmeyer, looked more worried than usual. She said, "If the crew and the passengers were entirely Ainge, don't you think heads are going to roll? I mean, the High Councillor is Ainge and so is most of the H.C. Council. Anybody in the ship corps who isn't Ainge could be out of work."

"Children," Rausch said. "If Mason Hildebrandt and the High Council want to fire us, they can come all the way out here and get us. The one thing I know for sure is that Alex Cleddman isn't going to hand the ship over to anybody for any reason."

A small row of yellow warning lights appeared along the bottom of one of the monitors on the giant wall before them.

"Good," Cutter said, almost relieved. "Something to take our minds off politics for a while."

"Unless the ship's about to blow up," Lisa Benn muttered.

"Wouldn't *that* be interesting," Rausch said.

They set about determining the source for the yellow warning lights.

Ben Bennett walked the halls of Eos University with a dead bear in his arms and trouble on his mind. Friday afternoon and the place seemed unusually quiet. Perhaps there *was* something to the Ennui. Perhaps it was spreading. Perhaps the little bear in his arms had gotten tired and somehow decided to stop living.

So what *was* an Avatka doing in Babbitt Hall?

Ben went door-to-door through Cowden Hall trying to find this Julia Waxwing person. He did come across several of her friends who recognized Jingle Bear and were sad to see that he had died. But they didn't know where Julia was. Jingles, Ben learned, was a polar bear from Earth that had been growth-locked in its infancy and gene-engineered to passivity, and had become a pleasant fixture in the dorm. The girls were deeply saddened.

Ben also learned that the bear was only three years old, so it clearly did not die of old age.

"Now what?" he muttered, alone at the end of the hallway, having run out of Cowden Hall rooms in which to look for Ms. Waxwing. She was probably on a date, having dinner in the student commons perhaps. . . .

His com/pager chimed out just then. "Go ahead," he said to the receiver in his collar chevron.

"Ben, this is Eve Silbarton. How far from a transit portal are you?"

"About ten feet," he said, bear in arms. "Why?"

"Get to Physics as soon as you can!"

Hugging poor Jingle Bear, Ben walked to the end of the corridor and entered the transit portal. "Physics, alpha lab," he said aloud to the portal's computer.

"Access to Physics, alpha lab, is denied," the voice said. *"May I reroute you to nearest portal that has access to the Physics lab?"*

"Sure," Ben said, wondering why regular access was blocked. "Why the hell not."

An energy tornado swallowed him. He and the dead bear were routed instantly, via fractal compaction, to a transit portal nearest the Physics main lobby and reception desk, a quarter of a mile from Cowden Hall and the other student dorms.

Ben's area of expertise, which he had studied at the University of Fresno-by-the-Sea and finished on board Eos, was in the field of data-bullet fractal compaction technology. In fact, he had come up with entirely new mathematics for fractal compression which made it easier to compress data to nanometer widths, increasing their lightness and speed. This same technology was also used in the operation of transit portals, making them much more efficient. One unexpected by-product of the new system was a very strange and as yet unexplainable euphoria.

This rush of the portal's energies was the first sensation of pleasure Ben had had all day.

The portal delivered him and the bear to the main reception area of the physics department. However, when the portal's sensational energies dissipated, he was met by harsh fire alarms and spinning red and yellow emergency lights.

Still carrying the bear, Ben raced through the reception area, stepping into an opposite hallway that led to the various physics labs.

He practically collided with Eve Silbarton and two of her research assistants as they were rushing out.

"*Whoa!*" Ben said, backing off.

Dr. Evelyn Silbarton stood five feet one and wore her black hair pulled behind her head in a girlish ponytail. She was sixty-one, but looked thirteen, a product of fierce anti-aging programs in her youth.

"Get back!" she shouted, pushing him out of the hallway.

The two research assistants—Brad Navarro and Peg Thiering—were in retreat right beside her. They were Dr. Silbarton's top grad students, and all three were frightened at what they had left behind them in one of the labs.

Shouting above the fire alarms, Dr. Silbarton said, "It's a disassembler! Someone turned loose a disassembler in the alpha lab when we weren't looking! It's spreading fast!"

"What?" Ben asked, not sure if he had heard correctly.

"Campus security's on their way, and so are the fire department and people from the physical plant!" she shouted.

"It's *that* bad?"

"It's *that* bad!" she said.

Disassemblers were the rarest of weapons and historically one of the most feared. To Ben's knowledge, the only known molecular disassemblers were supposed to be stashed in an arsenal of forbidden weapons somewhere deep inside an icy Pluto vault back in the Sol system. What was one doing here?

Several campus-security individuals quickly appeared at the opposite end of the hallway, having taken a different transit portal to the physics wing.

Because of the portals, there wasn't a place in the ship that could not be reached in less than four seconds. But four seconds in the life of a disassembler was a virtual lifetime of gorging and doing all sorts of damage to anything in its way.

The alpha lab, where the physics department did most of its grant work for the H.C. Science Council—multimillion-dollar grants were the mainstay of most universities—was presently dissolving in a cloud of sparkling gray mist. Ben watched as the mist stuck a deadly tentacle into the outer hallway, and Eve pulled him and his bear back. Molecules hissed and disappeared in nuclear fury. Structural supports in the floor and the ceiling began vaporizing as the cloud grew and grew.

At the opposite end of the corridor, a transit portal spouted several fire personnel who carried both compressed water packs and chemical foam packs. They saw instantly that there was little in their arsenal that could stop what they saw growing before them. Tiny iridescent sparkles danced in the air of the corridor, looking for something to destroy.

"Evacuate the floor!" shouted the fire chief. *"There's nothing you can do here!"*

The mist emerging from the wall of the alpha lab wasn't so thick that Ben couldn't see through it. Beyond it, very little remained of the lab—floor, ceiling, everything was gone.

Ben tried to recall how far the physics department was from Eos's outer hull. A hull breach in regular space would be bad enough. A breach while they were in trans-space would cause them to end up like the *Annette Haven.*

"How did this happen?" Ben asked.

Peg Thiering responded. "We don't know. We were in the beta lab when the alarm went off. Brad opened the door and almost walked right into it!"

"Was anybody in the lab when it happened?" Ben asked.

"No," Thiering said. "The place was deserted. Even the secretaries had gone home."

Ben watched. The police and fire crew at the other end of the hallway watched. There was nothing they could do *but* watch.

Some of the other fire crew had gone to the levels immediately above and immediately below the physics department to evacuate them. But the rest watched the coiling, roiling, voracious gas eat away at all it encountered.

To their relief, however, the deadly mist seemed to expend itself, easing back its ravenous advance. Moments later, it had ceased growing entirely and had begun to dissipate.

No one approached the area for a good five minutes, waiting for the crackling of disassembled molecules to die down completely. When this happened, everybody crept in for a closer look.

The mist had taken an enormous, completely spherical bite out of the alpha lab, taking with it part of the floor above and the floor below it.

"Wow," Brad Navarro said. "That's a *real* nasty weapon."

Clusters of pipes, bundles of wires, and packed optical fibers that were once hidden in the floors were now exposed and neatly severed. Water gushed, electricity sparkled, and gases bound for the chemistry labs on the floor below hissed into the air uncontrollably.

On the floor below in the chemistry department, several people were gazing up, just as startled as their colleagues in the physics department.

On the floor above them, only one person had witnessed the event. She was a slender, attractive young woman with commanding brown eyes quite unlike anything Benjamin had ever seen before.

The young woman looked directly at Ben from up above. She pointed to the animal in Ben's arms. "Is that my bear?"

Ben could only read her lips, since the fire alarms were still clamoring about them, but he understood.

He had just located the elusive Julia Waxwing.

5

Julia Waxwing, a mixed descendant of Apache and Zuni Indians from distant Earth, had almost vanished. She had almost been swept into the arms of Death—like a titmouse taken in the claws of an Arizona sparrowhawk.

The twenty-three-year-old archaeology student had escaped that fate. But the incident with the disassembler did remind her how her grandfather, Stan Chasing, had once described the death of a human being: a fading from human memory, with nothing to show that he or she had ever walked the Earth.

Julia understood the manifold perils of space. Ships blew up, colonies died out, explorers soared into the abject blackness of the unexplored Alley, never to be seen or heard of again. But a *man-made* catastrophe was something no one should have to put up with. That was just bad manners, totally unbecoming of the dignity of *Homo interstellaris*.

However, the strange silver fog that took out nearly all of the physics department below as well as part of the archaeology department above was no longer of interest to her. Her little bear, a going-away present from her family, had been her only link to that familiar world. Now that link had been destroyed.

As the ship's crisis-control people surveyed the damage done by the weapon's bite, interviewing those who had witnessed the event, Julia descended into grief. She hugged the body of Jingle Bear where she sat next to the corridor wall in the physics department.

The young man who had brought the bear to her stood by, as if not knowing what else to do.

"Listen, I'm sorry about your bear," the young man said to her.

His back to the wall, he slid down beside her. "I tried looking for you in your dorm, but your pager was switched off and nobody knew where to find you."

An intentionally disengaged com/pager was, theoretically, a university misdemeanor. The com/pagers in the chevrons on the collars of everyone's tunic were *supposed* to be turned on at all times. This was for cases of emergency where university officials might need to know where their three thousand wards were.

But Julia honored her American background by defying authorities in minor, but annoying ways, and she had taken some of that with her when she came to Eos University two years ago in order to study with the famous Albert Holcombe. This was to be Professor Holcombe's last Alley circuit and Julia couldn't pass up the professional opportunity of studying under so famous a scholar. The death of Jingle Bear, however, had taken some of the wind out of her sails, leaving her demoralized.

"My name's Ben," the boy with the ponytail said. "I teach in the physics department. Or what's left of it, anyway."

"I'm Julia," she said softly, cradling her bear. She did like his smile. And his eyes. They hinted of intelligence and the possibilities of great mischief. He seemed more like a jock than a physics teacher.

"I'm a lecturer," he said, as if feeling the need to qualify his last remark. Or perhaps just to make conversation.

"I'm just a research assistant," she said. "It pays my way."

Ben nodded.

People kept arriving to assess the damage, the Grays of the administration as well as campus security, some of whom were armed with the ship's only weapons—crowd-control stunners.

Off to their right, a transit portal glowed and a major Gray appeared in the iridescent ring. Julia recognized the head of campus security, Lieutenant Theodore Fontenot. He sported a black mustache of military smartness, and his snappy gray tunic had nary a wrinkle or crease. He was accompanied by an assistant with a shoppingcam already sweeping the area. The story was that Lieutenant Fontenot was a lineal descendant of Ixion Smith himself—Smith and his eleventh wife. Mom and Dad often sent their kids to

Eos University *because* of Mr. Fontenot's pedigree. They knew Bobby and Suzie would be safe in his care.

"This should be interesting," Ben whispered, also seeing the lieutenant appear on the scene.

"Why?" she whispered back.

"That woman there?"

"Yes?"

"That's Eve Silbarton," Ben said. "She was my advisor on my dissertation."

"So?"

Ben looked at her. "So, Fontenot is supposed to have had a 'thing' with Dr. Silbarton some time ago. She hates him now."

They watched Mr. Fontenot survey the damage. Eve Silbarton stood beside him, arms crossed.

"Do you have any idea what happened here?" Mr. Fontenot asked.

Silbarton gave her account, mentioning specifically how the work seemed to be that of an outlawed disassembler. Her two graduate students then gave their account of what happened. Meanwhile, Fontenot's assistant with the shouldercam diligently took everything in. The camera, to Julia, looked like a parrot on the shoulder of a pirate.

Fontenot then glanced down at Julia and Ben on the floor. He pointed to the bear in Julia's arms.

"Is that animal dead or alive?" the lieutenant asked.

"He's dead," Julia told him.

Fontenot indicated the spherical cavity that used to be the physics alpha lab. "Did he die in this accident?"

"I found him dead in my dormitory," Ben said. "I was bringing it to her. Actually, that's not entirely true. Eve called me and—"

"What is your name?"

"Benjamin Bennett," Ben said. "I'm a—"

"And what's your business here?" Fontenot said, interrupting.

Ben rose to his feet with surprising agility: he *was* a jock. "What do you mean 'what's my business here'? I *work* here."

Fontenot seemed unimpressed. He stared down at Julia. "And who are you? What are you doing here?"

Ben moved closer to Fontenot. "Hey, man, what the hell kind of question is that?"

"Ben—" Eve Silbarton said, rushing over.

Julia watched and said nothing.

"She's in the archaeology department. Up there," Ben said heatedly, indicating the offices of the archaeology department visible through the eight-foot hole in the ceiling.

Lieutenant Fontenot glared at Ben. "Sit down and cool off, son. I'm just asking questions."

Ben relaxed, then sat back down beside Julia.

Fontenot again addressed Dr. Silbarton. "You said you thought this was the work of a disassembler. What made you think that?"

"I've worked with them before," Eve Silbarton said.

"Really?" Fontenot seemed truly surprised.

"Yes," Silbarton said. "I was a research technician at Europa DuPont for three years."

"They gave a common *tech* security clearance to work with disassemblers?" Fontenot asked.

"Stranger things have happened, Ted," Silbarton responded.

"Hmm," he said, deep in thought. "Was someone working on a matter disassembler in the lab?"

"If they were," Eve said, "they would have been breaking about twelve laws, all of which are felonies."

"They're probably dead, too," Ben added.

"There's that," Eve acknowledged.

"We're in the process of doing a head count now through the computers," Fontenot told them. "Did the lab contain any kind of project or experiment that could have *resembled* a matter disassembler?"

Dr. Silbarton shook her head. "We have nothing in any of our five labs that even comes close. Dr. Harlin wouldn't sign on with a project that could cause this much damage, or any damage for that matter."

"Tell me again what *you* were doing when this happened," Fontenot queried.

"My students and I were in the beta lab checking the results of some of the work we did yesterday on our Casimir field separator.

We had prepped the separator, but its energy levels were well below the start-up phase. Then the alarms went off."

"This 'Casimir field separator,'" the lieutenant said. "Could it have done this?" He waved a hand at the damaged lab.

Eve Silbarton scowled at the lieutenant. "Only if someone turned loose a disassembler while we were operating it."

"Are you absolutely sure?"

"Look, Ted," Silbarton went on. "The energy created in a Casimir vacuum would be sucked back into trans-space if it ever got out of control. It's the cleanest form of energy we know. And it *can't* blow up."

"What is your separator for?" Fontenot asked.

"It's to power the stardrive I'm working on in the gamma lab," she said.

"Whose projects were being tested in the alpha lab?"

"Gan Brenholdt and his students have exclusive use of the alpha lab," Eve said. "He was apparently at Friday-night services. He's on his way here now."

"What was he working on?"

"A stardrive system based on modified Alcubierre equations."

"Which is . . . ?"

Eve said, "You'll have to ask him, Ted. He can explain his work better than I can."

"What you're saying is that you don't think I could understand it," Fontenot said.

"No, I don't. But maybe Dr. Brenholdt can explain it to you, who knows?"

The security chief did not seem particularly perturbed by Dr. Silbarton's manner. He then asked, "How many of these star drives are you people working on?"

Silbarton said, "Mine, Gan Brenholdt's, and one by Dr. Ossam Hamdeen, but his is still in its design phase. He's at evening prayer, but he will be here shortly, too."

Julia and Ben watched as the adults pondered the extent of the damage and wondered who or what had caused it. BEN 1527!

After a long pause, Eve Silbarton voiced a question they were all thinking, including Julia. "So who would have done such a thing? Who would even *want* to?"

"Well," Fontenot said, looking at her. "*You* might."

Several onlookers gasped at the remark.

Eve Silbarton glowered blackly at the man. "The men and women who work here are *colleagues,* Ted, and I wouldn't think of sabotaging their work any more than they would think of sabotaging mine. So get that stupid notion out of your head right now."

"Let me ask you this," Fontenot said. "How important would you rate your project over those of your colleagues?"

"Fuck you, Ted," Eve responded. "I'm not going to answer any more of your dipshit questions."

Lieutenant Fontenot surveyed all that was before him—the technicians going over the crime scene, the various witnesses to the event being interviewed at the far end of the hallway—then nodded as if agreeing to his own thoughts. "Of course, if this was a *political* act, it might look very bad for someone who has publicly expressed sympathies for the policies of the KMA."

"*What?*" Eve Silbarton stammered. "What are you implying?"

Fontenot's assistant switched off his shouldercam, taking a signal from the lieutenant's wink.

Dr. Silbarton saw this. "Turn that damn thing back on! I want a record of this!"

Fontenot said, "We have to consider all possible motives here. And we all know where the KMA comes out on the Enamorati Compact *and* the Ainge, don't we?"

"Hell, Ted, you just got here!" Eve said. "You haven't even *begun* your investigation. Who knows who did this or why? Forget Jack Killian's Mobile Army or his Mad Assassins or whatever the hell they're called. We've got a situation right here, right now. This thing might have eaten through a bulkhead, and if that had happened, you wouldn't be standing here right now looking like an idiot."

"You think I look like an idiot?" he asked.

Eve Silbarton put her hands on her hips and gave Fontenot the evil eye. Two of them, in fact. "You *are* an idiot, Ted," she finally said. "Get used to it."

Fontenot turned to his crew of investigators. "Gentlemen, escort our witnesses to security detention so we can get their stories in a more comfortable setting."

"Lay a hand on me, Ted," Dr. Silbarton snarled, "and I'll break all eight of your legs."

"Are you resisting arrest?" Fontenot asked.

Eve Silbarton's eyes went wide. "You're *arresting* me? What the hell for?"

"For resisting arrest," Fontenot said. "Among other things. Conspiracy would be another."

Dr. Silbarton said, "You can't arrest anybody for resisting arrest if you haven't *arrested* them yet, you worthless sack of shit. And nobody is conspiring against you!"

"We can start, though," Ben said, surprising even Julia. "If that'll make you feel better."

Julia punched Ben as hard as she could, but the boy with the ponytail and the mischievous grin merely smiled up at the security chief.

Julia had read Ben's character correctly from the start.

And Fontenot took them all to jail, Jingle Bear included.

6

What originally started out as arrest and detention turned out to be nothing more than an "investigative interview" wherein nobody was actually charged with anything and no one had to spend too much time in campus security's holding cell. Julia and Ben had the Cloudman to thank, for he had intervened on their behalf, once he got wind of it.

Julia had never met their pilot before, but Cleddman in action was a wonder to behold. The captain stormed into the campus security offices, read Mr. Fontenot the riot act for being such a cretin, and subsequently got everybody released.

Jingle Bear also helped in getting their release. Julia wouldn't let anyone take him away from her and it seemed to make their guards uncomfortable with Jingle Bear's eyes rolled up in his head, his small pink tongue hanging out. As a consequence, Julia was the first of the prisoners to be let go.

Back in Cowden Hall, Julia began thinking about how she was going to dispose of her little bear. She found a small blanket her mother had made for her years ago and this made a perfect funeral shroud.

On her bookshelf stood a line of animal fetishes Julia had made when she was a teenager. She found a whale she had carved from black serpentine just two inches long. A whale would make a good otherworld companion for an Arctic bear, she thought. She took the serpentine whale and, along with some dried herbs and two peregrine feathers, she placed them in the shroud next to Jingles and began sewing up the whole affair.

Once the shroud had been sewn, Julia gave some thought as to how she was going to dispose of it. Incineration was out of the question. So was dumping him into the ship's recycler. Jingle Bear deserved a much better fate. Julia then decided she would return his body to the soil somewhere on their next stopover.

However, Eos was not scheduled to leave trans-space for another two weeks. Their next port of call was to be an Earth-like world of an M-type star. This world, discovered long ago by the Enamorati, was in a late Cambrian stage of biotic development, with most life still being submerged in its murky seas. Because of this, there was no plan for archaeology to go down to Paavo Juuoko 4's surface. There was nothing for them to do.

Nevertheless, being a graduate student, Julia could get a pass on just about any gondola heading to the surface. There, she could inter Jingles, perhaps dropping him in a stainless-steel canister into one of the oceans. The canister would not affect the planet's biosphere any, and if intelligent life managed to evolve on Paavo Juuoko 4 aeons hence, the canister would probably be so metamorphosed that it would be unrecognizable to those future fossil hunters.

In the meantime, she was going to have to keep the body preserved. For this, she transited to the archaeology department, where she found an unused vacuum chamber in one of their forensic labs. The vacuum chambers were designed to hold artifacts in a perfect vacuum where destructive bacterial or chemical agents could not get at them until they were ready to be analyzed.

So with a very heavy heart, Julia placed Jingles's coffin into the chamber and sealed it. She then put her name onto the lock's panel so the other students would not open it by mistake.

Julia stepped out into the hallway and walked the short distance to the area the disassembler had taken out earlier that day. Campus security, however, had sealed the region off.

She turned and started looking for the nearest transit portal.

That was when she heard the music. The pulsating rhythms of a StratoCast drifted down the hallway, a strange kind of music for any adult in the archaeology department to play.

It seemed to be coming from one of the faculty offices, specifically Dr. Holcombe's office.

Julia found the Regents professor staring at a 2D screen, which depicted a forested landscape. But this was not an Earth forest. The trees were much, much taller, and the sky was a brilliant, luxurious green, filled with floating chlorophyll clouds. The music was synthetic, minimalistic, and energetic—not at all the kind of music a man of Holcombe's years normally listened to.

Dr. Holcombe turned in his chair, lowering the audio. "Hello, jailbird. I see they didn't keep you long. So how did it go?"

"Fine, I guess," she said. "They decided that we didn't look like saboteurs so they let us go."

"You kids should *really* give them something to worry about. Stage a student riot. Take over the administration building. Have a panty raid. They deserve to have their gray feathers ruffled."

Julia could hardly believe what she was hearing. Was this the way the man grieved? He seemed more angry than sad.

"Is that a StratoCast you're watching?" Julia asked.

Holcombe nodded. "It's one my clone-son had made about three years ago."

"What group was he in? Anybody famous?"

Holcombe leaned back in his chair. "Well, I don't know how famous he was, but he sure made a hell of a lot of money. More money than I'll ever see working on this boat. He was a BronzeAngel. I guess they were one of the best."

Julia had heard of the BronzeAngels. They were a "sky-runner" group who recorded their feelings while skimming treetops and racing down small canyons on antigravity shoes. The technostrobic music that accompanied their emotional highs was implanted on data tiles and the tiles sold in the millions, as did the technology that came with them. StratoCast tiaras amplified the theta waves underneath the music, which, in turn, magnified the feelings the StratoCaster imprinted onto the tile. StratoCasts were particularly popular for people on lonely outposts or on faraway planets for whom a bit of escapism was essential.

Julia was impressed that Professor Holcombe had a StratoCaster in his family.

"This was done on Lehi," Holcombe said, indicating the 2D screen. "Lehi's the southernmost continent on Tau Ceti 4. I camped in that very forest with my father and my brothers."

He said nothing for a moment. He then switched off the 2D. "So what are *you* doing here? Shouldn't you be out on a hot date or what?"

"My bear died," she said in a low voice. "I put him in one of our storage chambers until I can give him a decent burial."

Professor Holcombe sat forward. "Your bear died? How?"

"I don't know," Julia said. "A student found him lying before his door in Babbitt Hall."

"I'm so sorry to hear this, Julia."

"Actually, Ben said that one of the Avatkas found him."

"Ben? Who's Ben?"

Julia brightened. "Ben Bennett. He's a lecturer in the physics department. He teaches two courses in Van Flandern physics. I just met him."

"Ah," said the professor, and ran a hand through his shock of white hair. "Well, this month will probably go down in the record books. All sorts of people dying. And bears."

"What are we going to do about the hole in the lecture hall's floor?" Julia then asked.

"I've been thinking about that. The only people using that hall this semester are Chad Rutledge and Raymonda Moore. We'll shuffle them around to other rooms until we can repair the damage. We're lucky this happened on a Friday. We've got the whole weekend to make repairs."

"You're not going to cancel classes?"

"I don't think so," he said. "They might down in physics, where the damage was, but—"

A sudden fist of nausea hit Julia in the stomach and Professor Holcombe suddenly lurched forward in his chair.

"Oh!" she said, gasping in pain. It was as if a hand had bunched her intestines and suddenly twisted them. *Hard.*

It seemed as if something had struck the ship like a clapper to a bell and now the sound, though inaudible, was ringing throughout the spaceborne university.

Holcombe turned a whitish green. He stood up. "What the *hell* was that?"

"I . . . think it's the ship," Julia said. "Something's happening to the ship!"

The chorus to those remarks came in the form of a series of alarms that Julia had never heard before, not even when the gray mist ate away part of the physics department just a few hours earlier.

Another wave of nausea hit her and this time she thought she was going to throw up.

Dr. Holcombe braced himself against the edge of his desk as all sorts of items rattled and crashed to the floor.

"Dr. Holcombe!" Julia cried.

"We've been blown out of trans-space!" Holcombe said. "It's the Engine! I think the Engine's going to explode!"

7

Ben had never been in trouble before, at least the kind of grown-up trouble that required the intervention of lawyers. Thankfully, Eos University had an aggressive Rights Advocacy Office whose lawyers took umbrage at just about everything university Grays— or Grays anywhere—did. Eve Silbarton instantly summoned Captain Cleddman, who, in turn, called on the Rights Advocacy Office, who, in their turn, sent Messrs. Kerry Wangberg and Winn Sammons, who came *tout de suite*. They demanded that Mr. Fontenot show cause for his arrests, and since Mr. Fontenot really couldn't, he was forced to downgrade the charges to a mere reprimand, which Ben didn't like either. He told Fontenot so, but Mr. Fontenot was persuaded to let them all go anyway.

Once Ben's interview with campus security ended, he found himself half a mile from Babbitt Hall with nothing to do. It was, by then, late Friday night and it was far too late to see about finding a female for companionship. But considering his recent performances—or lack thereof—it was probably just as well that the women he'd had in mind were out of range. Melissa Lozinski, a math major; Colleen Lamb, a seriously sexy Navy ROTC student; and Peggy Shumaker, a mask-maker in Fine Arts whose breasts, when unmasked, were said to be legendary. They would remain such, thanks to the Ennui or saltpeter or whatever it was that plagued him.

So he decided instead to go to the student health center. A young man his age shouldn't be having performance problems, and the staff at the student health center usually had the answers to everything. Or most everything.

To his surprise, Ben found the student health center fairly busy at that hour. He counted eight miserable-looking students in the lobby waiting to see the next available doctor.

At first Ben wondered if the students in the lobby had suffered side effects from whatever it was that destroyed the physics lab—burns, broken bones, and the like. But that didn't seem to be the case. Mostly, these students just seemed depressed. There were five young men, three young women.

Triage got him in to see one of the doctors an hour after the others were cycled through. On his way to an examination room he passed a ward filled with sleeping students. He couldn't count the number of students held there, but he guessed it was over twenty. That seemed high to him, for a university the size of Eos. But what did he know?

Ben climbed into a gown, feeling like a little kid putting on his jammies. The door to his cubicle opened and an attractive woman in her late thirties entered. A faint aura of perfume had come in with her and its caressing fingers surrounded Ben where he sat on the examination table.

"You must be Benjamin," the doctor said, consulting her chart. "I'm Katrina. Katrina Larsen."

Ben blushed. She wore no wedding ring and smiled at him familiarly. Even so, the woman's aura, hint of pleasantly large breasts, even her shapely mouth, could not rally his "boys." Inwardly, he bewailed his fate.

"So what brings you to me tonight?" she asked in a very musical voice.

Ill at ease, he said, "Are there always this many students in the health center?" Ben jerked a thumb over his shoulder. "There must be twenty or thirty students in that ward we passed."

Dr. Larsen began probing Ben's ears, flashing lights in his eyes. "Let's don't talk about them. Let's talk about us."

" 'Us'?"

"Why *you're* here tonight. With me."

"Actually, I don't know if—"

"Sure you do. Tell me."

He swallowed and told the beautiful doctor his problem. Dr. Larsen listened patiently. She scribbled a few notes on Ben's file sheet.

"I'm almost twenty-eight years old," he said at the end of his pitiable disquisition. "This isn't supposed to be happening to me."

"You'd be surprised how often it does happen," Dr. Larsen said.

"You mean this is normal?"

Dr. Larsen nodded. "College students display a wide range of reactions to stress, particularly when exam time approaches."

"But, I'm not a student anymore," Ben insisted. "I finished my dissertation program two semesters ago and I'm just teaching now. That's it."

"Well, have you been depressed lately? Are you homesick at all?" the doctor asked.

"No," Ben said.

"To which?"

"Both."

"Hmm." The doctor scribbled more notes into Ben's file. She was nodding slightly as well.

"Listen, Doctor," Ben then asked. "I have to know about those people in that ward back there."

"If you must know," she said, lowering her clipboard. "Many of them are here with the same stress-related symptoms you have."

"No kidding?"

"Except for the one who just had her baby."

"A baby?" Ben said. "I guess that's normal. There are a lot of married students traveling with Eos University."

He then saw the empty look on Dr. Larsen's face. "Isn't it?"

The doctor hugged Ben's file. She seemed momentarily sad. "It might be normal if there were five or six births a year on Eos. But it isn't."

Now that he thought about it, Ben couldn't remember seeing any infants, even among the students who lived in married housing one floor above Cowden Hall.

"Then they *are* putting saltpeter in the food," Ben said with a startled whisper. "Those evil motherfuckers!"

"Dr. Roden—Rob Roden, our director—would *never* allow such a policy on the ship," Dr. Larsen said. "But, historically, our birth rate has always been low."

There *were* children on Eos. Many staff and faculty were traveling with their families, children included. But Ben couldn't recall the last time he had seen a pregnant woman anywhere on the ship, let alone a baby in a stroller.

"Then it's the Ennui," Ben said. "It *is* real!"

"I would bank on saltpeter before I accepted the Ennui," Dr. Larsen said. "That myth has been studied for a hundred years and no one has proven a thing. It's just an old wives' tale."

Ben knew from newscasts that the general human population in the Alley was not advancing the way most growth specialists had anticipated. Despite its three Earth-like worlds—Earth, Tau Ceti 4, and Ross 244 3—the H.C. had a population of around ten billion persons, eight billion of whom were on Earth. The population should have been three times that and rapidly expanding, but it wasn't. Perhaps more ships than they knew were being blown up in trans-space.

"But let's get back to you. Now, when was the last time you were 'successful' with a woman—or a man. Whichever."

"Woman," Ben said quickly. "Or women. Definitely no men."

"Then when was the last time you had normal sex with a woman? And use your own definition of 'normal.' "

"The last time?" *Now* Ben felt truly humiliated. "Last year. The university stopped at Kaikkivallan 5. A bunch of us had gone down to a ski lodge for a week."

"And?"

Ben wondered how he could say it. "It, uh, took me longer than usual to, uh—"

"Reach a climax?"

"That's it."

He had been with Page Stauffer, whose breasts were speckled with very delightful freckles, and had to work for three hours to achieve an orgasm. When they were finished, he fell asleep, exhausted; Ms. Stauffer put on a tiara and went StratoCasting with Prince Namor and the SubMariners. He had gotten his rocks off, but she hadn't. He never did see her again.

The doctor penned a few more notes. "And the time before that?"

"That would have been—" That would have been Jamie Schisler the semester before. But Ms. Schisler had certain fetishes she had never warned him about. He found out about them when he was bound and gagged and Ms. Schisler brought out the whips. She did look great in high heels, however.

"I can't remember," he said. "Sorry."

The doctor scribbled more notes.

"Look. Are there any medicines I can take for this?" Ben asked. "That would be the easiest."

Dr. Larsen nodded agreeably. "Well, yes, there are a few things I could prescribe. Some stimulants as well as a few behavioral exercises you can do two or three times a day—"

She dropped her clipboard.

Ben felt his stomach lurch.

The room seemed to heave slightly.

"Oh!" Dr. Larsen said. She stumbled backward. She then folded her arms across her stomach and bent over.

Ben jumped off the examination table. Something was terribly wrong. In the outer ward, glass objects crashed to the floor and several people let out cries of bewilderment or screams of terror.

Dr. Larsen fell back into the only chair in the room, her face gone chalk white, and the air in front of Ben's eyes shimmered. It seemed as if the ship itself—the actual vessel—had become violently ill, convulsing at an atomic level.

Then the nausea went away and the room ceased vibrating. All was still.

Ben knew exactly what had happened: The Enamorati had shut down the Engine and the molecules of their bodies had rushed to reposition themselves back where they ought to be from their trans-space compressions.

Ben stood up shakily. "Someone's just shut the Engine off."

"We're not supposed to leave trans-space for another two weeks!" the doctor said, rising from her chair.

Ben thought of the ill-fated *Annette Haven* . . . and of the large hole that had so recently been gouged in the physics department's alpha lab.

He fervently hoped that he wouldn't blow up in the middle of his next thought.

8

Transition into and out of trans-space usually caused a mild disorientation, which was why transition couches were fixtures in every room of the ship. But *this* transition had been downright *ugly.*

Recovering his poise, Ben ripped off his examination gown, stepped back into his clothing puddle, then made his way out of the student health center. Dr. Larsen would have real afflictions to deal with now.

In the outer corridor, Ben found every wall flush with the Cloudman's visage and the sound of his voice ordering everyone to buckle into their transition couches, which in Ben's case was in his dorm room.

Ben found a transit portal and shot back to Babbitt Hall. There, he found Jim Vees on his knees in the hallway, dazed. He was wearing a T-shirt and a pair of underwear, having been yanked from a deep sleep.

"Do you know what happened?" Vees asked.

"I think the captain's turned the Engine off. We're in real-space now."

"Why?"

"I don't know," Ben said.

On the 2D in Ben's room, they caught Cleddman in the middle of some sort of explanation. The pilot was saying, "—we now have word from the Kuulo Kuumottoomaa that the Engine has been stabilized. The Kaks are determining our new position in real-space, and as soon as we know where we are, we can begin calling for assistance, if we need it."

"Ix on a stick!" the former astronomy student said. "Something happened to our Engine?"

Ben nodded.

On the screen the Cloudman said, "I've called for a Code Three emergency. Stand by. Watch your screens."

The 2D went blank.

"Isn't he going to tell us what happened to the goddamned Engine?" Vees asked. "And what is a Code Three emergency?"

"Let's find out," Ben said. To the video screen, Ben said, "Screen on. Main menu. Emergencies. Definitions. All codes."

The 2D scrolled out: EMERGENCY CODE ONE: MALFUNCTIONS; INTERNAL THREATS TO THE SHIP—I.E., GRAVITY; ATMOSPHERE; ELECTRICAL; WATER SERVICES. EMERGENCY CODE TWO: EXTERNAL THREATS—I.E., COLLISION WITH EXTERNAL OBJECT OR OBJECTS. EMERGENCY CODE THREE: POSSIBLE, PENDING, OR UNAVOIDABLE DESTRUCTION OF VESSEL FROM INTERIOR OR EXTERIOR SOURCE.

Eos University had been around for a hundred years and was as massive as an asteroid. Its shields were state-of-the-art. But they only worked in real-space. Something had killed their Engine in trans-space.

"And we're at Code Three?" Ben said, astounded.

Into Ben's room burst George Clock. With him came Tommy Rosales, their other Bombardier. Though of average height, Rosales had a peculiar muscular condition that gave him the strength of three human beings without the attendant muscle grotesquerie. He excelled in all things physical and failed in all things academic. He only recently had quit Eos University's architecture program, having lost interest in it.

Tommy Rosales was excited. "Did you hear? We're going to have to abandon ship!"

The Bombardiers were always happy for any sort of disruption in their daily routines.

"We're *not* going to abandon ship," Ben said.

"That's what everyone is saying," Rosales said.

Ben faced the 2D. Speaking directly to the screen, he said, "ShipCom. Eve Silbarton, please."

The 2D opened on Eve Silbarton. From what Ben could see in

the background, Eve wasn't at her apartment at all. She appeared to be in the gamma lab in the physics department.

"Eve? Do you know what's going on?" Ben asked.

Eve Silbarton looked up from her work. She appeared to have been quite engrossed. "The captain thinks there might be something going on in the Engine compartment, some sort of disagreement among the Enamorati. There may even be fighting. No one knows yet. Whatever it is, the Kuulo has shut the Engine down."

"They're *fighting* in there?" George Clock asked.

"That's what's circulating," Eve said.

"What about the Auditors?" Ben asked. "They live on their doorstep. The Auditors would know."

"I'm sure President Porter is conferring with Bishop Nethercott as we speak," Eve said. "But if the problem's mechanical, then there's little good those two guys can do."

"Are we going to blow up?" Ben asked.

"No one knows that either," Eve admitted grimly.

Jim Vees cursed. "Ix! The one thing we *don't* need is a bunch of Ainge Auditors interfering with the Engine. Somebody ought to throw them out a window."

"Nobody gets near the Engine but the Enamorati," George Clock said. "Let Porter and Nethercott confer. We should head for the lifepods."

"I still say we ought to throw them out a window," Jim Vees insisted.

Dr. Silbarton looked off to one side, consulting another screen. "I've got a message coming through here. You'd better switch over at your end. Out."

The image of Dr. Silbarton vanished and was replaced by a series of words. On Ben's screen appeared: EMERGENCY. CODE THREE. ALL PERSONS TO THEIR ASSIGNED ESCAPE PODS. ALL PERSONS TO THEIR ASSIGNED ESCAPE PODS. . . . And out in the halls, alarms rattled a newer tune, commensurate with the gravity of the situation.

"Here we go," Ben said, switching the screen off.

With that the Bombardiers raced for the nearest transit portal, which would now automatically send them to the escape pods.

Portals could only take three people at a time, so there was a line of young men from the dorm already there at the end of the hall.

The line, however, shortened fairly quickly and the young men of Babbitt Hall were shunted via optical cable to the lifepod bays that ringed the ship.

All but Jim Vees made the transit.

"What an idiot," George Clock said, stepping into the pod bay.

Humans were limited to only ten transit jumps a day. Any more than that and molecular degradation would begin. Beyond ten jumps, transit portals would automatically refuse to transit people whose chevrons had registered ten jumps. But many students, including the Bombardiers (and including Ben), often used transit jumps to get high.

Jim Vees now had to hoof it.

This particular section of the lifepod bay contained three lozenge-shaped ships capable of holding fifteen people each. But so far, the three boys from Babbitt Hall were the only evacuees in the bay.

"Who else is assigned this bay?" Ben asked, looking around. "Any of you guys know?"

George Clock nodded. "I think we share these 'pods with the Ainge Auditors."

"But they're not here," Tommy Rosales said, looking around.

Outside in the hallways, the ship's alarms were caterwauling dramatically; red and yellow lights blinked rapidly.

"I can see that," Ben said.

"Then that means we get a lifepod each," Tommy Rosales said.

"Goody," said Clock.

Red lights over the hull exits indicated that none of the 'pods had the go-ahead signal from the command deck to be released into space, nor had Ben heard the telltale sounds of airlock decompressions from neighboring lifepod bays. That meant that the Cloudman was still assessing the situation, preparatory to actually giving the "abandon ship" call.

Several minutes went by, but no command came. The alarms had been cut off, but the emergency lights continued to twirl their crimson capes in the hallways.

And in that period of time, none of the Ainge Auditors transited to the 'pod bays.

"Why aren't the Auditors here?" Ben asked.

"Who cares?" Tommy Rosales said.

"I do," Ben said.

"No you don't."

"Okay," Ben admitted. "But I'd like to know why they're not here."

"Forget those guys. Let's wait for Jim," Rosales said.

"Well, *I* think Cleddman's not going to call an evacuation and I think the Auditors know that, which means they know why."

"So?" Rosales asked.

"Let's go look," Ben said.

"No," Rosales said. "I'm staying here."

"I'll go," Clock offered. "I think you're right. Something's going on and the Auditors know what it is."

"You're both idiots," Rosales retorted.

"Where's your sense of adventure?" Ben said to him.

"It's right here, where the lifepods are," Rosales told them.

"All right," Ben said. "When Jim shows up, keep him here. Keep him out of trouble."

"I should keep you guys out of trouble," Rosales mumbled.

Ben and George Clock headed for the nearest pedestrian corridor. A transit portal would be quicker, but they were set by default to shunt people to lifepod bays in times of emergency. They jogged for an eighth of a mile to the Auditor quarters, and while some people were still heading to their assigned bays, no one appeared to stop them. No one seemed to care.

The Ainge Auditors lived in a large compound that separated the Enamorati's living spaces—and the Engine—from the rest of the university. The entrance to the Ainge Sanctuary was through a highly impractical set of oaken doors. These opened up to a small anteroom, which, in turn, opened onto a two-hundred-seat auditorium that faced a podium. This podium was used by High Auditor Nethercott for regular services, but was normally not in use at any other time.

Behind the podium was a specially treated glass wall. On the other side of the wall were what the Enamorati called their "empath stations." These flanked a long, thick rod—called the "communion rod"—which resembled a massive drive shaft, the kind that might propel a waterborne ship. Its true purpose was unknown, but students and parishioners alike would come to the Sanctuary and watch the empaths, the Avatkas, sit at their stations, plugged into the communion rod.

Ben and George Clock entered the auditorium and found the place deserted—which they expected. However, on the other side of the glass wall there were also no Avatkas sitting at their empath stations and the communion rod itself wasn't glowing.

That was unusual.

"Wow," Clock said. "Where *is* everybody?"

"Maybe something *did* happen to the Engine," Ben said in a low voice.

Suddenly from just behind them a shadowy figure appeared and spoke to them in a stern voice. "Gentlemen," the elder said. "Can I help you?"

"Oh, shit," Clock said, whirling around.

Behind them stood High Auditor Joseph Nethercott. He was a tall, pale man in a crisp gray long coat and prim priest's collar.

"We heard that something happened to the Engine," Ben said. "We happened to be nearby."

Nethercott came down the aisle like the specter of death.

"The Engine has simply been taken off-line for the time being," Nethercott said. "There is nothing to worry about." He smiled at them with thin, bloodless lips.

"Where is everybody?" Ben asked. "Where are the Avatkas? There's always somebody at the rod." Ben pointed to the deserted communion rod room, which, he just now observed, was also devoid of the greenish gases the Avatkas normally breathed. "Looks like the atmosphere's gone out, too. What happened in there?"

The High Auditor said, "Nothing's happened. The Enamorati have merely been—"

A loud *pop!* sounded out just then and the three jerked around to see that a giant silver crack had appeared in the wall separating the communion room from the Sanctuary auditorium. The crack, thirty feet long, looked like a frozen bolt of lightning.

"*Ixion!*" Nethercott exploded.

"Jesus!" Ben said as he and George fell into defensive crouches. The sound had been quite loud.

The partition, however, held. It did not explode and no trace of the Enamorati's toxic atmosphere came hissing out at them. Seconds later, vents on the Enamorati side in the ceiling began oozing a sealing solution that raced down the crack. The viewing window would be as good as new within a few minutes.

"What the *hell* was that?" Clock said.

"Boys," Nethercott said, gathering himself together, "this is not for you. Return to your lifeboat stations and wait for the captain's command to go back to your rooms."

"But what about—" Ben started.

"Leave," Nethercott said insistently, "or I will have campus security come and drag you away. There is nothing for you here."

Ben stared at the communion-rod room and the empty empath stations *and* the long crack etched by some disturbance deep inside the Enamorati compound. But no further explosions were heard; no more cracks appeared in the glass partition.

"I'd tell someone about that," Ben said, pointing to the disappearing crack.

"I plan to," Nethercott said.

With that, they left the Sanctuary. Whatever the Ainge were up to, it was unlikely anyone else knew anything about it. Ben thought he'd try and find out.

9

That following Saturday morning the Grays made official what every human being and Enamorati on the ship already knew: Eos University was stranded 118 light-years from Earth at the Alley's inmost point in the galaxy with a permanently disabled Engine. Few people slept that night and a lot of them wound up in the health center with complaints of acute nausea and disorientation.

Eos's piloting and communications personnel reacted swiftly by firing a mayday data bullet to the Enamorati home world of Virr, which was twenty-three thousand light-years away in the inner Sagittarius Alley. That bullet, a bare description of their situation along with their stellar coordinates, was made extremely small so it could travel through trans-space as fast as possible. Despite that, it would take at least ten hours to reach Virr. Acknowledgement of the mayday, however, would likely take a little bit longer. It all depended on how long it took the Enamorati ruling council to assess the news.

In the meantime, ShipCom became very busy sending data bullets back to the worlds of the Human Community, apprising the nearby settlements of their status. Once the maydays went out, ShipCom allowed the students, faculty, and staff to file their own letters. These were shot out almost as soon as they were compacted in the rail queue, in the hope that Mom and Dad would see that everything was under control.

For Julia's part, she decided against sending a letter of her own to her mother and three sisters back on Earth in Flagstaff, Arizona, telling them of her adventures. And after the Engine had broken down, Julia had a very good adventure. As it developed, fourteen lifepods had managed to launch themselves from Eos during the

Code Three emergency and it took Eos's EVA squad several hours to maneuver the pods back to the ship. Julia had managed to find herself on one of those pods with twelve women from Cowden Hall, and they stayed up all night talking about it when they got back to the dorm.

Julia had managed a little sleep by 0900 hours the next day. She had just stepped from the showers when an announcement came that the president of Eos University was going to address the student body at 1000 hours. This gave everyone time to get some breakfast and get to their assigned meeting halls.

Eos University had six assembly halls where students were corralled on special occasions to be briefed or debriefed, depending on the occasion. The William F. Nietmann Hall was quite crowded when Julia arrived, but if the several hundred students gathered there were uneasy, she couldn't tell. The place had a carnival atmosphere to it. Students were laughing and poking each other like children. Which was strange, she thought, since they almost had been blown to smithereens. But no one seemed to care.

Julia wore her usual tunic, with its twin collar pins denoting her area of study and that she already held a bachelor's degree. This allowed a seat down with the adult faculty in the front of the hall, separate from the rowdy undergrads behind her, who were busy throwing paper airplanes into the air, firing off spitwads, blasting raspberries. Julia hadn't seen a spitwad since she was in high school. *Something,* she thought, *is definitely in the air.*

The group quieted down, however, when Albert Holcombe arrived. He came down the short flight of steps like a shaggy, white-headed bear, looking as if he wouldn't stand for any foolishness at that hour of the day.

Everyone suddenly shut up. The silence that filled the place was practically deafening.

Holcombe looked up at the six hundred or so assembled students. "You don't have to be quiet on my account. It's Saturday, for Christ's sake," he said. "Make all the noise you want."

The students started up again, returning to normal.

Julia watched as Professor Holcombe found a place next to his colleagues two rows in front of her. He plopped into his seat almost exuberantly.

"Good show, old man," said a geology professor.

"What did you have for breakfast, Albert?" a woman sitting to the other side of him asked.

"Wayhighs," Professor Holcombe told her. "A whole plate full."

"Christ, Al," the geology professor said in a lowered voice. "Watch what you're saying. The Grays don't have a sense of humor. They might think you're serious."

Holcombe smiled at his colleagues, but kept his silence. To Julia, it was all cryptic. She didn't know what to think of Professor Holcombe's buoyant, almost cavalier manner.

Moments later the lights in the auditorium dimmed and the giant 2D screen filled with the visage of President Porter.

"*Boo!*" shouted several students.

More airplanes flew. And a shoe hit the screen.

Nolan Porter, Ph.D., was the Big Gray, a man born and bred among the Ainge on Tau Ceti 4, an Auditor himself, and a third-rate scholar—at least according to the student gossip Julia had heard. Half the students of Eos liked the man because he was Ainge; the other half didn't for the same reason. That half seemed to fill every seat in the William F. Nietmann Hall that morning. Julia almost felt giddy with a renewed sense of excitement.

His hair silver-gray, his eyes blue-gray, President Porter sat calmly at his desk, pictures of his three wives and thirty children in the background. For the occasion, he wore a long, coal gray herringbone tunic of standard cut. Everything gray. He also wore a smile.

"Oh, shit. The son-of-a-bitch is smiling," somebody said far behind Julia in the darkness. "We're in for it now!"

Giggles followed this, and several of the assembled faculty shushed them fiercely.

The giant image of President Porter began speaking down to them. "I want to thank all of you for gathering like this on such short notice. And on a Saturday morning when so many of you have papers to write and tests to study for—"

"Eat me!" someone shouted in the dark.

A female professor jumped up quickly. "Quiet! All of you!"

"—so I'll make this as short and as informative as possible: For those of you who haven't heard the news or read about it in the latest edition of *The Alley Citizen,* our student newspaper—" Porter handled his copy of *The Alley Citizen* as if it had come with a fish in it. "—a number of things have happened to the old girl, our university."

He placed the newspaper off to the side. "Late Friday afternoon, a weapon similar to old-style disassemblers destroyed part of the physics lab, causing millions of dollars of damage. I mention that because, as most of you know, a few hours later our Engine broke down and we had to return to real-space, which I'm sure you all experienced. It certainly caused Mrs. Porter a little scare."

Somebody hooted. Somebody else made farting sounds with his hands in his armpits.

"Hey!" the female professor shouted over her shoulder.

The president went on. "According to the Kuulo Kuumottoomaa, the Engine suffered an unexpected energy drain which caused a systemic ripple effect, destroying the Engine completely."

"Yeah? Well, at least we didn't blow the fuck up," someone else shouted.

The female professor jumped to her feet and shouted, "If I have to go up there, mister, you're going to really regret it!"

A mock-frightened hush fell over the crowd.

"The Engine failure *may* be linked to the damage done to the physics lab," Porter continued. "But we don't know yet. We are looking into every aspect of the case—"

The auditorium filled with snickers and somebody yelled "Blow job!" and now several professors down in front were actively scanning the auditorium for the scattered malcontents.

Porter said, "The Kuulo did say that the Enamorati will cooperate fully in all of our investigations, providing that our need for information doesn't violate the Enamorati Compact. I find no trouble with this."

For an anxious moment Julia thought that the president would next mention something about Jingle Bear, since her bear's death seemed to be part, in some vague way, of what had happened. But Porter either didn't know about it or hadn't thought it important enough to mention.

"Since the Enamorati Compact forbids us to interfere with Enamorati affairs, we have no choice but to let them conduct their own investigation of the Engine's failure. We will wait for their report. In the meantime, we will be conducting our own investigations and I urge everyone to give campus security your fullest cooperation, especially those of you who might happen to have been in the science wings when the weapon was set off. We're all in the same boat, after all."

The president's smile reappeared. "Once the cause of the Engine malfunction has been discovered and analyzed, the Enamorati will be jettisoning the old Engine and replacing it with a new one. Depending on the availability and location of the nearest Engine, we estimate that we can be back on our Alley circuit in three weeks."

A collective groan went up through the crowd, but this time no faculty member tried to quell it.

Somebody threw his other shoe at the screen.

"We aren't exactly helpless out here, however," the president said calmly. "Physics and Engineering, who were up all night working on the problem, have informed me that we do have a means of getting us to the nearest human-habitable planet. Astronomy tells me that we are just three light-days away from what appears to be a main-sequence M-type star that has at least one habitable planet. We were very lucky in this.

"As you know, our part of the Sagittarius Alley is very, very small. There are thousands of stars within a hundred light-years of the Earth and we've only explored a fraction of those. So this new star and its planets will be a wonderful opportunity for us all. Who knows? We might even make a little bit of history.

"Therefore, under the university charter, I am immediately directing our pilot, Captain Cleddman, to divert us to this nearby system. In the meantime, contrary to any rumors you may have heard—" Here, Porter gestured to the copy of *The Alley Citizen* on his desk. "—classes will continue as scheduled. So, enjoy your weekend. That is all."

Even before the 2D screen winked out, all sorts of debris was hurled at the fading vision of Nolan Porter, including a squash racquet.

The lights came on and the babbling began again. Julia looked around. She hadn't thought about the possibility of classes being canceled, but it was clear that several students had hoped they were going to be.

The boisterous crowd got up and started filing out into the adjoining hallways, ready to start their delayed weekend.

Behind Julia, in the crowd that had been sitting high in the rear, was Ben. He seemed to be walking gingerly and he looked a tad shorter than she remembered him being.

Unless, of course, he was walking barefoot.

And he seemed to be in a hurry.

She was about to call after him, but he and his friends had disappeared. Besides that, two professors were already heading in their direction, one of whom held a shoe in her hand. She was looking for the foot that fit it.

Julia decided to contact Ben later. They had, after all, three weeks on their hands.

10

Colin Hollingsdale, who lived in an earlier century, probably never imagined his discontinuity breeder reactor as a means of moving ships through the interstellar void. The Hollingsdale reactors were typically designed for instructive purposes and were found in schools such as Eos University, or on planets far from either Tau Ceti 4 or Earth. This was because the Hollingsdale reactors created very small black holes in free space, so students and scientists alike could study their effects.

Ben had some experience with Hollingsdale-breeder technology back when he was working on his master's degree at UC Fresno-by-the-Sea. The breeders created artificial black holes—discontinuities—by using a form of C-gravitaton compression at distant projection points, tapping into the same energies that powered the Onesci Engines. Depending on the relative motion of the breeder—the ship it was within or the moonlet it was on—a powerful black hole with the same angular momentum could be created—well away from the projection source to prevent the hole's intense gamma radiation from killing its users, of course. But the gravity effects of the discontinuity itself *could* be felt, and that was the whole point.

Ben hadn't known that Eos University had a Hollingsdale discontinuity breeder until Eve Silbarton had told him that this was going to be their means of limping to the nearby planet where they could reprovision themselves until the new Engine arrived.

So while the students celebrated their good fortune to have a habitable planet nearby and the means to get there, Captain Cleddman sent a bullet back to the H.C. Council, giving directions to the star Kiilmist, which the Enamorati had just named, and its target

planet called, for the time being, Kiilmist 5. More detailed data
bullets would be sent with more information, once they achieved a
stable orbit around the planet. For now, they had a tricky maneuver to make and all of the rail guns were going to be shut down for
the duration.

At 1400 hours the following Monday, Eve Silbarton and her
handpicked crew activated the Hollingsdale breeder reactor. Ben
was among those invited; so, too, was Tommy Rosales. Ben had
convinced Eve that Rosales's experience with fusion-reactor technology might come in handy, even if Rosales had dropped out of
Eos's nuclear engineering program.

Dr. Silbarton and several engineers had spent the weekend setting up communications links from the nuclear engineering alpha
lab, where the Hollingsdale resided, to both ShipCom and the
command deck. This last was done at the request of the Cloudman.
If the ship was going to move, regardless of means, he wanted to
be in control of the means by which they were going to do it.

Though some of the best engineers on Eos had been called to assist with the experiment, Ben hadn't anticipated that the Kuulo Kuumottoomaa, one of his Kaks—a navigator Ben had never seen
before—and High Auditor Nethercott would be invited to observe.
They were standing in the back of the room, staying as much out
of the way as possible. But nothing escaped their scrutiny.

"What are *they* doing here?" Tommy Rosales whispered to Ben
when the spectators arrived at the last moment.

"I don't know," Ben remarked. "Let's ask."

Ben walked up to a gathering of technicians going over the large
Hollingsdale breeder—a reactor the size of a small house—and
buttonholed Dr. Silbarton.

"Eve, what are those people doing here?" he asked.

The High Auditor had had his eye on Ben the moment he had
walked into the lab. Apparently, Ben's little venture into the auditorium the other day had cost him anonymity among the Auditors.
Nethercott glared at Ben. Ben glared back, and the High Auditor
came over, having heard Ben's query. "I can assure you that we're
here as advisors only, Mr. Bennett," the Auditor said cordially.

"Advisors?" Ben said. "You're going to *advise* these people?
What qualifies you or . . . them"—Ben pointed at the Kuulo and

the Kak standing mute in their enclosed environment suits—"to advise anybody on anything?"

"They're just going to observe, Ben," Eve said.

"They shouldn't be here," Ben insisted.

Nethercott's eyebrows rose somewhat, but he did not seem to mind Ben's effrontery. He said, "President Porter invited us to observe the ship's use of energies it will be taking from trans-space, the realm of Mazaru."

"Horseshit," Ben said.

Several engineers had heard this and looked up. Even Rosales seemed surprised.

"Ben!" Eve said.

Ben felt his blood start to boil, although he wasn't sure why.

"They have *no* reason to be here," Ben stated. "That's all."

The High Auditor said nothing, but did not take his eyes off him.

Eve Silbarton pulled Ben aside. "What did you do? Trade your brain in?" she whispered harshly. "If you did, get it back. This one's defective." She tapped him hard between the eyes with a forefinger.

"Ow!"

"Look, this is Porter's idea. Nobody's done this before and he thinks it will make history—if we can pull it off. And it might be good for us to have several highly placed witnesses."

It was the Kuulo Kuumottoomaa's turn to voice an opinion on the matter. The voice box at his collar said, "We traveled in space for thousands of years using sublight-speed technologies before we came across the Onesci Lorii's mathematics and could build her Engines. But this maneuver you are attempting is new to us, at least the way your engineers have described it, and we may be of some help if something goes wrong."

Several of the workers in the room had paused to witness the exchange between Ben and the Grays.

"Then why not share Onesci mathematics with us so we can manufacture our own Engines and get the hell out of here?"

The High Auditor took in a breath sharply. But the Kuulo didn't seem to be offended. "When you are ready for them, they will make themselves known to you. That is how Mazaru works."

"He helps those who help themselves," Ben said. "What kind of help is that from the Almighty?"

"I'm sorry," the Kuulo said. "I do not understand—"

Dr. Israel Harlin, the head of the physics department, broke up the philosophical fracas. Harlin was a tall, white-haired man with a heavy beard, and a way of walking stooped as if he feared ceilings. "Gentlemen, please. We need everybody at their stations for this. We can argue later."

The two aliens and the Auditor backed away as if conceding some sort of minor victory to Ben. But Eve kept looking at him strangely—as if he had just had a personality overhaul, one that came with less common sense than the one it replaced. Maybe she was right, Ben admitted to himself. But it didn't cool his resentment.

One of the techs announced, "I've got a parallax focus at one thousand miles, dead ahead."

"C-graviton expansion point?" Dr. Harlin asked.

"Eighty miles behind us," the tech said. "We're ready to poke a hole in space on your command, Dr. Harlin."

The tall department head nodded. "It's the pilot's call. On his mark."

"*And you're sure we can use the beta-projection point as a brake?*" Captain Cleddman asked from the command deck.

"Yes," Eve Silbarton said, switching on her own com/pager. "The black hole ahead of us and the C-graviton expansion point behind us will give us enough pull and push to get us moving toward Kiilmist 5. We'll activate a second discontinuity to slow us down."

"*Behind us,*" Cleddman said.

"That's right. If we can stay outside the Schwarzchild limit of the alpha collapse point in front of us," Silbarton said, "then the thing will pull us toward it and quadruple our speed. We'll do the same to slow us down."

Tommy Rosales whispered to Ben. "How long is the discontinuity going to stay out in front of us?"

"Just a few seconds," Ben said. "But that's all we'll need to get us up to relativistic speeds—that is, if we don't get sucked into it directly or near enough to it to catch its gamma radiation."

"Has anyone ever done this before?" Rosales asked nervously.

"Only on paper," Ben replied.

"Swell."

"It's worse than that," Eve Silbarton said, having heard the two. "Time's going to pass us by on the outside. We're going to lose both contact and time with the rest of the Alley. But it can't be avoided."

"How much time will we lose?" Ben asked. "Has anyone done the math on that yet?"

"I did," Dr. Harlin said. "Depending on our top velocity, we should arrive at Kiilmist 5 in about four days. On the outside, however, we'll be out of contact for about two months."

"Mom and Dad aren't going to like *that*," Tommy Rosales said.

Dr. Harlin glanced back at their "advisors" standing at the rear of the room. "The good news is that it will give our Enamorati friends back at the Yards enough time to find us an available Engine or build us a new one."

"*If* this works," Ben said.

"That's right," the department chair said.

"Okay," Eve Silbarton announced, scanning her monitoring board. Lights became all green across it. "I think we're ready. Let's put Mr. Hollingsdale to work."

11

The Hollingsdale maneuver, as complicated and dangerous as it was, actually worked. The discontinuity, brought into existence and traveling well out ahead of them, stayed in place long enough to coax Eos up to the required velocity they needed to reach Kiilmist 5.

Perhaps more politically desirable was the outcome on the High Auditor and the two Enamorati witnesses. The two aliens had agreed that Mazaru had not been violated, concluding, in fact, that the success of the maneuver was an indication of how much Mazaru approved of it.

Which, Ben thought, was hogwash. This time, however, he kept his opinions to himself.

Ben left with Eve Silbarton soon after that, leaving it to the human engineers and Tommy Rosales—who decided to stay behind—to explain to a couple of nosy reporters from *The Alley Citizen* what they had just done and why every student on board should be proud. They were part of history now.

Ben and Eve Silbarton went straight to the gamma lab in the physics department. Ben was feeling buoyed by the experiment's success, but Eve was much less sanguine and kept silent.

Once they were in the gamma lab and the outer door closed—several undergraduate students were in the delta lab next door working on their own projects—Eve cornered Ben. "Look," she said sharply. "We're the focus of an intense investigation by campus security and God knows who else, and we don't need any more heat right now."

"What heat? It was *our* lab that got wiped out," Ben said.

"Listen, stupid. There are people on this ship whom the administration *and* the Ainge would rather see floating in space without their helmets."

"Like who?"

"People who are sympathetic to the KMA."

"People like you?"

"Exactly," Eve said. She lowered her voice and looked around the equipment-filled lab. "And I'm not the only one who feels this way. The captain does and so does Dr. Harlin. In fact, most of the science personnel on the ship have KMA sympathies."

"So?" Ben said. "They can't persecute you for your political beliefs. That's against more laws than I can count. The Ainge haven't rewritten the Human Constitution."

"Not yet they haven't. But they're trying," Eve said. "The fact is that they *can* affect the disposition of grant money for the university. They could dry us up if the political winds shift. And if you keep acting like a fourteen-year-old, they'll *really* come down on us. And that's what we don't want."

"So what *does* KMA stand for?"

"Forget about that!" she snapped. "Politics is the name of the game and you've got to think and *act* responsibly if you want to survive."

"I understand that," Ben said. "But no one can convince me that thirteen Ainge Auditors should have more status on this ship than any other religious group. Why isn't the Newman Center or Hillel or the other student religious groups located right up against the Enamorati compound? They should *all* be there. Who made the Ainge so special? They had no business being present when you activated the discontinuity reactor. Not one of them has any science or engineering experience."

"You really are an idiot, aren't you?"

"Only when I start thinking about things."

"Well, for now, *don't*. We can't afford to have campus security breathing down our throats. At least *I* can't."

In the middle of Eve's harangue, she had begun going about a security check, making sure the doors were locked and that no one was eavesdropping, at least electronically. She then threw a static cloak around them that would have stymied the best eavesdropping device known. Ben couldn't recall having ever seen Eve this intense before.

"So what's this *really* about?" he asked.

Eve turned to him. "What it's about is that Captain Cleddman doesn't want a new Enamorati Engine installed and he's going to do everything he can to prevent one from reaching us. That's what this is about."

"You're joking," Ben said.

"I've never told a joke in my life," Eve said. "The fact is we're almost ready to install our own stardrive system and getting to Kiilmist 5 will buy us the time we'll need to install it and get it working properly. *That's* why we can't have the heat."

Ben suddenly saw her in an entirely different light. "Dr. Brenholdt was working on an Alcubierre drive system in the alpha lab. Were *you* the person who took it out?"

Silbarton opened a locked door leading to an adjoining room, one that Ben never knew existed. He followed her.

"Are you out of your mind?" she asked fiercely. "That surprised me much as it did everyone else. In fact, I was worried that the disassembler might come this far and destroy *this* lab."

In the center of the smaller room, suspended above an antigrav plate where it could be worked on, was a device that looked as if it might have been the drive shaft taken from an automobile. It was seven feet long, two feet wide at one end, tapering off to just a few inches in width.

"*This* is the prototype of your engine?" Ben asked incredulously.

"It's not the prototype," Silbarton said. "This is the real thing."

Ben's own area of expertise was in fractal-compression technology. It was a technology that took naturally occurring fractal configurations, particularly in metals at the crystalline levels, and arranged them so that there was very little space between their molecules. *This* machine, however, was a masterpiece of compaction: Eve's engine, size-wise, was to the Enamorati Engines as a flea was to an elephant.

"*This* will power a ship as big as this one?" he asked.

Eve crouched down and inspected the underside of the floating device. "No. It would take six of these to power a ship as large as Eos. Maybe eight, depending."

"Onesci Engines are supposed to take up to eight hundred thousand cubic feet of space," Ben said. "These things are a fraction of that."

Eve stood up, dusting her hands. "We know so little about the Onesci Engines. We've always assumed that their Engines were as large as they are because of the way they processed energy taken from trans-space. Their reaction chambers would mostly be empty space. Combustion chambers, if you like."

"That could account for accidents," Ben said.

Eve shrugged. "Depends on where the combustion occurs. Mine take place *within* trans-space itself. We just tap into it."

Eve walked over to a nearby console and began activating a certain screen. "Come over here. I want you to see this."

Ben found a chair and slid over beside his teacher. "What have you got?"

On the screen appeared the words SHIPCOM—TRANSIT PORTAL LOG #99-2970.3.59—FOR UNIVERSITY USE ONLY.

Eve moved the video record forward. "Cutter Rausch dug this up this weekend. Campus security wanted it for their investigation. It's a video record of recent transit-portal jumps from portal number fifty-nine. It's the one nearest the alpha lab at the end of the reception hallway."

The video text was that of the individuals who had used the portal closest to the alpha lab in the hours preceding the disassembler attack. Since it had been a Friday afternoon—and classes weren't held on Fridays—the images were mostly of staff and faculty coming and going. Nothing incriminating there.

The chronometer passed 1200 hours, when everyone apparently went to lunch. So far, so good. Then a pile of students tumbled out of portal 59, laughing from the transit high. Ben blushed. There were Bombardiers all over the floor before portal 59 and one of them was him. Oops. As it was, right after that he had gone to pick up Ms. Borland, taking another transit jump to her dorm and getting higher still. He made a mental note to see if transit-portal jumping led to sexual dysfunction. . . .

The video text then showed the Bombardiers, minus Ben, doing the same thing later. They dove out of the portal, ran hell-for-leather for portal 60 at the far end of the hall, laughing all the way.

Ben swallowed. "I guess I can't persuade you that these are transit flashes of my friends?"

"Nope."

When a particular transit portal became overused, "flashes" often occurred in nearby systems, which would be portals 56 to 63. Sudden afterimages that lasted several seconds, transit flashes often would leap out of a portal ring in another hallway and scare the Ix out of anyone who happened to be nearby. It had happened to Ben a number of times.

"But these aren't important," Eve said as she forwarded the playback to where she wanted to be. "But these *may* be."

Eve slowed the playback. The portal's ring glowed with energy and there stood, to Ben's considerable surprise, the Avatka Viroo. The alien, in his usual environment suit, stepped from the portal, but only for a moment. He glanced around, then stepped back inside and was gone.

At first, Ben thought that the alien had taken the portal to the wrong destination, recognized the fact, then stepped back in. It happened frequently enough. But the playback showed the Avatka doing it two *more* times, each time stepping out, then stepping back.

"Now *those* are transit flashes," Ben said. "That portal could easily have been overloaded."

"Maybe," Eve said. "Now watch."

Once again, the Avatka made a transit appearance, but this time he stepped all the way through. And this time he carried Julia Waxwing's little polar bear in his arms.

The Avatka stepped completely out of the portal and walked swiftly out of sight of the video camera. This was no transit flash.

A quick check of the time and Ben saw that it wasn't too long after that when the Avatka showed up at his doorstep with the little dead bear.

"What about portal sixty at the end of the hall?" Ben asked. "It should have a video record of where he went."

Eve shook her head. "He didn't take it. He must have walked from this last exit point."

"Julia Waxwing should see this record," Ben said.

"You can take this copy," Eve told him. "But just remember, Ted Fontenot saw you with the bear in the aftermath of the alpha lab's destruction. He *might* think that the two of you are connected in some way—you and the Avatka. If there is dissension in the Enamorati ranks and the Avatka is one of the dissenters, then you could get some real heat from campus security."

"Dissension among the Enamorati? I thought that was a rumor."

"The Enamorati aren't talking," Eve said grimly. "But we think something like that has happened in there. In any case, if there *was* a revolt or insurrection among the Enamorati, the administration might think there's a connection between us. They could decide that our new stardrive is endangering both the ship and the Enamorati Compact. Porter will shut us down in a second. I don't want that to happen."

"That's a hell of a leap to connect me with radical elements among the Enamorati," Ben said.

"Maybe," Eve said. "Just *don't* draw him to me. I can't set up my drive system if I'm in jail."

"I get the picture," Ben admitted.

"Good," Eve said. "Stay the hell out of trouble."

"I'll do my best."

With that, Ben went in search of Julia with the data tile containing the video recording of the Avatka Viroo and her dead polar bear.

12

Julia Waxwing brought in two cups of freshly brewed coffee and set them both beside the viewing station where Professor Holcombe was making adjustments to a specialized StratoCaster tiara. The monitor screen on the desk was already showing the video content of a BronzeAngel 'Cast his clone-son Seth had made long ago.

Holcombe seemed intense, fired by demons Julia couldn't guess . . . or it just might have been that the Engine breakdown crisis had somehow energized him. It might also have something to do with the possibility of exploring a new world, one that even the Enamorati had never known about. The faculty senate had, that day, authorized its exploration by any university department interested in taking students to the surface. Holcombe had already reserved a gondola for his students.

Holcombe took the cup of coffee from Julia. He then lifted it in salute. "Cheers," he said, popping a small white pill.

"What was that?" Julia asked.

"It's a wayhigh," he said. "Twenty milligrams in sugar. Want one?"

So the man *wasn't* making it up.

Julia looked over her shoulder to see if anyone had heard. "A wayhigh? Aren't those illegal?"

"They're illicit, not illegal. There's a difference."

"How are they different?"

"Wayhighs are not covered in the *Controlled Substances Registry*. The Ainge merely frown on their use. They're against all stimulants. Heaven forbid that their followers should have open and active minds, thinking for themselves."

"Where did you get them?"

"An acquaintance of mine makes them."

"Here? On Eos?"

Holcombe nodded.

"Is it the same person who's selling the cigarettes?" she asked. Rumor had it that someone on Eos was dispensing cigarettes and other prohibited items on the black market.

Holcombe shook his head. "I don't think so."

Julia pulled up a chair. "How long have you been taking them?"

"All my life," Holcombe said.

Surprise blossomed on Julia's face.

Holcombe smiled slightly, pushing back a lock of white hair. "Everybody my age has some experience with drug use. It comes around every few generations. But mostly I did it because of my father. I've been doing it ever since he died."

Julia knew that Holcombe's father had been a High Auditor and that his whole family was very prominent on Tau Ceti 4. But she didn't know what the man's death had to do with wayhighs.

Holcombe handed Julia the tiara he'd been adjusting. "But enough of me," he said. "I called you down here because I thought you might want to experience an unedited StratoCast Seth made when he was starting out. It's very unusual and made me think of some of the work you've done."

Julia took the tiara.

"I wanted you to see what Seth ran into on Kissoi 3. Remember, this was taken about ten years ago. This might be the only copy in existence."

Julia leaned back in her chair, letting the tiara's spider-clamps press themselves to her temples.

Holcombe engaged the tiara and Julia jerked with surprise. The neural spike was immediate and she felt the 'Cast's euphoric energies tickling up her spine. Music started in, uncoiling in rapid-fire microtonal bursts, filling her sensory universe.

Then the visuals kicked in. She started to experience—see, feel, hear, and even smell—what Seth Holcombe had experienced.

Kissoi 3 was an Earth-like world, with blue skies that rushed with gorgeous cumulus clouds the size of asteroids. Julia could feel Seth Holcombe's surge of excitement as he leapt the crowns

of trees, swooped into small creek-filled canyons, skated above
alpine meadows. Sometimes he'd be running just inches off the
ground, other times he'd be half a mile high. Experiencing a StratoCast was not for the vertiginous or the agoraphobic.

Holcombe had been following the 'Cast, at least the visual and
musical part, on a smaller monitor screen on his desk. "Now, pay
attention to this section," he told her.

Off in the distance Julia saw—as Seth had seen—a storm taking
shape. It appeared to her—and Seth—almost like a living thing.
Julia even felt the sudden adrenaline rush that Seth Holcombe had
felt upon noticing the storm. The BronzeAngels running with him
came to a halt as they wondered what to do.

"Ix! Look at that!" Clark Evans, leader of the BronzeAngels,
cried out.

*"There was nothing in the weather specs describing anything
like that!"* Tim Stamets, another 'Caster beside him, said.

"Back to the ship, guys!" Seth shouted.

The BronzeAngels turned and ran—music still playing, veins
ablaze with fear-launched adrenaline. The cloud front moved like
a gigantically grotesque tornado, squat and ugly, churning with
sparkling lights flung out in streamers like deadly bolos. *It was
coming for them.* Ball lightning danced out from the cloud and
pummeled the meadowlands below them. *It was hungry. . . .*

Julia felt Seth's fear as he raced above the trees and slid down
to the valley where their gondola waited. The cloud, Seth felt, was
some sort of *animal* guarding its territory.

Julia took off the tiara. "Wow."

"This particular 'Cast was never marketed," Holcombe said.
"None of the other BronzeAngels had decent recordings of the
event. They were all scared."

"I can see why."

"Did those clouds remind you of anything?"

She nodded, having recognized them from the start. "Firebirds,"
she said.

Julia's first scholarly paper had been on cross-cultural thunder-
bird folk legends, tales of sky beings whose anger was easily
aroused. Native American tribes had them. So, too, the Australian

Aborigines. The Bedouins of the Sahara Desert had them as well. Theirs were called *jinn,* and were not to be dealt with lightly.

"It might be interesting," Julia said, "to go back to that planet to see what they were. Does anybody know anything about Kissoi 3?"

Holcombe shook his head. "The Enamorati stopped there once, at least long enough to put it in their catalog. But they never explored it. So many worlds, so few Engines," he said wistfully.

"Anybody home?" came a voice behind Julia.

Julia turned to see Ben Bennett standing in the doorway to Holcombe's office. "Ben!" Julia said.

Holcombe turned as well. "This is your jailbird friend, Ben, I take it."

"Oh, yes," Julia told him. "This is Ben Bennett. This is my advisor, Dr. Holcombe."

Ben came in and shook the professor's hand. "Hi," he said.

"Glad to see you out of jail."

"Glad to *be* out," Ben said.

Julia didn't know what to say. Her mind had been on Seth Holcombe's experience. Ben's appearance had been a jolt.

"I thought I'd show you this," Ben said, holding out a video tile. He also nodded at the activated monitor.

"What is it?" Julia asked.

"Eve Silbarton gave this to me. It's a transit-portal record she got from ShipCom. I think you should see what's on it."

"Let's see what we've got here," Holcombe said, taking the tile and slotting it into the 2D unit.

Ben inched close to Julia as Holcombe queued the tile. Her senses seemed unusually keen as they watched the 2D. She could discern the aroma of the soap he used that morning, his deodorant, and the dab of cologne he put on before he left his room.

What was on the screen made her stop thinking of Ben, however. She watched the video play itself through . . . and through again as Dr. Holcombe ran it back several times, just to be certain.

Ben finally said, "This last appearance of the Avatka with your bear *could* be a transit flash. I checked other transit-portal records and this very same image occurred four other times. So the real

Avatka could have been much closer to the dorms than it appears from this flash."

"Yet, he *was* in the physics wing," Professor Holcombe said.

"We don't know that either," Ben said. "They *all* could be transit flashes. But he *did* have the bear when he came to my room and it wasn't too long after that when the alpha lab was destroyed."

"What could this mean?" Julia asked Professor Holcombe.

Holcombe leaned forward. "It was a few hours after this the Engine went out. Maybe the Engine went out because this Avatka wasn't at his station."

"But what was he doing in Ben's dorm with my bear?" Julia asked. "Jingles never wandered out of the dorm, the girls' dorm, I mean."

Ben said, "I think the Avatka found him somewhere else."

"But why would he take it to your room?" Julia asked.

"My room is right next to the stairwell. It would be the first one he came to when he came out into the hallway."

"Has anybody asked the Avatka about this?" Holcombe said.

Ben shook his head. "I tried. But the Auditor I spoke with said that the Enamorati are preparing for *'Makajaa,'* some sort of religious ceremony, and none of them could be disturbed."

"Which Auditor was this?" Holcombe asked.

"Orem Rood," Ben told him. "He said that the Enamorati would be secluded until both the *Makajaa* ceremony and the *Sada-vaaka* insertion ceremony were finished."

"That second ceremony," Julia said. "I've never heard of it before. What is it?"

"It's a three-day-long ceremony that involves the insertion of the new Engine," Holcombe said. "Since Engines tend to be inserted into ships at the Enamorati Yards, few humans have been anywhere near a *Sada-vaaka* ceremony."

"He also said something about *rakkavan*," Ben told him.

"That's an 'adjustment to Mazaru' period when the Enamorati tweak the Engine in trans-space to make sure everything's in working order. That lasts about ten days."

"Rood said that my interview could begin after *rakkavan*," Ben said. "He told me not to bother the Avatka until then."

Holcombe looked to Ben. "So they just gave you the runaround?"

"That pretty much describes it."

"I know Rood," Holcombe said. "He's a poltroon."

Julia popped out the video tile. "Well what about now? This isn't sort of sacred period for them, is it?"

"I don't think so," Holcombe said. "If it was, I'm sure it would have been announced in the student newspaper or in a faculty bulletin."

"Then let's see if we can talk to him now," Julia said. "I want to show him *this*." Julia held the data tile between her thumb and forefinger.

"Try it," Holcombe said.

"I will," Julia said, getting to her feet.

Holcombe then said, "Orem Rood is the son of my uncle's fifth son by his fourth wife. If he causes you any trouble, tell him that I know what he and Pamela Farthing did on Marlin Place and that I will personally tell the High Prophet on Tau Ceti 4 in very graphic detail. Don't say anything else. Just that."

"All right," Julia said, although she didn't know what that meant any more than Ben did.

"He seems like a nice man," Ben said as they approached the portal. "I didn't know he had it in for the Ainge so badly."

"His father was a High Auditor for eighteen years. His whole family is worth billions of dollars throughout the Alley."

"What's he doing running the archaeology department? Why isn't he an Auditor himself?"

"He got excommunicated from the Church when he was in college," Julia said. "Nobody really knows any more than that."

"Was his dad High Prophet then?"

"Not for a few more years."

"Wow."

"But, you know," she said slowly, carefully, "ever since we've come out of trans-space, his mind's gone weird. He's acting like . . ."

"Like what?"

"Like one of those friends of yours."

"The Bombardiers?"

She nodded.

"They're just idiots," Ben said. "And Professor Holcombe is *not* an idiot."

They transited directly to the Ainge compound, far aft in the ship. The large ornamental oak doors of the Ainge Sanctuary stood open; but just like the other day when he and George Clock ventured there, Ben and Julia found the place empty.

Once they were inside, Ben could see that the giant silver crack in the window of the viewing chamber had completely healed itself. The "communion rod" beyond the wall, however, was still inactive, and it looked as if some sort of calamity had been unleashed in there. Some of the eerie Enamorati "art" on the walls of the communion-rod room—strange moon shapes, odd crescents of silver, long scythes of a rust-iron color—had fallen to the floor or were hanging loose as if popped out of place by some stifled explosion in the Engine compartment itself.

"Where is everybody?" Julia asked.

Ben looked over his shoulder, half-expecting High Auditor Nethercott to pour out of the shadows. But no one was lurking there. "Maybe they *are* in seclusion," he said.

Ben walked down the aisle then off to the left where a door led to the Inner Sacristy. Few people went this far; even Nolan Porter, the president of the university, had never entered the inner chambers. He venerated them too much.

But Ben didn't venerate them and apparently neither did Julia.

The door to the Sacristy opened and they stepped inside.

The Auditors lived like monks and their decor showed it. The place was drab, soulless. There was no art on the walls and the rooms they passed led to apartment quarters of Spartan character. And they were all empty. As were the main dining center and the library. They heard no sounds, saw no one.

"Where do you think they are?" Julia whispered.

They came to the end of a corridor whose airlock seal was wide open. *Here* they heard voices. Ben and Julia stepped through the archway, hugging the walls, both their hearts hammering.

What they saw took their breath away. This was the fabled Inner Temple of the Ainge Auditors—an amphitheater of wooden pews that faced another large glass wall similar to the one in the public auditorium. Beyond this wall, though, was a very strange machine. To Ben, it looked like a dynamo, a dynamo that apparently was connected to the steering-rod facility visible from the auditorium. But whatever it was, parts of it were now smoldering.

The Auditors—all thirteen of them—were at the bottom of the amphitheater, their faces pressed against the glass wall like children at an aquarium, each trying to get a better look in the room beyond.

The scene inside the "dynamo" room was horrific, a bloodbath, a hell pit. Enamorati bodies, perhaps as many as a dozen, were everywhere, with blood on the walls, entrails on the floor. The odd decorations on the walls and the ceiling had been blasted from their stays, much of the art now covering the Enamorati bodies. Nothing moved in the smoke and haze.

By their astonished expressions, Ben guessed that the Ainge themselves had only just discovered the bloodshed. And they, too, were stunned by what they saw.

"Ixion!" Ben blurted out uncontrollably.

Every head in the room turned toward them. Seconds after that, the corridor seal behind them closed.

Ben tried to recall what the Eos University handbook had to say about trespassing, and how many years in prison they could get for it.

13

Four Auditors, led by Nethercott and Rood, hustled Ben and Julia out of the Inner Temple as fast as they could, away from the carnage in the "dynamo" room. Ben was surprised at how strong his captors were. Auditors—whose rank was the highest one could attain in the Ainge Church—spent their waking hours listening to the hum of God in their Auditor boxes. Where had they found the time to work out? The guy that gripped Ben came close to possessing the strength that Tommy Rosales had.

But Ben didn't go easily or quietly. Both he and Julia struggled as they were escorted out of the Auditors' domain.

However, just when they reached the outer auditorium, the entire escort halted. For standing in the middle of the aisle that led to the oak doors and the nearest transit portal were two ominous men. Ben recognized them from their photographs in the general university catalog, but this was the first time he had seen them in the flesh: Messrs. Sammons and Wangberg from the Rights Advocacy Office. Behind them was a deadman who also wore a black suit, but whose metal eyes and ears recorded every detail of the encounter. Deadman details were very much admissible in a court of law and mere sight of them often caused the potential malefactor to think again.

"What do *you* people want?" High Auditor Nethercott asked.

Winn Sammons, tall, toothy, with jet black hair, stepped forward. "Albert Holcombe called us to look in on these two people. He said that you might be persecuting them. It appears as if he was correct in that assumption."

The deadman leaned in a bit closer.

"This is none of your business," the High Auditor said, tugging at the hem of his gray tunic. His chin thrust out from the tight, white collar.

"So far," Sammons said, "you have committed battery and possible illegal detention."

"These two people trespassed into the very heart of the Temple, and *that* we don't allow," the Auditor exclaimed. Two more Auditors came from the Sacristy and joined Nethercott's crowd.

"We weren't trespassing," Ben said. "No one met us in the anteroom—the Sacristy—so we just went on inside. We didn't know what to think."

Julia faced Nethercott. "And I want to know what *you* know about the Avatka who killed my bear!"

The deadman trained its eyes, ears, and olfactory senses on the Auditors. Deadmen were a hundred times more efficient than old-style lie detectors, for they were able to detect sweat odors and the pheromones of fear.

"What bear?" High Auditor Nethercott said. "What are you talking about?"

"An Avatka killed my little bear!" Julia said. "I *demand* to speak to him!"

Nethercott blinked several times, not making any sense of Julia's words.

Advocate Wangberg stepped forward. He was shorter than his partner, but more muscularly compact. He looked as if he'd rather wrestle with an opponent than litigate him. "And this is the reason you sought out an Auditor. To help you speak with this Avatka whom you believed killed your bear. Is that right?" Wangberg asked.

"You're leading the witness!" Auditor Orem Rood burst out.

"I'm merely getting to the heart of the matter the fastest way possible," Wangberg said. "Besides, we're not in court."

"That's it, exactly," Julia said. "We couldn't find anybody, so we went looking. There's no law forbidding us to enter their chambers without their permission. It's only the Enamorati who have that rule."

"But . . . these people were *trespassing*," Nethercott sputtered.

Advocate Sammons faced Julia. "Did you announce your presence?" he asked.

"Yes!" Julia said swiftly, defiantly, lying through her teeth. Ben was impressed. This was a side to her character he hadn't seen yet.

"And when they didn't answer," Julia continued, "we went looking for them. We thought they could help us. And now they want to *arrest* us! They're supposed to be the servants of humanity! Now look at them!"

Nethercott stammered. "That's not . . . they were . . . don't you understand? They were *trespassing*!" Nethercott was livid with barely contained rage.

"They were in the Inner Temple!" stressed Auditor Rood.

"Are either of you registered members of the Ainge Church?" Kerry Wangberg asked.

Ben knew that he didn't have to answer any question regarding his own civil liberties, but he also knew where Mr. Wangberg was going with such a question.

"No," Ben said. "I'm not."

Julia shook her head.

Wangberg faced the Auditors. "If these two people belonged to the Ainge religion, then you *might* have some jurisdiction over them. But since they aren't, and since you have sequestered them without immediate access to counsel, it seems that *you* can be held on charges of false imprisonment and perhaps attempted kidnapping." Wangberg then turned to Julia. "Did they physically assault you?"

Julia pointed to Auditor Rood. "He did! He *grabbed* me!"

Ben was, frankly, amazed. Jeannie Borland had the personality of a dishrag compared to this extraordinary young woman.

"We now have charges of assault," Mr. Wangberg said.

"Whose side are you on?" High Auditor Nethercott exploded. "*We're* the aggrieved party! *They're* the ones who committed the crime!"

"Then press charges," Sammons said. "But if you do, then I must encourage these two young people to press charges against *you* which are far more serious than your charges."

Nethercott's eyebrows knitted angrily. "If you were Ainge, I would have your job."

"I don't think you'd want it," Sammons said. "The pay is lousy and the hours are terrible and you'd have to deal with people such as yourself."

Ben heard a commotion behind them and he turned around to see a bunch of people enter the auditorium. Lieutenant Ted Fontenot and three of his associates appeared. So did Eve Silbarton and two student reporters from *The Alley Citizen,* and one from the student-run radio station, KEOS. Albert Holcombe was a hell of a cagey old coot, Ben decided. The Marines had landed, and the Auditors saw that the battle was all but lost.

A while later, Captain Cleddman came down from the command deck and the Ainge became so occupied with defending themselves that Julia and Ben were able to slip away to let the adults play this one out.

Julia, however, was still driven by her anger and her need to know what *exactly* had happened to her little bear. An autopsy might have supplied a few answers, particularly if the Avatka had perhaps poisoned Jingles. But Julia abandoned the idea of subjecting Jingle Bear's body to an autopsy, feeling that such an ordeal would be too much for the little creature's spirit. Still, she wanted to know what killed the bear.

It was clear now that she wasn't going to get any answers from the Auditors or the Enamorati. But the arrival on the scene of the student reporters suggested to her that *The Alley Citizen* might have more expertise in seeking out the sources that might supply her with the answers she needed.

So she and Ben went to the offices of *The Alley Citizen.* The *Citizen* was part of the communications department, which also operated KEOS and had its own staff of reporters. Between these two media sources, they could blanket almost the entire student body. What also gave this team their strength was the fact that none of the students or faculty were members of the Ainge Church. They would, therefore, be less inclined to soft-pedal the misdeeds of the Auditors. Assuming there were any.

Julia and Ben met with the editorial staff of *The Alley Citizen* and told them everything they had experienced, from their first meeting in the disassembled physics lab to their explorations of the Ainge Inner Temple—emphasizing that they knocked before entering. They finished with the account of the "dynamo" room. During their recitation, the two reporters who had been sent to the Ainge quarters had finally returned and they had juicy video of the warring parties, particularly High Auditor Nethercott.

The faculty advisor of the student newspaper was a man in his sixties named Kevin Dobbs. He had been present when Julia and Ben walked in, and throughout their interview he merely puffed away at a Red Apple cigarette, Jeannie Borland's brand, saying nothing.

But the senior student editor, a woman named Elise Rutenbeck, and her top reporter, Mark Innella, were all too taken with the story. Their eyes lit up when they sensed that blood could be spilt with the Auditors and quite possibly the administration.

It was at this juncture that Dr. Dobbs spoke up. "Of course this is all anecdotal. We can report it as eyewitness accounts, but we've got to have hard evidence, something corroborative."

"You should have taken a shouldercam in with you," said Mark Innella, a rail-thin boy with ferretlike features. "Then we could have really nailed them. It's about time somebody whittled the Auditors down to size."

Elise Rutenbeck was a heavyset young woman whose temperament was much less incendiary than Innella's—which was probably why she was editor and Innella wasn't. "You said you didn't get close to the window to this 'dynamo' room."

"We didn't have to," Ben said. "There was blood everywhere. On the walls, the floor. And we saw at least a half-dozen bodies on the floor."

Julia nodded at this. "All of the Auditors were there, gathered at the window. It must have just happened."

"Do you know *how* the Enamorati were killed?" Innella asked.

"The bodies looked as if they were hacked up. But the dynamo itself, or whatever it was, was scorched and burned."

"But the Enamorati were hacked up?" Rutenbeck asked.

"That's what it looked like to me," Ben said. "To us, I mean."

"Perhaps this fire in the dynamo room," Dr. Dobbs said, "was part of our Engine malfunction and the Enamorati in the room were killed by it."

"But that was a few days ago," Julia said. "*This* looked like it happened a few hours ago."

"Yes, but," Dobbs observed, "there is the possibility that the aliens you saw today *were* killed by some factor relating to the Engine malfunction. A part could have been blown loose, anything might have happened to them."

"Well, *something* happened in there," Ben said.

Rutenbeck turned to her faculty advisor. "Dr. Dobbs, look what we've got. We had our Engine breakdown, a disassembler weapon went off in the ship, and now we've got an eyewitness account of some kind of slaughter in an engineering room visible from the Auditor's Inner Temple. That's a hell of a story."

"And my dead bear," Julia added. "Don't forget that."

"And a dead polar bear," Rutenbeck acknowledged.

"And nothing to link them conclusively," Dobbs said.

"Connected or not, this should go out in tomorrow's paper," Mark Innella said.

"Only what Ben and Julia have seen themselves," Dr. Dobbs said. "To say they are connected is pure conjecture."

"But we could suggest a connection in a student editorial," Rutenbeck offered. "It would be just my opinion."

"If you do," Dobbs said, "you'll call down the wrath of every Gray in the university. Remember, we exist at the behest of the university charter. In campus struggles on Earth, the journalism department is the first to be purged. On Eos, 'purging' could mean something altogether different. I'd watch it, if I were you."

"But these two people have been *in* there!" Innella insisted. "At the very least we can report that."

In the background, various students were at their design boards working on the next issue of *The Alley Citizen*. Layout, typesetting, ink chemistry, multimedia lithography, even papermaking were required of all journalism majors. Julia had never given any thought as to how the student newspaper was put together—or how fragile its existence was in the eyes of the administration. Now she knew.

"Even if it is the truth," Dobbs said in a nimbus of smoke, "it'll cause trouble. You might want to consider the real possibility that they might disband the newspaper if not the entire department."

"It's worth the stretch," Innella said.

"Incoming!" one of the students announced.

A chime went off and the large wall screen in *The Alley Citizen*'s office came alive. The president of the university, Nolan Porter, appeared, and he did not look at all happy.

"Faculty and students. I have an important announcement to make. Until further notice, all classes are hereby canceled and students are restricted to their dorm rooms. Faculty and staff are to stay in their apartments. All classrooms, laboratories, and workstations are closed. This includes the student newspaper and the student radio station. I am declaring a state of emergency, and emergency bylaws are now in effect. If you are not familiar with those, consult your student handbook. Thank you for your attention."

"Well, shit," said an undergraduate at her editing board.

"Looks like something *did* happen back there," Dr. Dobbs said. He stubbed out his cigarette.

"Maybe it's spilling over into the ship," Ben said aside to Julia. "The fighting among the Enamorati, I mean."

At that juncture, a bookish-looking student appeared at the door. Julia had never seen the young man before this.

"This is Scott Nessa," Dr. Dobbs told them. "He's the student manager at KEOS. I'll bet he has something wonderful to tell us."

Nessa walked over to Dobbs's desk and helped himself to an illicit cigarette, which he lit expertly. "You should see it. Campus security is pulling our broadcasting equipment."

"What?" Dobbs said.

"They're pulling it right out of the wall," Nessa said. "They took our keys, music tiles, computer files. Everything."

"Can they do that?" Ben asked.

"Apparently," Scott Nessa said.

Dr. Dobbs stood up, pocketed his cigarettes, and said, "That means that we're next. All right, boys and girls. We're going samizdat. You know the drill."

" 'Samizdat'?" Ben asked. "What the hell is that?"

"You're going to find out," Dobbs said.

14

Whatever had transpired in the Enamorati "dynamo" room, it hadn't spilled over to the rest of the ship. President Porter's campus-wide shutdown might have been a response to the rumors of an Enamorati revolt, but for Ben there was no way of knowing what the Enamorati were up to. At the very least, the Auditors weren't talking.

Also part of the campus-wide shutdown was the data-bullet rail-launch system. Although data bullets could be written and compressed and placed in the rail queue for launch, they could not be sent. The rumor mill suggested that President Porter didn't want Mom and Dad to get wind that the Enamorati might be running amok on Eos. A more reasoned approach suggested that Porter thought the university needed a cooling-down period and opted for a "holiday" period . . . at least until the ship reached the inner planetary system of Kiilmist. Still, what it meant was that no news was going out and none was coming in.

However, in the communications department, Dr. Dobbs had managed to scatter his journalism students throughout the ship, taking with them what equipment they could. Since all networked computers and printers had been blocked on President Porter's command, the journalism students had to improvise. They made their own printers as they had been trained to do, and they made their own paper by tapping into the ship's food-processing system in the student commons.

This was samizdat. In the tradition of the anti-Stalinists in the old Soviet Union, the students published *The Alley Citizen* in the Eos University equivalent of basements and backrooms, entirely underground. Copies were then delivered on foot and by hand while the editorial staff dismantled the press and moved it to another locale for the next edition. That Kevin Dobbs was a member of the KMA didn't come out until it was all over.

Ben found a copy of the newly named *The Alley Comrade* before his door the next day. In it were editorials excoriating the administration Grays for hiding the truth about the Auditors and the Enamorati. *The Alley Comrade* printed his and Julia's adventure in the Inner Temple and what they had seen there, but the articles did not mention Ben and Julia by name. They were called instead "reliable sources." None of it was verifiable and all of it libelous. However, no one at the *Comrade* gave a shit.

Still, most of the students were quite happy to have classes canceled and the greater majority of them spent their time in the student commons playing pool, video games, and the like. It was a nice holiday.

Ben, however, was in the grip of a personal dilemma. Part of him wanted to track down Julia and spend more time with her—she was unlike any woman he had ever met. After all, what kind of a girl would have a *bear* for a pet? But another part of Ben knew that the events of the past five days were unprecedented and that he'd had a major role in it. He wanted to know if there was anything new regarding the Enamorati or what the Auditors didn't want him to see in the Inner Temple. Curiosity won out.

After breakfast in the student commons, Ben, with little else to do, headed for the makeshift offices of *The Alley Comrade*. He'd heard a rumor that they were operating out of a vacant room behind a barber shop and beauty salon in the student commons. Since there was no reason for him to go to his office to prepare for the two classes he taught as a postgrad, he decided to look in on *The Alley Comrade*.

When Ben reached the offices, he found that the student staff had already packed up and moved on. Ben paused before a corridor wall screen and summoned up the campus directory menu. Not knowing what else to do, he asked the directory for the whereabouts of Mark Innella. Which he got.

And that surprised him. A real revolutionary would have covered his tracks better. Yet the directory showed Innella's com/pager giving a location in the university library, the only other place on the ship to which students still had free access. Classes might have been canceled, but homework still had to be done.

The library was approximately 350 yards from Ben's present position. But part of the shutdown included the transit portals, and without the transit portals in operation people had to walk wherever they wanted to go. So he did.

The menu indicated that Innella was in a back room that was part of the Special Collections department of the library. No one stopped him from entering the library technical-processing area, and he found a side room that appeared to be the place on the directory where Innella could be found.

Ben walked right in without knocking.

A dozen students were busy pecking away at word processors, polishing the stories of the next edition. Several people gasped when Ben stepped inside.

"Shut the door!" Innella said, rising from his seat, pencil behind his ear. He rushed behind Ben and pulled the door closed, but not without checking to see if anyone had followed him.

"How did you find us?" Innella asked.

Ben pointed to the reporter's collar chevrons. "Through the university's main directory. You left your pager on."

"Shit!" Innella said, tweaking it off. Other students doublechecked to see if theirs were turned off.

"Now they'll find us for sure!" one student said.

"I think if they wanted to track you down," Ben told them, "they would've done it by now."

"Then maybe the rumor is true," another student said.

"What rumor?" Ben asked.

"That there's a rift among the faculty," Innella told him.

"A rift? What kind of rift?"

"There's a big stew whether or not we should continue the circuit and go home," Innella said. "Some of the staff and the faculty want to go back to Earth and let the H.C. Council in Geneva straighten everything out."

"Straighten what out?" Ben asked.

"What you and your girlfriend saw in the Inner Temple," Innella told him. "That, and the Engine breaking down. That's upset more

faculty than has been let on. That's one of the things we're looking into right now."

"The natives are getting restless," Elise Rutenbeck said, an ink
smudge on her forehead. "And if there *is* a fight going on among
the Enamorati, word has it a lot of people want to seal off the entire Auditor quarters so the Enamorati can't get through to the rest
of the ship."

"They should seal the Auditors inside there with them," muttered a discontented student.

"Should have done it a long time ago," someone else added.

Ben thought about this. He was only a lecturer, not privy to the
dealings of the tenured faculty in the physics department. His only
real contact with the rest of the university faculty was Eve Silbarton, and she hadn't mentioned anything about faculty or staff unrest. On the other hand, she had been busy. Canceling classes was
probably the best thing that could have happened, under the circumstances. It now gave her the time to work on her stardrive system around the clock.

"We've been racking our brains trying to figure out a way to interview the Avatka you saw," Innella said. "We even thought of
mailing him a letter, like the old days. But we couldn't figure out
a way to deliver it. The courier system is shut down, what with the
administrative offices closed."

"They'd have to get through the Auditors," Ben said. "And
they'd be suspicious of a letter."

Scott Nessa, the former manager of KEOS, had been over in a
corner reading a book, *The Discourses,* by Meher Baba, which
Ben recognized from a humanities class he had taken long ago.
With the radio shutdown, Nessa had absolutely nothing to do.
"Have you tried speaking with one of the Tagani? Anyone can contact them and you don't have to go through the administration or
the Auditors."

Another student said, "We had a Tagani historian talk to us two
weeks ago in Mr. Wharton's class. The Enamorati historian caste
is always eager to talk with humans."

"Let's find out," Mark Innella said.

The first thing they had to do was find a history graduate student
who knew how to contact the few Tagani who traveled with Eos.

They didn't want a member of the history department faculty in on the ploy. About half of the history faculty were members of the Ainge Church, and right now the students needed to stay away from the Ainge.

They found a sympathetic ear in a graduate student named Paul Wierenga, who was sitting in a study carrel just outside the library tech center. When he was told what *The Alley Comrade* was looking for, he was only too happy to help.

In a darkened office in Special Collections, they opened a computer link to the Enamorati quarters, which, surprisingly, went through. Ben guessed that the library's tech computers were on the same com links as the physical plant, and the physical plant never closed or had any of its necessary functions belayed.

Wierenga, a tall, balding young man in his thirties, spoke to the 2D screen. "This is Paul Wierenga summoning the Tagani Veljo Tormis. Please acknowledge."

Ben half-expected nothing to happen. But seconds later, the visage of the Tagani historian Veljo Tormis appeared on screen.

"This is Veljo Tormis," the being said. "I wish to assist you." The eerie greenish yellow atmosphere swirled around the Enamorati's head and his nostrils took the vapors in with small inhalations.

"Hello," Wierenga said enthusiastically. "We met last semester when I scheduled you for Professor Patterson's lecture series."

"I recall this," the alien said.

"We would like to continue the lecture series when classes begin next week, but we're afraid that too many of your colleagues have been killed. Is that true?"

Ben had devised the cover for their call. As Wierenga spoke, everyone else remained out of the reciprocal camera's range, making it seem as if Wierenga were acting alone.

"No Tagani has died," the alien said. "We will be able to assist you in any way."

Wierenga did not miss a beat despite the shrewd evasiveness of the Tagani's answer. "We were thinking of interviewing an Avatka for the lecture series. One of our teachers suggested the Avatka Viroo. Will he be available?"

"I am afraid that our catastrophic Engine failure has made the entire Avatka caste unavailable until the new Engine is installed and flight-tested."

Wierenga faked disappointment. "I'm sorry to hear that. The Avatka Viroo was High Auditor Nethercott's favorite. Bishop Nethercott's going to be at the lecture series, you know."

"I did not know that," the alien admitted.

"We would really like having the Avatka Viroo speak to our class," Wierenga insisted. "Is there any possible way this can be arranged?"

With no trace of emotion, the creature said, "The Avatka caste is presently being cared for and will be unable to speak with any member of the human community probably until we reach Wolfe-Langaard 4. The matter can be taken up with them at that time."

The students flanking the 2D screen, trying to stay out of the reciprocal camera's view, looked at each other. One young reporter started scribbling frantically on her notepad.

"Wolfe-Langaard 4?" Wierenga asked. "Are we going to leave the Alley Circuit?"

The Tagani said, "Given the recent changes in our own . . . administration, we have decided that we also need a new class of Avatkas and Kaks. It will be a journey of some months, but it will allow for a more efficient Engine crew."

"Sir, I would hate to think that something terrible has happened to the Avatka Viroo. Has he been hurt in any way? I hope you understand that we are your friends and there isn't anything we wouldn't do for you."

"I am sorry to say that this member has been killed," the Tagani said. "Many of us perished in the Engine's breakdown. But I do thank you for your offer of help. Perhaps we can arrange something for the upcoming *Makajaa* ceremony. Though it is forbidden for you to witness the Engine's removal, we could use your support and prayers."

"I can rally the students whenever you wish. Will you let me know when your new ceremony starts?" Wierenga asked.

"I shall call you in forty-eight hours," the Tagani said.

"Please do so," Wierenga said enthusiastically.

The Tagani said the Enamorati equivalent of "goodbye" and the transmission came to an end.

The students gathered around Wierenga.

"The new Engine will arrive in forty-eight hours?" Innella asked. "I thought the new Engine was *weeks* away. Why haven't the Grays told us about this?"

"Maybe they don't know," someone suggested.

"Where is Wolfe-Langaard 4?" another student asked. "Have any of you heard of it? Is it in the Alley?"

"And since when are we going there instead of our next scheduled port of call?" Elise Rutenbeck asked.

"Let's print it all and find out," an undergrad suggested.

"That'll liven things up," Ben said.

"Let's hit the presses," Rutenbeck ordered. "This is going out now. Today. Are you in on this, Bennett?" she asked.

"I think I *started* it," Ben said.

15

The eagerness of the staff of *The Alley Comrade* to get the news out at any cost was their undoing. The issue, again hand-delivered, carried the news that the Avatka Viroo had been killed and that his "caste," or what remained of them, were being cared for. The paper also contained the news that the new Engine would be arriving *very* soon—much sooner than expected—and that Eos University was about to begin a months-long journey to some place called Wolfe-Langaard 4 after their new Engine was installed.

The Grays went nuclear and conducted a shipwide crackdown. Campus security, aided by members of the ROTC, undertook a thorough search for the comrades responsible for the illegal newspaper. They rounded up the editors, the reporters, the fact-finders, the photojournalists, and the printing staff, confiscating their printing equipment and laptop computers and throwing most of the staff into detention so they could be grilled more closely.

They also went after the Enamorati who had been the source of the information. High Auditor Nethercott reluctantly put them into contact with the Tagani Veljo Tormis. The High Auditor did not want to disturb the Enamorati in their time of crisis, but President Porter told him that they'd have an even bigger crisis on board the ship if he didn't.

The Tagani did not disavow the content of the articles, saying that the business about Wolfe-Langaard 4 was a bit premature, and he apologized for the grief it might have caused. The staff of *The Alley Comrade* was finally set free, but they were no longer journalism students and the journalism department had been dissolved. The staff of *The Alley Comrade* had become de facto Bombardiers.

News of this fracas might have inflamed the student body of any normal university to protest, but the students of Eos now had a greater, and much more hopeful, distraction: Eos University had finally reached the planet Kiilmist 5 and had pulled into a three-hundred-mile-high orbit above the Earth-like world. Whatever else was going on in the university could not rival a brand-new planet to explore. Even the members of campus security were interested.

Viewing an orbital insertion—regardless the planet—was a tradition in the university. Students gathered throughout the ship, wherever giant 2D screens were available, to watch the slow orbital ballet as the Cloudman guided the giant ship into a stable orbit. No lecture was involved, no sermon from President Porter—just the blue-white limb of an undiscovered planet turning slowly below them on giant 2D screens everywhere.

Ben found Julia with Professor Holcombe in a seminar room used jointly by the physical sciences. Ben was joined this day by the Bombardiers who took time out of their farting-around schedule to view the planetary unveiling.

The surprises started coming almost immediately. Captain Cleddman earlier had released several satellites and landsats into various orbits to begin scanning the planet for raw, environmental data. Kiilmist 5 was half again as big as the Earth and its yearly cycle around its star-sun was about sixteen months. It had two moons, one of which had its own debris ring. People were already talking of going to the beta moon, if only to figure out how such a small body could have a ring around it at all.

Ben sat next to Julia while George Clock and Tommy Rosales sat behind them. Professor Holcombe sat off to one side where he had access to the controls to the video equipment that would allow him to switch between satellites. Several other faculty had seated themselves close to Holcombe and conferred among themselves, just as excited as any student to see this new world.

Tommy Rosales poked George Clock. "Hey, take a look at that blue sky. Maybe they'll let us take down a couple of kites."

One of the professors down in front had heard the remark. She turned and said, "Doesn't look like there are any mountain ranges, boys. It's mostly low hills and erosion canyons."

"So?" a freshman student sitting behind Rosales and Clock asked.

Clock turned around. "Without mountain ranges you could have surface winds in excess of two hundred miles an hour. Go kiting in a breeze like that and you'll get your wings clipped."

"Or worse," a graduate student added, "you might never touch ground. At those speeds, the winds could keep you aloft forever."

In the upper right corner of the screen was a full-image view of Kiilmist 5 taken at a distance of a million miles. A reddish orange band of airborne gunk—or so it seemed to Ben—girdled the equator. It was easily a thousand miles in width, and was no telling how many miles deep. It looked similar to Jupiter's Great Red Spot, probably a stagnant jet stream.

A closer view of the planet's northern hemisphere showed that it had several more continents than did the Earth, and a feed from a landsat in polar orbit revealed ice caps at the poles. But the continents near the mid-latitudes away from the stagnant jet stream seemed to be quite congenial, with green forests, large lakes, and diverse river systems.

"By the way the continents are distributed I'd say that continental drift may have come to an end," someone said.

"Especially if there are no mountain ranges," added a vigilant student.

Along the side of the large viewscreen appeared readouts of measurements and other data. Another student had been examining this and said, "Look at its axial tilt. It's nearly perpendicular to the ecliptic. If it ever had any axial tilt in its past, it doesn't have one now."

"A rotational period is almost seventy-two hours long," a female student added. "With an oxygen-nitrogen mix at twenty-three to seventy-six, the planet is very, very old."

"Strike a match," someone else said, "and you might set whole continents on fire."

"But *how* did the oxygen level get so high?" another student asked.

Throughout the lecture hall, students were busy at their computer notebooks analyzing the data—everyone, that is, except the Bombardiers. And Ben. Ben was torn between the many 2D screens of Kiilmist 5 and the woman by his side—Julia.

Julia suddenly spoke up. "That one continent there. What are those formations? Do you see them? They look like craters."

Everyone craned forward. Through the haze of slowly drifting clouds their landsat picked up the distinct images of small speckles, circular formations that peppered most every continent, particularly along the seacoast edges.

Professor Holcombe was already typing in commands for a zoom image on the one large continent that was slowly turning beneath them. The view, much enhanced by their computers, brought the landmass into better focus.

Julia grabbed Ben's arm with surprising ferocity. "Look at that coastline! It looks like we've got signs of a civilization down there!"

Voices rose as excitement raced through the room. The new images were revealing the distinct characteristics of surface engineering: roads and bridges, rerouted river systems—probably for irrigation purposes—even the rectangles of tilled or partitioned land were all too evident now.

And a dozen small cities.

"Bingo!" someone shouted triumphantly.

If these markings were signs of intelligent beings, then they would be the first race discovered since humans had encountered the Enamorati two centuries earlier. The discovery was historic and no doubt the other lecture halls, seminar rooms, and auditoriums throughout the university were thinking the very same thoughts.

From behind Ben and Julia, George Clock spoke down to the gathered faculty. "Has ShipCom picked up any kind of signals? Like radio or television signals?"

Professor Holcombe pointed to the left side of the screen, where a column of statistics was illuminated. "ShipCom hasn't detected any signals on any known bandwidth. The entire electromagnetic spectrum is dead."

"It's possible they may never have discovered radio," Ben said.

"Or bypassed it altogether," George Clock said. "They might have gone directly to optical cable or line-of-sight laser communication."

"Or discovered it and decided they didn't need it," said a student behind them.

"Or are using some other means of communication," someone else said.

"Telepathy?" said a student.

"How about semaphores?" suggested another.

"Unless," Ben said, squinting at the screen, "those circular formations are what's left of a war of some kind."

Professor Holcombe began typing quickly. On the left side of the giant 2D screen appeared a column of different numbers.

"If they had a nuclear war," Professor Holcombe said, "it happened a long, long time ago. Our landsats aren't showing any kind of radioactive materials in the air."

"What about that equatorial band?" a young woman asked in the back. "If it happened a long time ago, the trade winds could have easily trapped airborne debris at the equator. If that's an active system, it could be highly radioactive."

One of the landsats had been sent directly to investigate the ugly ring at the planet's equator. But its reading of the equatorial debris belt indicated that nothing radioactive was being held in suspension there.

"If a war happened a hundred thousand years ago," Julia said, "then the half-lives of debris would have expired by now."

"That would depend on what sort of fissionable materials they used in their weapons," Professor Holcombe said. "The purest grade of plutonium would take millions of years to decay."

"And yet there are green forests," Tommy Rosales said. "The plants could have easily recovered in that length of time."

"Can you get a higher resolution, Dr. Holcombe?" one student asked. "I want to see the cities, if that's what they are."

Their screen jumped to its highest power of resolution until the seaboard cities came more fully into view. And cities they were. But cities that were lifeless and deserted. There were no industrial smokestacks, no power plants, no high infrared readings of factories in use of any kind. No cars or vehicles on the roads. No carbon by-products of fossil fuels being burned. No planes in the air, no jet contrails, no ships at sea leaving visible wakes. There weren't even any signs of pollution beyond the equatorial band thousands of miles away from the continents of the upper mid-latitudes.

"The place couldn't be *dead,* could it?" Julia asked.

The pall that descended upon the lecture hall instantly dashed everyone's spirits. To have come all this way to find a dead civilization—and one that had possibly been dead for hundreds of thousands of years—was obviously a letdown.

"Well," said Professor Holcombe, leaning back in his chair. "I guess this means that we'll just have to go down and find out for ourselves."

16

"Hey, man. Are you up for some trouble?" came George Clock's voice from the com/pager at Ben's collar.

"What?" Ben said, tweaking his com.

The verification that Kiilmist 5 was human-habitable, and that the requests of several university departments to send gondolas down to explore it had been granted by the Grays, was the talk of the day. Ben had spoken with Julia about it over lunch, then spoke about it some more while escorting her back to the archaeology department, where she was going to help Dr. Holcombe provision their gondola for a trip down to the planet.

Ben left Julia at the archaeology department, promising to pick her up later, at dinnertime. He was on his way down to the next level in a regular elevator to look in on Eve Silbarton. Eve had made herself scarce over the last twenty-four hours and he was curious as to why. That was when George called him.

"We're in astronomy pod number three," Clock's voice returned. *"You've got to see this."*

"See what?"

"Just get here as soon as you can."

Ben reversed the elevator's course and rerouted it to the astronomy labs.

The astronomy department was the only department on campus that had actual access to the outer hull of the ship. It had six different viewing blisters, each manned with several kinds of telescopes for both students and faculty. Besides the usual optical scopes, there were infrared and ultraviolet telescopes, X-ray and gamma-ray telescopes, as well as solar-mapping telescopes. All of these telescopes came with the best photographic equipment available, all of it operable from inside the ship or outside it.

"What's this all about?" Ben asked when he arrived at the lab. President Porter had lifted his ban on student, staff, and faculty travel in the ship, and so many students and faculty had gone back to their labs to work on their various projects. Therefore, their presence in the astronomy lab 3 wasn't technically forbidden.

It's what the Bombardiers had in mind that was forbidden.

Ben found Clock and Rosales sitting at a monitoring station next to the entrance to the number-three telescope blister. Standing next to the blister was Jim Vees, already suited up in standard EVA gear.

George Clock turned to Ben. "Want to see the Engine?"

"What?" Ben asked.

"Jim thinks the Enamorati are getting ready to remove the Engine," Tommy Rosales said. "It'll take two to monitor the extension pod from in here while the other two are inside it. That'll be you and Jim."

"Are you nuts?" Ben asked. "Do you have any idea how much trouble we're already in?"

Jim Vees had always been a difficult young man for Ben to read. His dorm room was right across from Ben's, but he mostly kept to himself. They only got to know each other through intramural football games, which Jim enjoyed.

"We know exactly what we're doing," Clock said.

"No, you don't," Ben countered.

Vees clipped his utility belt shut. He said, "The Enamorati have just detached the Engine from its moorings and I think they're going to remove it today. If they haven't already."

"How do you know this?" Ben asked.

"I have my sources," Jim said.

"What sources are these?"

"I'd rather not say just now. But they're very reliable," Jim said.

"And you guys are buying into this?" Ben asked Clock and Rosales.

"It's foolproof," Rosales said.

Rosales may have been their muscle powerhouse; he was also their most cautious Bombardier. If Tommy was in on this, the chances of getting caught must be minimal.

"What else have your sources told you?" Ben asked Jim.

Jim said, "I was in the department's computer this morning and discovered that most of our satellites will be on the other side of the planet for the next forty minutes. The landsats are far too low and can't be retasked to higher altitudes. It's perfect for an Engine removal. No one on Eos will be watching."

"And?"

Jim looked at him. "And the Enamorati haven't locked down any of Astronomy's extensor pods, nor have they been shut down from the command deck. I've sent the pod out and back twice now very slowly and no one's noticed."

Ben considered George Clock, the only other Bombardier whose judgment he could trust. "What do you think about this?"

"Well, the gondola bays and service bays definitely are locked. This is routine for the ship in a standard holding orbit, but it's also routine for the *Makajaa* ceremony. *I* think they're pulling a fast one. I say we take a peek."

"Besides," Tommy Rosales added to Ben, "what have you got to lose? If you're caught, what are they going to do? Make you a Bombardier? You've already completed your program."

"They could send us all to prison for breaking the Enamorati Compact. My degree would be useless there," Ben said.

Clock merely smiled, and at the monitoring console Tommy Rosales seemed assured that they could get away with it.

"Time's awastin', bud," Clock said.

"Easy for you to say. You're going to be in here, where it's safe," Ben said.

"We can do this and *not* get caught," Clock said, "because technically we won't be physically leaving the ship and the systems override will read as if the whole thing is being done automatically. No one's going to know that *people* are in the pod or here in the lab. What do you say?"

"Why do we have to go outside?" Ben asked. "Why not just extend the pod and watch it from in here?"

"Because I want to see it with my very own eyes," Jim said.

"And so do you," Tommy Rosales said to Ben.

He had him there. Despite the alleged effects of the Ennui, humans still had a trace of primate curiosity in them. There were just some things they *had* to know. Eventually, something like this was going to have happened in the Human Community anyway.

Ben took the EVA suit from the wall and began climbing into it.

While they secured their suits, Tommy Rosales prepared the airlock's pressure sleeve and brought the observation pod's hydraulics on-line, including all optical systems.

Jim said, "The Enamorati don't have any control over the astronomy department's equipment. Plus, our observatory blister is forward of the ship's equator, which they normally can't see anyway. All we're going to do is extend the pod high enough 'over the horizon' to take a peek aft."

"Except that you and I will be going for a ride in it," Ben said.

"That's the plan," Jim said.

It took them another twenty minutes to flight-check the suits and climb into the pod extension arm. Clock and Rosales then sealed Ben and Jim Vees into the extensor pod and unhooked the extensor arm's lock restraints. When Ben and Jim were finally ready, Clock slowly extruded the extensor arm.

When Ben deopaqued the main viewing ports, they saw the full blue-white splendor of Kiilmist 5 three hundred miles below them. It left Ben virtually speechless. Clock rotated the extensor pod, so its main telescope faced aft. When they were ready, Clock gently coaxed the extensor arm just far enough 'for Ben and Jim to see over the horizon of the hull. At the same time, Tommy Rosales engaged the video recording equipment.

No human being in all the years of Enamorati relations had ever seen an Onesci Engine. When Engines were sent to the H.C. Yards, one near Earth and one near Tau Ceti 4, each came enclosed in a massive casing that was hauled by a large tug. Engines that had outworn their usefulness were always destroyed, never towed back to Virr or refurbished, nor were they recycled in any way.

It was all a big mystery, and now a small part of it was about to be revealed.

The Enamorati had been hard at work already and had most of the Engine removed from the immense Engine nacelle. Captured in the full light of the star-sun Kiilmist, the Engine was almost entirely black, barely visible at all. Tongues of fire damage coated much of its hulk with soot and it trailed behind it massive pipes and loose wires.

George Clock's voice sounded in their ears. *"We've only got seventeen minutes of sun left. When we go into shadow, we won't be able to see a thing."*

"Affirmative on that," Ben said after Jim did not respond. The quiet young man beside him already seemed consumed by the spectacle before them.

Ben noticed that there were no space-suited Enamorati assisting in the process of jockeying the Engine away from Eos. Instead, small, single-individual Enamorati EVA craft glowing bright yellow moved here and there like gnats in a slow ballet, settling to one side or another of the big dead Engine, pushing here or pushing there.

Several moments later, however, three larger EVA craft, these glowing a bright blue, appeared from the nacelle and encircled the Engine.

"Tugs?" Clock asked.

"I don't know what they are," Ben admitted. "We certainly don't have anything like them."

The trinity of blue orbs took equidistant positions around the Engine and began to rotate slowly.

"Wow," Ben said.

The trio of bright blue orbs, however, did cast enough light about the Engine that the Bombardiers could see more details of the Engine, or at least its cowling. To Ben, the Engine resembled a blackened—and very *big*—almond seed the size of a small, sleek asteroid. It probably took decades to build. Ben felt a new respect for the Enamorati. This was an astonishing feat of engineering.

"Look at it!" Jim said in an excited whisper.

The Engine also had an opening, like that of a ramjet scoop, or a jet intake valve at its front. It was impossible to see inside it.

They watched in silence as the small EVA vehicles made a fairy ring of pretty lights around the Engine and escorted it away from Eos. The ceremony was beautiful, majestic, and quite mysterious. Whatever lack of respect Ben may have had for organized religion in general, and the Ainge religion in particular, he gained a whole new level of admiration for the Enamorati. This was a machine that took them into the realm where their god lived. Humans had nothing like it.

The EVA vehicles then turned the Engine facing the star-sun, ninety-four million miles away. Then all the vehicles—the smaller, bright yellow craft and the three large blue orbs—began to spin around the dead Engine. Faster and faster the ring of vehicles raced until they were almost indistinguishable as single points of light.

The dead Engine began to move away from Eos, out of orbit. The peculiar halo of circling EVA vehicles was apparently acting like some sort of catapult or energy funnel.

Tommy Rosales suddenly said, *"I'm getting an infrared signature deep inside the Engine amidships. Very small but it's definitely there."*

"It probably hasn't cooled down all the way yet," Ben said.

"Maybe it's a reactor fire," Tommy Rosales said. *"Ix! Maybe that's why they're in such a hurry to get rid of the damn thing."*

George Clock began to pull the extended observation pod down as the Engine and its fairy entourage moved past Eos, retracting the pod so as not to attract any attention.

"Look!" Ben said. "Look what's following the Engine!"

Behind the fairy-ringed Engine escort appeared small, erratically moving lights, much, much smaller than the smallest EVA craft. These came almost out of nowhere as if they had been trailing the giant university at a great distance and were only now catching up. These "lights" humans had seen before, but no one knew what they were.

"Wakesprites!" George Clock said. *"Look at them go!"*

Wakesprites were a peculiar side effect of Engine acceleration. They mysteriously appeared just as Engines revved up for transition into trans-space and pursued Engine-driven ships when they raced off. What they were, no one knew. Not even the Enamorati. Their best guess was that wakesprites—called *moira* by the Enamorati—were a product of trans-space insertion, an aftereffect of trans-space engagement.

The halo-shrouded Engine suddenly shot off straight toward the sun, taking the madly racing ring of EVA craft with it. The wakesprites followed as well.

"*Wait a minute! Were there Enamorati in those EVAs?*" George Clock asked. "*You think they sacrificed their priests?*"

"Unless the EVAs were being remotely piloted," Ben said. "On the other hand, if they weren't, *that means they engage in blood sacrifice.*"

"Get us back inside," Jim Vees said.

"*You got it,*" George Clock said.

The observation module jerked with a sharp, rearward jolt as Clock retracted them back into the Astronomy blister of the ship a little too fast for Ben's tastes. "Hey, asshole," Ben quipped. "We're not in *that* much of a hurry. Slow down! This has got to look robotic and casual."

There was no response. The pod bumped and jounced violently.

Ben stared at Jim, whose brown eyes were slowly filling with panic. Ben felt his stomach sink.

The pod finally retracted and locked itself back into place inside the blister. Atmosphere hissed into the pod and the seal was then popped open.

Standing at the open door to the pod were Lieutenant Fontenot and elements of campus security. Standing behind them were High Auditor Joseph Nethercott and two junior Auditors, Orem Rood among them.

George and Tommy were already in handcuffs.

"Hello, Bombardiers," Fontenot said, looking directly at Benjamin. "End of the line."

17

Albert Holcombe brooded. His latest wayhigh was running low and it would be a while before he could take the next one, unless he wanted to endanger his health. Heart disease had long ago been eliminated by medical science, but no one knew what wayhighs did to neural cells, they were so new to pharmacology.

From his chair in his office, he gazed at the wall-sized 2D screen, pondering the vast Earth-like world below. *So many worlds to explore, so little time. . . .*

The other viewscreens, those of cameras facing the rear of the ship, had been switched off. The Enamorati had notified Captain Cleddman that they were going to proceed with their *Makajaa* ceremony and Cleddman, in turn, accommodated them by locking the service bays and the gondola bays for the duration of the sacred ceremony. *Yes,* he thought. *Very sacred . . . and very secret.*

The entire Human Community needed a wayhigh, he thought bitterly, a jolt to get it moving again. Books and scientific articles had been written on the Ennui, but no psychologist, sociologist, or philosopher could get a handle on it. It remained evasive, and still humanity slept. And the Ainge, he thought, were part of the cause, not the cure. "Be in the world, but not *of* the world" was their credo. There was a countersaying among the Gentiles: "A laughing Auditor is an Auditor a day away from excommunication." It was so true. Holcombe had never seen his father—or any of his many uncles—laugh. Ever. Rumor had it that the First Prophet Ixion Smith never laughed, even as a baby. He had just been happy to have arrived to do his work—which was serious work indeed.

Holcombe couldn't remember feeling this bleak in his life.

He picked up a secure fax that had just arrived. It was from

Nolan Porter, the real inspiration of his present mood. The fax was a response to a request from Bishop Nethercott, who had respectfully requested that no science teams go down to the planet's surface until the new Engine was installed, which could take weeks. Nolan Porter acquiesced without consulting any faculty member or even Captain Cleddman.

The fax reeked of Ainge influence. They were the only group of humans to actually venerate the Enamorati. After all, hadn't Ixion Smith *proven* the existence of God? Hadn't Smith *found* the realm within which He lived? Didn't this almost require a privileged relationship between the Ainge auditors—humanity's "Listeners-to-God"—and the Enamorati?

"Blow me," Holcombe said, wadding up the fax and tossing it into a nearby waste chute. Tomorrow, six research gondolas would be leaving Eos as planned, and the only person who could stop them was Captain Cleddman, not Nolan Porter.

Holcombe stepped out of his office and walked to the faculty lounge, thinking to get a bite to eat. Wayhighs tended to burn calories and often required a person to seek immediate replenishment before torpor set in.

He heard a transit-portal chime ring out. He was the only one on the floor and he found it odd that anyone would be transitting to the department now that classes had been canceled.

Somebody started calling his name frantically. "Professor Holcombe! Professor Holcombe!"

Before he could respond, Julia came running into the lounge.

"Dr. Holcombe!" she said. "They've arrested Ben and his friends! It's all over the university!"

"I hadn't heard this. What did they do?"

Julia gulped air. "Campus security says that Ben saw the Engine being removed. About thirty minutes ago."

"It's all over the university?"

"Two reporters from the student newspaper followed campus security to the astronomy department's telescope pod bays. There was a fight and they say campus security beat them up!"

Holcombe activated the wall screen in the lounge. Instead of the menu appearing, what he got were four pages of *The Alley Revolutionary.*

"What's this?" he asked.

"It's the student newspaper. They figured out how to run the newspaper without the need for a printing press," Julia said. "They've got an illegal tap into the computer's main com system. This way everybody gets the news whenever they log on."

"I'm impressed," Holcombe said.

The paper told of the capture of Benjamin Bennett and his friends, as well as the fight that ensued, a fight, the *Revolutionary* stressed, caused by exuberant members of campus security. One other detail emerged: The Auditors helped physically restrain the four boys. There were photographs of this: the sneaky reporters had shouldercams. Holcombe's rage went up a couple of degrees when he saw one photograph of Ben wrestling two Auditors to the ground, each of whom he had in a hammerlock.

"Those motherfuckers," Holcombe snarled. "So now the Auditors work for campus security. We've got to put an end to this nonsense."

They made for the nearest transit portal.

There might have been four Bombardiers in the detention cell, but the Accuser only had eyes for Ben.

An *Accuser.*

Ben had never seen an Accuser before. He hadn't even known that the Enamorati had such a caste. The Accuser was of average Enamorati height, but his—*her? its?*—environment suit was made of a dark bluish chitinous substance hard enough to be body armor. Inside the alien's helmet, a collar concealed the creature's mouth and tiny nose, leaving only its small eyes exposed.

And all it did was stand outside their jail cell and stare.

Ben rose from the cot and stood at the bars of the jail cell. "If you've got something to say, you worthless piece of shit," he said angrily, "say it!"

The alien Accuser said nothing. It just stared at him.

Ben tried to grab the alien through the bars, but the Accuser was just inches out of reach. Ben turned around. "George, let me have the cot. I need something to poke this guy with."

Clock didn't move from the cot where he lay. He had bloody

knuckles, a bruised rib, and a torn shirt. "No way am I sleeping on the fucking floor."

Ben turned to Tommy Rosales. "Tommy, help me take the cot apart. All I need is something long enough to get this guy."

Dour Rosales was sitting calmly on the floor. He had two black eyes. "You want to add 'destruction of university property' to whatever else you've got coming? I don't think so."

Their captors were currently in the outer rooms debating on what to do with the Bombardiers; what sorts of punishments to levy; and what they could do to keep the Enamorati Compact. Their grumbling voices could be heard like distant thunder, the Fates at work building the scaffold of the Bombardiers' doom.

"I thought you said we wouldn't be caught," Ben said to Jim Vees, who was standing against the far wall, hands behind his back. He looked like St. Sebastian.

Vees was their noncombatant. He had gone quietly. "My mistake. Sorry."

"But how did they catch us?" Ben asked.

Vees pursed his lips and looked away. "Nethercott read my mind. They say all Auditors have that skill. All those years in their Auditor boxes . . ."

"What are you talking about?" Ben asked.

Jim looked at him. "If they can read minds, then we might be in more trouble than I thought."

"Well, *that's* good to know," Ben said.

At that juncture, several individuals emerged through the door that led to the detention center. The group included Professor Holcombe, Julia Waxwing, Lieutenant Fontenot, and several of his staff—but no Ainge Auditors. The security staff had crowd-stunners in their hands. They came directly for the cell in which the Bombardiers languished.

Then the newcomers saw the Accuser.

Julia fell back. "What is *that*?" she burst out.

Ben watched everyone's response to the creature.

"This is an 'Accuser,'" Ben said, hands dangling through the bars of his cell door. "But it doesn't do much of anything except stare at us."

More people were crowding in the corridor beyond. Two reporters from the nonexistent student newspaper were among them. Their shouldercams craned upward like cobras to get a better view.

Dr. Holcombe faced Lieutenant Fontenot. "I want these men released. I'm posting bail, whatever it is."

"You can't afford it," Fontenot said.

"What is it?"

"Ten million dollars," Fontenot said with a lizardly smile. "More than you've got."

"That's unconstitutional," Holcombe said. "They didn't do anything to warrant such an exorbitant bond. That would be harassment. And I don't think that'll look good in court."

"Who's going to file charges of harassment against campus security?" Fontenot said with a laugh. "You? If you do, then I'll throw *you* in jail for jeopardizing an investigation into high crimes against the Human Community and the Enamorati Compact."

"You can't do that," Holcombe said.

"I'm going to do it right now," Fontenot said as he stepped toward Albert Holcombe.

"I wouldn't," came a voice from behind them.

Making their way through the mob came Messrs. Sammons and Wangberg, their ominous deadman standing behind them. The deadman's neck had elevated itself by eighteen inches in order for its eyes to take everything in.

"Who let those guys in here?" Fontenot shouted back to his people in the outer offices.

"That doesn't matter," said Advocate Sammons. "You've broken a few laws yourself."

Lieutenant Fontenot's face seemed to turn crimson and spittle began to gather at the corners of his mouth.

Sammons spoke before Fontenot could erupt. "You've held these men without immediate access to counsel. You've denied them bail, which, given the nature of the crime you're accusing them of, is unconscionable. You've then denied third parties in posting bond in lieu of the accused doing so on their own."

"And I want to know what the hell *that* thing is," Ben said, pointing to the alien. "It could have *killed* us while you guys were playing squid!"

Fontenot leveled an accusatory finger at Ben. "*He* assaulted the High Auditor and I witnessed it."

"That's horseshit! Nethercott and his javelinas tackled me!" Ben said. "And since when do the Auditors work for campus security? They're a *religious* order! They can't do *anything* to *anybody* on the ship! And those motherfuckers *jumped* us!"

"They were acting as concerned citizens of Eos," Fontenot said. "I deputized them."

"You *deputized* them? You can't deputize them! They're fucking *priests*!" Ben said.

Sammons raised a hand. "We'll let the courts decide the issue." He looked at Fontenot with absolutely no hint of fear on his face. "Right now, we've got enough evidence to put you in there with them, Mr. Fontenot. Is that what you want?"

Fontenot's eyebrows came together belligerently. "These . . . *men* constitute a threat not only to the ship but to the Enamorati Compact! They witnessed the Enamorati's sacred Engine-removal ceremony."

"Were they outside the ship?" Mr. Wangberg asked.

Fontenot hesitated. "Technically, no. We caught them inside a telescope pod just as it was returning to its bay."

"Were the bays off-limits?" Sammons asked.

"Well, no—"

"What other proof do you have?" Sammons demanded.

Fontenot stammered. "They were outside the ship! That's all the proof I need!"

"Yes, but, how do you *know* they were?" Sammons asked.

Fontenot's fists clenched. "Listen, Winn. These men have committed one of the most heinous crimes against the Enamorati in human history! Was I supposed to sit back and let them do it?"

Mr. Sammons stepped in front of Fontenot. "Then *you* made the first move in the astronomy lab."

Fontenot blinked. "We *had* to, because we thought that—"

"So these men were *provoked*," Sammons interrupted. "They were forced to defend themselves. That's assault and battery right there. Let me ask you this, Lieutenant. Has Mr. Nethercott filed charges of aggravated assault against Mr. Bennett or any of his friends here?"

Fontenot thrust out his chest. "The Ainge are not vindictive. This isn't about revenge, as far as they are concerned."

"Then you are holding these men illegally," Sammons said. "And *that* fact will be used if or when this goes to trial."

Fontenot could barely stifle his rage. "But they *saw* the ceremony! That's the *one* law *nobody* can break!"

"Do you have proof that they witnessed the event?" Sammons asked once more. "I'm sure that these men would have been smart enough to have made a video recording of the event, if that's what they had intended to do. Did you confiscate a data tile with the video record?"

"They made a tile," Fontenot said. "But one of them erased it. I think it was Clock. That's him right there."

"So you have no proof that they did anything wrong?" Mr. Wangberg asked with the deadman right beside him.

"I guess we don't," he finally admitted.

Everyone had been ignoring the alien. Upon Fontenot's admission, the Accuser turned and headed for the doorway. He made no comment. He merely walked out of the room.

Sammons said, "You have nothing to hold these men on. Charge them with a crime for which you've got immediate *cause* or let them go."

"Fine," he said, throwing his hand in the air. "Fine! Turn them *all* loose. They only *broke* the Enamorati Compact!"

"Prove that," Dr. Holcombe demanded. "Right here, right now. Especially in front of this guy." Holcombe pointed to the deadman whose head was now back in place.

Fontenot gave Holcombe a fierce stare. "*You'd* better watch it, old man," Fontenot said. "You pick the wrong side in this and you'll suffer the consequences."

Holcombe, a bear-sized man, stood before the head of campus security. "Any time you and your pet squirrels want a piece of me, just ask. I will pull out your *liver* and eat it while you die."

The room filled with tense silence.

But the beleaguered lieutenant merely turned and pushed his way out of the room. The skirmish had been lost, but not the war. The war had simply entered a new phase.

18

"Is Holcombe always like that?" Ben whispered to Julia as they left the campus-security detention center.

The group was led by an energized Albert Holcombe. The man now seemed like a walking dynamo, fired up by his rage.

"No," Julia whispered. "I've never seen him like this."

Her breath, Ben noticed, smelled of peppermint; her hair had the aura of a springtime wind drifting across the prairie just after the rain. She filled his senses.

In fact, Ben had noticed lately that all of his senses seemed to be a bit sharper. His hearing was more acute and his mind seemed to work faster. Either he was in love or the excitement of getting a glimpse of an Engine had cracked the calcification in his brain from having been in school so long.

Or perhaps it was the simple pleasure of punching a major Gray—High Auditor Joseph Nethercott—in the snoot and getting away with it.

Holcombe waited for them at the transit portal. He looked around him—the walls and the ceiling, the dreary brownish gray confines of campus security. "This place is for the birds," he said.

"You mean the detention center?" Julia asked.

"No," Holcombe said. "I mean the ship. It's run by a bunch of deadmen. They've let the life drain out of themselves long ago."

They followed him into the transit portal and within seconds they were back in the archaeology department. Ben's friends had decided to go back to their dorm rooms to recuperate. Holcombe headed for the department's main offices and Ben and Julia followed.

Holcombe stood before his own 2D and said, "Screen, open. President Porter. Regents' Priority Override."

"*Contacting. Stand by,*" the voice of the computer said.

"What's this about?" Julia asked.

Holcombe stood like a Viking, arms crossed, ready to do battle. "There's a famous quote by a Roman historian that I've always loved. Tacitus once said, 'They make a desolation and call it peace.' Tacitus was speaking about the Romans, bringers of civilization to England. It's always reminded me of the Ainge Church."

The 2D screen came alive. The view was President Porter's personal quarters. Holcombe had caught the man at home. However, in the background was the hovering 3D image of the Kuulo Kuumottoomaa, with whom Porter must have been conversing.

Porter asked, "*What is it, Albert? How may I help you?*"

Ben and Julia stood beside each other next to Professor Holcombe, well within view of the reciprocal camera's eye.

Holcombe spoke. "Just moments ago, campus security arrested several students for no reason whatsoever and detained them without allowing them proper access to counsel or to medical treatment. They needed medical treatment because they were physically assaulted by that fascist Fontenot and his men. If the Rights Advocacy Office hadn't been available, Fontenot would have thrown us all in jail and it would have been days before you would have heard of it."

A momentary look of confusion passed across Porter's face. "*Albert, Ted doesn't act rashly. I'm sure that whatever he did was in the best interests of the ship.*"

"Do you know what the situation was?" Holcombe asked.

"*Well, I'm sure he would have informed me as soon as the situation was stabilized.*"

"The son of a bitch is a cowboy!" Holcombe shouted. "Look, he not only tried to arrest four students who were conducting experiments in an astronomy lab, but he enlisted several Auditors to help him out. Hasn't anyone told you this?"

Nolan Porter held out his hand helplessly. "*Albert, I can't be on top of every little fracas on the vessel.*"

"*Fracas?*" Ben said.

He stepped in front of Professor Holcombe in full view of the televisor lens.

"Do you know that there's another class of Enamorati on this ship? They're called 'Accusers' and they put one of them in detention with us. Its e-suit was body armor."

Ben felt some of Holcombe's rage. He went on. "And since when is there another class of Enamorati? We've known the Enamorati for over a hundred and fifty years! What else are they hiding from us?"

Holcombe gently pushed Ben aside. "Ted Fontenot is a loose cannon. He's deputized the Ainge Auditors into the ranks of campus security and he's allowing these Accusers, whatever the hell they are, in on civilian detention matters. Is Fontenot running the show now?"

"*Albert . . . Albert, there has been a misunderstanding,*" Porter insisted. "*Lieutenant Fontenot would never incarcerate anyone unless circumstances warranted it.*"

Ben jumped back into the frame. "I want to know what that creature was! I want to know how many of them are back there. There could be a whole fucking *army* back there!"

"*Watch your language, young man,*" Porter said stiffly. "*You do not speak to an Auditor that way.*"

Holcombe held Ben back. "Nolan, I called you because I don't think our students are safe anymore. The Accuser is only part of it. From where I'm standing, it looks like campus security, the Auditors, *and* the Enamorati are running the ship. And that's in clear violation of Eos University's charter. And that thing *was* wearing body armor, Nolan. I think it's from a warrior class the Enamorati haven't told us about."

Behind Nolan Porter the image of the Kuulo Kuumottoomaa hovered. He had been listening to the discussion. The alien said, "*The armaz-paava are sentries, not soldiers. Their duties include being observers in legal affairs. Perhaps 'Accuser' is not the right word in your language to describe them, but they are most definitely not warriors. Our sentries are devoted to everyone's protection, including yours.*"

Ben said, "Hey, that guy had *no* intention of protecting anybody! I was there!"

The Kuulo went on. "*As for the other matter, I would respectfully counsel everyone to remain on the ship until the new Engine arrives. We don't yet know the date of its arrival and it might be awkward if too many of your people were coming and going from the university."*

"I don't care," said Holcombe. "As a Regents Professor I have certain rights and duties that allow me to act in times of crisis. We've got six gondolas already fitted for descent tomorrow. Six more can be outfitted within twelve hours. We've got fifteen inflatable biodomes for surface habitation. If the Ainge and the Enamorati are running the ship, that's in clear violation of university charter. I demand that you allow all those who want to go, to go down to the surface and wait in our habitats for rescue from the H.C."

The president protested. *"But Albert, if hundreds of students are on the planet when the Engine arrives, they will just have to return again until the insertion ceremony is over."*

"We won't·see a thing if we're on the surface of the planet," Holcombe said. "The atmosphere's too thick at sea level and none of the gondola scanners have the necessary visual resolution to see ships in orbit. We won't see a thing."

Here the Kuulo spoke. He said, *"But it may take days to retrieve hundreds of vessels. We should be on our way as soon as the Engine is fitted and passes its first test cycle. The planet below can be explored by a later expedition."*

Ben stepped back into the frame. "And what's this business of taking Eos University to some place called Wolfe-Langaard 4?"

President Porter frowned. *"Son, don't believe anything you read in the newspaper. Those are very troubled students—"*

"I was there when the Tagani Tormis told us the Enamorati had decided to take us there. I don't think the Tagani was lying or misinformed."

The Kuulo spoke immediately. *"The Tagani was mistaken. His caste does not sit on our Council. He probably had heard a rumor or two and accidentally passed it on."*

Kuumottoomaa paused and spoke to someone at his side, someone out of the camera's eye. He then faced outward. *"Please don't think I'm being evasive. We, too, have suffered from the Engine malfunction and we want to make sure that no further lives, human or Enamorati, are lost. Any interruption of the* Sada-vaakaa *ceremony might caught further distress among us, especially among our remaining Avatka class, whom we need so desperately."*

Porter nodded. *"If it will expedite matters and help with the new Engine's installation, then I say we stay put and let the Enamorati do what they have to do so we can get out of here. Because of the new time dilation caused by the Hollingsdale maneuver we are already two months behind schedule."*

Julia, who had remained silent all this time, stepped forward. "Sir, why not substitute Kiilmist 5 for our next port of call? How hard could it be to fashion our spring curriculum around Kiilmist 5? That's what Eos University is for."

"But the parents of our students expect us to be at Paavo Juuoko 3 for the entire semester," President Porter argued. *"And many of our staff and faculty have relatives there. We are already missed."*

Holcombe countered with, "We can take both in. Split the semester. Besides that, I don't want to wait up here until the insertion ceremony is over. We're wasting time and the opportunity to do what we do best. The folks at Paavo Juuoko can wait. The planet below is a gold mine. We should probably stay and colonize it."

"This is not advisable," the Kuulo insisted. *"I must protest in the strongest possible terms."*

Holcombe then said, "Doesn't the Enamorati Compact say specifically that we can go wherever we want and do whatever we want, just as long as it doesn't involve anything illegal?"

The Kuulo hesitated. *"That is correct. All I wish to suggest is that our present circumstances require caution and a bit of patience until the new Engine arrives."*

"Fine," Holcombe said. "We'll exercise caution. Down on the planet. When the Engine arrives, we'll just stay grounded."

True to his word, Porter took the proposal before the University Council that evening and the Council voted. The majority of votes went for the change of port of call to Kiilmist 5.

President Porter was not at the Council meeting, nor was the Kuulo Kuumottoomaa. Nor were any of the new "sentinels," the Accusers.

It made Ben wonder what the Grays were now up to.

19

Like any schoolgirl, Julia Waxwing had grown up studying the great adventures of the Human Community in space. The discovery that life once existed on Mars spurred further explorations of the solar system's other planets and moons. They found life within the seas beneath Europa's ice mantle. On Ganymede and Io they found a kind of lithoautotrophic bacteria similar to that found on the Earth in deep-sea vents. But those environments were extremely hostile to life as it had evolved on Earth. Only Tau Ceti 4, Ross 244 3, and Paava Juuoko 3 came close to being Earth-normal.

Now they could add Kiilmist 5 to that list.

To Julia, the discovery of a human-habitable planet wasn't quite as interesting as discovering a planet that once had a civilization advanced enough to have built cities and roads. More than that, for Julia and the rest of the archaeology team the signs of life—the patterning of their farming tracts and the layout of some of their building structures—indicated that Kiilmist 5 had produced a race of beings remarkably similar to *Homo sapiens sapiens*. It was a veritable gold mine of knowledge they would be studying for years to come.

Now Julia could feel the excitement of the other students and faculty when the various gondolas of Eos left the bays of the enormous vessel, carefully avoiding the sacred spaces around the empty Engine chamber—particularly the now-empty Engine nacelle. Everybody seemed buoyed by the mere fact that they were getting *out*. Julia only wished that Ben and his friends could have come along with them.

Well, Ben anyway.

The chatter among the students in the main viewing bubble rose excitedly as the gondola dropped out of orbital space and began its careful antigravity descent to the planet's surface. Professor Holcombe came in from the cockpit holding what appeared to be a printout. He, too, was clearly excited.

"I've got some reliable statistics on the planet," Holcombe said to the group. "Gravity is point nine Earth-normal; atmosphere, however, is nearly half again as thick as the Earth's. The lighter gravity we'll feel will be countered by a slightly higher specific gravity at sea level. From the planet's weak magnetic field, we estimate that the world is about five or six billion years old. She would be an older sister to the Earth."

Nearly all of the undergraduates in the archaeology department were from prominent Ainge families, most of whom came from Tau Ceti 4. One of these was Bobby Gessner, a blond boy of nineteen with a nearly invisible blond beard. Gessner interrupted Holcombe's recitation. "Dr. Holcombe, the planet would need an active magnetic core to generate a field strong enough to deflect cosmic rays. Life can't exist without a shielding upper atmosphere."

Holcombe nodded. "Sediment samples taken from lakes at different altitudes will help us figure that mystery out. Or perhaps the atmosphere is so thick that it's able to block out cosmic rays. That's one of the things we'll be looking into."

Holcombe consulted his watch. "We'll be making landfall in about forty minutes and we'll start our hostile-environment check immediately after that. If it turns out that we'll have to wear our Van Houten suits, you can add another hour."

The students groaned. Van Houten suits were extraordinary environment suits, but they were difficult to put on and messy to remove. They had to be dissolved with a chemical spray that was also a bactericide and the removal process took about forty minutes. Julia hoped it wouldn't come to that.

"So are we going to land near a city?" one of the eager undergraduates asked.

Holcombe nodded. "We've located a city that has a river next to it and some structures that look like bridges which seem to be intact. We've chosen a level area between the river and the city to set up our base camp. The gondola will stay behind as we explore on foot. If it's safe, we'll set up camp there and make excursions into the city's outskirts. But *only* if it's safe. If it isn't safe, we'll move somewhere else."

Bobby Gessner wore an old-fashioned pith helmet. "How do we know that the cities down there are dead, Dr. Holcombe?"

The twenty students in the gondola stared expectantly at the Regents Professor. Holcombe said, "Recon photos and bioform scans from the landsats didn't find signs of animal life higher than what we would call rodents. Its flora, however, is quite extensive."

"Maybe the rats *are* the intelligent life," Gessner said jokingly, and everybody laughed.

"Yes, but why would rodents build buildings a hundred times larger than their own nests?" Julia said.

"Or roads," another student added.

"Maybe they're really *big* rats," someone else said.

"Let's hope they aren't *that* big," Holcombe said.

"What about reptilians or mammalian forms?" a young woman asked.

"Nothing," Holcombe told them. "Not even in the seas, at least as far as our cursory scans were able to detect. Of course, there could be life in the deep benthic regions of the oceans. But we're decades away from exploring the oceans here."

The only other graduate student besides Julia on the expedition was a brown-haired, full-figured young woman in her early thirties named Marji Koczan. Like Julia, Koczan was not from an Ainge family, but, unlike Julia, she was much more cosmopolitan, having traveled widely on Earth and other worlds. Ms. Koczan said, "The city builders would have to have evolved from a long chain of biological ancestors. If the world is a billion years older than the Earth, maybe they're a civilization that just ran out of energy, or just wound down. It could happen to us."

Proudly, young Gessner said, "Humans are firmly established on three Earth-like worlds and have habitats on dozens of moons. We're not going to devolve into lobsters at the end of time."

"Not unless the Ennui is real," Julia said. "Maybe it's true that empires run out of steam. Maybe *these* people ran out of steam."

"Perhaps we'll be able to find out," Holcombe said. "If we do commit ourselves to a whole semester here, there's no telling what we might come across."

The descent seemed to take forever.

The students, Julia included, couldn't take their eyes from the viewscreens. Holcombe's strategy was to set down at their target location sometime before sunrise, local time. This was done with the expectation that if anyone (or anything) was down there to do them harm, they would more than likely be asleep, assuming that sleeping was something "they" did.

The gondola dropped down through the predawn darkness. Ground radar easily penetrated the haze of the thick atmosphere, and they found a treeless plain next to the river they had originally chosen from space.

Then they saw the "highway." Or what was left of it.

The thoroughfare, if it was such, seemed to be fashioned from a dull gray substance similar to concrete. It led directly to the city that, by their estimation, began about a mile or so to the north of their position, easily within walking range.

The gondola set down carefully next to the road in the mauve light of dawn, the antigravity engines of the gondola purring softly. Out went the landing gear, and the gondola settled gently in the loam of the ground beneath them.

Their deadman pilot went through a quick systems check to see how the descent had affected the small craft and also to see if the engines were able to lift them back off the planet. The deadman then signaled Professor Holcombe, telling him that the descent check was complete and that their systems were in good shape.

"Now, boys and girls," Dr. Holcombe said as the gondola's biohazard analyzers went to work sucking in air and scooping samples of soil to sift through for nasty creepy crawlies.

"Now, we wait."

Ben had never seen the university so close to unraveling, with students wandering the corridors more boisterous than usual. Even the students from Ainge families were mixing it up more than usual. Students played transit tag and chased each other all over the place. The only thing that kept the university functioning was the levelheadedness of the day-to-day staff—the secretaries and the physical plant employees, most of whom couldn't care less about politics or religion. They rather enjoyed the sight of the students running loose in the halls, something they had never seen in all the years of Eos University life.

The faculty, however, were becoming as unruly as the students, and Ben did not know what would happen if *they* decided to protest. Learning institutions much older than Eos University had gone up in flames over much less than had befallen them.

Thankfully, the rest of the student body, those who stayed behind, did not seem to be aware that tensions had risen between the Ainge and non-Ainge adults on the ship. None seemed aware that, if the rumors were true, they might be bound for a place called Wolfe-Langaard 4 instead of Paava Juuoko 3. More worrying was that the most influential professors from the hard sciences and engineering—and Eve Silbarton was one—were conspicuously absent during the last twenty-four hours that saw the exodus of six research gondolas.

Ben was in the middle of lunch, brooding about all this, when he received a call from Eve. She was in her lab in the physics department and she needed to see him right away. She wouldn't go into details, but the tone of her voice seemed uncharacteristically grim. He abandoned his tray, hoping that this didn't mean that another disassembler was loose in the ship.

In the physics wing, repairs were proceeding on the alpha lab. A dozen techs were positioning great plates for the floor. Many of the severed wires, cables, and pipes had already been replaced. The hallway also had several security officers, who frowned at Ben the moment he emerged from the nearby transit portal but did not prevent him from seeking out Eve Silbarton.

Ben went directly to the gamma lab and found Eve and several other individuals standing around Eve's stardrive. The drive was floating above its antigravity plate, making it easier for everyone to examine it. Which a number of people were doing.

Eve turned around when Ben entered. He couldn't read her mood. She did seem hostile. "Have you been working on the prototype here without my permission?" she demanded.

Everyone stared at him.

"Good God, no," he said. "Why do you ask?"

Dr. Cale Murphy, the youngest full professor in the department—he was twenty-four and absolutely brilliant—said, "We've got a fog that lasts fifteen minutes on the security tape."

Murphy nodded at the ceiling, where their security camera was hidden. "Someone blanked out the camera so they could get at Eve's drive."

"You're kidding."

"Nope. And it had to have been someone smart enough to get around our security system as well as someone who could get past the guards out there," Dr. Murphy said.

"Do you have any idea who that person might be?" Ben asked.

"It could have been you."

"Well, it *wasn't*."

"Where were you yesterday?" Cale Murphy asked.

Ben glared at him. "In jail. I've got witnesses who'll vouch for me."

"Well, *somebody* got in here," Cale Murphy said.

"Maybe it was campus security," Ben suggested. "If they're in with Fontenot, they'd have reason to sabotage Eve's work."

"If they could get past our security systems," Dr. Israel Harlin, the department chair, said. "Which we doubt."

"So I was the first one you thought of?" Ben asked.

"No," Eve said. "You were the last."

"Thanks for including me."

Eve Silbarton said nothing. Instead, Ben asked, "You think this might have been the same person who took out the alpha lab?"

Eve looked at him, exasperated now. "Odds are that it was."

Of the stardrive itself, it looked as if parts of it had been removed for inspection or even cleaning. But as far as Ben could tell, the prototype appeared undamaged. Nothing was cut or broken or smashed in any way.

Ben stepped closer to the hovering stardrive. "So what was done to it?"

"The calibration of the flux sequencing system was thrown off by a few degrees," Eve said. "If Cale hadn't run a systems check, we wouldn't have known it until we went to full activation of the phase array tomorrow. At such a setting, one of two things would have happened. The first would be that the drive unit itself would have been thrown across the galaxy."

"The second?" Ben asked.

"Nothing," Eve said.

"It all depends on the settings for the C-graviton separator pump," Cale Murphy said. "We think a guard on his rounds spooked our guy before he could finish his tinkering."

"But they did enough," Dr. Harlin said. "The energies the unit's going to tap into are on the order of a million joules."

Eve nodded. "When you separate C-gravitons their energies immediately open a hole into trans-space and disappear into it. The problem has always been how to trace the vector those particles take. Lord Bowden's mathematics say that these vectors, if tracked, would allow for the creation of transfer analogs between two sets of real-space and trans-space coordinates. A series of phase array units, like the one here, should be able to position the C-gravitons to coordinates set up by a basic navigation program. At least, that's the theory."

"So what were the settings?" Ben asked.

"That's what we can't figure out," Dr. Harlin said. "The initial energy buildup was decreased in Eve's unit."

"It was adjusted *downward*?" Ben asked.

"Looks that way," Dr. Harlin said.

Ben thought about this. "Maybe this guy doesn't want to be transported to the other side of the galaxy with us."

Ben knew that Eve's stardrive, so completely unlike the Onesci Engines, would allow for a ship to reposition itself in space by shifting from one set of coordinates to another instantly. Eve's work was based on the late-twenty-first-century theories of Europa's first president, Michael Bowden. Lord Bowden had always maintained that the Onesci Engines wasted extraordinary amounts of energy that could be used to help the C-graviton pump create and maintain the coordinates in trans-space. Eve's stardrive, theoretically, could do just that.

"This doesn't make any sense," Ben said. "They had to have known you would be running checks on the system . . . unless they just wanted to slow you down."

"If that's what they tried to do," Eve said, "it worked. We're going to take the whole engine apart, check each component, re-calibrate everything."

One of the older professors said, "What if our 'burglar' comes back to finish his work?"

Eve nodded. "We'll have to double up on cameras and sensors. Put them in places they'll never suspect."

"Yet," Ben said, "last week, someone got into the alpha lab and none of our sensors or video cameras caught it until the disassembler had already gone off. They obviously have a way around our security system."

"You make it sound as if 'they' aren't human," Dr. Murphy said.

"If the shoe fits," Ben said. "And you guys actually thought that *I* had lowered the calibration settings on Eve's machine?" he asked.

"We had to consider all of our options," Cale Murphy said. "It all came down to you."

"Perhaps," Ben said, peering at the aborted mischief, "you haven't run out of as many options as you think."

Perhaps, Ben thought, it was time to confront the Enamorati directly.

And perhaps an Auditor or two. . . .

20

By the time the archaeology team had prepared itself to step outside, the gondola's biohazard scanners had detected nothing hostile to humans, or at least nothing their AllPox implants couldn't handle. Still, there was nothing in the animal kingdom nearby sizable enough to come their way looking for lunch.

Everyone was a bit jittery, including Julia. This could have been the simple anxieties most explorers feel upon setting foot on new territory. After all, the ports of call on the Eos University circuit were already much explored. *This* was the real thing, and it had no youth hostels, no beach resorts, no amply provisioned way stations. They were on their own.

The ground beneath their gondola was covered by a rugged, ground-clutching ivylike grass similar to that found on a number of worlds. The place also had trees, or life-forms similar to trees. They were hundreds of feet tall, taller than any known tree species. But there were no birds or flying reptiles or anything that flew. Young Bobby Gessner was at the windows the entire two hours it took to run the biohazard scans, and he gave everyone constant reports on what he saw or didn't see.

Dr. Holcombe was given the honor of being the first human to set foot on Kiilmist 5. He was followed by Julia and Marji Koczan, the next-ranking humans. The rest of the students followed, with Bobby Gessner volunteering to bring up the rear. This was because he was guiding the field data kit, a hovering platform that contained their heavier equipment and larger instruments. It floated a foot off the ground, using a triad of antigravity plates.

Once the students left the gondola, the deadman set his antigravity engines to a moderate idle, elevating the small craft to an

altitude of one hundred feet, both to monitor weather conditions
and to stay in touch with Eos above. The plan Holcombe had devised was for the group to reconnoiter the best place to make base
camp, then mark the position with a transponder. If their deadman
couldn't find them, then the other gondolas could.

Holcombe scanned the horizon. He wore a pith helmet with UV-
screening sunglasses. Julia, standing beside him, brought up her
binoculars. The whole class gathered around, admiring the expan-
sive green fields and the gigantic "trees" beyond.

"This area looks like it had been cleared for agriculture at one
time," Julia said. "Look at how flat it is."

"A very long time ago," Holcombe said. "There are sloughs here
and there."

He pointed to an irregular depression at the far end of the field.
"Water's gathered there and the ground's sunk. No one came back
around to repair it."

The gondola had intentionally set down to the south of a gathering of ruins they had sighted from the air. It was their immediate
goal. Holcombe wanted to get the lay of the land—the "suburbs"—before they actually entered the city beyond.

They moved out single-file, their personal shields aglow. The
ground, covered with the broad-leafed grass, was a soft carpet for
their boots and muffled most sounds they made. But hardly anyone spoke. There was too much to see, too much for their shouldercams to record, too much to be on the lookout *for*. Even though
their instruments couldn't find anything large or terrible—or *small*
and terrible—that didn't mean they weren't there.

"No insects," one student in the line said.

"But plant life without insects doesn't seem possible," someone
else said.

"Insects evolved when flowering plants evolved," Julia said. "This
planet might not have flowering plants. No flowers, no insects."

"And no spiders!" young Gessner added from the rear.

Marji Koczan adjusted her sunglasses. "It's kinda creepy. No
bird sounds or insect sounds. Just the wind and the leaves."

Holcombe paused. "A lady doesn't give up her secrets easily.
We've only been here a couple of hours. There's no telling what
we'll find."

They came to the edge of the ivy-covered field and climbed a small ridge. Professor Holcombe paused on the top of the ridge. "This is what I wanted to see," he announced. "I spotted it as we were coming in."

At the base of the ridge was an old, beat-up road. From what Julia could tell, the road hardly seemed wide enough to hold a horse-driven cart. But it *was* an artifact, their first. The team clambered down to the road and began inspecting it, shoulder cams peering down with the same eagerness.

"This looks like badly pressed asphalt," one student said.

"It could just be old," another student suggested.

"Acid rain could do this, don't you think, Dr. Holcombe?" said another.

Holcombe nodded. "Bobby, get a sample of the road. We'll analyze it when we're back on the ship."

Young Gessner came around and bagged a sample of the stony substance of the road, then placed it into an airtight locker in the hovering field kit.

Holcombe faced them. "Okay, try to cross the road as carefully as you can. Don't disturb it too much. People long after us will be studying it for years."

The wind had picked up slightly and it bore with it an alpine coolness. It reminded Julia of the aspen meadows surrounding Hart Prairie near Flagstaff, Arizona. Her ancestors had worshipped that land. They believed that their gods roamed it when people weren't looking. But her ancestors were gone. So, too, the denizens of Kiilmist 5.

They proceeded to the ruined city.

Knowing that the planet below them was human-habitable and that it harbored the remains of a civilization set the entire university abuzz. It was probably fortunate that classes had been canceled because most of the students were spending their time glued to the giant video screens in the student commons, watching the various video feeds coming from the gondola teams below or the landsats above. They wouldn't have attended classes anyway.

The only group of people who weren't interested in the gondola

teams was campus security. Campus security seemed more interested in watching Ben.

When Ben left the physics department to go to dinner, two
Grays were at the far end of the hall. While he was eating, several
students ran past them playing transit tag, but the Grays ignored
them. Campus security didn't appear to be interested in anyone
other than him.

Two more guards followed him through the student commons.
And two more were in his dorm when he went back to his room,
where he had planned to take his usual after-dinner nap. They did
not approach him or bother him or even make eye contact. They
were simply shadowing him.

Rather than take a nap, Ben decided to go for a walk, to see how
far campus security would go to tail him. He left Babbitt Hall and
wandered down one corridor, then another, entering one transit
portal, going from the library to the media center to the student
commons . . . and all the while a campus security guard seemed to
be nearby to intercept him.

And these were the ones wearing their gray campus security
uniforms. There might be an equal number of campus-security personnel wearing civilian clothes. There was no way to tell.

Outside the faculty commons, Ben paused. The only bar serv-
ing liquor was in the faculty commons. Older students fre-
quented the place and Ben fit right in. But when he stepped
inside the Zoo Club, a female campus security guard entered
right behind him.

Ben got a beer and walked through the crowded bar, listening to
the music from the jukebox. He finally came to stand next to the
club's transit portal.

The beer had been making him sleepy, but suddenly the portal
flashed and Tommy Rosales jumped out.

"Right on target!" Rosales said.

Ben clutched his heart. "You scared the shit out of me!"

"You're a hard man to find," Rosales said.

"Not to them," Ben said, pointing to guards playing darts over
in a corner. "They know where I am no matter *where* I go. And
those are the ones wearing uniforms. There's no telling who is in
this place."

Rosales pulled Ben aside. "It might not be you they're after. Have you seen Jim today?"

"Not that I can remember. Why?"

"We can't find him. He's turned off his pager."

"Maybe he's in the field house, working off steam."

"I checked there," Rosales said. "But I don't think he wants to work off steam. That's the problem. After we got out of jail, George heard him talking about getting even with Nethercott's goons. We were hoping he was with you."

"Maybe he's back in jail," Ben said.

"If he is, he's not listed in the computer. And I called the Rights Advocacy Office. They said that campus security isn't currently holding anyone."

"Have you tried his *room*?" Ben said.

"We did, but he didn't answer."

"He could still be in his room, then."

"That's why we need the key he gave you."

Ben didn't like where this was going. "What's he doing in his room that's so dangerous?"

Rosales appeared uneasy and glanced around the bar to see if anyone was listening. "You're not going to like this."

"I'm counting on it," Ben said. "What's he doing?"

"Jim thinks he's figured out a way to listen in on the Ainge at their Auditor stations. The setup's in his room. If he's listening in on them and in some sort of trance state, then he's practically incommunicado."

"He's been listening in on the Auditors?" Ben asked, incredulously. "Are you serious?"

"What do you think he does all day? He's had it with the Auditors. He didn't want to tell you about it because you're in enough trouble."

Ben considered the dart-throwers. He noticed two other campus-security people—two women—sitting at the bar.

Tommy Rosales said, "Can you imagine the trouble we'd be in if they can prove we've violated the Enamorati Compact *and* tapped into the Auditor box technology? They're both sacred ground. That's why we need your key."

"And probably a couple of good lawyers," Ben said. He finished his beer and set it down on a nearby table.

"We'd better unplug that boy before he gets us all thrown in prison," Ben said.

They stepped into the transit portal and disappeared.

21

The transit portal took them back to Babbitt Hall, and they walked the short distance to Jim Vees's room. Ben kept a lookout for campus security, but they had moved too quickly, it seemed. If they were *seriously* being tailed, then it would only take a campus security official a few minutes to contact ShipCom to find out where the transit portal 44 had sent them. On the other hand, maybe they were merely keeping an eye on Ben. In that case, they just might have let him go back to the dorm, where he could do little harm.

Ben and Tommy Rosales went straight to Jim's room and knocked softly. There was no answer. Ben pulled out his key and passed it through the lock.

Jim Vees's interest in astronomy went all the way back into his childhood, when he learned how to build telescopes, of both the optical and the radio kind. Jim could make his own equatorial mounts, his own autoguidance systems, his own lenses and billion-channel frequency scanners. His room showed it. Parts of telescopes and CPU boards held together with duct tape lay about the room. One whole wall was a small library of books on every aspect of astronomy and celestial mechanics.

"A clue," Ben said, pointing at a table that held a strange machine resembling a radio transmitter. Wires and cables led from this into the bathroom and into the suite next door. Babbitt Hall's dorm rooms shared a common bathroom facility. A few students, and Jim Vees happened to be one, were lucky enough to have an empty suite next door. Pick the lock and you had a cozy two-bedroom apartment. This is where they found Jim Vees.

"No wonder he didn't hear us knock." Ben said.

Jim sat, eyes closed, in a chair, wallowing in some sort of trance state. Around his head was clamped a headset with multicolored wires snaking back to the unit in the first suite. Jim's mouth hung open and his fingers twitched.

"Unplug this thing," Ben said.

"Right," Rosales said.

Rosales picked up the cluster of wires and gave it a good yank. Things in the first suite fell over.

Ben whapped Vees on the head. "Hey, asshole. Snap out of it!"

Jim jerked in his chair, opening his eyes. It took him a moment or two to realize where he was and who stood before him.

"What the hell are you doing?" Ben demanded. "Do you know we've got campus cops all over us?"

Vees blinked. "Are they here?" he managed to say.

"I don't think so," Ben said. "Tommy told me you're listening in on the Auditors. Is that true?"

Tommy Rosales signaled Ben that he was going to step outside to see if campus security was sneaking up on them.

"Well?" Ben repeated.

"Sort of, I guess," Vees admitted.

"How long has this been going on?"

"A while now."

Vees rose from his chair and went into the bathroom to wash his face in cold water. "I got the last bit of equipment I needed when we were at Chandos 4, several ports back."

Ben had always known of Vees's intense dislike for Auditors. The Ainge civilians he didn't mind; they were as normal as Catholics or Jews or anybody else. But Auditor boxes seemed to generate in the Auditors themselves more than just a confidence in the existence of God. To Jim, the boxes generated arrogance and condescension, and he didn't like it. Even so, as far as Ben knew, he never said he was going to *do* anything about this dislike of his.

Vees ran some cold water in the sink and gave his face a good splash. He then tossed the towel into the sink, where it dissolved and disappeared down the drain.

"Do you know that eavesdropping in on the Auditors is a serious offense?" Ben asked. "In fact, eavesdropping in on *anybody* is a serious offense."

Vees merely nodded.

"I don't think I'll be caught," he finally said. "Besides, I got the boot today. So I don't think it'll matter."

"You got the boot?"

Vees pulled a letter out of his tunic pocket and gave it to Ben. The fact that the letter was sent to Jim on actual paper indicated to Ben the seriousness of its contents.

"Ix," Ben muttered as he read the letter. It said:

Dear Mr. Vees,

We regret to inform you that your persistent refusal to reinstate yourself in your degree program here at Eos University compels us to ask that you be prepared to leave the university at Paavo Juuoko 4. The liner *Hyapatia Lee* will take you back to Earth. We regret writing this letter and we regret losing you as a student. Your intelligence scans and high test scores had put you in the top 2% of the student body. Should you decide to reinstate yourself, you will have to go through the regular admissions procedures and begin your program anew.

We wish you luck in your future endeavors.

The letter bore the official seal of Eos University and it was signed by the chair of the astronomy department, the dean of the College of Liberal Arts, the provost, and finally President Porter himself—the major Grays of Eos University.

Vees smiled wistfully at Ben. "As of now, I am the Bombardier par excellence."

Ben handed the letter back. "You can still be reinstated."

"Yeah, well, I don't know if I want to," Vees admitted. Here, he nodded at the strange helmet connected to all the wires leading back into Vees's suite. "Not after that."

"What have you seen?"

"I don't *see* anything," Vees told him. "Mostly I just tap into the same frequencies that are translated to theta waves inside the Auditor box. I'd make a real Auditor box if I could, but the alloys

Smith used when he invented his are only found on Tau Ceti 4. This is the best I can do."

"I'm surprised you've gotten this far," Ben said. "People have been trying to duplicate the Auditor technology for a hundred and fifty years."

"Rumor has it that they've killed those who've come close," Tommy Rosales added. "I'd watch it, if I were you."

"They don't know I'm nosing around. Or if they do know, they haven't done anything about it yet."

"How does it work?"

"It's simple, really," Jim said. "I rigged a passive trans-space nexus projector in my room. When the Auditor station is activated, it sends out signals like ripples from a fishing line in a still pond. I pick up the 'ripples' and trace it back to the point of contact. I can't read their minds, exactly, but I can pick the sensations coming from trans-space. You should see them. They fight each other to take a turn in the box."

"They fight each other?"

"It's more like bickering," Vees said. "But it's an incredible high. I can't imagine what the full force of contact is like. I've calculated that I'm getting about ten percent the levels the Auditors are getting. It's better than sex."

Ben was impressed. "Sounds to me as if you've invented a practical means for artificial telepathy. That alone should get you reinstated. Hell, that'll get you an interview with the personnel people of my father's corporation. BennettCorp is always looking for new talent."

Vees shrugged. "Maybe when I get back. Who knows."

Tommy Rosales was standing in the bathroom hallway, taking all this in. He said, "So you've plugged into Mazaru. What's it like? What's the Big Guy have to say?"

"He doesn't say anything," Vees told them. "It's mostly a feeling that comes across. But it's very powerful, alluring. The Auditors can't take more than twenty minutes of it at a time. Any more than that would probably kill them."

"Didn't Ixion Smith die after being in his Auditor box for three days?" Rosales asked.

"It's like having an orgasm nonstop," Vees told them. "Pretty soon, you just implode."

"That's one hell of an addiction," Rosales said.

Ben was thinking. "So this thing basically focuses on the spatial location of theta waves produced by an Auditor box?"

"Actually, I can project the nexus point anywhere," Jim said. "It took me two and a half weeks to find the location of the Auditor station. I had to do it at night while the Auditors were asleep. From what I gather, the station is a couch you lie on. Then they surround you with—"

Ben was already along a different track. He couldn't rid himself of the scene of the carnage in the "dynamo" room he and Julia had witnessed just a few days ago. "You know, there's a rumor that the Enamorati are fighting each other. Not bickering, but fighting. Have you picked up anything?"

Jim nodded. "I pick up whatever the Auditor picks up when he's in the box."

"What have you heard?"

"A few days ago I heard an explosion. Yesterday, I heard several loud bangs, but those might have been the Enamorati unbolting the Engine from the ship. There's no way of knowing without actually going over there."

Ben, however, had fallen silent for a long moment. Rosales caught this and asked, "What is it?"

Ben looked at them both. "Let's see if we can find out."

"What?" Rosales asked.

Ben said, "What if we used a fractally compressed camera probe, put it in an artificial trans-space tube, then sent it back there using Jim's nexus locator? If we can send the probe over there and back fast enough, we might be able to do it without anybody noticing, especially if the probe is small enough."

"What if they *do* see it?" Rosales asked.

"If the probe's source of origin can't be traced, who cares?" Ben said. "Besides, we can yank it back so fast they'll probably think they imagined the whole thing anyway."

Jim stared at him. "So you want to eavesdrop on the Enamorati?"

"Absolutely."

Tommy Rosales frowned. "Now, *that's* trouble. Not the kind that might get you thrown out of school, but the kind that gets you thrown off the *ship*."

"Julia and I got far enough into the Ainge compound to see several dead Enamorati inside a chamber that was connected directly to the main Engine. Jim says he's heard sounds, maybe explosions. Something *is* going on in there and I think it's in our best interests to find out."

"At least that's the excuse we can use when they arrest us," Vees said.

"Exactly," Ben replied. "I'm just surprised that no one's thought of it before."

"That's because most normal people don't want to go to jail," Rosales said.

22

No human ever got over the thrill of discovering new worlds. It was ancient and visceral. It inspired awe and not a little bit of fear.

Julia walked several yards behind Professor Holcombe, who led the archaeology team at a somewhat incautious pace down from the tree-lined ridge onto a large field. The nearest set of ruins lay just three hundred yards ahead of them, and their irregular outline was quite visible.

Earlier, one of the students had voiced the opinion that the tall, pink-skinned trees might themselves be "animals." But Professor Holcombe tested a nearby "tree" and it seemed thoroughly rooted into the earth. If something was going to come after them, it wasn't going to be the "trees."

Julia paused with Professor Holcombe at the far end of the field—the ruins just in sight. "A war," she said to Professor Holcombe. "Maybe a war wiped everything out. From the top of the food chain to the bottom. These plants could be all that's left."

"That's what I was thinking," added Marji Koczan, standing just behind Julia and smoking a Red Apple cigarette.

"Except there isn't any residual radiation in the air or on the ground," Bobby Gessner said.

"It wouldn't have to have been a nuclear war," Professor Holcombe said. He wiped heavy perspiration from his forehead. "It could have been biological or biochemical. It could even have been a planet-wide industrial accident, perhaps a toxic spill."

"Like what the Enamorati did to their own planet ten thousand years ago?" Koczan said.

Julia said, "There are probably dozens of ways a civilization fades away."

Professor Holcombe adjusted his helmet. "However, we don't know if there aren't any people left on the planet. The cities in this region might be dead, but its people could be hiding out some-where."

Shouldercams scanned the terrain while personal voice recorders took in what each of the students was seeing, thinking, and feeling. They were the first on Kiilmist 5. All this would make history.

"You know, maybe the place is just *old*. Maybe the ecosphere wore itself out," someone then said.

"Gaia is not quite dead here," another student said.

"*Something* happened here," Marji Koczan said. "It's been des-olate for a long, long time."

They moved on, crossing the leafy field of the strange, ground-hugging ivy, heading toward what initially appeared to be a row of immense ivy-covered hedges. They knew, however, from the land-sat pictures, that they were the outer edges of the nearest of the ruins. They weren't hedges. They were very old and very hidden walls.

The slight breeze trembled in the ivy clutching the bricks of a wall ten feet high that appeared to surround the ruins. An opening in the veiled wall led the Holcombe expedition into a random clus-tering of buildings. Most of the buildings, however, had just one or two walls remaining of their skeleton and none of them seemed to have their roofs intact. The green, leafy everywhere-ivy gave the place a melancholy aura of great antiquity: nothing on two legs—let alone four legs or six—had come here in quite a while.

Cautiously, they moved along a narrow, cobblestoned avenue that ran between two clusters of ruined buildings. The students were agape.

Holcombe pointed to the building on their right. "It looks like they had developed principles of the arch. Notice the doors and windows."

Koczan poked her head in a low window of the building. "No glass," she said. She ran her hand along the base of the window, just inside the sill. "And no place *for* glass. They got as far as the Romans or the early Byzantine Empire."

"That's possible," Holcombe said.

The thick ivy made it hard to tell much about the architecture of the buildings or even what purpose they served. Later expeditions would be given the honor of figuring that out.

The group of students followed Professor Holcombe down the path that passed between the two buildings huddled in overgrowth, emerging in an open area that appeared to be a cul-de-sac with only narrow sidewalks—of cement or cobblestone, they couldn't yet tell—leading between each of the buildings.

"You think this might be a courtyard connecting family units on either side?" someone suggested.

"Hard to tell," Holcombe said, pondering the crumbled remains of the old buildings.

The students were itching to get into one of the ancient buildings, but Holcombe held up his hand, stopping them. "We'll do this by the book. Julia, you and Marji follow me," Holcombe said. "The rest of you stay here, shields up, and keep an eye out. Bobby, if the field kit peeps, raise a perimeter shield."

"How big?" Bobby Gessner asked.

Holcombe looked around. "A fifty-foot radius should do."

"Gotcha," the undergraduate student said happily.

With a collapsible handheld rod, Professor Holcombe began probing the strange ivy of a nearby wall. It looked like the most logical place to put a doorway or an entranceway into what seemed, from their angle, to be the largest of the buildings in the cluster. As he did, Julia, who was right behind him, made a slight adjustment—upward—in her personal shield. It was almost impossible *not* to fear that something with stingers or fangs or deadly breath might be lurking within the overhanging growth— because on Earth there *would* be. Her intuitions told her not to trust the assessments of their field kit, their scanners, or the land-sat photos.

"Found it," Holcombe announced. He disappeared into a curtain of lush green. "It's a open archway. Come on through," he called back to them.

Julia followed Holcombe and behind Julia Marji Koczan pushed her way through. Both women had shouldercams activated and following the tracks of their masters' eyes.

"If this were on the Earth," Julia whispered, "I'd say this region definitely experienced a war . . . some sort of major civil disruption."

Holcombe and Koczan nodded in agreement.

Whatever purpose the building may have served, it had but a single, very large room, and part of the ceiling had collapsed into it. Ceiling timbers were scorched from ancient fires and the ivy had insinuated itself into the bricks of the wall here and there with tendril fingers, loosening them.

Because of the large aperture in the ceiling, the ivy-grass flourished on the inside and covered everything inside the room. Whatever kind of furniture the Kiilmistians had used was now covered in soft, leafy green.

"A lot of Native American tribes had one-room structures like this," Julia said.

"The Norse and their longhouses," Holcombe added. "They were large, communal gathering places where whole extended families lived. Livestock included."

"But there are at least seven of these houses in this cul-de-sac," Julia observed. "If they lived communally, they must have numbered in the millions. The landsat photos show that the city to the north has tens of thousands of houses just like this, maybe hundreds of thousands."

"So where are all the people?" Marji Koczan asked.

The professor made his way through the ankle-deep ivy to where a heavy curtain of ivy obscured a wall near the rend in the ceiling. He pulled the ivy back.

"Here we go," he said.

To their surprise, the walls were covered with graffiti. Eerie pictoglyphs of strange, humanoid beings—and quite possibly larger animals—were carved in the wall or scrawled with charcoal from long-dead campfires. This could have been a wall in the Lascaux caverns in the south of France.

"Wow," Julia said, completely awed.

"Jesus Christ. We could be here for years studying this one wall," Marji Koczan said. "We wouldn't have to go anywhere else. It'll take decades to decipher this."

There were arrows pointing this way and that; there were etchings of what had to be animals. There were hieroglyphics and actual writing. Among the writing were numerals—or what appeared to be numerals—and all of it placed there over a long period of time.

"If it's graffiti," Julia said, "we might not be able to decipher it without a living language for idiomatic referents."

"We don't know if they are dead yet," Marji Koczan said. "This place could just be the victim of urban flight."

"Except," Julia countered, "these *are* the suburbs."

Professor Holcombe tugged away at the ivy, pulling down a large section of the green veil so that their cameras could take better pictures in better light. Marji Koczan, meanwhile, circled some of the ivy-covered remains of the broken "furniture" piled in the center of the room. She carefully pulled apart a section of the strange growth, exposing white stones and ash underneath.

"I think they had a hearth here," she said. The ash and plant debris underneath had long since become mulch.

Julia had extensive experience with kivas of the American Southwest. She pointed at the ceiling. An ugly smudge blossomed like an dark flower there.

Julia said, "This building wasn't built with a hearth in mind. There would need to be a ventilation hole and there is none. The roof over there collapsed because of the rain."

Holcombe inspected the fire. "Different fires at different times. This has been used as a bivouac by wandering groups."

"After the people who built it were killed or were run off," Julia said.

"Could be," Holcombe said.

Bobby Gessner appeared in the doorway, his personal shield glowing. "Dr. Holcombe," he said, breathing excitedly, "I think we've got something important out here."

They retreated back through the leafy canopy, stepping into the bright morning light. Across the peculiar quad, the rest of the students had gathered behind a building whose whole north side had completely fallen in. That side faced a broad field of the ivy-grass. Beyond the ivy was the "city," the goal of the expedition.

"We were looking for a communal garbage dump," Gessner said. "We thought it might be out here, away from the dwellings. We came across this."

They had found a body.

The desiccated remains of a clearly humanoid creature lay sunk partway in the field grass. Julia guessed that the being, when it stood, probably stood over seven feet. It had multi-jointed arms, and while its hands had five fingers, there were no opposable thumbs. It had two eyes and a nose in the right place, but its ears were small flaps. Its mouth was a very wide slit and probably was fairly gruesome when eating.

The creature, dried to a pale gray color, also wore a bodice of brownish rawhide and boots that concealed long, narrow feet. It looked as if every ounce of moisture had been sucked from it by years of lying in the field.

"Can I turn it over?" Bobby Gessner asked. Cameras clicked and shouldercams whirred.

Holcombe nodded. "Be careful. I want this thing intact."

"Are we taking it back?" a young woman asked.

"If at all possible," Holcombe said.

They carefully rolled the creature over. It was remarkably light. Underneath it, they saw, were no insects or worms in the soil. Just more ivy. Layers of it.

"It looks like he died right here," Marji Koczan said. "It looks like it was crawling away from the buildings."

Julia glanced into the sky. "No predators. This person should have been consumed by the ecosystem here. But all he did was mummify."

"Unless the summers are fierce," Bobby Gessner said. "You know, drying everything out?"

"But *how* did he die?" another student asked. "It doesn't look like he had a wound or anything."

"Poisoning? Disease?" Julia speculated. "That might have stricken him suddenly."

"What about a heart attack?" Marji Koczan said.

"If they *had* hearts," Holcombe told them.

The other students had begun to fan out over the large field, with some moving off toward the north where a single, gigantic "tree" stood. The tree was at least ninety feet tall.

Someone shouted out. "Hey! Over here! We've got another one!"

"Keep your shields up," Holcombe advised. "And stay together."

The group walked across the meadow, their feet hissing through the ivy.

Beside the flesh-colored tree lay a body almost identical to the first one. This one, however, had been wearing a clothlike toga that had long since frazzled into dry threads. This creature had rolled itself into a fetal position and died that way.

Holcombe lifted the folds of the creature's toga with his extended probe. A small, leatherlike pouch fell out.

"Maybe it's his lunch," said one of the younger students.

Using his probe, Professor Holcombe gently lifted back the pouch's ragged flap. Inside they found globes about three inches in diameter made of some sort of shell-like material.

"Ix!" a student said.

"Eggs, you think?" Julia asked. The students gathered around.

"They might be," Holcombe admitted.

"You think they could have been his lunch?" asked another.

Julia stood up and stepped away from the giant pink-barked tree and the toga-clad being beneath its boughs. There were no roads or sidewalks or fences to mark out territory, and the communal houses seemed to be random constructions, arranged haphazardly.

But then, these people *were* alien. They didn't *have* to make sense.

Julia, on her own, started walking north.

23

Making certain they weren't dogged by campus security, the Bombardiers went in search of a place where they could conduct their experiment without attracting too much attention. They found an unoccupied suite in nearby Peterson Hall where they lugged Jim Vees's nexus locator. Next, they borrowed a small data-bullet compressor unit from physics, a model designed for fractal-compression studies. Ben then installed his own software—the process that his dissertation detailed—whose algorithms allowed for a more efficient compression of data with virtually no corruption in the defragmentation process.

Ben then dug up the design schematics for Anira-class vessels, of which Eos was the last. There was no way to know how extensively the Enamorati had reconfigured their living area over time, but they wouldn't have fooled with the major support structures of the ship itself. Those would be their guide.

This effort had taken the Bombardiers several hours, and sometime after dinner they were ready.

"Okay, where to first?" Ben asked.

"What about that 'dynamo' room you guys saw?" Tommy Rosales suggested. "You said there was blood all over the place. We could move aft from there."

Ben shook his head. "Anyone in the Inner Temple can see right into the 'dynamo' room."

"It's not going to be around for long," Rosales said.

"I don't want to risk it," Ben said.

The probe they chose to use was the size of a pearl, a standard video "bug." With Ben's fractal-compression unit, the probe would be compressed to the size of a large molecule, then "repositioned" elsewhere in the ship, via trans-space, using Jim Vees's nexus locator. The probe would then return to its default configuration, take forty pictures, and be yanked back. If done right, the whole thing should take only a few seconds.

"You know," George Clock offered, "the Enamorati might have the means to detect the trans-space transfer."

Ben said, "But if they're fighting a war in there, they could be too occupied to go looking for the projection source of our probe. And that's assuming that they would have the means to trace it in the first place."

"And," Jim Vees said, "they would only be able to trace it *if* a detector was in the room itself to measure its appearance."

"Campus security could have given them something," Tommy Rosales pointed out.

"Why would they?" Jim Vees said. "We just now thought of this. You're paranoid."

"Tommy's good at being paranoid," George Clock said, standing off to one side, arms crossed.

"Blow me," Rosales quipped.

Ben said. "Our little guy will be gone before anybody can register its appearance. Even if they do detect it, they still won't know who sent it. I think we can get away with it."

"Easy for you," Rosales countered. "You've got the weight of BennettCorp behind you. Your family will send a liner full of lawyers to defend you."

Ben smiled. "We're in this together. And I've got an aunt who sits on the Rights Advocacy Council in Geneva. She'd sue God if she thought she'd get a hearing."

Tommy Rosales raised his hands, giving in. "Okay. But I still think we'll spend the rest of our lives in that prison on the surface of Tau Ceti. What's it called?"

"Hyperion Station," Clock said.

"Right," Rosales acknowledged. "Where the H.C. keeps all its malcontents."

"If we're careful," Ben said, "it won't come to that."

Jim Vees pointed to a location on their map to a position just aft of the "dynamo" room. "What about here?" he asked.

The area Jim had suggested was in a hallway that, according to the schematics, was near an airlock.

"Look," Clock said, "if we're going to go to jail for this, I think we should go as far in there as we can."

"Fine with me," Ben said. "Let's do it."

They calibrated a nexus point where their map—and their best guess—said there were no walls or bulkheads. Then, a narrow, trans-spatial tube extending to the nexus point was created. Once that was stabilized, they were ready. George Clock stood guard at the door as Ben pressed the "engage" button.

The probe went POP!, disappearing from the space above its antigravity plate. A slight puff of air took its place.

Just a few seconds slid by, and then the probe reappeared.

"Let's see what we've got," Ben said as he took the probe and downloaded its visual scan data into their small computer. The Bombardiers gathered about as images began appearing on their monitor screen.

The probe's camera and massive storage capacities allowed for amazingly clear photographs. The probe had appeared in a hallway filled with an eerie, yellowish fog. This may have been the normal Enamorati atmosphere or it may have even have been smoke. But the hallway was littered with all kinds of debris. Parts of the wall and some decorative ceiling tiles had apparently been blown from their positions. Strange scimitar-scythe-crescent decorations were everywhere underfoot.

Ben scrolled through the photographs. It was more of the same. But there were no bodies, no Enamorati wandering the halls—at least in this part of their compound.

"Did the breakdown of the Engine do *this*?" Rosales asked.

"Unless they live this way," George Clock said.

"Enamorati are supposed to be fastidious," Rosales asked. "Look at the mess!"

"Yes," Ben said. "And where is everybody?"

"Maybe most of them are dead, because of the Engine," Clock said. "Remember that the Tagani said we were going to take on new Avatkas when we got our new Engine."

"And Kaks," Ben added.

"Right," Clock said.

Then Rosales said, "What about those ships that went with the Engine into the sun? If they were manned, they could have taken dozens of their kind with them."

"Even so, there's still plenty of room back there for several hundred Enamorati," Ben said.

They printed out forty digitally enhanced photos of astonishing clarity and laid them in a line along the floor. Taken together, the photographs gave them a 360-degree scan of a corridor intersection.

"Let's do another scan," Ben said. "This time thirty feet farther in."

They prepared the probe for its next journey, then sent it off with another POOF! as it disappeared.

It came back almost immediately.

The second set of photographs, of another corridor in the Enamorati compound, showed the same kind of destruction. Except this time there were bodies.

They printed out the second set of photographs and laid them out on the floor as well.

"Look at this!" Rosales said. "These guys are wearing environment suits."

"So?" Clock said. "They always wear their e-suits."

"Except that it's in their own territory," Rosales pointed out. "Why are they wearing e-suits in their own quarters?"

Ben crouched above the second set of photos. "They're wearing body armor," he said. "The same armor that Accuser wore."

Ben noticed that several of the photographs showed pockmarks or gouges in the walls. Ben looked at Jim Vees. "You've heard loud bangs back there. Could it have been gunfire?"

"Some of the Auditors think so," Jim said darkly.

"*This* looks like the results of a hand grenade," Rosales said.

"Let's go in deeper," Clock suggested. "Let's go in three corridors farther aft, and laterally about a hundred yards."

"I'm game," Ben said.

They immediately reset the machine. Once they calculated the next nexus location—approximatley 90 feet farther aft and 280 feet to the port side of the grand ship—Ben pressed the Engage button.

The pearl-like probe vanished in a puff of air. A few heartbeats later, it reappeared. They downloaded the data into the computer and started the printing process once again.

The probe this time had manifested very close to a wall—inches from it, in fact. The first set of frames were of that wall where a long, slender, scimitar-like tile had fallen out of place and was, presumably, on the floor just beneath the probe.

The next set of images showed more of the same kind of destruction they'd seen in the first set. But here the walls and ceiling looked as if they had been shredded. Several lighting fixtures dangled, though some were still functioning.

They moved to the next set of ten, where the probe was looking fully down one corridor—and they nearly jumped out of their boots.

"Whoa!" said George Clock.

"Jesus Christ!" said Jim Vees.

An Enamorati—apparently a Tagani, a historian—stood squarely in the center of frame 26, from the elbows up, standing, staring right at the camera. The alien couldn't have missed it. The rest of the frames were shots of him standing there, staring, perhaps not sure that he had seen what he *thought* he had seen.

Tommy Rosales stood up from where he had been kneeling on the floor and stretched magnanimously. "Well, I guess that's it. Break out the suntan lotion. I hear it's hot on the surface of Tau Ceti."

Ben wasn't ready to give up. Though the lone Enamorati seemed to be staring at the probe, not much else was happening in the corridor. Moreover, the Enamorati did not appear overly alarmed by the probe's nosy presence.

"Let's send another probe to the other end of the same hall. I want a different perspective on this guy."

"What difference does it make?" George Clock said. "We're all going to jail. I can't believe you talked us into this."

"It will take them a while to figure out it's us, *if* they figure it out," Ben said. "We've got some time yet. Let's make use of it. If we're really fast, we can get these pictures to the student newspaper. They'd love this."

"We can read it when we're in jail," Clock said.

Ben swiveled around in his chair, reset the probe, reset the nexus to a position just twenty yards down the hall, then launched it. When it returned Ben immediately downloaded the probe's data, printing them instantly.

Privately, Ben had expected to see nothing but an empty hallway. Enough time had gone by for the armored Enamorati to have gone off to tell the Kuulo Kuumottoomaa what he had seen.

However, what *had* happened in that span of time—probably no more than ten minutes—was that the first Enamorati, the one who had seen the probe, was now leaning against the far wall in a position that suggested violent death.

But now there was a second Enamorati. This being, also in body armor, held what appeared to be a sword in its right hand—one of the wall "decorations," a graceful slice of composite material approximately four feet long. Not only was he using it *like* a sword, the decoration had all the look of a *real* sword. And the halls had been decorated with hundreds of them!

"I guess we don't have to worry about the first guy," Clock said.

The newcomer had just slain the first Enamorati when the probe had appeared and scarfed its sequence of forty photographs. The attacker was just turning around when the probe caught him, but had vanished before it could have been seen.

Been looked closer at photo 40, the last containing a discernible profile of the alien.

Ben turned back to the computer, jumped to frame 40, then magnified and enhanced it. "*This* is an Accuser," Ben said emphatically. "He's in full battle armor and those things on his belt look like weapons to me!"

"Then they *are* soldiers," Tommy Rosales said.

"And we've been carrying them around in space with us for a while now," Ben said. "Question is, how many of them are there?"

None of the Bombardiers could answer that. None wanted to.

24

Through the phalanx of the magnificent flesh-colored trees, Julia saw a Mound to the north of their position. It was easily within walking distance, so she set out for it. Its flattened pyramid shape seemed to beckon her, reminding her of the jungle-covered ruins the Maya had left behind in old Mexico. Even in their desolation, those stone edifices still had power to evoke forgotten eras. So, too, did the Mound in the distance.

Julia recognized quickly that it was artificial, not just another hill rising above the ivy-covered plain. Its walls were too steep, too angular *not* to have been constructed.

Holcombe brought the other students to Julia's position at her call, and everyone paused to examine the distinctive structure.

Bobby Gessner took out his high-powered field binoculars and zeroed in on it. "It looks like there's a series of low buildings just to the west of that Mound," he announced. "They're covered with the same ivy or grass or whatever it is. It looks like there might be hundreds of buildings underneath the stuff."

"Dr. Holcombe," one of the students asked, "is this the city we saw on the landsats?"

Holcombe was just catching his breath from the brisk walk. "I believe so."

The Mound itself wouldn't have shown up on any of the landsats. The green ivy-grass was everywhere and Kiilmist had been close to the zenith when the landsat photos had been taken two days ago, so the Mound would have cast only the barest of noon shadows. Only the strange, crumbling roads and long-abandoned agricultural fields and drainage ditches pointed to a civilization of moderate evolution in this region.

"It looks like one of the Wessex burrows near Stonehenge," Julia said. "The way it's shaped, it looks like it could be a burial mound of some kind. Maybe it's a ceremonial pyramid."

"We'll make our base camp near that Mound," Holcombe told them as he wiped his brow with a handkerchief. "The way the buildings and the fields have been organized around it, I'd say it's the geographical center of the town."

Julia had turned off her personal shield. She wanted to feel the wind on her face and smell the aromas of this new world.

But the very air smelled of death, and she frowned.

"Your thoughts," Professor Holcombe asked, coming up to her.

Julia felt slightly embarrassed to answer with so many undergraduates looking on. "We talked earlier about flowers and insects or their equivalents being missing from this Gaia-system."

"We did," Holcombe said.

"The air should be filled with odors of all sorts of living things," Julia said. "Especially microorganisms, pollens, and spores. There would be by-products of both plant and animal life. But I don't smell a thing."

"And our biohazard scanner back in the gondola registered nothing," Bobby Gessner chimed in. "Remember?"

Holcombe faced the Ainge boy. "Our scanner only indicated that there was nothing in the air that was hostile to us. It didn't say there was *nothing* in the air. It's not even programmed to do that."

Marji Koczan came over. "You mean there's only *air* in the air?"

"What would be wrong with that?" a young female asked.

Holcombe looked at Julia and she felt a slight peak of pride. Holcombe seemed to be handing her a baton of some kind, a public acknowledgment that she was already maturing as a field archaeologist.

"It would mean," Julia told them, "that something has scoured the ecosphere clean, taking out the smaller life-forms, leaving only the plants."

The students were becoming somewhat more agitated the farther they got from the gondola. Julia noticed that while she, Marji Koczan, and Professor Holcombe had switched their personal shields off, the other students had turned theirs up several notches. Fortunately, the Mound was not that far away and a pitched camp with the field kit's perimeter shield up and running would go a long way toward easing the minds of the younger students.

The distance was a little more than Holcombe had estimated and he slowed his march toward it, mostly to make sure that young Gessner and the floating field kit did not fall too far behind.

Julia was walking beside him, her eyes on the Mound that seemed the center of the world, so much did it dominate the landscape.

"So what do you think of the Ennui?" Holcombe asked after a few moments. "Do you think it's real?"

"I don't know. I've never thought much about it. Why do you ask?"

Why *did* he ask? Holcombe's mood had gone from blithe melancholy to a darker shade of depression. He wasn't his usual self.

"The sky is full of stars," he said. "You'd think that once humans got off the Earth, civilization would have spread like wildfire."

"Civilizations come to an end," Marji Koczan said, having pulled up to Holcombe's left side. "Nothing lasts forever."

"You think this planet suffered from the Ennui?"

"Something like it," Holcombe said.

"I'd say it's just entropy," Marji Koczan said. "Civilizations can get *tired*. In 700 C.E., at the very beginning of the Dark Ages, southern Italy was virtually deserted because of the barbarian invasions of the previous three centuries. Everybody moved away, tired of being run off their farms and orchards."

"That's not entropy," Bobby Gessner responded. "History is a flow of forces. To us it only looks like they ran out of steam. The barbarians must have thought they were riding high on their good fortune. It depends on where you're standing."

"Unless there is a larger force moving through history," Holcombe said.

"The Ennui is a force?" Marji Koczan said.

"Or fate," Holcombe said.

"Nobody knows what it is," Julia said, "or even if it's real."

"Entropy is real," said Bobby Gessner.

"Right," said Holcombe. "But notice how when humans don't

understand why something happens, we call it fate. However, if we understand it, then it's destiny at work. We're in control."

"Are you saying destiny is an illusion?" Koczan asked.

"Perhaps."

"Then you're saying that *someone* is responsible for the death of this planet's ecosystem?" Julia asked.

"Or some*thing*," Holcombe told her. "I'm just very suspicious of entropy and 'accidents' and the Ennui. They make complicated historical processes seem easy to understand."

Some of the students had begun branching out in their walk rather than simply following Holcombe and the two graduate students. Here, the ivy-grass was somewhat more spongy but offered no real obstacle. The Mound ahead of them seemed to lie in a shallow valley just over the next ridge.

"Found one!" a female student shouted off to their right.

The students gathered around a patch of loose ivy in a depression in the field. A dried-out forearm of a Kiilmistian stuck partially out of the ground like a strange plant. It was clutching some sort of wooden rod with a set of leather bindings attached at the top.

Holcombe crouched down. He carefully took hold of the exposed arm and attempted to move it. But it held firm. The body had been there so long that it had become petrified.

"Bobby," Holcombe called.

"Right here!" the Ainge youth said, coming forward.

Holcombe pointed. "Flag this guy. And you'd better call the deadman. Have him bring the gondola to this location. We'll set camp just over this rise."

Holcombe stood up. He removed his helmet and scratched his head. "I wonder if the other study teams are finding the same things we are."

Just then, behind them, one of the female students cried out. "*Help!*" she shouted.

Everyone turned. One of the undergraduates had fallen up to her waist in a hole that the ivy had concealed.

"Mark this guy," Holcombe said again to Gessner. The rest of the group ran over to the girl who had sunk through the ivy-grass.

She was in no immediate danger, however. She had simply been surprised to have stepped into a hole when she had been expecting solid ground underneath. She shucked off her backpack and launched it out ahead of her. Two male undergraduates helped her out of the hole.

"I almost broke my leg," the young girl said, trying to calm herself.

The rest of the troupe gathered around the depression in the ivy. Holcombe called back to Gessner. "Bobby, bring the grapple. The pole, not the hook. I want to look at this."

Bobby Gessner unslung the grappling pole from the side of the hovering field kit and hurriedly brought it over.

Holcombe sunk the hooked end of the pole deep into the ivy where the student had fallen in, then carefully pulled the green curtain back.

"*Oh, my God!*" shouted the girl who had fallen into the hole.

"*Jesus!*" someone else said.

Another said, "*Ix!*"

Underneath the ivy was layer upon layer of what were clearly bodies, many of which had already become clusters of bones.

And by the look of it, they had been there for a very long time.

The students immediately looked around them. To their horror, they discovered that they were standing in the middle of a field that contained the composted remains of tens of thousands of Kiilmistians.

The students ran like crazy for a nearby ridge. Apparently, they had been walking on a cemetery that covered that whole part of the continent.

25

In a moment of uncharacteristic foresight, Ben thought it wise not to press their luck with probing the Enamorati compound. The evidence from the photos they had so far suggested that at the very least the Engine's destruction may have caused—or have been caused *by*—deadly factionalism among the aliens. George Clock thought that since humans didn't know anything about the Enamorati, maybe it was possible that they *always* fought among themselves. The blood, the bodies, the debris *could* have been normative behavior for them. They were *aliens*, after all.

Ben told Clock that he was an idiot. Even if hand-to-hand fighting in the corridors *was* normal for the Enamorati—and the humans found out about it—they'd risk the wrath of all the moms and dads back home who wouldn't take very well to their kids flying around the Alley with a boatload of warring aliens. This *had* to be an aberration. The Enamorati *were* fighting among themselves, and it was quite likely the Bombardiers were the only humans who knew about it.

So the Bombardiers hastily broke down their probe projector and, in the tradition of the former student newspaper, hid the various parts at different locations in the ship. Each Bombardier hid a component in a location the others knew nothing about, so they could plead ignorance if caught.

Ben, though, soon came to realize that they had to show the photos to someone in authority whom they could trust. Certainly their pilot, Captain Cleddman, would need to see them eventually. Before that, however, Ben thought he'd take them to Eve Silbarton. First, she was on better terms with the captain and could probably account more easily for the mere existence of the photos. Secondly, Eve—or someone else among the stardrive team—might have a better perspective on the meaning of the photographs.

Construction personnel were still at work on the gap in the floors of the physics department. Only this time they were under the watchful eye of campus security. This, however, was Eve's doing, given the security breach the other day. Still, the presence of the police only heightened Ben's uneasiness. They were just *waiting* for him to slip up. And any little thing would do.

But the guards let him through and they made no attempt to search him. Had they done so, they would have found a data tile in his tunic pocket and about forty-five photographs in the leg pockets of his pants, which he would have a hard time explaining.

Eve soon managed to assemble more than two dozen faculty and staff to hear Ben's story and examine the photographs laid out on a long table. Ben pointed out the ripped metal of the wall decorations and the dangling strips from the ceiling.

"This is incredible," said a professor from computer sciences. "I thought it was just a rumor the students were passing around. The Enamorati really are fighting each other in there."

"They were supposed to have given up actual physical combat ten thousand years ago," Dr. Israel Harlin said, his thin arms folded across his chest. "I guess they didn't."

"Unless the Accuser caste turned against everyone else," Ben said. "Look at what they wear. I've seen their body armor up close. It's more than just an environment suit."

" 'Accusers'? What are Accusers?" someone else asked.

Apparently information about this new class of Enamorati hadn't reached Eve's stardrive army in the physics department. At the very least, they hadn't occasion to use the ship's main computer and thus get *The Alley Revolutionary*. The *Revolutionary* had put that little item on page one. It would have been hard to miss.

Avoiding certain incriminating details, Ben told them of his little adventure in the astronomy observation pod.

Dr. Cale Murphy, standing beside Dr. Harlin, asked, "What are these Accusers supposed to do? Did it accuse you and your friends of anything?"

"Not really," Ben said. "It just stood there. But the e-suit it was wearing looked just like the one in these photographs. It might not make much difference if we get a new Engine or not, if they're still fighting in there."

Eve Silbarton rubbed her eyes. She looked as if she hadn't slept in days. "A civil war," she said. "That's all we need."

"Then," Ben went on, "there was all that blood Julia and I saw in the 'dynamo' room the other day when we got into the Inner Temple."

"Wait," one professor interrupted. "Blood in the 'dynamo' room? What's that all about?"

Since that little adventure hadn't been made public, Ben had to tell them about the carnage they witnessed in the "dynamo" room, adding that he did not know what the giant machine's purpose was on the other side of the Inner Temple's glass wall. He did say that the Ainge Auditors were also horrified by what they saw. So, in his mind, the destruction had to have been recent.

"Ixion's blood," one of the older professors swore. "You sure have been nosing around in all the wrong places lately."

"Sorry," Ben said.

One of the other professors said, "Revolt among the Enamorati had to happen sometime. Jack Killian's equations of fractal dynamics in social systems said they would. They're not immune. Maybe it's time we did the same."

Eve Silbarton held up her hand. "Let's not sound the call for revolution just yet. We've got to decide what to do about Ben's photographs. No matter who we show these to, someone's going to ask where we got them. They could incarcerate everybody with knowledge of these photographs. They'd close down the lab, probably disavow the whole department, and that's something I don't want to happen."

Dr. Cale Murphy then said, "And that's assuming that they think the scans are real and not a hoax. They come from the Bombardiers, after all. How likely is it that Porter or the Governors' Council would believe them?"

"Why wouldn't he?" Ben asked. "Our Engine malfunctioned when we were in trans-space and we were forced to return to real-space. That has *never* happened before to a starship fitted with an Onesci Engine. Usually, ships are retired and scrapped, or—"

"Or they retire themselves by blowing up in trans-space," Dr. Harlin said.

One of the senior space-science engineers, Dr. Mike McCollum, spoke up just then. McCollum was a man who knew everything there was to know about conventional propulsion engines in starships. When McCollum spoke, everyone listened. He said, "I think we should show these photographs to Captain Cleddman as soon as possible. There are governance protocols that can come into play if the situation is truly dangerous. Porter won't have any authority if Cleddman thinks we're in danger. The overrides can only respond to his voice."

"And then what?" a female graduate student in structural engineering asked. "We get fitted with a new Engine and fly around with them still fighting each other in there?"

McCollum frowned. "Unless we can persuade him to head back to the Earth or the nearest safe port so we can unload our kids and families."

"Ix," someone then said.

Cale Murphy scratched the stubble of new beard on his chin. "I guess this might explain a few things."

"What sort of things?" Ben asked.

"Do you remember the tampering that was done to our drive system the other day?" Eve asked.

"Yes, and I remember that you thought *I* did it."

"My mistake," Eve said. "Sorry."

"So what about it? Did they come back and finish the job?"

"It may not have been an attempt at sabotage."

"Then what was it?"

"It looks now like an act to get us to make sure of the calibration settings for the system's residual energy net. Israel saw that the drive might work more efficiently if we could harvest the residual energies from the C-graviton pump to the projection points rather than just dump the excess in trans-space."

Ben nodded. "This would mean a more accurate focus of the C-gravitron stream to the coordinate points."

"We would, theoretically, get to the projected destination with greater efficiency and accuracy," Cale Murphy said.

"And we wouldn't have even known we could do that," Eve

said, "if we hadn't taken a second look at our original calibrations for the residual energy net."

"So they *improved* it?"

"I don't know if even *they* knew what they were doing," Eve said. "We would have discovered it eventually, in about a year. Maybe sooner. But they jump-started us."

Ben held the photograph taken of the Accuser in the gas-filled hallway where he stood holding a bloody sword over the two halves of his countryman.

"What is going on back there?" he said in a low voice.

"Maybe we should ask them," Cale Murphy suggested.

"I'd talk to an Avatka," Dr. McCollum said. "Forget the Kuulo. Go to someone who has hands-on experience with Engines."

"I'd like to talk to the Avatka we captured on the transit-portal record. He'd have to know something," Eve said.

"The Avatka Viroo is dead," Ben then said.

"How do you know?" Eve asked.

"A historian told us."

Dr. Harlin shook his head. "Well, we can't risk calling attention to ourselves right now. The work is more important than knowing who's fighting whom back there."

"Except," Ben said, "there might be an *army* back there just waiting to get out. If Mom and Dad knew that, Eos University would lose its charter and we'd be out of jobs."

"Or dead," Dr. McCollum said.

"There's that," Ben agreed.

"Then our best course of action," Dr. Harlin said, "is to stick to our plan. With any luck, we can get back to Earth in one piece. Then if the rebel faction wants to fight, we'll cripple the ship and let the Space Marines have a go at them."

"I agree," Eve said. "We've got to follow through on our original plan and hope that nothing slows us down."

"What plan?" Ben asked.

"I don't know how much of a plan it is. It's just come together. But we think it can work. So does the captain."

"What is it?"

Eve walked over to her stardrive as it hovered above its anti-gravity plate. She said, "As soon as we get our units installed and calibrated, we're leaving. Captain Cleddman doesn't want to be anywhere near Kiilmist 5 when the Engine and its escort arrives."

"You make it sound as if that might happen soon," Ben said.

The entire room, filled with twenty-five or so of the most gifted physicists, engineers, and mathematicians anywhere in the Human Community, became deathly quiet.

Eve said, "Our sources tell us that Kuumottoomaa has convinced Nolan Porter to forestall our Alley circuit once the Engine is installed and head back into Enamorati space, perhaps to Virr, the Enamorati home world itself, or some other destination."

Ben recalled the accidental reference the Tagani Veljo Tormis made to a world called Wolfe-Langaard 4.

"Why?" Ben asked.

"Word has it," Eve said, "that Porter's worried that we've broken the Enamorati Compact and he wants to argue the case himself before the Enamorati Council. Taking Eos University there would be an enormous show of faith."

"Can Porter *do* that?" Ben said.

"He's done it," Eve said. "He says he's received a data bullet giving him full authorization from the H.C. to let the Enamorati Council conduct an investigation into the possibility that some humans might have violated the Enamorati Compact. They want to put those people on trial. They think it's the only way to salvage the E.C."

The eyes of the physics department were upon Ben. He suddenly didn't feel very well.

26

The discovery that the archaeology team had probably been walking over mashed alien bodies ever since they had left the gondola cast their undertaking in an entirely different light. The students scrambled to a stony outcrop that rose above the fields and sat on it as if washed ashore on a desert island.

The one positive outcome of the race to the stony outcrop was the animal skull Bobby Gessner found by falling into an ankle-deep hole. Withdrawing his boot, he pulled up the skull of a beast that might have been a horselike creature. It had a long narrow skull but also had a horn—tooth?—where its nose might have been had it been an Earthly Pliocene mammal. The Ainge boy left the skull where he found it, flagging it for possible analysis later. They had enough to deal with at the moment.

At the top of the stony ridge, they could now see the Mound quite clearly. It seemed to squat directly on the top of a large rectangular plaza that, to Julia, resembled some of the classic landsat photographs she'd seen of the buried Mayan cities in eastern Mexico. Farther to the west were low hills covered by the same ivy. The irregular contours of the hills suggested to her the obvious remains of buildings long abandoned.

Professor Holcombe finally reached the top of the rocky outcropping, breathing hard from the climb. He had been trailing Bobby Gessner, making sure every last student was accounted for.

When he caught his breath, he said, "We're going to have to get the landsats to radar-map this whole region. I want to know how deep the bones are."

"*I* would like to know what killed them," Julia asked.

"And when," Marji Koczan said.

"We can probably find out from the maps," Holcombe told them. "But it looks like the surrounding topsoil is made up of bones. And no telling what else."

The bones of the plain were dry, but were not yet compacted to dust. That suggested to Julia that only a few centuries had passed since they were laid down. Radiocarbon dating would help nail down the exact time.

Julia watched as Professor Holcombe considered the "plaza" and the Mound on top of it.

"What do you think it is?" Julia asked. The other students looked on.

"It's too big for a burial mound," Bobby Gessner said.

"And it's at the center of this 'plaza' area," Holcombe told them. "There's never been a culture that's buried their dead on top of a market place or shopping mall."

"Or even in the center of their main village," Julia said.

"Except that we don't even know what the 'plaza' is," Holcombe observed.

"More bones, I bet," Bobby Gessner said. The Ainge students had clustered together and were generally silent, sipping water from their canteens.

"Could be," Holcombe said. "Let's find out."

The lower level of the ivy-covered plaza appeared to be approximately ten feet thick, to judge by the ground immediately surrounding it. It had gently sloping sides and it was thoroughly draped with the strange ivy. The Mound itself sat on top and in the exact center of the plaza, looking to be easily a hundred feet tall.

They left the outcrop and walked to the plaza—stepping on bones all the way.

The sloping sides of the plaza weren't as steep as they had thought they would be, and a number of students were already racing for the top of the plaza. Once at the top, several students discovered that the plaza was also made of bones and cartilage, but was much older. It had the density of limestone. The bones in this area, they decided, had been laid down much longer ago than the outlying bone fields.

Again at the top of the plaza they had to stop for Professor Holcombe. Julia and Marji Koczan exchanged worried looks between them, but Holcombe himself said nothing when he finally mounted the roof of the plaza.

As the rest of the students fanned out to examine the Mound up close, Julia remained behind with Dr. Holcombe.

"Should you be doing this, Dr. Holcombe?" she asked. "You don't look well."

"I'm all right," he said. "Too much time cooped up in the ship. That's all it is."

Julia watched Holcombe walk toward the Mound. He seemed hypnotized by the Mound the moment he saw it up close.

So, too, had Julia. The Mound would tell them everything they would need to know about these people and what happened to them.

She could feel it in her bones.

Cutter Rausch sat on a tatami mat in his quarters, legs crossed, hands in a *zazen* mudra, and wondered if he would ever see the Kobe Gardens of Hokkaido again. On the other hand, it was possible that he would never see *Earth* again, if the laws weren't changed soon. He missed the Gardens, he missed the temple, and he missed his teacher. Rausch had never married and had little family left in the H.C. The Kobe Gardens were all that he ever called home, all that he ever *wanted* to call home.

An incident one fateful day in those Gardens had forced him into exile, and all because he hadn't acted appropriately. Or in time. He would never again let that happen.

"Cutter," came Lisa Benn's voice over the com. *"I'm sorry to bother you, but we've got a problem here. I think you should see this."*

"Are we getting data-bullet replies yet?" he asked, eyes still closed.

"We're decompressing some of them now," Benn said. *"But something's gone wrong. You'd better see for yourself."*

He rose with a sigh and readjusted the folds of his kendo gi, leaving his slippers off for the time being.

The ShipCom Arena was nearing the end of the first shift, so most of the staff had gone home. The only ones remaining were Lisa Benn, his second-in-command, and their lone intern, TeeCee

Spooner, a former Bombardier recently reinstated after she had cleared her academic probation period successfully.

"What have you got?" Rausch asked, still a little light-headed from his meditation.

Lisa Benn held up to him three hard-copy sheets that she had just printed out. "We're starting to get replies from the first bullets we sent back to the H.C. when the accident happened."

"And?" Rausch squinted at the printouts.

"I think our bullets are going out scrambled. Three messages in a row arrived at their destinations D.O.A."

"Were the destinations ships or outposts?" Rausch asked.

"Ships," Lisa Benn said. "But if they went out scrambled, all of the others we've sent since then might have gone out scrambled, too."

"Ix on a stick," Rausch muttered as he examined the printouts of the three messages.

The printouts were standard "Fatal Error In Transmission" responses indicating that a bullet had not arrived intact and had thus been untranslatable at the receiver's end. The three reports in question had to do with bullets sent from Eos several days ago to three relatively nearby ships. The first was to an Ainge missionary vessel, the *Lili Marlene*; the second went to a cargo ship named the *Ginger Lynn*; the third went to the *Shelene*, a newly commissioned exploration vessel. They were private bullets, and should have been routine.

Rausch sat at his console. "Lisa, bring up the Bullets Out file. Let's start there."

A list appeared on their monitors. Rausch studied it carefully. "It looks like these bullets went out within hours of each other. But they all arrived D.O.A."

TeeCee Spooner considered her console. She was a tall young woman with bright orange hair cut very, very short. She said, "The target spread in real-space was only a few degrees of arc. Could something have gotten in the way of the bullets that might have distorted them?"

Lisa Benn shook her head. "When data bullets travel through trans-space, they pass right through anything in real-space."

"What about in trans-space itself?" TeeCee Spooner asked. "Could these bullets have been deflected there?"

Rausch shook his head. "Trans-space is all energy. It exists only as potential to any other moving object. Collisions can never occur."

TeeCee considered the arrival times of the return messages. "These three messages were returned to us almost one on top of the other. Isn't that significant?"

Lisa Benn shook her head. "An error-in-transmission note would have been instantly returned if our bullet came in scrambled. It would be an automatic computer response. No one at the receiving end would probably have noticed its arrival in the first place."

"Is this common?" TeeCee asked.

"It happens, now and then," Benn responded. "Usually when the target is far away. Bullets have been known to degrade at extreme distances."

Rausch added, "We use a Thompson-Kwaitkowski rail gun with a Cochran queue suspension system for the data bullets themselves. It's the best there is. So the fault shouldn't be ours."

Rausch pondered the printouts. "Did you do a systems check on the Kwaitkowski?" Rausch asked.

"Right before I called you," Benn said. "From my board here, it looks like it's working fine."

"What about bullet compaction in the rail queue?" Rausch then asked.

"Checked that," Benn responded. "BennettCorp hardware is top-of-the-line, including their fractal-compression software. It's all working according to specs."

TeeCee Spooner then asked, "Could it be a reception problem, and not a transmission problem?"

Rausch thought about this. "If it was a single message going to a single source. But we've got three different sources reporting the same phenomenon. And these sources are separated by several light-years."

"The only thing I can think of is that something happened to our bullets *before* they went into trans-space," Benn said. "At our end."

"But how could anyone get at the rail gun?" Spooner asked. "I thought that was impossible."

"It's supposed to be," Rausch said.

He consulted the entire BULLETS OUT list. Forty-four data bullets had been sent from Eos University from the moment their Engine broke down and they had to return to real-space. The first bullet had been sent directly to the Enamorati Yards to apprise the engineers there of the condition of the ship. After that, Eos started sending out bullets to dozen of sources including all nearby ships in case a massive rescue operation was needed.

Rausch brought up the BULLETS IN file. The very first bullet received by Eos University was a reply to the mayday sent to the Enamorati Yards right after the accident. It had arrived twenty hours after it had been sent. It was a ten-hour transit one way, and it took the smallest, tightest data bullet BennettCorp's software could compress in the rail queue. The Engine Makers in orbit around Virr would have responded almost immediately in a bullet of smaller size. It would have said something simple, such as "Acknowledged. Engine is on its way."

However, the next three data bullets sent out after that first mayday had apparently arrived at their respective destinations D.O.A.

"But the reply from the Engine Makers came back intact?" Spooner asked.

Rausch leaned back in his chair. "Several days ago, in fact."

"Who decompressed the return bullet?" Spooner, asked.

"The Enamorati did," Rausch said. "All we do is send the bullets out or catch them when they're sent at us. The Enamorati decompress and decode their own messages."

Rausch turned in his chair and saw that Lisa Benn had already leaped to the obvious conclusion that they might now be in very serious trouble. He said to her, "How many bullets are being decompressed now?"

"Two," Benn said, consulting the monitors at her station. "One arrived just as I called you, the other just a few seconds ago."

Rausch had seen the last reception register on his computer screen and thought nothing of it. Until now.

Rausch brought up the data on the fifth bullet, the one now being decompressed.

Lisa Benn, seeing the same thing on her screen, said, "It's a reply from one of the bullets sent by President Porter back to Ala Tule 4, our last port of call. The one that just came in seconds ago is a reply to the bullet Porter sent to Vii Vihad 4 right after the Ala Tule 4 message."

Rausch didn't have to consult his monitor screen to see the report on the bullet from Ala Tule 4. It came on screen: FATAL ERROR IN TRANSMISSION.

Rausch sped up the decompression of the bullet that had just arrived. An accelerated decompression of a bullet often compromised the data quality of the message, depending on the terabytes of information stored in it. But Rausch didn't think the message from Vii Vihad 4 had anything more than the few data bits it took to say FATAL ERROR IN TRANSMISSION.

Which it did.

TeeCee Spooner was only now getting the picture. "Bullets two through six went out damaged," she said hesitantly. "Then only the Enamorati at the Engine Yards know what happened to us. Or where we are or what we've done since. They don't know about the Hollingsdale maneuver or about Kiilmist 5."

"That," Rausch said slowly, "seems to be the case."

"Ix," Lisa Benn breathed. "We're out here. All alone."

"I'll take this to the captain myself," Rausch said. "It looks like we're in a bit of trouble."

27

The eager undergraduates of the Eos archaeology department circled the mysterious Mound on the leaf-carpeted roof of the "plaza." They had out their cameras and shouldercams taking snapshots and scans of the structure from every angle. Several students attempted to pull back the ivy-grass shroud that covered the Mound to see if they could find steps or some sign of masonry that would tell them what purpose the Mound originally served.

Julia, meanwhile, stood beside Professor Holcombe, watching the man closely. He was seventy-two, long past his physical prime, but he nonetheless had a lifetime of field experience on several planets and dozens of different climates, environments, and altitudes. Hiking *should* have been second nature to him. But he seemed exhausted, drained now; whereas on their last field trip, on Vii Vihad 4, he had seemed much more vigorous, much more outgoing.

But then he hadn't lost a clone-son, he hadn't survived an unprecedented Engine breakdown that could have killed us all. And he's been using wayhighs.

Julia did not like what this foretold.

Bobby Gessner and Marji Koczan had been taking core samples of the hardened surface of the plaza just underneath the layer of ivy-grass.

"We've got a preliminary reading on the composition of the plaza," Koczan announced. She pulled a printout from the field kit's computer. It was the results of a series of electronically induced seismic soundings.

"First of all," she said, "it's a much more compacted version of the surrounding field of bones. Not much of a surprise there."

"But," Bobby Gessner added excitedly, "the scans show that there are three distinct layers of debris under us and between each layer is strata of lighter material."

"That would be this ivy-grass," Holcombe said.

Young Gessner gave the printout to Professor Holcombe, who studied it closely. He then said, "It looks as if they came here to live in three waves or migration. They clustered, then died. The ivy covered everything up for a time, then the same process was repeated."

Julia was thinking. She then said, "When Schleimann found Troy, it was part of a mound that contained at least nine layers of cities built on the same spot. When invaders came along and destroyed the city, it was abandoned. Then a new city was built by the next group who came along decades or centuries later."

"Well," young Gessner said, "*this* place wasn't abandoned. The people just died here."

"But *why* are the bodies so clustered?" Marji Koczan wanted to know.

Julia watched as Professor Holcombe pondered the sky to the south of them. Everyone's attention turned.

"Hadn't noticed that before," Holcombe said.

"Neither had I," Julia said.

Massive cloud shapes had gathered ten miles off, perhaps the prelude to an afternoon storm. If this were back home, Julia knew, rain would be less than an hour away. But Professor Holcombe seemed more concerned than usual over *this* storm.

Holcombe touched the com/pager at his belt and spoke into the chevron at his collar. "Pilot Six, are you there? Report on your status."

From the speaker in the chevron came static, but the voice of their deadman pilot broke through. "—*avionics malfunctioning . . . am relocating to your transponder coordinates . . . storm approaching . . .*"

Julia considered the storm. The cloud formation, several thousand feet high, seemed strangely coherent for a mere afternoon storm. It was more of a giant taking shape in the sky.

"Pilot Six," Holcombe said into his com. "You will find a large earthworks mound a mile to the north of your position. A stone

outcrop two hundred yards to the south of the mound will be a
good place to land. We are at the mound. You will see us."

"—*acknowledged*—"

The other students had now gathered around them.

"Are we going to get caught in the rain?" one student asked.

"The gondola will be here," young Gessner said.

"Maybe," said the professor. He faced them. "Before it arrives,
let's see who can figure out this big boy here."

The sun was otherwise bright above them and the wind was
calm. The students only needed Holcombe's permission to tackle
the mystery of the Mound.

This gave Julia an opportunity to speak privately with him. "Is
there something wrong, Dr. Holcombe?"

Holcombe nodded. He was very grim. "The atmosphere here
might be chemically more complex than we thought. There should
have been no static with the deadman."

"Could that be bad?" she asked.

"It might affect the gondola's antigravity plates," he said. "If the
atmosphere is too highly ionized, it might even affect communications with Eos."

For the first time since their landing, Julia felt a twinge of actual
fear—the fear of being stranded on a world they knew nothing
about.

"The deadman knows enough to avoid the storm or get word to
Eos if there is the slightest hint of danger to it or to us."

"We can ride out any storm under the field kit's shield," Julia
said. "We've done it before."

"Possibly."

Holcombe took his binoculars out and gave the storm to the
south a closer look. He then said, "I don't like it."

"Maybe we should vacate the area," Julia said.

"Let's wait for the deadman," Holcombe said. "We can easily
stay ahead of the storm if the gondola is still maneuverable." He
checked his watch. "It won't take him long to get here. I think we
have time."

The worried expression on the man's face belied the confidence
of his words.

Some of the students were now climbing the Mound. The ivy-grass offered excellent purchase. Other students were looking to see if there might be a door into the Mound.

One of these was Bobby Gessner. He drew their attention, calling out from the base of the ivy-covered Mound.

"Hey!" he shouted. "Over here, you guys! Look at this!"

The boy was wrestling back a curtain of ivy where he had found an entrance to the strange structure.

"Look what I found!" he exclaimed proudly.

Captain Cleddman closely studied the printouts Cutter Rausch had just delivered to him on the command deck. The second shift was ready to come on, but several members of the first shift had lingered behind when they saw the disturbing news about the rail-gun system.

"So there's a real possibility that every data bullet we sent has gone out damaged," the Cloudman said. "Is that right?"

"All except the first one we sent," Rausch informed him. "The mayday seems to have made it to its destination intact."

Alex Cleddman had a reputation of being one of the most steady and unflappable pilots in the Pilots' Guild. This time, however, he seemed neither steady nor unflappable.

"Son of a bitch," he snarled. He rattled the printouts before him. "Are you sure about the mayday?"

Rausch nodded. "Reasonably. Everything seems to indicate that the mayday was received and taken to the proper authorities, then answered. Minus the travel time for its return, they took twenty-eight minutes to make a decision and respond."

"But the others—"

"Apparently D.O.A., whatever their destination."

A member of the first shift, Lawton Blythe, a rugged ex-constable in the Earth Services, was a naturally suspicious man. Blythe leaned forward in his chair. "How many of the other bullets sent out were from the Enamorati? Or were they all just ours?"

"They were ours," Rausch admitted.

"So ours went out scrambled and theirs didn't?" Blythe said, nodding to himself. "That seems to point a finger at the Enamorati, if it was sabotage. You think the Enamorati are stupid enough to pull a fast one on us?'

"I'm not sure they have pulled a fast one on us," Cleddman said. "We still need an Engine. Why would they sabotage the rail-gun system? Remember, they use it to send messages too."

"Have we received any bullets from the H.C. sent to us as independently sent message packets? Packets that *weren't* responding to a bullet we sent?" Cleddman asked.

"So far, no," Rausch told him frankly.

Eos's second pilot, boss of the second shift, spoke up just then. Rene Udice was a redheaded, fortyish woman, somewhat on the heavy side, but she made for a very capable pilot. She said, "What do you think would be Porter's reaction if he found out that the H.C. *doesn't* know what's going on here?"

"That's hard to say," Cleddman said. "He'd speak with the Kuulo for sure. At the very least he'd want us to fix the bullet system. And probably as soon as possible. At least, that's what I would do."

"We're taking apart the queuing system tonight," Rausch said. "Tomorrow, we'll physically inspect the rail gun. But in order to do that, we'll have to shut it down so we can get past the antimatter shield surrounding the rail itself."

"We should do that before we go off making any accusations," the second pilot said. "Maybe it wasn't sabotage."

"That's a possibility," Rausch said.

"You know," Lawton Blythe said, "if the students find out that none of their messages home have been getting through, it could get nasty. I suspect even the Ainge students would be alarmed."

Cleddman's brow furrowed in thought. "If the Enamorati *are* fighting among themselves *and* if *they* sabotaged the data-bullet system, it makes me wonder if an Engine convoy is on the way or something else altogether."

"Such as?" the second pilot asked.

"A troop ship?" Cleddman said.

"We would still need an Engine," Blythe said.

But the men and women gathered on the command deck were all thinking the same thing. Rene Udice said, "Maybe they have no intention of refitting us with an Engine. Maybe they're coming to wipe us out. They could tell the H.C. that we suffered an accident similar to what the *Annette Haven* experienced."

Lawton Blythe added, "Look what's happened so far. There has been an Engine breakdown and rumors of Enamorati unrest. And if it's true that some of our students may have seen the Engine being removed, it's possible that we've pushed the Enamorati Compact too far. From the Enamorati Home Council's point of view, Eos University could be a liability. Maybe instead of an Engine on its way, executioners are coming."

"*Ix*," someone mumbled.

Cleddman paced the room. "Not executioners," he said. "Maybe police."

"How do you figure that?" Lawton Blythe asked.

Cleddman said, "If the Enamorati are fighting among themselves, the Kuulo would naturally want to stabilize the situation. New personnel coming with a new Engine would do that."

"So the rebel faction, if there is one," Blythe suggested, "might be responsible for the scrambled data bullets."

"That's what I was thinking," Cleddman said.

"Yes, but," their second pilot offered, "what if the Kuulo's faction sabotaged the data-bullet system?"

Cleddman said, "That's also a possibility, but I think it's less likely than the first scenario. Remember, there are forty-five hundred human beings on board Eos and less than a hundred Enamorati. I don't think Kuumottoomaa would risk an uprising."

"So are we going to pass this information along to Porter?" Lawton Blythe asked.

Cleddman shook his head. "For the moment, let's pretend this is a ShipCom technical matter. If we can't straighten it out before morning, I'll tell the president what's been going on. For now, mum's the word."

The meeting ended with the second shift coming on duty. All the other personnel went to their quarters, but Rausch, at Cleddman's request, remained. Cleddman had just asked him to go over the details of the data-bullet inspection process when the door to the command deck hissed open and President Porter's personal assistant, Kennedy Ridlon, entered. Two campus security officers had come with him, but they remained outside in the hallway.

"What can I do for you, Mr. Ridlon?" Cleddman asked.

Ridlon gave Cutter Rausch a quick, distasteful glance. Rausch was still in his gi.

"President Porter has convened an emergency meeting of the Governors' Council in the Colonial Suite. He asked me to escort you there personally."

"What about Mr. Rausch?" Cleddman asked, indicating the communications chief. "He's on the Governors' Council, too."

"This is an impromptu meeting, nothing official," Mr. Ridlon said. "He's only talking with a few members of the Council, the more important ones."

"What the hell am I?" Rausch asked. "Chopped liver?"

Ridlon's eyes were as gray as his tunic. "Dr. Porter only requested the captain. Sorry."

"Then let's get on with it," Cleddman said.

He returned the printouts to Rausch and said, "Get these to physics. See what Eve Silbarton has to say about them."

Rausch looked confused for a second or two, but recovered quickly. "Right," Rausch said.

The First Secretary did not seem to notice.

Cleddman followed the president's personal assistant off the command deck and into the outer corridor. But it seemed that the two campus-security men had decided, for whatever reason, to remain behind at the entrance to the command deck.

Cleddman made note of that. And didn't much like it.

28

Cleddman and the First Secretary walked to the nearest transit portal, which whisked them amidships, where the university's administrative offices were located. When they arrived they were passed, going in the opposite direction, by Lieutenant Fontenot and three of his people. They had apparently just come from the Colonial Suite. This, Cleddman found odd. The Governors' Council was composed of the heads of all departments on the ship, including campus security. Fontenot's business with Nolan Porter, then, must have already been concluded.

One entire wall of the Colonial Suite was a real-time 2D projection of the blue and white planet below them. About thirty individuals had gathered in the suite, and all of them seemed to have been waiting for the Cloudman to arrive. Cleddman found a seat closest to the door.

The mild chatter in the room ceased when Cleddman and Mr. Ridlon walked in.

President Porter was conversing with the Kuulo Kuumottoomaa at the opposite end of the room in an area set aside for the Enamorati representatives on the Council. Rather than use chairs, the Enamorati usually relied on a series of upright supports that made it easier for them to stand for long periods of time. That the Kuulo was here in the flesh, and *not* in 3D, seemed particularly ominous to Cleddman.

The next surprise came when, from a door behind the Kuulo, an Enamorati Cleddman had never seen before stepped into the room. From the whispered mutterings of the other humans in the room it was evident that some of the governors hadn't seen it before either. This Enamorati was a few inches taller than the Kuulo and had a pronounced ridge running from its nose to the back of its head. Its e-suit was an olive green and, to Cleddman, it looked an awful lot like battle armor. Its high collar, inside the transparent helmet it wore, concealed every facial feature but its eyes.

It immediately made eye contact with Cleddman, staring at him accusingly.

Cleddman made other observations in quick order. This new Enamorati notwithstanding, there were no other Enamorati present—no Avatkas, no Kaks. The Kaks, the Enamorati's navigators, were always at Council meetings, and so were their human counterparts. Yet, first-shift navigator Peggy Harris wasn't there, nor was Linda Kasperzak of second shift. Also missing was the head of the physical plant, Lewis Arendall, and, of course, Cutter Rausch. In fact, *this* Council seemed to be made up entirely of the friends of President Porter who were all from prominent Ainge families. And sitting off to his left were Auditors Nethercott and Rood. By charter, Ainge Auditors—or any religious official—were forbidden from attending Governors' Council meetings.

Cleddman grasped the situation instantly.

He leaned back in his chair. "I take it that this isn't *quite* the emergency Mr. Ridlon said it was."

Nolan Porter gave him that condescending half-smile the Ainge were so famous for. "It's not an emergency that threatens the ship, if that's what you mean, Captain."

"That's not what I mean, Nolan, and you know it," Cleddman said. "Who's the new creature?"

President Porter bristled slightly and the half-smile lost what little warmth it had. "This is a member of the Enamorati *armazpaava* class. They are bred with eidetic memories. They remember everything and are used as witnesses in legal proceedings."

"Since when?"

"Since we have known the Enamorati," Porter said. "They have always been around."

"That's horseshit and you know it," Cleddman said. "We've been studying their culture for, what, two hundred years? I've *never* seen anything *like* this guy before. And I don't think anyone else in this room has seen it, either."

The assembled group looked at each other, muttering under their breath. But Cleddman had read the situation correctly.

Porter started to speak, but Cleddman cut him off. He rose from his chair. "Look, maybe no one's ever explained this to you, Nolan, but most captains of spacegoing vessels like to know what they're hauling around. It makes them nervous because they don't know if they're hauling around something that might kill the crew and passengers and blow them up out in the middle of fucking *nowhere*. I want to know what this thing is and what is it doing here in body armor."

Several of the well-heeled Ainge gasped at the captain's effrontery.

"Captain, I can *assure* you—" the president sputtered.

Cleddman poked Nolan Porter in the chest. "I'm also bothered by the fact that half the Council is *not* here. So what's this all about? Have you finally decided to turn Eos University into a theocratic state or what?"

President Porter drew back. "If you are speaking of our guest here, it is absolutely harmless. The coloring of its e-suit has to do with its caste. It is *not* body armor."

"I don't buy that and neither do you," he said to the president.

The Kuulo raised his gloved hand. "Captain Cleddman, we have a very grave matter before us, I'm afraid. These other issues can be dealt with on another occasion."

The captain crossed his arms defiantly. "Then let's get down to business. What sort of hand job are you people giving me?"

Speaking carefully, the president said, "As you know, Captain, events over the last few days have taxed the Enamorati Compact and we believe that some sort of intervention is required in order to prevent further damage to our relationship with the Enamorati. I'm sure you can appreciate the fine line I am walking in trying to find a solution to our problems."

"What is it you're trying to say, Nolan?" Cleddman said bluntly. "We're all acquainted with the English language here. Except maybe them." He gave a curt nod toward the two aliens in their braces.

"Captain, we've had several students who we think managed a

few days ago to witness the Enamorati's *Makajaa* ceremony, which would be in clear violation of the Enamorati Compact."

"As well as a possible infringement of Enamorati religious rites and rituals," Auditor Rood added, one row away.

Cleddman leveled his arm at Rood. "You aren't even supposed to *be* here, let alone open your mouth."

The Auditor turned bright red, as if slapped.

Cleddman turned to the university president. He hadn't heard about students violating the Enamorati Compact. If any had—and if the campus security or the faculty senate had proof of the transgression—the whole ship would have known about it by now.

This was a dodge.

"Students will be students, Nolan," Cleddman said.

"Not *our* students, Mr. Cleddman," High Auditor Nethercott said, his voice cracking with barely suppressed anger. "Our students would never do such a thing."

"Captain, we are not talking about student pranks here," Nolan Porter said.

"Then what *are* we talking about?"

Bishop Nethercott stood up defiantly, his fists balled with impotent rage. "For your information, *Captain*, for some time now we've been tracking what we think is an eavesdropping signal or probe coming from Babbitt Hall. It's probed us; it's probed the Enamorati compound. And that we will not tolerate."

"What are you talking about?" Cleddman asked.

Nethercott told him. "Someone's been remotely eavesdropping on our main Auditor station. It comes and goes, but we got a fix on it yesterday. The Kuulo Kuumottoomaa reports detecting the same phenomenon in their chambers. We *know* this is going on."

"If you can prove that this is happening," Cleddman said, "then I'll make every effort to locate the people responsible for it and bring them to justice. If you have that proof, then I'll back you all the way in court. If you don't and all this is about is retribution or harassment of non-Ainge students and faculty, I will throw all of you off this boat myself."

The room was his, and for several long moments no one said anything. "Do you have proof that this has taken place?"

The two Ainge Auditors and the Kuulo considered one another.

Nethercott said, "We don't have it yet. We can only estimate the distance of the return signal. All we know is that it's coming from Babbitt Hall."

Cleddman nodded. "Well, we can find its source easily enough. Cutter Rausch might be able to come up with the equipment to locate the signal precisely. But I want neutral faculty or staff to witness the signal capture. This ship runs by law, gentlemen, not divine dispensation."

Cleddman turned back to President Porter. "What else is on your mind, Nolan?"

Nolan Porter pulled out two letters from one of his pockets. "Several days ago, I sent a data bullet back to the H.C. Plenary Council apprising them of our situation here. Their reply came in this afternoon."

It was Cleddman's turn to blink. "That's it, I take it."

"Yes, it is."

"May I see it?"

"Certainly."

Nolan Porter gave him one of the letters, newly printed from a recently uncompressed data bullet. It bore the official seal of the Human Community Plenary Council and was signed by Mason Hildebrandt the Seventh. The letter seemed authentic.

Which was impossible.

Data bullets were going out damaged, impossible to decompress, thus impossible to read. Mr. Rausch had precise records of all bullets sent to Eos. And as they had just recently discussed, no independent bullets had arrived intact.

Porter spoke as Cleddman read the letter. "The Council has given us permission to proceed to Wolfe-Langaard 4, once our new Engine is installed. There, the Enamorati will be able to determine for themselves if the Compact has been violated. They also need to compare their test results on the old Engine with test results on other Engine failures which they have at Wolfe-Langaard 4."

Cleddman raised his eyebrows. "Wolfe-Langaard 4? That's an eight-month flight, one way. What're Mom and Dad going to think when they get wind of this? For they will, you know."

"The Plenary Council will be meeting to consider that issue very soon," Porter said. "No one takes this lightly, I assure you, Captain Cleddman."

"And what are the students, faculty, and staff going to do while we're taking an extended vacation to Wolfe-Langaard 4?"

Here, the Kuulo Kuumottoomaa spoke. "We believe that your esteemed faculty will be able to fashion lesson plans that do not require your planetary stops. They can probably make up their lost work on Wolfe-Langaard 4 itself. It is a very habitable planet—the first extrasolar planet we settled when we first started traveling in space. It is the equivalent of your settlements on Tau Ceti 4."

"Mr. Kuumottoomaa," Cleddman said, "I don't think you should presume to speak for our faculty, unless you want a full-blown insurrection on your hands. That's the first thing. The second is that I'm not taking this ship anywhere until I see proof that the Enamorati Compact has been compromised. We're not going to make a long trip out of our way just because you *think* someone is probing your quarters or that some student *maybe* has seen the Engine being removed."

Nolan Porter drew himself fully erect, jutting out his chin. "Captain, what happens next on Eos will affect the rest of humanity. The Plenary Council is all too aware of that fact."

The university president held out the second letter, which Cleddman took.

Porter went on. "As you can see, Mason Hildebrandt has granted our request to take over flight operations of Eos until the crisis is resolved to the Enamorati's satisfaction. I'm very sorry about this, Alex, but the order has the H.C. Plenary Council's approval and you see that they've affixed their seal."

Cleddman read the second letter, now understanding why the two guards were left outside the command deck. It also explained why the other members of the Governors' Council weren't there with them in the Colonial Suite.

The letter, completely bogus, had placed him on administrative leave for a period ten months—the exact length of time it would take to reach Wolfe-Langaard 4.

He'd just been fired.

29

Those archaeology students exploring other parts of the mysterious Mound immediately chucked their own ventures across the roof of the "plaza" when young Gessner had announced his discovery. Those students climbing the sides of the Mound slid back down in a rain of shorn leaves; the others came running.

Julia, however, stopped them all from storming the entrance, plunging headlong into no telling what. "Hold on, people," Julia said. "Not so fast. Everybody back off."

"Thank you, my dear," Professor Holcombe acknowledged as he came up behind them. Holcombe seemed to have caught his breath and was no longer wheezing with even the simplest effort.

Two students helped young Gessner peel back the ivy curtain, tying it in place with a length of rope off to one side. Several shouldercams took all this in. Julia stood aside as Professor Holcombe approached the aperture. His flashlight came out and a long beam of white light surveyed the dark opening in the Mound.

With the fall of ivy-grass pulled back, they could see that the Mound was not made of compacted bone and dried cartilage, but had been constructed with tightly packed cobblestones of pinkish quartz composition. The entrance itself, they found, was an excavation, a tunnel six to seven feet in diameter. Someone had gone at the Mound in this one spot with pick and shovel.

"Grave robbers, you think?" Julia wondered out loud.

"Let's get some probes from the field kit," Holcombe said. "I don't want to walk into a giant Venus's-flytrap."

"But this place has been dead for a thousand years," one impatient student claimed. "What could be living here?"

"Booby traps last forever, son," Holcombe replied. "Let's do this by the book. Okay?"

Despite their disappointment, the students backed off and let the careful probing proceed.

Organic life-forms gave off various body odors or chemical residues of their metabolic processes. Holcombe, Bobby Gessner, and Julia ran several checks at the entrance to the tunnel, but found that the tunnel was dry as bone. This did not rule out dangers of a mechanical kind, but Holcombe was satisfied with their initial biotic scans enough to proceed.

"Bring the float lights," Holcombe said.

Marji Koczan and young Gessner brought in several small antigravity lanterns. These would hover inches above the tunnel's hewn floor about every ten yards or so to mark the way.

The soft illumination in the tunnel revealed that the cobblestones were in fact made of an opaque and very hard pinkish glass, not rock-solid quartz as they first thought. Moreover, they were completely round.

"Do we know of any civilization that's used *round* bricks to build their pyramids?" Julia asked as she studied the ceiling.

"And what would be used to hold them in place?" Marji Koczan asked. "Glue?"

Professor Holcombe took out a small pick from his utility belt and teased a thin edge of chalky-white material from the matrix between the stones. "Aliens do alien things," Holcombe said slowly. "Who knows why they built this Mound?"

"Who knows why someone else would want to tunnel into it?" Julia asked.

Nobody spoke for several moments. Julia watched Holcombe study the further depths of the tunnel.

Holcombe then said, "Wait here."

Everybody waited as Holcombe slowly walked to the end of the tunnel. He walked slightly hunched over because his head was inches away from the ceiling, and, Julia noted, he had turned his personal shield up slightly. He disappeared around a corner like a bear returning home to its own cave.

Julia, meanwhile, began examining the cobblestones in the

walls. With her own pick, she coaxed out one of the cobblestones. It was remarkably light. It might even be hollow.

She held it up in the light. "This looks like one of the objects that alien had in his pouch. Remember?"

She handed the stone to Marji Koczan.

"Except that these are bigger," Marji Koczan said.

Professor Holcombe reemerged from his short jaunt to the end of the tunnel. "The tunnel is quite extensive. It goes on for several more yards and leads to a central chamber."

"Look at this, Professor Holcombe," Marji Koczan said. She held Julia's cobblestone before him. "Doesn't this look like those objects we found in that first alien's pouch?"

"It does," he remarked.

Julia noticed that Holcombe seemed pale. But that, she thought, might have been a trick of the light from the floaters.

"What do you think they are?" Koczan asked.

The archaeology professor seemed almost reluctant to answer.

However, just then, from behind them, back near the entrance to the cave, a student in the rear started shouting. "Dr. Holcombe!" The student pushed his way toward the head of the line. "Dr. Holcombe, you'd better take look at that storm outside!"

They hustled back to the mouth of the cave. Stepping out in the open they found three other students standing beside the hovering field kit, which had been left outside. The students were staring off to the ominous south.

An electric storm cloud the size of a large asteroid had seemingly coalesced out of vague vapors and high-altitude winds. And it had done so in the space of twenty minutes. Around its edges sparkled balls of brightly colored lighting. In the distance, they seemed to Julia like angry gnats.

One of the students at the hovering field kit turned to them. He looked very frightened. "I tried reaching our gondola but all I got was static. Then I tried to reach Eos. The call wouldn't go through."

Thunder started trampling the landscape, coming up from the south, and Julia felt the living presence of negative ions in the air.

"Everybody inside!" Holcombe rapped. "The field kit, too!"

She stood there, mesmerized, by the strange formation of clouds. It almost seemed alive. It seemed . . . familiar.

The students maneuvered the floating field kit into the opening of the hidden cave. Julia came in last, reluctant, tugging at the rope that held the fall of ivy-grass. They were completely concealed. But concealed from *what*? A mere thunderstorm?

She looked at Professor Holcombe and saw that he had been thinking the same thing. He nodded at her without saying a word: The bizarre lights that were being generated by the massive buildup of clouds seemed to resemble what Seth Holcombe and his StratoCaster friends had encountered on Kissoi 3.

Julia's intuitions had been sparked by the memory of Seth's own terror that had been ingrained on the StratoCast tile Professor Holcombe had shown her.

Holcombe turned to Julia. "The Mound *may* protect us. But we'll turn the field kit's personal shield up to its highest setting and use it to block the entrance to the tunnel."

"Do you think it will work?" Julia asked as the students looked on, perplexed.

"It better," Holcombe said. "Because we don't have any anti-gravity shoes to outrun it. In the meantime, I want to show you something."

When Captain Cleddman was a little boy, he had dreamed of piloting a space vessel. The reason? Life was so boring. Humanity no longer seemed to be *achieving*. But the Ainge would say that humanity no longer *had* to. It had *arrived*. The starving were fed; the homeless were housed; the sick were healed; and anyone who wanted to go to another world could. The Ainge, the largest Christian religion sect in the H.C., would even pay their way. Still, Cleddman found life boring. Only space held the promise of excitement, discovery, and adventure.

Now he had all three. In spades.

Cleddman undoubtedly surprised everyone on the Council by taking the news calmly and walking out when it appeared the meeting was over just a few minutes later. According to university charter protocol, Cleddman would continue overseeing the daily functions of the ship. But actual command relating to traveling would be given over to someone of Nolan Porter's choosing. This could be anyone, from Rene Udice, the ship's usual second pilot, to someone in campus security or even the physical plant. There were about six or seven individuals who could stand in for a debilitated pilot. So it was Porter's call.

This didn't mean that Cleddman walked away angry. He simply had an ace or two up his sleeve.

To President Porter's credit, he did not place a guard on Cleddman, thus allowing him to go back to his quarters unescorted. Also part of protocol: Porter was kind enough to give him the letters that had supposedly come from the Earth just hours before from Mason Hildebrandt, permitting him to redirect the university to another part of the Alley.

Once in the outer hallway and finding that he was alone, Cleddman opened his com and in a quiet voice said, "Mr. Sammons, this is the captain. Could you and Mr. Wangberg meet me on the command deck as soon as possible. I would appreciate it. Out."

Once inside the nearest transit portal, Cleddman went directly to the command deck rather than his own quarters. Had Nolan Porter any military experience, he wouldn't have allowed him to roam free at all. Trust and docility, though, were stock Ainge characteristics—virtues in earlier Christian eras, vices when an infinity of death surrounded you. He would personally see to it that Porter was hoisted on a lanyard when this was over.

Cleddman exited the portal nearest the command deck and, to his surprise, he did not find anyone standing guard.

However, stepping inside the command deck—the door still recognized his chevron—Cleddman found three of Mr. Fontenot's guards unconscious on the floor. Cutter Rausch, still in his gi, was just now calming down. The man's hair was slightly mussed.

The second-shift crew was looking on in absolute amazement.

"What happened to them?" Cleddman asked.

And Rausch said, "One guy accidentally hit the ceiling. That guy there hit that wall over there. And this guy was bounced upside down on the floor. Several times."

"It probably won't matter, in the long run," Cleddman said walking around the unconscious guards.

Cleddman then explained the situation to them, showing them

the falsely constructed letters that had been allegedly sent from the Plenary Council all the way from the solar system.

"Do you think the president knows what he's doing?" Rene Udice asked.

Cleddman nodded. "He does if he concocted these letters. And I think he did."

"But *why*?" Lawton Blythe asked.

"The Ainge view the Enamorati as kin," Cleddman said, "probably because they commune with the same God. It's inconceivable to Porter that the Enamorati would do us harm. He thinks we'll be exonerated when we go to trial."

"There is a rumor," Rene Udice said, "that when Porter's stint as president of the university is over he wants to be elected Highest Prophet in the Ainge Church."

"Ix," Lawton Blythe mumbled. "What do we do?"

Cleddman said, "I've called Wangberg and Sammons, but those guys might not be able to help us if we do end up taking off for Wolfe-Langaard 4."

"But those letters are fakes," Rene Udice said.

Cleddman handed Cutter Rausch both of the letters. "Porter says they're fully restored uncompressed bullets. As you can see, their time of receipt by Eos is at the top of each letter. As you can also see, both bullets arrived just hours ago and they arrived intact."

Rausch had by then brought his breathing under control from the tussle with the three guards. He said, "These letters are frauds. And even if they weren't, Mason Hildebrandt could never have convened the Plenary Council in less than a week. They meet face-to-face and in real time on Luna. They would probably debate the issue for a week. By that time, Mom and Dad would have heard what was happening out here and created a firestorm of criticism. Hildebrandt would have called us *in* to stand trial, not *out* to Wolfe-Langaard 4. Do we even *know* where that is?"

Lawton Blythe indicated his screen. "I've just brought it up. It's way the hell in toward the galactic center."

"What do you think the Rights Advocacy Office can do?" the second pilot asked.

"If we can get the data-bullet system up and running," Cleddman said, "we'll need all the clout we can get."

He turned to Cutter Rausch. "For whatever reasons, Porter's concocted this letter so he can take over the ship. What I want you to do, Cutter, is facsimile both of these letters down to the last molecule. They've got Porter's fingerprints on them and maybe the people who actually made them. So if he denies ever seeing them, then we'll be able to nail him in court."

Rausch nodded. "I'll remove mine, then."

"But first we've got to fix the data-bullet system and get word out to the nonaligned worlds and let them know that Porter just took control of the ship when there was no reason to do so, particularly when the Kuulo hasn't registered a violation of the Enamorati Compact. Somehow Porter's convinced that he's doing this in *our* best interests."

"A show of good faith?" Rausch said.

"Perhaps."

"Then could it be possible that the Enamorati sabotaged the data-bullet system?" one of the techs asked. "They could have sent out their mayday, *then* hit the rest of the system."

"But that begs the greater question 'why,' " Cleddman said.

One of the techs, who had been listening to the conversation, had been sitting idle at her console. Suddenly, she sat up as a yellow warning light appeared on her board.

"Captain!" she said. "I think someone's trying to override our boards."

"I've got it, too," Rene Udice suddenly announced, swiveling around in her chair.

Cleddman stepped around to Udice's station.

The female tech who had announced the first alarm said, "I'm tracking a systems signal diagnostic. It shot right through my board like someone was testing it. It's gone now."

Rene Udice said, "It looks like someone activated the auxiliary power network."

"Where did the signal originate?" Cleddman asked.

"Not from the physical plant," the female tech said.

Cleddman smiled wryly. "I'd say somebody's testing the system to see if they can bypass the entire command deck up here."

"But why?" the female tech asked.

"Probably to see if they can take control of the ship if they need to at some point in the future," Cleddman said.

"But who would be doing such a thing?" she asked.

"Lieutenant Fontenot," Cleddman said.

"But he couldn't do anything without power from the physical plant," the tech said. "Is Lewis Arendall one of them, too?"

Cleddman frowned. "If Fontenot could convince Lewis of the legality of this coup, then Lewis would be bound to go along. I know Lewis very well. He would never do anything to endanger the students."

Cleddman turned to Rausch. "Cutter, get those letters duplicated. Get copies to the Rights Advocacy Office, get copies to the student newspaper, if you can find them; then, when you figure out what's wrong with the data-bullet system, get copies into the Alley with a summary of what's going on. Include the facsimiles. Fire it to every nearby ship and outpost."

The door to the command deck hissed open and two men stepped in. They wore their usual black tunics with shouldercams and they carried with them their quasi-intelligent briefcases.

"Ah, Mr. Sammons. Mr. Wangberg," Cleddman said.

The two lawyers stared down at the guards spread-eagled on the floor and still unconscious.

"We've got a problem," Cleddman said. "And it involves these gentlemen here."

"I should say so," Sammons said in a voice resonant and commanding.

"But not in the way you think," Cleddman said, pulling the two men inside. "Let me explain—"

30

Holcombe had seen enough of the approaching storm to comprehend the magnitude of what was about to befall them. He should have known it from the sly frizziness in the air while he was walking across the ivy-covered fields. But *Homo interstellaris* had long lost the intuitive hunting skills that had gotten them out of the plains and jungles and to the stars. *This* was the somatic caress of the Ennui, just now something very real.

Holcombe pushed the kit's force shield to its maximum setting, which would easily protect them and much of the Mound as well. *But for how long?* He wondered.

By the time they were all back inside, the storm had already begun to spit upon the land. Wind and rain started pushing at the Mound, but inside, silence reigned.

"We never checked the sky for predators," Marji Koczan said, hunkering down by the dim light of a floater.

"What about the gondola?" someone else asked.

"The deadman might have seen it coming," Holcombe responded. "One of the landsats might have seen it forming. Someone in Eos could have gotten word to it."

"Is that storm out there . . . *alive*?" someone asked.

"Perhaps not as we would understand it, but living nonetheless," he admitted.

Julia, he noticed, had been looking at him as well, but she was merely waiting on his lead. "Why don't you tell us what you think is out there, Julia."

Julia faced the watchful students. "Professor Holcombe had a clone-son who was part of a group of StratoCasters. They were sky-runners and had encountered a cloud formation like the one outside. Except that this one was on a planet called Kissoi 3. It chased them but they managed to outrun it."

"You had a StratoCaster clone-son?" a student asked. He was a freshman and came from a prominent Ainge family on Tau Ceti 4. "He was in *your* family?"

Ainge rarely listened to StratoCasts. They did not go in for deep-mind introspection. To them, all a person needed was an Auditor, a church nearby, and a beneficent Mazaru to guide him.

The ivy curtain concealing the cavern began to shudder with the storm's fury. "If what I *think* is out there, it's been reported in scientific journals as appearing on two other worlds—Pahad Suuva 6 and Konaean 4. I think we can now add Kiilmist 5 to that list." And he hadn't even told them yet what lay at the other end of the tunnel.

"This thing couldn't be indigenous to *all* of those planets," Marji Koczan said. "That would imply that it's a phenomenon that goes from planet to planet. Is that what you're saying?"

"Yes," he said.

A deeper *rumbling* began to resonate through the Mound, coming from above. It danced and harried the Mound, but the structure, protected by the kit's shield, seemed to withstand it easily. Unfortunately for the expedition, as long as the kit's shield was up, they couldn't contact Eos or any of the other gondolas for assistance.

"Bobby," Holcombe said. "Print out a star map of the inner Alley. Highlight Konaean, Pahad Suuva, Kissoi, and Kiilmist. I want a top-down view."

Young Gessner eagerly drew up the map from the kit's data banks and printed out a two-foot-square map. He then spread it on the gravelly floor of the tunnel so all could see for themselves. He then drew a line connecting the stars of Kissoi, Pahad Suuva, Konaean, and Kiilmist. The line resembled a nearly perfect "wave" or ripple that might have emanated from the galactic core itself. Earth was approximately 120 light-years out ahead of the "wave" front.

Holcombe pointed to the "wave." "These four star systems are roughly the same distance from the galactic core." He tapped a section of the map with his pointer that was awash with millions of specks of ink.

"Where is the Enamorati home world in all of this, do you think?" he then asked.

One of the Ainge children blasphemed. "Ix!" he said with a gasp. But no one admonished him.

Virr lay at the very Inner Alley. The "wave," the migratory path of the living lightstorm outside—or whatever it ultimately turned out to be—seemed to come from there.

The physics team and the other renegade faculty managed to break Eve Silbarton's stardrive down into modules so they could refine some of the more problematic parts of the engine while beginning the process of duplicating the others that were ready. This took time. Their materials duplicator had to be reconfigured for the larger parts of the drive, particularly the drive "shaft" itself, a seven-foot assembly that resembled a miniature data-bullet rail gun. This "gun," however, would shoot C-graviton particles through trans-space that Eos itself would come to occupy once the coordinates were established. Ben had been in on the effort since breakfast.

They had just begun duplicating the stardrive components when Captain Cleddman surprised them by walking rather nonchalantly into the lab.

The captain looked over his shoulder, back the way he had come. "How long has the corridor out there been deserted?" he asked.

The ten or eleven people in the room looked to one another.

"We didn't know it *was* deserted," said Dr. Israel Harlin.

Cleddman darkened. "Fontenot, that son of a bitch." He activated his com. "Ship Security," he commanded.

"*Ship Security, here. Go ahead,*" came the dutiful response.

"This is Captain Cleddman. Where are the two guards that are supposed to be watching the physics wing?"

There was no hesitancy in the response. "*We're just changing shifts now, sir. The new shift will be on momentarily.*"

"Have them report to me first," Cleddman said. "I am on the physics floor. Out."

Eve Silbarton, wearing a pair of welder's goggles on her forehead, came over. "So what's the news?"

Everybody set their tools down and listened to Cleddman's update, particularly the switchover of command to the university president and his appointees. He made special mention of the data-bullet problem and the phony letters of command-transfer that could not have been sent, let alone received.

"But *why* is Porter doing this?" young Cale Murphy asked at the end of Cleddman's briefing.

"Because," Cleddman said, "the Auditors think that some of the students have been eavesdropping on both them and the Enamorati. The same students supposedly violated the Enamorati's sacred Engine-extraction ceremony—which is probably why we've been ordered to go to Wolfe-Langaard 4 to stand trial."

Everyone looked at Ben. Eve Silbarton prodded him. "I think you'd better tell the captain what you've been up to."

Which Ben did, rather contritely. He then dug out the photographs the Bombardiers made from their probes. "We were going to get these to you anyway."

Cleddman threw up his hands. "Jesus fucking Christ," he said.

"Sorry," Ben said. "It just came over us."

Cleddman glared. "Something seems to have come over *everyone*. No wonder Porter wants to grab the boat."

"But you said that he had no concrete proof that anything was done. Right?" Ben asked.

"If he finds these photographs of yours," Cleddman said, "he'll have all the proof he needs."

Ben then said, "But he'd have to explain the damage in the corridor and the one Accuser killing the other Enamorati. That *cannot* be normal for them, even if they *are* aliens."

Dr. Israel Harlin, standing tall and thin in stained coveralls, said, "You know, this is going to be in court for years and years. It'll take forever to straighten it out."

"Like I said," Ben told him. "Something just came over us. The opposite of the Ennui, maybe."

"You remind me of *me* when I was your age," Cleddman said. "Reckless as hell and damn lucky no one shot me every day of my life."

"If there *is* a battle going on inside the Enamorati quarters, then we're *all* in danger," Ben said. "We don't know what factions are in there or who is in power. For all we know, the Kuulo's group could be on the losing side."

"Which could explain why the Kuulo wants to get us to Wolfe-Langaard 4 in such a hurry," Cleddman said.

"But the trip is ten months long," Dr. Israel Harlin said. "I wouldn't call that a hurry."

"But in that time they can quash any sort of rebellion, particularly if the Engine convoy is bringing in reinforcements. That's why we're going to need your engines in place as soon as possible," Cleddman said. "The new Engine could arrive at any point during the next forty-eight hours."

"What if Mr. Rausch fixes the data-bullet system," another tech asked. "If we can get word back to the H.C.—"

Cleddman waved him off. "But that wouldn't help our situation here. I've got the lives of forty-five hundred people to think about."

"What about our gondolas?" Ben asked. "Six or seven of them went planetside this morning. It'll take at least a day to get them back."

"I've put Mr. Rausch on that," Cleddman said. He then faced Eve Silbarton. "Our second problem is that I think Ted Fontenot is setting up a secondary command center in the Hollingsdale facility. We picked up a scan from the facility about an hour ago. It was sneaky, but we picked it up."

"So you want *our* drive in place as soon as we can arrange it," Eve said.

"Sooner, if possible," Cleddman responded.

Eve rubbed her forehead. Everyone there was exhausted already.

"I need something in place, *anything* in place," Cleddman went on. "Even if we can only relocate a few hundred thousand miles in this system, that would do."

At that point, they all heard a *thump*! It seemed to come from out in the hallway.

"What was that?" Eve said.

Dr. Harlin turned to one of his students, standing beside the door. "Check that out, Wilson."

Wilson returned, alarmed. "I . . . think someone's placed security locks on the doors and the two transit portals have powered down. Their 'Not in Use' signs are on."

Ben edged past everyone. Several faculty members followed into the corridor.

Ben went one way, the engineers the other.

"Locked!" an engineer shouted from his end of the hallway.

"He's right," Ben said.

The corridor seals were locked and the overrides to the transit portals wouldn't work.

Cleddman tapped his com. "Security! This is the captain. I am in the physics wing, which has been sealed off. I want to know why."

Lieutenant Fontenot's voice appeared over the com. *"I'm sorry, Captain. We have deemed it necessary to remove all of you to the detention center. Since it will take us about two hours to prepare the center, we have decided to keep you where you are for the time being."*

"Are you out of your fucking mind?" Cleddman said.

"No, Captain. President Porter's given us the authority to detain you. As soon as we are ready, we will arrive to escort you down to the center."

"Listen to me, you moron," Cleddman snarled. "You have no such authority! The letter Nolan Porter got from the H.C. is a fake! The data-bullet system hasn't been functioning properly since the Engine accident a week ago!"

"—will be accompanied by several Enamorati armaz-paava. They will be witnesses—"

"Fuck you, Fontenot!" Cleddman shouted. "Didn't you hear what I just said? That letter—"

But the captain's voice became an empty echo in the hallway. The conversation had been terminated at Fontenot's end.

"Shit!" Cleddman swore.

"Well then," Israel Harlin said, "if we're stuck here for the next two hours, we might as well make the best of it."

Cale Murphy then said, "What's the use? If we can't install the units, why should we finish them?"

And Ben said, "If you finish just two of them, we might be able to outfit a gondola that could get back to the H.C. A friend of mine here, George Clock, is an excellent pilot."

"It won't matter if we're in jail," someone else added.

"Wangberg and Sammons are on the case," Cleddman said. "I know they'll be—"

Ben had not been listening. Instead, he had been staring at the far end of the corridor, to the transit portal with the red NOT IN USE sign blinking.

"What's that?" he asked, pointing.

Everyone stopped talking. The wall near the transit portal seemed to be a little "fuzzy."

It was a mist, a greenish blue miasma that sent out tendrils and wisps. At the end of the tendrils were small sparkles of light.

The mist started eating.

"It's happening again!" Eve Silbarton said. *"Everybody back into the lab!"*

31

Ben stared incredulously at the mist growing at the far end of the corridor. It seemed innocent enough, with its bright sparkling lights and its gentle hissing. Yet the innocent mist had atomizing teeth. Alarms began sounding throughout the hall.

Captain Cleddman turned, facing the engineers. "Get back into the lab, close and seal all doors."

The captain engaged his com. "Ship Security! Fontenot, you son of a bitch! What in God's name are you doing?"

A dreadful moment passed before Fontenot responded. When he did, a note of derision was in his voice. *"Can't you people keep quiet for twenty seconds? We need the com clear. If we're going to have an orderly transition of power, we need to make sure that all parts of the ship—"*

"Fontenot, you worthless piece of shit," Cleddman snapped. "What the hell are you doing? Do you want us dead? The mist is coming right for us! Is that what you want? Is that what this is all about?"

"The mist," Fontenot said. *"What mist?"*

"Fontenot, if you think you can get away with murder, think again!" Cleddman shouted. "There are people in this room who have family and connections back in the H.C. Those people are going to ask questions and someone's going to trace this back to you, you sniveling little sewer rat!"

"What are you talking about?" Fontenot asked. *"You people started this. I'm only doing what I've been sanctioned to do. Calm down."*

Ben watched—*everybody* watched—as the captain shook with monumental rage.

"Ted, that letter Porter gave you is *fake*! And even if it was authentic, it wouldn't give you the authority to assassinate us! Open the fucking doors on the physics wing before the disassembler kills us!"

Ben edged back from the mist, keeping an ear tuned to the captain's efforts. The deadly gas with its fairy lights had now filled much of the far part of the corridor—the whole wall having fallen behind the thick, silent smoke.

Dr. Israel Harlin stepped next to the captain and spoke loud enough to be heard by Fontenot. "It was your people, Mr. Fontenot, who brought the disassemblers on board, wasn't it. And it would be so easy. Nobody searches the luggage and stores of campus security. It's really quite beautiful. Thank you, Mr. Fontenot, for being the death of us all."

"What?" came from campus security.

"I'll bet they fucked up the rail system, too!" Cale Murphy shouted. "They have access to the entire ship and they answer to nobody. Hey, Ted! I hear your momma is so fat that when your daddy is done with her, he has to roll over twice just to get off!"

"What are you—? Who said that!"

Ben jumped in. "And, of course, your people were conducting the investigation into the alpha lab's destruction. No wonder they hadn't found out who did it. *They* did it."

"Listen," Fontenot said, sounding genuinely perplexed. *"This has nothing to do—"*

Eve Silbarton clutched Cleddman's arm. "It makes sense, Al. They took out the alpha lab because Gan Brenholdt's engine was close to completion."

"But then why not take out yours as well?" Cleddman countered.

"Maybe that was the plan," Ben said. "There are three stardrives being developed here. It was Friday afternoon, the staff had gone home. Maybe it *was* meant to spread. It could have taken out the entire department without killing any of our staff."

Cleddman waved everyone quiet. "Ted, you hear the alarms in the background? They're going off for a *reason*! Open the goddamn doors!"

"This isn't going to work," Fontenot said. *"Fooling with the alarm system is another felony count against you—"*

Cleddman stepped across the hall to a command panel and

popped it open. Fontenot had undoubtedly cut off the power to the panels, but there was a default override that only a ship's captain knew about. Everyone watched as Cleddman pulled the entire panel out, exposing a secondary unit within. He tapped in his private code and spoke loudly into the speaker.

"Mr. Arendall, this is Captain Cleddman. We have a Code Two emergency in the physics department! The doors and transit portals have been deactivated by campus security and there are fifteen people trapped in the physics department. We need all fire personnel here *fast!*"

"Acknowledged," came a voice from the ship's power plant. *"We're on it."*

Cleddman turned to everyone standing in the doorway to the physics department. "Let's hope that Mr. Arendall hasn't made a decision as to which side he's going to be on."

Ben had been watching the mist eat its fill of molecules as Cleddman called for help. Then, quite unexpectedly, the alarms braying overhead were suddenly cut off. Silence collapsed around them.

But the mist kept coming at them.

Meanwhile, everyone in the physics lab was rushing to the fire extinguishers. They had extinguishers filled with water; extinguishers filled with chemical foams; they even had extinguishers that wrapped a vacuum around the combustion source. All of these came into play.

Ben pulled a large floor-model extinguisher from its hidden cubby in the outer hall and dragged it down the hall, joining the others. He held up the wide nozzle to the deadly vapor as it approached. Several streams of water, choking chemicals, and bursts of oxygen-strangling vacuum flowers roared at the mist.

None of it worked. The mist disassembled everything cast at it and it seemed to operate perfectly well in a vacuum, so that extinguisher was of no use to them.

"To hell with this," Ben said in frustration. He lifted the floor model and threw the entire unit into the gray fog.

The red canister flashed once then disappeared. However, the sheer mass of the extinguisher had gouged a massive hole in the mist before it had been entirely dissolved. Ben stared, astonished. Through the hole the extinguisher made, Ben had seen movement on the far side of the fog. Someone was standing there in the opposite hallway, now visible though the gap in the gray mist.

Ben turned to Captain Cleddman beside him. "Did you see that?"

Cleddman said, "I certainly did."

"I think the mist is slowing," Dr. Israel Harlin said, coming up behind them.

The rapacious mist seemed to dissipate into nothingness before their eyes, as if the extinguisher Ben threw took all of its residual energy.

To their surprise, the floor, ceiling, and supporting walls to either side of the hallway survived unscathed, unlike the episode last week with the alpha lab. This bomb was meant for the corridor seal at the end of the hallway: the one Fontenot had locked from his offices in campus security. The wall had been completely disassembled. A big hole in the metal hung there, mist trailing from its edges.

Through the large opening, they could see into the next corridor.

Fragments of the mist still remained, but that didn't stop Ben from getting a better look at the *person* on the other side of the mist—the person who had clearly set off the disassembler.

"Bennett, wait!" the captain called out.

Ben was out ahead of them now, and, fired up with the need to exact some sort of revenge, he simply hurdled through the opening in the gone wall. He felt the ends of his ponytail sizzle slightly as they encountered stray disassembler molecules. But he did not stop.

Captain Cleddman stepped through the newly eaten hole in the wall and followed Ben. The two reached the end of the hallway and they finally saw their attacker.

It had been an Accuser.

Not someone from campus security.

The creature, wearing the distinctive olive green body armor of the *armaz-paava* class, fled down the adjoining hallway, running as well as it could in its environment suit. And the thing was *fast*, faster than Ben thought an Enamorati could run. The Enamorati were used to a .9 Earth-normal gravity, and it should have been encumbered by the extra weight of the humans' gravity as well as its bulky suit.

Ben turned to the captain. "I'm faster than you are. Get everyone out of physics and tell Mr. Rausch to fix the goddamned bullet system. We've got to get word back into the Alley."

Cleddman hesitated, probably realizing that under normal circumstances they could rely on ship's security to chase down the saboteur. But campus security, it seemed, was part of the problem, not the solution.

"All right," Cleddman said. "Report your position when you get him. But be careful. That thing is armed and dangerous."

"Right," Ben said.

Cleddman turned back to the physics wing as Ben raced off in pursuit of the Accuser.

Ben shot around the nearest corner. The Accuser was well out ahead of him, dodging into stairwells, shooting through rooms that were unoccupied at that hour. The creature appeared to know exactly where it was going.

Moreover, things jangled at the alien's belt. Were they weapons? Were they tools? Ben had to be careful as he ran because the Accuser could easily drop one of his disassemblers, and Ben, in his eagerness, might round a corner and plunge right into a disassembler mist and never be seen again.

Though the creature had a head start, Ben was catching up with it. Now the two were approaching the student commons and more than just a few Eos students were left in their wake, mouths open, completely surprised. Some students jumped out of the way, others screamed at the sight of an absolutely new kind of Enamorati being.

Ben noticed that the Accuser did not take any of the transit portals back to the Enamorati chambers. They would have been the fastest means of flight, but the Accuser ran right on past them.

Ben then realized why: Transit portals had computer records and video scans. It could be recognized by the system the humans had made just for an incident like this.

So this guy knew the system well, Ben realized, and had thought through his escape. It had now become a footrace.

The Accuser burst into the main causeway, past the student cinema. Students were filing out of *Mayberry Agonistes* just in time to feel the gusts of wind Ben made as he chased his would-be as-

sassin. Students fell backward; others just dove for cover. Someone punched an alarm and Ben thought he heard a whistle blow.

But now he had the Enamorati on a straightaway where Ben
knew he could catch it.

The thrill of the chase soared in his veins. He was his old self
again, the person he used to be, the young man who used to play
football and soccer, who felt the fires of pure testosterone in his
blood, pushing him farther, faster. He couldn't recall being this
charged up.

The creature only ran with more determination.

And Ben knew exactly the course the creature would take. It
was headed aft in more or less a straight line, regardless of who
saw him. It was trying to reach the Auditors' sanctuary, where, if it
got there in one piece, it would be safe.

But Ben knew these corridors inside and out. He turned suddenly into a corridor to his right. If he was fast enough, he could
cut the creature off. But he had to be fast!

He put on extra speed, feeling his heart pound, his lungs burn.
Anger and revenge soared in his blood.

He overshot his goal. He had originally intended to have about
five yards of space between him and the Accuser, enough room to
capture the alien in his arms before the Accuser could reach for the
disassembler globes at its belt, release one, and kill them all. That
was the plan.

Instead, Ben came bursting out of the last hallway and collided
head-on with the Accuser.

They made an ugly smacking sound, with Ben's nose flattening
violently on the faceplate of the Accuser's e-suit. Ben's momentum carried them both to the nearest wall, where they both struck
hard—the glass from the Enamorati's helmet falling about them
both like stars.

The hall instantly filled with toxic gases as the creature's e-suit automatically started pumping more of the Enamorati's breathable air.

Death hissed around Ben and there was nothing he could do, for
he was out of air himself and was forced to take in the deadly
fumes the Enamorati breathed.

Death from asphyxiation was just seconds away for both the
pursuer and the pursued.

32

Ben saw stars.

His sight filled with phosphenes of intense, pain-generated light and the metallic, putrescent fumes he breathed left him dizzy, his head spinning. He had, perhaps, thirty seconds to live.

Instinctively, he pinched his com/pager, which sent out an emergency distress signal that would also give ShipCom his location in the ship. He scrabbled away from the wreckage of the Accuser and its shattered helmet. The alien, which had taken the brunt of the tackle, seemed just as disoriented. It, too, began gasping for its own air, horrified to discover that its helmet had been obliterated.

Several students had witnessed this and gathered in the corridor but kept their distance. However, one student approached them. This was Mark Innella, chief reporter of the renegade student newspaper. It did not take an ace reporter to see that they had a whopper of a story before them. His shouldercam came alert at his urging.

Ben held up his hand, stopping Innella's approach.

"Get back!" Ben shouted. Glass from the alien's helmet crunched underneath him as he rolled over. He almost vomited from the smell of the Enamorati's air, an odor somewhere between rotten meat, burnt rubber, excrement, and an Earthly camel's really bad breath.

Ben tweaked his com/pager. *Physical plant*, he thought. *They have access to the ship's ventilation grid . . .*

"This is Benjamin Bennett on level twenty-one, corridor eight. Track my position and close all filtration vents immediately. We've got Enamorati atmosphere in here."

More students had gathered at the nearest corridor junction. This time, however, the Bombardiers were among them. Tommy Rosales and George Clock apparently had been in the commons eating when Ben and the alien had shot past them.

Clock and Rosales rushed to Ben's aid, but the other students stayed where they were. The Enamorati's breathing air was drifting toward the ceiling.

"Hey, man, what's going on?" Clock asked, lifting Ben to his feet, pulling him away from the Enamorati.

"What happened to this guy?" Rosales asked. Then he saw the broken helmet, the scattered bits of glass. Then he *smelled* it.

"Well," Rosales muttered, cupping his nose and mouth. "Now we're gonna die."

The three backed away from the alien. "I broke open its environment suit," Ben said. "Get those people out of here."

Some of the students were already backing away, and overhead the air ducts began closing off. Seconds later, the doors to the adjoining corridors clamped shut. The message had gotten through to the physical plant. Unfortunately, at least ten other curious students had remained with them in the corridor with the Bombardiers, Mark Innella being one such.

The humans backed off like a wave advancing in a pond. But the seconds went by, becoming minutes, and the Enamorati atmosphere hadn't done any more than make the humans turn up their noses at the ungodly stench. Curiously, the alien on the floor didn't seem much bothered by *their* air either. By the twitching of its hands and feet, they could see that it was still alive, and its respiration seemed normal.

"So how come we're not dead yet?" Clock asked.

"Beats the hell out of me," said Ben.

Mark Innella came over and the four of them stared at the creature, which lay several yards off, back turned to them, trying to sit up in its olive green e-suit. The humans wouldn't go any closer.

"What the hell kind of Enamorati is *that*?" Innella asked.

"It's called an 'Accuser,' " Ben told him. "Theoretically, the Accuser caste has been flying with us for decades."

"What's it supposed to *do*?" Innella asked.

"It's supposed to be a witness to events," Ben said. "But I think it's a soldier. It tried to kill us."

The air ducts whistled overhead as newer, cleaner air was frantically pumped into their section of the corridor.

"But I *still* want to know why we're not dead yet," Clock stated.

"That guy's alive, too," Rosales said, pointing to the Accuser, now sitting up in the ruins of its e-suit.

The Enamorati supposedly found the air humans breathed ten times more toxic than humans found theirs, and the unfortunate Enamorati was supposed to perish if he ever chanced to breathe a single lung-bladder of the nitrogen-rich stuff.

This apparently wasn't going to happen.

Even more astonishing, the alien slowly began to climb to its feet, the glass of its helmet falling like loose diamonds to the floor.

It rose awkwardly, like a stunned insect. It then turned, facing them. The jagged splinters of its helmet's remains jutted up from the suit's collar, and dark blue blood had emerged from a minor scratch, nothing serious.

The Accuser faced its pursuers. But it did not reach for any of the various weapons at its belt—indeed, if they *were* weapons—and it did not perish from the air. In fact, the alien seemed invigorated by it.

Ben stood speechless. This wasn't an Accuser.

It was an *Avatka*. More specifically, it was the Avatka Viroo.

Ben had spent plenty of time in detention studying the only Accuser he had any experience with. That Accuser had a pronounced reddish crest rising from between its wide eyes over the top of its skull. *This* being, though, was the Avatka Viroo. He never could have mistaken the two. Castes among the Enamorati were like racial features among human beings.

The alien moved toward them. Ben, Tommy, and George spread out instinctively. Mark Innella simply watched, dumbfounded.

"You are in great danger," the Avatka Viroo said in clear, slightly inflected English. He had raised up an arm as if to signal a momentary truce.

So they breathe air and speak English fluently. What else can they do? Ben wondered.

"We're in danger because you keep trying to kill us," Ben told him.

The creature's voice sounded a bit wheezy, shrill. The air had *some* effect on him. "I was not trying to kill you. I was trying to set you free."

"That's not what it looked like to us," Ben said.

The alien said, "A *vehenta* has a short life span and was dying the moment I released it. None of you would have been hurt. You needed to be free."

"What's that guy talking about?" Rosales asked.

Ben said, "I was in the physics department until this guy here turned loose another disassembler. I chased him from the physics wing to this spot."

"That's about a half of a mile," Clock said admiringly.

"I was in a hurry," Ben said. "This is the second time he's tried to kill me."

"It was not an attempt on your life, this second time," the Avatka said. "You needed to be free."

Ben noticed how weak the creature had become from the chase . . . or it could have been from the humans' regular atmosphere.

"You want to explain that?" Ben demanded. He was keeping an eye out for any movement from the alien's hands. There wasn't an object clinging to the creature's belt that couldn't be a weapon and he had no idea what a *vehenta* was.

The creature said, "The Engine's breakdown propelled certain forces among the Enamorati to turn against each other. Those who are now emerging as the victors have allied themselves with your president and his allies."

"We know that," Ben told the Avatka.

"What you don't know . . . is that *all* of you are in danger. I was hoping that the . . . nonaligned humans of the ship would have seen the real struggle before now."

"We have seen the inside of your chamber," George Clock said, pushing forward. "So you people are fighting among yourselves? All that wreckage we saw, it was recent?"

The Avatka's face was unexpressive, but veins were now beginning to appear on his forehead. "We are . . . and it is."

"*Why* are you fighting?" Ben asked.

The creature said, "We are fighting over . . . something I did, a most deplorable act."

"What was that?"

"I am the one who destroyed the Engine."

"*You* destroyed the Engine?" Tommy Rosales burst out. "Why?"

"Because a little white bear died and I knew that it was time," the Avatka told them.

The group of students looked to one another, uncomprehending. Even Ben was taken aback. "You did this because Julia's pet bear died?"

The Avatka's breathing now was coming in uneasy gasps. He started to wobble where he stood—he was very close to fainting.

"A vast deception is being played out on the ship and it would have led to your death. The little bear was just another casualty in a horrible war which must now come to an end."

"A war?" Mark Innella asked, his shouldercam peering close.

But the Avatka collapsed before he could add any more to his cryptic pronouncement.

33

The protective shield generated by the archaeology team's field kit hunkering just inside the entrance to the tunnel seemed to be holding up against the storm outside. At the very least, the Mound seemed solid enough to take just about anything the planet had to throw at it. It would probably last through this particular storm. Or so Julia hoped.

The semidarkness of the tunnel, the terror of the storm outside, and the sheer eeriness of being trapped in an alien-dug tunnel begun to get to a few of the younger students, making them nervous in ways they had never experienced on any of their other ports of call. But Julia had done a great deal of spelunking when she was younger—caves had always been vital to the native cultures of the Desert Southwest in America—so she didn't feel as claustrophobic as the rest of the students.

Instead, she considered Dr. Holcombe, who stood at the rear of the group. His shoulders hunched as if he felt the gravity of their situation and his face, lit eerily by the floaters scattered in a line about fifteen yards into the tunnel, seemed haggard and drawn. Much was on the man's mind.

"Do you know what this is about, Dr. Holcombe?" Julia asked as thunder walked the world outside the Mound. The other students looked on.

"I have an idea," he admitted.

"That lightstorm outside," Julia said. "Is it responsible for killing off the higher life-forms in this region?"

"Not at first," he said. "But it would have eventually."

The undergraduates looked at one another, mystified.

Holcombe paused for a moment, taking a long, hard look to the darkness at the end of the tunnel. He then said, "I think you ought to see what's in there."

Most of the students remained huddled on the floor, their personal shields aglow. Only Marji Koczan and Bobby Gessner had any interest in doing any more exploration. The rest only wanted to go home.

Holcombe led the way with Marji Koczan and Julia right behind him. Bobby Gessner brought up the rear, dropping the occasional floater to light the way for the others, if they chose to follow.

"So, tell me," Holcombe said to Julia as they edged along. The tunnel now seemed to be narrowing. "Do you believe in fate?"

"Fate?" she asked. "I haven't given it much thought. Why do you ask?"

Holcombe shrugged, flashlight held forward like a bright crystal lance.

Julia responded almost cavalierly, "You couldn't have any kind of legal system if our lives were fated. No one would be responsible for anything they did. We'd be creatures of our desire."

"I'm talking about the way things happen in our lives," Holcombe said. "Outside factors. What some people might call 'acts of God.' You know, a lightning bolt out of nowhere. That sort of thing."

Julia couldn't quite read the expression on his face and couldn't see where he wanted to go with this train of thought. So she said, "Well, if God plans everything or at least knows how things are going to turn out, then I would say, yes, our lives are fated." This was an old Calvinist saw that few humans held to anymore. Certainly fate had no place in Ainge theology. They believed that once a person "hears" God in an Auditor box, he knows what to do for the rest of his life.

Holcombe paused as they seemed to be near the end of the tunnel. Just behind him, beyond the range of light, appeared to be some sort of obstruction on the floor.

"Let me ask you this," he then proposed. "What are the odds that Eos would suffer an Engine breakdown just a few light-hours from a star system with a human-habitable planet?"

Marji Koczan and young Gessner paused right behind them.

Several of the other students had, by then, also decided to follow. They listened raptly to the unusual philosophical discourse.

Koczan said, "If pure randomness governed the universe, then the odds would be astronomical that we'd be anywhere near an Earth-like world."

Julia looked at Professor Holcombe. "Are you trying to suggest that our Engine was destroyed just so we could find this particular planet?"

It took Holcombe a few long seconds to say so, but in the end he said: "Yes."

"Then what's all this talk about God and fate?" Julia asked.

"Because humans have gotten lazy," Holcombe said. "We've taken too much for granted, we've gotten used to asking far too few questions. We've lived too long on faith alone, trusting that everything will turn out for the best because it always seems to."

"The Highest Auditor says that faith is what holds life together," young Gessner said.

Professor Holcombe nodded slowly. "The Ainge will tell you that God speaks only to those who listen. But if the Auditors are the only people who can hear God, what does that say about the rest of us?"

"We don't have Auditor boxes," Marji Koczan said.

"Lie in an Auditor box just once, and you'll see," a male student in the rear said. "Ixion Smith *was* hearing God move through the cosmos. I've heard Him. So has everyone else here."

"Speak for yourself," Marji Koczan said.

"Up until Ixion Smith built the first Auditor box, the only way we've ever learned anything about ourselves or the universe is through our mistakes, our failures," Holcombe told them. "I've been in an Auditor box three times in my life. But I'll tell you one thing Ixion Smith never knew and that is that success is a greater enemy than failure. Success can deceive you, but your failures will never lie to you."

"Dr. Holcombe, what's this all about?" Marji Koczan asked. Julia almost asked the same question.

"Come this way, children," Holcombe said.

The tunnel had narrowed to a width of three feet and a height of about six. Most of the lingering students had caught up with them by now, drawn to the resonance of his storytelling voice.

"Our first order of business," Holcombe said, stopping at the very end of the tunnel, "is to determine how this gentleman fits into the great scheme of things."

Professor Holcombe pointed to the desiccated remains of a humanoid being at their feet. Very old and very dead, this individual clutched a crude pick, and a blunted shovel lay beside him.

This entity was not, however, a Kiilmistian.

"Oh, my God," Marji Koczan gasped. "This is an Enamorati!"

Julia immediately recalled that some of the wall graffiti they had found at the first ruins had stick-figure-like images of short, squat humanoids—Enamorati?

Bobby Gessner knelt down and carefully turned the Enamorati over. He was as light and as brittle as papier-mâché. A grimace of terror was his death mask. Some of the underclassmen backed off.

"What is an Enamorati doing *here*?" Bobby Gessner asked. He looked up at Professor Holcombe. "Didn't the Kuulo say that the Enamorati had never explored this world?"

"He did," Holcombe said.

"Then, what—"

The students stared, awestruck, by the body before them and the myriad questions its very existence posed.

Holcombe then said, "It would also be an interesting question to ask why this character *isn't* wearing an environment suit. The atmosphere, even in this tunnel, should have killed him. Yet he made it in this far, digging and scraping."

"Maybe it *did* kill him," young Gessner suggested.

"No," Julia said. "He was digging when he died. It looks like he might have just broken through when he collapsed."

"Then," Gessner said slowly, "maybe this is an ancestor of the present-day Enamorati, someone who had come here long ago *before* their planet's environment went bad and they had to use e-suits."

"Except," Julia said, "that the Enamorati destroyed their ecosystem centuries *before* the Onesci Lorii was even born. How could a civilization with slower-than-light technology have come this far from their home world? Virr is more than two thousand light-years from this planet."

"I think it's safe to say that this gentleman got here *after* the Enamorati invented trans-space travel and *after* they bred themselves to breathe their current atmospheric mix," Holcombe told them.

The children of the Ainge looked confused. Julia and Marji Koczan were as well.

"That can only mean that some of them *can* breathe our air," one of the male students in the rear said.

"Perhaps *all* of them can breathe our air," Holcombe responded. Upon further inspection, they found that this creature also had a pouch full of the same strange egglike objects they had come across in the grasp of the second Kiilmistian in the ivy-covered field. These, too, were dry and brittle and yielded nothing of their purposes.

"I think you people should see this," Holcombe said in the darkness beyond the end of the tunnel. He was now standing in what appeared to be an immense cavern—the goal of the hapless Enamorati grave robber.

Julia stepped over the Enamorati tunneler and entered the Mound's capacious interior. She dropped a floater behind her, just inside the Mound. Marji Koczan came in behind her, and behind Koczan came young Gessner. The other students followed.

They brought up their flashlights, filling the interior cavern with all manner of dancing beams. More floaters were thrown about and the contents of the Mound were finally revealed to them.

"Ixion Smith!" young Gessner blurted out. *"Look at that!"*

"It *is* a temple," Julia breathed.

"Or something," Holcombe added.

They had emerged onto a ledge about four feet wide that seemed to be made of the same cobblestones. It completely circled the interior of the Mound, which was a large pit perhaps thirty-five to forty feet deep. A large dome made of the same glassy cobblestones arched over them at a height of fifty feet.

However, it was the object *in* the pit that commanded their attention.

In the pit huddled a hemispherical structure like the giant shell of an Earth turtle. It was sleek, the size of two or three houses, and out of its sides, plunging into the ground below it, were numerous limbs bunched together, giving the impression of arms or legs, though it was far too massive to be a once-living thing.

The students aimed their flashlights at the imposing object.

"What *is* it?" Julia said in a barely audible whisper.

Professor Holcombe, standing off to one side, said, "I don't think you want to know."

34

Someone once said that idle hands were the devil's playground. They must have had Jim Vees in mind.

As the university entered the slow hours of the evening shift, the halls became quiet and Jim became bored. Tommy and George had gone to the student commons while Ben had taken the probe photographs to his advisor in the physics department. Jim was left to his own devices, sitting in his dorm room in Babbitt Hall.

Jim had always admired Ben both for his sense of daring and his instinct for caution when caution was required. Ben seemed a natural leader that way. But Vees could not shake the images the probe captured of the mayhem inside the Enamorati compound. Nor could he shake the strange sense of trust the Auditors had for their alien neighbors—neighbors who had all manner of weapons disguised as wall decorations.

A very violent civil war was under way inside the Enamorati compound, but the Ainge refused to acknowledge it. *Why?*

Vees had revised some of his thinking on his Auditor box locator that occupied the second suite of his dorm room. It occurred to him that not only could he pick up the brain waves of individual Auditors in their holy box, but he might even be able to duplicate them if he could maintain a strong enough lock on the Auditor box itself. The experiment with the probes showed that a nexus signal could be sent and returned at much higher power gradients than he'd thought possible.

Vees soon reconfigured his nexus projector and plugged it into an amplifier that had been gathering power in modest increments over the last few hours. He donned the headset, reclined in his special chair, and switched on his system.

Vees let his mind drift with the theta-wave rhythms the nexus beam picked up as it probed the sacrosanct world of the Auditors. The nexus probe drifted as light as a dream through walls, down corridors, into rooms—quiet as a shadow searching for the theta waves in the main Auditor box. High Auditors and bishops could spend as much time as they wished in the Auditor box, listening to Mazaru doing His work across the galaxy. Lower Auditors had to wait their turn, but wait they did. Patience was an Ainge virtue. Patience and obedience.

Vees was neither patient nor obedient.

Within minutes he found an intense source of magnified theta waves and knew that he had found it. The box. The Auditors more commonly called it the "station," and, to Jim's surprise, it wasn't a "box," but instead a simple chair—comfortable and plush—with a large headset. It was enclosed by four walls, giving it the appearance of a box from the outside.

And the Auditor taking his turn at the station was Orem Rood, one of the most privileged Auditors. Vees could feel the man's solemn pride mixed in with the headset's peculiar effects.

To Jim, it was like being in an opium den. Rood was nearly unconscious with the prolonged orgasmic titillations of the machine.

Vees focused on the endorphic charge Rood felt, letting his mind expand far enough to grasp the immense, impossible, energy-charged infinities of trans-space.

He saw God.

At least as Auditor Orem Rood saw Him. *Mazaru.*

He gasped with euphoric revelation, for he could actually sense God at work fifty light-years away in one direction, four thousand light-years in another, five hundred light-years in still another. *Dollops of joyful pleasure lightly touching here, lightly touching there throughout the galaxy. And it was intelligent, knowing, and all-powerful. . . .*

The mind of Orem Rood was calling out to God. A prayer. He was gently beseeching God to swing His righteous wrath back to their little corner of the Alley in this time of crisis. Time was of the essence, the situation deteriorating. . . .

Crisis? What crisis?

A loud *bang!* slammed against the door to Vees's room, the

sheer violence of it yanking him out of his trance. He ripped off his helmet in time to see long, slightly curved swords tear through the door to the second suite as if it were merely a paper partition. The swords, slender as those used by ancient Japanese samurai, had edges that were molecule-thin. And so did their axes. These came next and the door was sliced away from its hinges within seconds.

Alien soldiers came crashing in—four Accusers in their dark-green battle chitin and shielded faceplates, swords ready to slice up anything that got in their way.

"Jesus Christ!" Vees said, leaping out of his chair.

For the first time terror, *real* terror, gripped him. They came at him like a line of fullbacks. They had unexpectedly powerful hands and they snatched him from his chair as if he were a three-year-old.

"Help!" Vees shouted as the battle-armored Enamorati dragged him to the nearest transit portal. Four spiders. One fly. And no witnesses.

In the hallway, filled with the disappearing vapors of sleep gas, were the forms of six or seven unconscious students, caught in the wrong place at the wrong time.

Jim and his captors vanished into the transit ring.

Cutter Rausch stepped from his private apartment into the Ship-Com Arena, busily wiping his hands with a small towel. The fastidiousness he'd learned from the monks of the Kobe Gardens had stayed with him over the years. He did not like messes. But it would take several days to wash away the oil and grease from underneath his fingernails.

"Lisa, the diagnostics. What's the word?" Rausch asked his second-in-command.

Lisa Benn and several of Rausch's closest staff had been at their boards running a series of diagnostics on the entire data-bullet system, now that the problem with the system had been identified and fixed.

Lisa Benn said, "Just came in. The test bullet we sent seventeen minutes ago to Vii Vihad 4 arrived intact and returned intact. The system's back to specs."

Rausch sat at his chair and pondered the strange device that had apparently caused all of their communications problems. Between his thumb and forefinger, he held a gizmo about the size of a one-credit coin, three-fourths of an inch in diameter, an eighth of an inch thick. They had found no defect, or sign of sabotage, in their bullet compression software or in the magnetic suspension holding queue. That left the rail gun itself. Rausch had been on his knees for the last hour or so, wending his way through the maintenance tunnels that their servicing robots couldn't get into. The device he had found had been placed close to the center of the rail gun, but outside the antimatter barrier that surrounded the gun housing. It was a blind spot in the rail gun's construction.

"Do you know what it is?" Maree Zolezzi asked, pointing to the wafer-sized device in Rausch's hand.

Rausch nodded. "It's a computer chip designed to exert a slight magnetic pull on the antimatter shield surrounding the rail gun. When the gun powered up, this guy here would tug on the shield, warping it, causing the bullet to go into a wild spin. By the time the bullet arrived at its destination, its cohesion would have completely failed. Dead bullets."

Rausch passed it around the room.

Ms. Zolezzi pondered the little device. "I've never seen anything like this before," she said, passing it on to TeeCee Spooner. "Is it . . . one of ours?"

"Is it human, you mean? I'm sure we'll find out when we take it apart," Rausch said. "Unless an Enamorati got a human to make it, then we'd be in for a long and complicated investigation and I don't want—"

The door to the Arena suddenly hissed open. Lieutenant Ted Fontenot, two of his associates, and the Kuulo Kuumoottomaa appeared. The Kuulo, Rausch noted, was encased in a kind of e-suit he had never seen before. *Battle armor*, he realized. *No more charades. No more fooling around.*

Rausch turned to TeeCee Spooner and gave her the strange device that had fouled up their rail launcher. "Scan this and add it to your report, intern. Then proceed on that other matter we discussed."

"Yes, sir," TeeCee said. She placed the small device on their molecular scanner and turned it on. All this was done with a careful sense of nonchalance and business-as-usual regularity. Neither Mr. Fontenot nor the Kuulo Kuumottoomaa seemed to have noticed the transaction.

However, Rausch's attention was on the distinctive chevrons on Mr. Fontenot's collar: they were those of a ship's captain. By university charter Rausch had to obey the ship's captain, regardless of the particulars of succession. He could do nothing but obey the man's commands.

Or *pretend* to obey.

"Mr. Rausch," Fontenot said perfunctorily.

"Yes, Captain Fontenot," Cutter Rausch said, the words tasting funny on his tongue. "What can I do for you?"

"By direct order from the Plenary Council, I have been given command of the ship and am told to oversee the installation of the new Engine. We are then to proceed to Wolfe-Langaard 4, where Mr. Cleddman, several faculty, and a few students will stand trial for possibly violating the Enamorati Compact."

"I see," Rausch said. "And why are you telling me this?"

"Because," Fontenot said, "I want a total communications lockdown, nothing in, nothing out until the new Engine arrives and the Enamorati have completed their insertion ceremony. President Porter and I will have, by then, composed several communications to the worlds of the H.C. Everything will go by protocol from now on, because I will *not* let any of our actions further jeopardize our relationship with the Enamorati."

"I see."

"In the meantime, I want all transit portals switched off to human traffic and I want you to announce to the students, staff, and faculty that they are to return to their living areas until further notice. The Engine escort will be appearing soon and we don't want any interference this time from anyone."

Fontenot turned to walk away.

"Then shall I keep the transit portals open to Enamorati?" Rausch asked dutifully.

Fontenot paused, looking at the Kuulo Kuumottoomaa. The Kuulo said, "We have no use for them. You may include us in the shutdown, if you wish."

"As a show of good faith," Fontenot interjected, "we will allow the Kuulo full use of the portals, even if he does not avail himself of them." He made a slight bow to the chief Enamorati.

Rausch considered a light, now blinking, on his board.

"Then what about members of the Avatka class?"

Fontenot stood puzzled. He looked at the Kuulo. The Kuulo said, "The Avatkas are busy. None would be allowed anywhere until the *Sada-vaaka* is completed and the ship under way."

Rausch pointed to his data board. "Well, I'm showing that one of your Avatkas transited to the physics wing, oh, about ten minutes ago. What about him?"

The Kuulo looked about as perplexed as an Enamorati could be. Fontenot looked at the Kuulo Kuumottoomaa.

"Which Avatka would this be?" the Kuulo asked Rausch.

"The Avatka Viroo," Rausch said. "At least that's what we registered from his pager/transit chevron."

The Kuulo seemed surprised by this information. "There is a mistake in your tracking computer. Our Avatkas are preparing for the insertion ceremony and are in seclusion."

Before Rausch could respond to the Kuulo's obvious falsehood, Lisa Benn raised her hand. She had been pondering a new series of lights on her board. "Sir, I've got four unregistered Enamorati in Babbitt Hall. They've just arrived."

Rausch came over. Even Fontenot was taken off-guard by the revelation.

But then Benn retracted her remark. "I'm sorry. My mistake. They just transited back to the Enamorati compound. Never mind."

Fontenot and the Kuulo Kuumottoomaa looked wordlessly at one another.

Benn kept on speaking, however. "Oh, but now it looks like they were accompanied by a human being, a student. His com/pager is off but the transfer signal he left behind suggests the weight and mass of a human being. Male, I'd say."

"They transited back to the Enamorati compound with a *human being*?" Maree Zolezzi asked. She looked at Cutter Rausch. "Is that . . . allowed?"

Fontenot said, "The only way a human could transit into the Enamorati compound would be if an Enamorati allowed it. And none would. Like the Kuulo said, you're mistaken."

"Mr. Fontenot . . . *Captain* Fontenot," Rausch said. "Four Enamorati entered Babbitt Hall a few moments ago and returned with a male human student. Are you and the Kuulo trying to conceal the kidnapping of a human being through the transit system? If you are, I am duty-bound to prevent it. *I* oversee the transit portals. *You* don't. Now what the hell are the Enamorati doing in Babbitt Hall?"

Fontenot considered the Kuulo Kuumottoomaa. "Were you aware of this?"

The Kuulo seemed hesitant. He then said, "Of these four Enamorati, yes, I was aware of this. I cannot say for the Avatka in the physics wing."

"What were the four doing in Babbitt Hall?" Fontenot asked.

"A minor matter, Captain," the Kuulo said. "We are merely detaining those responsible for violating our *Makajaa* ceremony of a few days past. You and your agents have enough to do in securing the ship."

Cutter Rausch then said, "Unless you have a different perspective on this, I'd say that at the very least you've just earned a case of illegal entry, destruction of personal property, assault on a human being, and possible battery. Then you've got a charge of possible kidnapping that could be thrown at you, if that's what's happened."

Rausch and Fontenot had their eyes locked, but the Kuulo stepped in between them. He said, "I know this seems extreme to you, but we believe we are well within our rights to protect *our* privacy. The student taken from Babbitt Hall is the only human we know who is now capable of eavesdropping on us. We will return him when the insertion ceremony is over. We will detain him no longer than forty-eight hours."

"I don't think that's legal," said the intern.

Fontenot faced the Kuulo. "I insist that I know at all times what your people are doing. Do you understand? We live by the rule of law here. I *can't* have you acting on your own accord. Someone might get hurt or killed."

"I understand perfectly," the Kuulo said.

"All right, then," Fontenot said.

He turned to Cutter Rausch. "The Kaks have calculated that the new Engine will arrive in less than fifteen hours. One was much closer than they originally thought. We want all of the gondolas recalled immediately and the ship secured. This means students in their dorms, staff and faculty in their homes, and crew at their stations. Send that message out to everyone immediately."

"I can do that," Rausch said.

The Kuulo added, "It is also advisable that all of your probes and mapping satellites be destroyed."

"We can shut them down," Cutter Rausch said. "Their orbits will eventually decay and they'll be destroyed on reentry."

"I would prefer they be destroyed now—unless they can be captured and returned physically to the ship," the Kuulo said. "If the inbound crew escorting the Engine detects a satellite or probe nearby, they will withdraw and take the Engine with them. We will be stranded."

"Then those are your orders," Fontenot said to Rausch and his crew. "I want a communications blackout and every human accounted for in six hours. Do you understand?"

Rausch nodded. "And what about Captain Cleddman? Where is he?"

Fontenot said, "He has been ordered back to his quarters. He has demonstrated a willingness to follow this change of command, which will look very good for him, I'm sure, when we take this to court."

The two then left.

Cutter Rausch shook his head. He looked at TeeCee Spooner. "Did you have an open channel?"

The tall young woman nodded. "Yes, sir. The captain's waiting."

"Al, how much of this did you catch?" Rausch asked.

The voice of Captain Cleddman filled the room. *"Most of it."*

"What do you want us to do?" Rausch asked.

"Forget about Fontenot for the time being. Right now we've got to find out what those four Enamorati did with that student."

"His com/pager isn't sending out a signal," Rausch said. "Unless he has a pager, we can't track him."

"I'll figure out something. Right now get word down to the gondolas. We're going to have our own propulsion system in place in

the next eight hours or so. If we can do that, we'll be able to relocate ourselves in space and deal with the Enamorati at our leisure. What's the progress on our data-bullet system?"

"I have located the problem and fixed it," Rausch said. "We're set to go."

"The 'package'?"

"It's going out right now," Rausch said. "As we speak."

Lisa Benn pressed the button on her console, opening up the rail queue and activating the launcher. Seconds later, the bullets started going out—data packets that chronicled their situation—complete with photographs, video records, and voice testimonies. The package also contained an exactly duplicated version of the letters supposedly sent from Mason Hildebrandt, giving the university president the right to hand over the ship to campus security. Added at the very last moment by TeeCee Spooner was the molecule scan of the rail saboteur's chip, which was clearly not of human manufacture. And all of this was done under Lieutenant Fontenot's nose.

Those bullets, however, were very heavily compacted and would take days to reach the H.C.

And they didn't have days. They had perhaps hours.

No one could save them but themselves. And even *that* now seemed like an impossibility.

35

If ever there was trouble to be had, the Bombardiers had enough to last them several lifetimes—or consecutive prison sentences.

"Now what?" Mark Innella asked Ben as they stood above the nearly unconscious Avatka in the outer hallway of the student commons.

"Let me think," Ben said, down on one knee cradling the injured alien.

As Ben's mind raced with a thousand scenarios, most of them involving incarceration, Tommy Rosales and George Clock shooed away the onlookers in the hallway when the physical plant opened up the corridors and hallways.

"It looks like you've got a hell of a story to print," Ben said to Innella.

Rosales sneered. "You think campus security will let this story out? Not fucking likely."

"We need this guy alive," Innella said.

The Avatka seemed to be breathing easily enough, but none of them there knew the first thing about Enamorati physiology. For all Ben knew, the Avatka could very well have been dying. Its membranous eyelids fluttered erratically.

"Tommy," Ben said, standing. "You're the strongest. Throw this guy over your shoulder and let's get out of here. Mark—" He faced the reporter, who seemed stunned to have the story of a lifetime on his hands. "You have to get news of this incident to every single person on the ship. Faculty, staff—everybody."

Innella's Adam's apple bobbed a couple of times as he swallowed nervously. "I know," he said. He took off, threading through the gathered throng in the hall.

Ben turned to his friends. "I don't want campus security to catch us with this guy. We'd never leave detention."

Rosales effortlessly slung the Avatkas over his shoulder. "Okay. Where to?"

"The Cloudman," Ben said. "He has to know about this."

They ran back to the physics department taking as many short-cuts and detours as possible, always on the lookout for elements of campus security. But with their com/pagers turned off, there was little anyone could do to track them.

When they arrived at the physics department, the Cloudman was already orchestrating the dispersal of the physics team. Since Eve's unique stardrive created no propulsion ejecta, there was no need to place them in a cluster at the rear of the ship. They chose, instead, the central shaft of the vessel. There, the six small units could operate around Eos's center of gravity without the physics team having to factor in various equilibrium equations.

Most of Eve's people had left when Ben and his friends showed up. Curiously, no one from either the fire department or the physical plant had responded to the alarms that the second disassembler weapon had set off or their calls for help. But that was all right with Ben. He was just happy to find the captain.

Ben related the Avatka's confession to the captain, who in turn told him of the "student" from Babbitt Hall who had transited to the Enamorati compound in the company of four Enamorati—an apparent kidnapping.

"Jim," Ben said. "They wouldn't be after anybody else."

"They'll be coming after us next," Tommy Rosales said. "Just watch."

"Not if the transit portals are shut down," the captain told them. "They'd have to travel half a mile on foot and go through the student commons to get to us. They wouldn't risk it."

"Unless," Clock said, "they knew they could get away with it."

"They have enough swords," Rosales added.

"Yeah, but what do they want with Jim?" Clock asked.

"After what *he's* done?" Rosales said. "Hell, for all *we* know they may decide to *eat* him."

"We have to get Jim out of there," Ben said. "I don't want to

wait for the Kuulo to decide what he wants to do about this. It
would involve the Auditors, President Porter, and God knows who
all. It'd be the trial of the century."

"What about the air inside the Enamorati compound? The smell
in there alone could kill him. It might do to him what ours did to
this guy here."

Cleddman, watching it all, ran a hand through his ash gray hair.
"There are other matters to consider here."

"Like what?" Ben asked.

"I'm not quite sure yet just *why* Mr. Fontenot wants to take over
the ship. He stands to lose as much as the rest of us if we have to
face the Enamorati High Council on Wolfe-Langaard 4."

"What about the Governors' Council?" Ben asked. "Can't we
get them on *our* side?"

Cleddman shook his head. "Porter's got them by the short hairs.
They'll do anything he says if it will keep the Enamorati Compact
from falling apart. Our first concern is getting Eos to safety, out of
the reach of the Enamorati ruling council."

"But what about Jim?" Clock demanded.

Ben considered the Cloudman. "Let us go in and get him."

"Before they *eat* him," Rosales added.

Their former pilot crossed his arms and considered them evenly.
"Well, men, according to a whole bunch of laws—some real, some
imaginary—I'm not captain of the vessel anymore. I can't give
you permission to do much of anything, let alone go searching for
your friend."

"Would you try to stop us?" Ben asked.

"You'll get yourselves killed," Cleddman stated.

"I hadn't been planning on that," Ben said.

"Then we never had this conversation," Cleddman said. He
turned and headed back to the remainder of the physics personnel,
just now getting down to the task of duplicating Eve Silbarton's
stardrive parts.

"Okay, wise guy. How are we going to get *in* there?" Rosales
asked. "The Auditors aren't going to let us waltz past them."

"We're not going through the Auditors," Ben said.

"*We?*" Clock said.

"*We* are going to take a lifepod and go in the back way. The pods have docking collars that will fit any exterior airlock, and if we can't dock, then we'll use EVA suits. We'll take cutting tools, anything we'll need to get in there."

"Jim's pager is off," Clock said. "How are we going to find him?"

Ben had thought of this already. "First, we trace Jim's fractal signature from the transit portal in Babbitt Hall to the exit point in the Enamorati compound. Even if they moved on from there, that could be a good place to start."

"Then what?" Tommy Rosales asked. "Jim would be a needle in a haystack. We'd be looking around for hours. We'd be caught long before we could find him."

Ben pointed to the being at their feet. "That's why we're going to take this guy along with us. If we can get him into his own atmosphere, he might revive long enough to help us."

"*Then* what?" Clock asked.

"I haven't thought that far ahead," Ben said. "But we *have* to do something and we have to do it *now*."

Since Cleddman was supposed to coordinate the return of the planetside gondolas anyway, he went to the EVA bays and made sure that Eos's main computer didn't notice a lone lifepod pulling away from the ship. Ben knew that the risks they were all taking could mean their deaths. However, doing nothing and giving in seemed both inconceivable and unconscionable . . . and yet, one month ago doing *anything* daring seemed impossible for Ben. Now, they were out in the middle of fucking nowhere, at a crossroads in galactic history, flying right up the Enamorati's rear end.

For the first time in a long time, Ben felt *alive*.

The lifepod eased along, nudged by the gentle pulses of its thrusters until it drifted aft of the main section of the ship to the gigantic Engine nacelle section. No human had ever gotten this close to Enamorati territory, not even for minor maintenance and repair. The Enamorati themselves tended to all matters regarding their territory.

"I don't see any guards," Ben said, staring out the forward port of the lifepod. "And no shuttles."

"No wakesprites," Tommy Rosales said. "They must be asleep out there somewhere."

Ben was sitting in the copilot's seat. "I'm not picking up any security monitoring scans. That's good. I think."

George Clock expertly guided the lifepod, its lights out, over the edge of the vast Engine exhaust funnel, a forbidding, blackened cone more than a hundred yards wide. It was like floating over the edge of the famous Grand Canyon on Earth.

The black cave of the exhaust shield rose around them as the lifepod descended into the Enamorati abyss. Mr. Rausch in ShipCom had given them Jim Vees's transit pattern, from transit portal 61 in Babbitt Hall to transit portal 72 deep inside the Enamorati compound. That meant that the lifepod would be able to get quite close to Vees's position. Had Eos's massive Engine still been in place, their rescue plan would have been impossible.

As Clock ghosted the pod deep into the narrowing nacelle, Ben and Tommy Rosales climbed into e-suits. Though unconscious, the Avatka appeared to be breathing, if a bit shallowly. The alien had stirred a couple of times during the transit, eyes coming open, then closing again, but Ben didn't know what that meant.

Risking discovery, Clock turned on the lifepod's lights. Here the nacelle had narrowed to just fifty yards in diameter. However, instead of steel bulwarks and structural supports for a stardrive of mechanical design, this nightmare cavern bore rippled tubes and strangely calcified formations like tubers and roots. It looked absolutely *alien* to Ben, transformed by decades of chemical accretions and bizarre technology.

"I see a docking collar," Clock announced in a whisper.

"Is it one of the original locks?" Rosales asked as he pulled his gloves on and sealed them.

"We'll know in a minute," Clock said.

Clock turned out all of the lifepod's lights again. He threw a couple more switches and the Bombardiers saw the docking collar's tiny red guide lights come on. The collar's sensors had received the signal from the approaching pod and responded automatically.

"It looks like they haven't modified it much," Clock said. "Let's just hope that there isn't an army waiting on the other side. If there is, I'm heading home."

"When you pump atmosphere into the collar, George, keep its internal gravity at zero. It'll make it easier to haul our guide over there," Ben said.

"What if we get him over there and he doesn't revive?" Rosales asked.

Ben shrugged in his tight-fitting e-suit. "We might be able to use him for a trade."

"A trade?"

"Or a shield. *I* don't know. Quit nagging me."

Ben and Tommy wrestled the Avatka out of his seat. As they did, George Clock inflated the docking collar. "We're all set," their pilot told them. "The collar's secure, the lock at the other end is open."

"Did the computer over there ask for entry authorization?" Ben asked.

Clock shook his head. "It did, but I ran a standard go-ahead from my computer. No problem."

Their helmeted e-suits were lightweight and very flexible, but guiding the unconscious body of the Avatka through the narrow docking collar was awkward. However, the lock at the other end responded to their touch and the door hissed open, allowing them entry.

The airlock had its gravity setting at eighty percent Earth-normal, standard for the Enamorati's home world, Virr. Ben carried the Avatka as they boldly stepped into a dark and gloomy hallway from the airlock and found themselves in what appeared to be a maintenance corridor. The yellowish green Enamorati atmosphere made it all but unrecognizable. So did the gunk growing on the walls and the floor and the ceiling. It was a leathery substance, clearly organic, very much alive. They placed the Avatka on the floor.

"How long are we going to wait until he comes out of it?" Rosales asked.

"Don't know," Ben said. Both young men spoke in lowered voices which were projected softly over a secured radio frequency.

Their suits had collar speakers, but using them might spell their doom. Enamorati supposedly had excellent hearing.

Ben bent over the alien on the floor and placed his gloved hands on the creature's chest. Its armor was barely flexible enough for Ben to attempt CPR. He didn't know what else to do. The Enamorati had one central lung chamber and two hearts. Pressure in the center of the chest could theoretically stimulate the upper and lower hearts into action. Or perhaps it would just kill him.

It roused him. The creature coughed in a very human manner and opened his pupilless eyes. Ben sat back.

The creature began gabbling in his strange clicking language as he stared up at the moldy ceiling. He then saw the looming figures of the two Earth men standing over him.

"I have not been Translated," the Avatka Viroo said in perfectly intoned English.

Ben switched his collar speaker on. "If you mean that you're not dead, then, no. You're in your quarters."

They helped the creature to its feet. The atmosphere did appear to revive the Avatka somewhat.

"How did you get in here?" the Avatka asked, staring down the corridor at a closed seal that led farther into the compound.

"We took a lifepod in the back way," Ben told him. "It was the only way we could think of getting in."

The alien looked at his hands as if he were dreaming. "I see."

"Look," Ben said. "One of our friends is being held hostage here and we need your help in getting him out. He doesn't have an environment suit and we don't know what a prolonged exposure to your air will do to him. It's evidently not as toxic as your people have told us, but it's pretty thick. It could kill him."

"If your friends don't kill him first," Rosales said.

"The air would definitely make him ill," the alien said. "He would die eventually, if he were left alone. How did your friend come to be in here?"

"We think four Accusers got him," Ben said.

"They will do more damage to your friend than our atmosphere," the Avatka said. "It will not be a pleasant death."

"We're going to prevent that from happening," Ben said. "Can you locate him for us?"

"Yes," the alien said. "It should not be too difficult. If you think it can be done."

"We don't know if it can be done, but we're going to try," Ben told him.

"That seems to be a characteristic of your race," the Avatka said. "It is quaintly admirable."

"Why?" Tommy Rosales asked.

"Why? Because we learned a long time ago that one cannot change one's fate, either as an individual or as a species. You haven't learned that yet."

"We probably never will," said Ben.

The Avatka gave Ben a serious look. "Then I hope you make the best of it while you can."

"Why?"

"You shall soon see," the Avatka said. "Let us proceed."

The Avatka led them down the hallway, deep into the Enamorati living spaces.

36

The damage caused by the Engine's explosion had blackened all of the ports through which the Eos lifepod might be seen. With lights out and radio silence maintained, Clock might yet go undetected. It was still eerie for Ben to leave him there, docked so tenuously to the outer lock.

"We need to know where we are," Ben told the Avatka.

"And who we're gong to run into," Rosales added.

Wisps of the eerie, greenish yellow atmosphere ghosted around them. Strange, guttural sounds came from the walls and the floor, the sounds of fluids and liquids gurgling past them.

"We know that the kidnappers came back here, through transit portal seventy-two. Where they went from that point, we don't know. Can you tell us?"

"I know of only one place he could be," the Avatka said. "But if it is being held sentry by too many *armaz-paava*, there will be little we can do."

"Let's see what we *can* do first," Ben said. "We'll figure out the rest later."

Ben noticed how the Avatka appeared to have gained back his strength. Their racial fear of the atmosphere humans breathed must have some basis in truth. Still, the ruse had worked all these years: the fear humans had of Enamorati air had kept them from scratching the itch regarding Enamorati quarters, and what went on in there.

The Avatka walked out ahead of them in the preternatural light, guiding himself with one hand along the wall and wobbling just a little. They left the barely used maintenance tunnel and found themselves in a common passageway. There, they came across the definite signs of struggle, the same kind they had seen through their probes. Debris lay everywhere—slices and rips in the walls and ceiling. The peculiar wall ornamentations had been knocked loose and scattered along the floor.

They soon came across their first Enamorati body. It lay in two halves, neatly sliced from left shoulder to right hip. The blood that had pooled where it had fallen was now a dark, dried bluish purple on the rawhide floor.

"A Tagani," Ben said, recognizing the caste by the wizened, leathery look of the dead creature's face.

"Friend of yours?" Rosales asked the Avatka.

"I would have thought not," the Avatka said. "The *armaz-paava* do not kill their allies, usually. If they are doing so now, then matters have turned for the worse."

"The Accusers are in control?" Ben asked in a low voice.

"They are now," the Avatka said.

The Avatka kneeled down and removed the dead creature's belt. On the belt was what appeared to be a small handgun and a row of egg-shaped objects fixed to it. One of the eggs he locked in the barrel of the weapon.

"I thought the Enamorati had no weapons," Rosales asked.

"We have weapons," the Avatka said. "You would just not recognize them as such."

"Swell," Rosales muttered.

"What are those things?" Ben asked, pointing to the small, rounded leather-encased objects.

"*Vehenta*, at various stages. Perhaps 'calibers' is a better word to describe them," the alien said. "It is an unconscionable way to use them, but they have become our most effective weapon."

"You mean the disassemblers you set off in the physics department?" Ben asked.

"Yes," the Avatka said. "Both of them."

"So you *are* responsible for the first attack in physics," Ben said. "But why?"

"Why? Because your resources were being wasted on Dr. Brenholdt's project," the Avatka said. "I had to redirect your efforts. The mistake I made was overestimating the effects of the *vehenta* I used that first time."

"Were you the one who tampered with Eve Silbarton's project?" Ben said.

"I had to arrange it so that when reassembling the prototype, Dr. Silbarton would find a more efficient way to harness the necessary energy for her machine."

The Avatka stood upright as if ready to face a firing squad or walk the plank on a pirate ship. He said, "If you are to survive, you must do without Onesci Engines . . . and you must do it without us."

Ben and Tommy looked at one another, then shrugged.

The Avatka stared down the gloomy corridor. "We shall try the captivity cells first. If they have not killed him outright, your friend is most likely there."

"You have jails?" Rosales asked.

"That, and more," the alien said. "You will learn."

Evidence of the internal rebellion among the Enamorati was everywhere now. Bodies of one kind or another lay rotting—or recently dead—at every juncture they took. The dead still clutched their swords. They even found a sword sunk to its hilt in the floor: So thin was its blade that when it was dropped point-first, it had sunk through the floor's very molecules like a knife through soft pudding.

The Avatka approached a large reflective plate on one wall. It could have been a mirror. The Avatka touched it until luminescent symbols appeared.

"This way," he said. "We are very close."

They had yet to see any other living Enamorati, friend or foe, but now sounds could be heard coming from other regions of the compound: metal on metal, hissing gases, shrill screams, the death voices of warring Enamorati.

The Avatka plucked a long shard of metal from the wall and hefted it expertly. "Stand back," he whispered in English.

Ben and Tommy Rosales gave the alien a wide berth as the Avatka crept to the end of the gloom-shrouded corridor. He saw something there that galvanized him into action, and shot around the corner with eerie swiftness.

"Man, look at him go! That boy's faster than you are," Tommy said to Ben.

"I hope he's a better sword-fighter," Ben responded.

The two eased around the corner to find Viroo standing over the halved body of one of his shipmates. The Avatka had cleaved an Accuser from top to bottom. No sound had been made other than the squishy *ploop!* of the two halves of the alien sentry falling to the floor.

The Avatka laid his sword on the soft floor of the corridor. He then placed his palm on the lock of the door, which opened very quietly, exposing a long room, at the far end of which Jim Vees sat in a cone of intense light. Strapped to a chair and wheezing in the awful air, Jim was practically delirious from the heady fumes.

Several Accusers surrounded him, each holding an evil-looking sword or long graceful spear. There was no way past the armed Enamorati to get at him.

Ben and Tommy both looked to the walls around them, contemplating the possibility of fighting these beings with the super-sharp weapons. Ben had never killed anything more evolved than a pigeon before, and even that had been an accident. In planning Jim's rescue, Ben had never thought beyond the logistics of finding a way into the Enamorati's world. Now he had to face a very brutal fact: their adventure was about to turn ugly.

The Avatka took the strange gun from his belt and snapped one of the globelike objects into its stunted barrel. It looked like a popgun. Instantly, the leather leaves around the small globe sprang open like the petals of a flower, revealing a sphere of sparkling energy.

The Avatka stepped into the room and said nothing. He merely held the weapon before him. The Accusers turned to face him; then they saw the weapon in the Avatka's hand. Their swords settled gently to the floor and the armored aliens started backing off, their black eyes fixed on the globe that contained the mist of death.

Neither Ben nor Tommy had to be told to take advantage of the stand-down. They jumped into the room and ran straight to Jim's chair. His bonds had been made of the same leatherlike mix that composed the Enamorati compound. Ben lifted a sword from the floor and severed the bonds holding Jim to the chair. The blade was so sharp, Jim's shackles parted like pasta. Tommy, in turn, hefted the semiconscious Vees over his shoulder.

"We're outta here," Tommy said. He turned and ran for the door.

"Right," Ben acknowledged, facing the malevolent Accusers with the sword in his hand, the Avatka beside him.

He and the Avatka Viroo backed toward the door of the long room. The Accusers made no move to stop them, making instead the muffled cluckings of their language. Were they summoning more of their kind through hidden microphones or video lenses? Or were they communicating to the Avatka, who continually aimed the weapon in their direction?

"Let's go!" Ben said to the Avatka, letting his sword sink into the floor.

The Accusers in the room were not caught off-guard—Ben hadn't expected them to be—and they immediately rushed for their swords. Ben and Tommy turned and ran.

The Avatka emerged in the doorway, turning quickly and firing his weapon. Screams filled the air, drowned out by the hissing of the deadly mist as it unraveled every molecule it came upon in the interrogation room.

However, the Avatka was now limping. Behind him dropped bright coins of Enamorati blood.

"There is no time left," the injured Avatka said, limping up to Ben. "We have to move quickly."

But the halls were empty and no one challenged them. No alarms went off; no emergency personnel came from their quarters. The Avatka, however, ran as if opposition were imminent.

They made it to the airlock, but Ben had to support the Avatka. Blood had stopped flowing from the alien's wound, but it still looked bad.

They got to the docking collar without incident. But the Avatka was almost unconscious now. That, however, made it easier to coax him into the zero-g atmosphere of the collar. Tommy hauled Jim to safety, then took the Avatka from Ben. Ben closed the lock and scrambled back into the waiting lifepod.

"Get us out of here. Fast!" Ben said, sliding into the copilot's chair. Ben jettisoned the docking collar manually by pulling a simple disengagement lever. The pod lurched away, free.

That was when the opposition met them.

The pod rotated around and its bright guide lights caught several space-suited Enamorati Accusers drifting to meet them, each bearing a double-bladed axe. They came like slow flakes of black ash—a rain of barbaric death.

"We've got time to shoot through them!" Ben said.

"If we do that, we'll never have the power to get us back in orbit to dock with Eos!" Clock said.

The planet Kiilmist 5 filled their cockpit window. From all sides Accusers began to appear in the distance, pouring out exits the Bombardiers hadn't seen upon coming in.

A small *thump!* struck the pod.

"Well," Clock said grimly. "Somebody hit us from the rear. We just lost an engine."

More *thumps!* struck the pod's walls. No gashes appeared from the super-sharp axes, but Ben didn't want to wait around. "We can't have one of those weapons penetrate the hull," he said. "Just get us away from here!"

"Where?"

"That way!" Ben pointed to the blue-white planet that now filled the entire forward window.

With a massive burst of whatever power they had left, Clock plowed through the gathering Accusers, scattering them helplessly, and began a one-way tumble to the planet below.

37

"Now, *this* is interesting," Cutter Rausch said as he considered his main console in the busy ShipCom Arena.

Events were now unfolding in rapid order on the ship. Campus security and volunteers from Eos University's ROTC program were marching throughout the ship, ostensibly to maintain order among the increasingly restless students, among whom were unexpectedly—and unaccountably—rowdy students from high-placed Ainge families. Rausch and Captain Cleddman both knew that the police and their deputies were really searching for the original three guards placed on the command deck, whom Rausch had dismantled. Those guards were presently in a maintenance locker in Plumbing until the crisis could be resolved. Cleddman, in turn, claimed ignorance as to their whereabouts, as well as the whereabouts of most of the physics and engineering faculty. When Fontenot finally got around to searching the physics department, all he found there was Captain Cleddman and a gaping hole in one wall through which the insurrectionists had apparently escaped.

Now Fontenot had his hands full trying to quell the unrest caused by the editorial staff of *The Alley Revolutionary*, who were running pernicious lies about the administration, campus security, and the Enamorati. An editorial entitled "Mr. Fontenot's Hand Job" seemed to have been the cause of Mr. Fontenot's enforcement zeal. Rausch was therefore doing everything he could to keep track of Mr. Fontenot's progress throughout the ship.

As if that weren't enough, Rausch now saw on his monitor that deep within the Enamorati compound several vital communications cable clusters had been severed. If optical and transit-portal fibers were being severed, so too were the tubes and pipes carrying basic environmental necessities such as water, electricity, and the like. Something terrible appeared to be unfolding deep inside the Enamorati compound and there was a good possibility that only he knew about it.

Lisa Benn hovered over Rausch at his board. "What the hell are they doing in there? Tearing the walls out?"

Rausch opened the com. "Captain Cleddman, are you there?"

Captain Cleddman was back in his personal quarters under a mild form of house arrest: a dour-looking muscle-builder stood outside his door. Cleddman could come and go as he pleased, but his burly guard would go with him.

"Yes, Mr. Rausch," came Cleddman's voice. *"I'm here."*

"I've got indications on my board of some sort of massive malfunction happening on two decks in the Enamorati compound. Water, power, and sewage has been severed and I've rerouted what I can from here. Has Fontenot said anything to you?"

"This is the first I've heard of it," the captain said. *"Have you heard from the Kuulo? Protocol at their end requires him to contact either me or President Porter if there is some sort of problem."*

"If he's spoken with anybody about it, sir, they aren't talking to me. That's why I called you. I'm not showing any kind of communications traffic from the Enamorati compound."

"Hmm," the captain mused. *"Could be that Kuumottoomaa is dealing with it on his own."*

Rausch's crew looked at one another apprehensively. Rausch said, "Sir, our instruments indicated that the safety systems kicked in automatically. Our alarm here was automatic. It's possible that *nobody* knows what's going on in the Enamorati compound, not even the Kuulo. If that's the case, then the whole ship could be endangered."

"Contact Mr. Fontenot and see if he knows about this systems failure in the Enamorati compound. He won't talk to me, but he will talk to you. At least I think he will."

"All right," Rausch said. "Stand by."

Rausch touched a command switch. Under normal ship circumstances, Lieutenant Fontenot would be one of the most easily accessible individuals on the ship. Rausch had a direct line to

Fontenot's com on his main board, but quickly discovered that Fontenot was inaccessible.

He touched another button. "Campus security. This is Ship-Com," Rausch said. "I wish to speak with Lieutenant Fontenot, please. It's an emergency."

"Captain Fontenot is unavailable," said a deadman. *"I will take a message."*

"Take a message? This is an emergency. I want an open channel to Mr. Fontenot now."

The late-shift deadman would have the AI enough to recognize Rausch's voice patterns, and it would, as a consequence, clear a channel to Fontenot.

"Please stand by."

Rausch had to wait only seconds for Fontenot to get back to him. He was available to campus security, but was *not* available to ShipCom. To Rausch that could only mean that Fontenot was somewhere in the ship where he did not want to be found.

"Mr. Rausch," came the voice of Lieutenant Fontenot. *"What can I do for you at this hour?"*

"I am required to inform you that we have a major systems failure deep inside the Enamorati living quarters. We've got loss of all environmental services to two floors. Captain Cleddman wanted me to—"

"Mr. Cleddman's authority on this ship has been temporarily suspended," Lieutenant Fontenot said.

"That's why he had me call you," Rausch countered angrily. "He thought you'd want to know about this since you're the captain now."

"Thank you for the information, Mr. Rausch. I will consult with the Kuulo and will get back to you if it is necessary."

"Shouldn't we notify the fire department and the physical plant about this? We may have to go in there and—"

"Yes, Mr. Rausch. We will handle it from here. Thank you. Out."

"Ix," Rausch muttered.

He quickly went over his board and traced the source of Fontenot's call. "He's operating out of the room that houses the Hollingsdale discontinuity breeder reactor controls," he told his staff.

Cleddman, who had been listening in, said, *"That's probably going to be the new command center for the ship. His people have been in the process of rerouting all command functions to that location for most of the day. I wouldn't be too surprised if the Kuulo isn't with him."*

"And you're going to let him get away with this?"

"I have no say in the matter. Neither do you."

"Why wouldn't he just assume command on *your* deck?" Rausch asked. "That's what it's there for."

"I have no idea," the captain said. *"But it does locate his people closer to the Auditors and the Enamorati compound. They would be within walking distance of one another, whereas the command deck is two thousand linear feet in the opposite direction."*

"Makes sense," Rausch said.

"One other thing, you're going to have to be very careful to whom—" the captain started.

Bang! Something struck the outer door to ShipCom. Lisa Benn jumped in her chair, and Rausch was on his feet at the sound of it.

A long sword blade ripped an incredible gash in the metal of the door, tearing a seam straight down to the floor. Another swipe, then another of the same sword, and the door fell away in razor-sharp shreds. Boots kicked the remaining shards back in razor-sharp curls. Several people came in through the gap.

The first two were not people. The others were, but not the first two. These were Enamorati. All wore armor and all had swords at the ready.

Lisa Benn screamed and the other members of the crew fell back against the far wall.

"Captain, we've got company!" Rausch said into the still-open com.

Rausch sized up the situation instantly. Two Enamorati. Two men from campus security. And two Ainge Auditors, also carrying swords. *Good heavens,* Rausch thought, *Ainge Auditors ready to do battle!*

However, a different scenario appeared in Cutter Rausch's mind: Instead of these six invaders, he saw *an assassin breaching the walls surrounding the Kobe Gardens. Kendo master Yoshubi Takamitsu is taken by surprise. Rausch, the novitiate from Amer-*

ica, is meditating nearby. Rausch hears the song of a ninja's sword blade. The eighty-year-old national treasure of Japan is dead. There is only one thing left to do. It will mean exile, from the Kobe Gardens, from Japan, and possibly even the Earth. But it is the only honorable *thing left to do. . . .*

Rausch moved into the center of the room as his crew watched with undisguised terror. Two armored Enamorati of a caste Rausch had never seen before. Two Ainge Auditors. Two men from campus security. One man against six.

"Cutter, don't!" Lisa Benn shouted.

Cutter Rausch did then what he had done only once before in his life, in the Kobe Gardens of Japan. He *acted.*

It was how he got the nickname "Cutter."

Of all the Bombardiers, only George Clock had any sort of decent piloting skills. He came from a family whose wealth had been derived from providing vehicles for space construction firms. Clock could fly most kinds of EVA vehicles. In fact, since he had bombed out of Eos University's aerial photography and mapping program, he had been seriously considering a career in construction. The money was good and it took him places. A Ph.D. from Eos University would have been a nice shingle to hang in an office somewhere, but construction wasn't a bad life.

All of his piloting skills were needed now. Lifepod 27 was plummeting helter-skelter away from Eos, down toward Kiilmist 5 with either a spear or axe of impossible sharpness stuck in a dead starboard gravity engine. Clock wrestled the pod away from Eos's giant Engine nacelle, but he needed the onboard computer to help him land the small craft. He didn't know if lifepods could fly on one engine.

As Clock extruded the glide wings from the pod's oblong body and raised the tail assembly, Ben and Tommy Rosales attended to Jim Vees and the Avatka. Jim gulped pure oxygen from an emergency tank nearby and he was slowly coming around. Wisps of Enamorati atmosphere clung to his hair and filled the pod with its stench.

The Avatka, unfortunately, wasn't doing nearly as well. A human couldn't have survived a slash such as the one the Avatka had received. He was now drifting in and out of consciousness with every breath he took. It was impossible for any of them to tell how long the alien had to live.

"Where are we going?" Jim asked, pulling away the oxygen mask,

"Down," Ben said.

"Why?"

"*Why?*" George Clock shouted over his shoulder. "Because there's an axe in one of our engines, thanks to you."

"Me?" Vees said.

Ben looked at his friend. "I thought you said no one knew what you were doing with your machine."

"I guess I was wrong," Vees admitted.

"Now you tell us," Tommy Rosales said.

"We're in real deep shit, pal," Ben said. "You know that?"

Rosales added, "Just think of the human race as *all* Bombardiers. The Enamorati Compact is about as dead as you can get."

Jim gave Ben a look he had never seen before. Revelation? Surprise? Fear?

"Listen," he said to them. "I was *in* Orem Rood's mind. Mazaru is coming to us! The Auditors have been taking turns, around the clock, calling out to him for months now. Rood believes he is coming!"

"Look, stupid," Ben said, edging close. "We found you in a room surrounded by four of those Accusers and each one of them had a sword. I think they had every intention of killing you when they were done with you."

"So Mazaru is real?" Tommy Rosales asked.

"Who cares if Mazaru is real?" Ben snapped. "*This* is real. Right here. Right now."

Jim looked at Tommy. "I would have never believed it in a thousand years. Maybe Ixion Smith *was* onto something."

Vees swiveled around in his chair and noticed that they had an Avatka with them—one that didn't look well at all.

"What's he doing here?" Vees asked.

"He helped us find you," Ben said. "It turns out he's the guy who destroyed the Engine. It was this guy in the photographs we took from the last probe we made."

The Avatka was struggling to speak. "You should have left me back there. I might have been able . . . to do more. . . . "

A bony claw of a hand seemed to reach for something the Avatka thought was attached to his belt, but it came away empty. The strange "gun" that had been used to fire the *vehenta* had been dropped during their retreat.

"Look," Ben said. "You never told us *why* you had to destroy the Engine. Was it about to explode?"

"No," the Avatka said in a very strained voice.

"Then why did you do it?" Ben asked.

"Because . . . you had to find this planet, this one planet," the Avatka said. "The rest you would have figured out on your own. But I had to get you here."

"What are you talking about?" Ben asked.

"The truth," the Avatka said. "The truth that will set you free."

With that, he lapsed once again into unconsciousness.

38

The last time Eve Silbarton had gone tunneling, she had been eight years old, newly arrived at Tau Ceti 4 with her parents, who wanted to live in a more stable environment than was present on the Earth at the time. On the balmy southern isle of Tooele grew immense trees with convoluted tunnels in which she and her little friends played after school like woodpecker kin or squirrels. That sort of tunneling had been fun.

This sort most decidedly wasn't.

With the captain more or less under house arrest, Eve and her team had taken the initiative of setting up the six stardrive units throughout the ship. This entailed crawling through ducts and tunnels no one, outside of servicing robots, had been in for at least a century. This was the only way to reach the center shaft of the giant vessel. But what was once fun to an eight-year-old was now a regrettable chore to a woman in her sixth decade. Besides, it was cold and filthy.

She, Dr. Harlin, and two graduate engineering students had just crawled fifty yards through a maintenance shaft, trailing wires and optical fibers behind them. A small antigravity float platform held the sixth and last of the drive assemblies. Others of her group were setting the other drives in place roughly three hundred yards along the ship's core.

With Cutter Rausch's assistance, they had managed to circumvent the various security systems that protected many of the tunnels, but that was the easy part. What they had to do now was bolt the drive systems to the ship's core and get them synchronized. If they could get that far, they might have a chance of getting out of the Kiilmist system to a system closer to home, preferably one with facilities enough to sort out the legal mess the various human factions had gotten into with each other, to say nothing of the various charges the humans—united or not—were going to throw at the Enamorati. For Eve's part, all she wanted was to get back to the H.C. worlds of the Alley, and away from the Enamorati.

However, Eve quickly discovered that this particular tunnel was occupied.

She came across two students, a male and a female, bundled against the cold, working over various machines. What they were doing, Eve couldn't quite tell.

Trailing wires over her shoulder, Eve appeared at the lock and found the two students sitting in the semidarkness with laptop computers connected to what looked like a BennettCorp data-bullet compression unit. Several containment cubes, each holding a suspended microparticle data bullet, lay stacked to one side. The two students were making queue-ready, and quite illegal, data bullets.

"What are you doing here?" Eve asked.

They might have asked *her* that, but she had more rank than they did. "Well, uh," started the young woman.

Eve squirmed into the tunnel as Dr. Harlin came in behind her. "Eve, what's holding us up?" he asked. He then caught sight of the two. "Oh, I see."

The two students sagged as if they were balloons with the air just let out of them.

"I'm Elise," the young woman said. "This is Mark. We're the student newspaper. We were putting together the next issue. Do you want to see our IDs?"

The two conspirators were surrendering, finally, after four days of being hounded by campus security. A small food unit lay off to one side. What they were doing for bathroom facilities, Eve didn't want to know.

"That's all right," Eve said, stopping them as they rummaged in their tunic pockets for their ID cards. Eve pointed to the data-bullet compression unit. "What are you doing with that?"

"We're making data bullets of the student newspaper. Or at least the Alley edition of it," Elise told her. "Mr. Rausch said that he would send them out as soon as we could get them made."

"Does the captain know that you and Mr. Rausch are doing this?" she asked.

"I don't know," Rutenbeck admitted. "Probably not."

"Why are you doing it in here?" Dr. Harlin asked.

"It's the only place we could think of where campus security wouldn't look," Rutenbeck admitted. "We've had to relocate five times now. They've already shut down the journalism department and they've taken Kevin Dobbs into custody. Is it true that they're taking over the ship?"

"That appears to be the case," Silbarton said.

"You aren't going to report us then?" Rutenbeck asked.

"No," Eve said. "We're hiding, too. But you will have to find another place to do your newspaper. We've got to have these tunnels free."

The prospect of not going to jail was immensely more acceptable to the two students than having to relocate. That, they would happily do.

"Are data bullets are going out now?" Dr. Harlin asked them from inside his arctic parka.

"Every fifteen minutes," Rutenbeck told them. "The Human Community is going to get an earful in a few hours. The whole truth and nothing but the truth."

One of the graduate students behind Dr. Harlin in the tunnel shaft asked, "Using the rail launcher to send unscheduled data bullets takes a lot of power, Dr. Silbarton. Will we have enough for our units?"

"We should," she said. "But power to the rail guns will go off-line once we get started."

"Where are we going?" Mark Innella asked hopefully.

"*You* are going somewhere else," Eve told them. "And wherever it is, you will be sure not to mention the fact that you saw us in *here*. Got that?"

"Yes, ma'am," they said.

George Clock gripped the controls of the lifepod as it glided to the planet's surface. The one engine disabled by the axe was causing some drag—a cowling more than likely was exposed—and it took all the physical strength Clock had just to keep the pod's glide path aimed at the right continent.

From what little they could see from the pod's windows, the place they chose to land was currently suffering the rage of a massive thunderstorm. However, Clock had picked up a distress signal about three hundred miles to the east of them and he was using that as a homing beacon.

In the copilot's seat, Ben fiddled with the receiver, getting a better fix on the signal. "Looks like there's enough electricity in the air to fry everything in sight. Radio traffic is impossible."

"Are we near one of the gondolas?" Tommy Rosales asked.

"That's probably where the signal is coming from," Ben said.

"But it's a *distress* signal," Rosales pointed out. "*We're* in distress, too. Don't you think we should go to a gondola that *isn't* in distress?"

"It's a little late for that," Clock said, wrestling the controls. "One of the comsats will relay the signal to Eos, if they aren't already receiving it. They can send down a gondola to get us any time after that."

"It won't matter if you turn us into wreckage," Rosales quipped.

"Eat my shorts," said Clock.

The storm seemed to be moving north-northwest of the beacon's signal. Ben gave George instructions to bank farther to the north of their glide path, and took them in the opposite direction of the storm.

However, within minutes the signal suddenly got stronger and they sighted land through an unexpected break in the clouds.

"Land, ho!" Clock announced. "Signal source dead ahead."

" 'Dead,' " Rosales said. "Don't like that word."

The wide front windows of the pod showed them a landscape covered in green for miles in all directions. Ben could also make out the lines of ancient highways and the fractured ruins of a civilization.

"Cities," Rosales said. "Look, buildings!"

"Sit down," Clock admonished. "And strap yourselves in!"

Clock eased the pod down and for the first time they could make out the Mounds. Every ten or twenty miles in every direction were huge masses covered in deep greenish growth of some kind.

"Hey," Tommy Rosales asked, pointing through the window. "What's that?"

Clock leveled off the pod and extended the air brakes. All they needed now was a stretch of flat land near the beacon where they could enter into a hover mode and set down. Or lumber down.

"Isn't that a gondola?" Rosales asked.

They caught sight of what appeared to be a crumpled gondola glinting in the afternoon sun. The remains of the gondola were horribly battered, now smoldering and spitting fire, having been knocked out of the sky.

"Can't see any bodies," Clock said.

"The distress signal wasn't coming from there," Ben said, playing with the directional finder on the console.

"Maybe they got out," Rosales speculated.

"Those structures a mile off," Clock said. "They could be there. Dead ahead."

"That word again," Rosales said.

"That's the signal source," Ben said. "Put the pod down as close as you can to it and let's take a look."

What appeared to be an artificial "plaza" with a pyramid-shaped hill in the center of it rose before them. George Clock slowed the lifepod into a hover, using all the power the lifepod had left in it for the antigravity plates underneath.

"It's going to be rocky!" Clock said.

The lifepod came down on the surface of the "plaza" a dozen yards away from the Mound, landing gear sinking up to its hull. But they had landed in one piece and the storm seemed to be heading off to the west, to the far side of the sky.

39

The last of Holcombe's archaeology students had filed into the Mound's interior, carefully crowding along the ledge that circumscribed the enshrined object before them. The object had a deep blue sheen with traces of green here and there. It could have been made of stone. It was hard to tell. It could just as easily have been ossified chitin or skin or shell.

"What *is* it?" a student behind Julia asked in a whisper.

The floating lanterns provided sufficient light for them, but they still probed it with their flashlights.

"A Sphinx, maybe," Marji Koczan said in a low voice.

"It's organic," someone then said. "And it's dead now."

"Maybe *this* was the biggest creature on the planet," another student said. "The people here might have worshipped them!"

"No," insisted another. "This thing's made out of rock. Look at it! It's solid!"

Professor Holcombe remained silent through all of this.

Bobby Gessner, who had been attending the field kit, returned to the chamber very excited. "The storm's over!" he announced. "I think it's safe to go outside!" Then the Ainge boy caught sight of the Mound's treasure. His beam went up like a brilliant rapier. "And we have got to tell someone about this."

Professor Holcombe slowly sat down on the ledge, his boots extending just a few inches over the edge. "I don't think we're going anywhere for a while," he told them.

At the bottom of the abyss, they discovered, were more bones of Kiilmistians, highly ossified, covered with aeons of dust. Julia wondered if these were the remains of sacrifices.

Some of the students, unsettled by the artifact's eeriness, turned and headed outside. Julia remained with Dr. Holcombe, who seemed profoundly depressed. He sat on the ledge as if all his strength, perhaps even the will to live, had left him.

Holcombe closed his eyes and leaned back against the wall. He said, "I'd like to stay here for the rest of my life."

"What?" Julia asked, not quite understanding. Marji Koczan and several other students looked on.

"The wayhigh," he said. "It must be wearing off. I'm coming back to the real world and I don't like what I see there."

Even the sunny blue of his eyes seemed to be fading, like the onset of night.

"He's been on wayhighs?" Marji Koczan whispered to Julia.

"For years," Julia said.

Holcombe dreamily pondered the artifact as several students crouched close by. He said, "Children, try to imagine a predator that has learned to disguise himself as something benign or better yet beneficial to its prey. He tells you he's good for you, he's your friend. Then he gobbles you. Or perhaps he doesn't gobble. Perhaps he just . . . sips. He's even elegant about it, civilized. The next thing you know, you're working your way through his intestinal tract, making him strong, happy . . . fulfilling his destiny, confirming your fate."

Holcombe held them enthralled. "What do you think of that, boys and girls?"

"I don't understand," Julia said, probably speaking for them all.

He smiled weakly. "Your friend Benjamin . . . he'd know what I'm talking about."

"He would?" she asked.

Holcombe nodded. The hovering lanterns on the ledge gave a spectral glow to the artifact. He stared at it. "I guess I could rephrase the question and ask, 'When is a predator not a predator?' " he said.

No one knew what to say.

"When?" Julia asked.

And he answered: "When he charms you to sleep through your life as he consumes you. The art of it, though, is that he gives you a feeling of contentment . . . that this is the natural order of things;

that he is good for you . . . until you're bone-dry and as dead as you're ever going to get. Sort of like the Church."

A couple of students from Ainge families gasped at the blasphemous insinuation.

Holcombe looked at Julia. "You knew that I had been given a writ of excommunication when I was young."

Julia nodded. "It was a rumor. Nobody knew for sure."

"Do you know *why* I got excommunicated?" he asked.

Julia shook her head. A dozen dimly illuminated faces leaned in.

"When I was in college, three friends of mine and I witnessed an Engine-insertion ceremony. The whole thing, from beginning to end, and the Enamorati had no idea that we were there."

"You *saw* an insertion ceremony?" Julia asked. "When?"

"Fifty years ago," Holcombe said. "My friends were inside the shell of *Bountiful Bound* in orbit above Tau Ceti 4. We had gotten permission to study its architecture for a class project. The *Bountiful* was the ship that brought Ixion Smith and his followers to Tau Ceti 4 two hundred years ago.

"But we had forgotten to tell anybody *when* we were going to study it. We didn't think it was important. So we left the alpha moon by shuttle, pulled into orbit, and docked with the *Bountiful*, whose orbit had it on the night side of the planet. As it turned out, the Enamorati had decided to move the *Seka* also to the dark side and they ended up about two hundred miles behind the orbit of *Bountiful Bound*."

"I thought they cleared space for thousands of miles before Enamorati ceremonies," Julia said.

"Usually," Holcombe said. "But this time the Enamorati made a last-minute change and decided to tow the *Seka* to the dark side, where it met the Engine convoy."

"And you saw it?" Julia said.

"All of it. The Enamorati pulled the new Engine from the cargo ferry. We saw them insert it into the *Seka*. It took just under three hours and we watched it through powered binoculars from inside what was left of the *Bountiful Bound*."

"How did they catch you?" Julia asked.

"They didn't."

"Then who did?" Julia asked.

"My roommate confessed. The four of us were then pulled through a secret heresy court where they decided not to tell the Enamorati High Council. Instead, the Very Highest Auditor, the number one man himself, had me excommunicated because I was the oldest and should have known better. The other three were sent to Ross 244 3, which is almost all desert and the part that isn't is all swamps. As far as I know, they're still there."

One of the female Ainge students asked, her voice filled with awe, "So you actually *spoke* with the Very Highest Auditor?"

"Had to," Holcombe said. "He was my father. And not only was I kicked out of the Church, I was kicked out of my *family*. He never spoke to me again."

"But you went on to college," Julia said. "You did well."

"I had a dozen relatives who hated my dad, hated the Ainge, and helped me out, just to spite him. In fact, my mother's youngest brother was a close friend of Jack Killian. *He* was excommunicated, too. But that was before my time."

"Your family had a Very Highest Auditor *and* someone high up in the ranks of the KMA?" Julia asked.

"Stranger things have happened," Holcombe admitted.

"No wonder you dislike the Auditors so much," Koczan said.

"Actually," he said slowly, "I thought I had gotten over it. Until today. Until now."

He aimed his flashlight at the artifact.

A female student suddenly appeared in the tunnel, pushing everyone aside. "Dr. Holcombe, there's a lifeboat come to rescue us outside!"

"We've got to get you back to the university," Julia said, helping the aged professor to his feet.

"It doesn't matter," Holcombe said. He leaned unsteadily against the wall of the compacted glass cobblestones. "You have to tell the Alley worlds about this thing in here."

Professor Holcombe fell heavily against the wall of the tunnel, a lock of white hair drooping across his face. It reminded Julia of the color of Jingle Bear's fur . . . and how Jingles had looked in Ben's arms a few days ago.

The one image was transposed over the other and Julia felt a tremor of dread: As Jingle Bear had died, so, too, might Professor Holcombe.

In fact, it seemed inevitable.

Death filled ShipCom.

Of the six attackers Cutter Rausch had to face, only two now remained—the junior Ainge Auditors. Their backs were against the wall and their swords were on the floor. They were alive, the others were dead—and in several pieces.

In just four seconds, Rausch had sidestepped the first Accuser's sword thrust, put an arm around the creature's waist, and spun it around, facing his armored comrade. The long sword sliced off the arms of that alien. Rausch then did a gavotte on one foot, flinging the first alien into one of the campus-security attackers. Rausch then grabbed the fallen sword, minus the forearms that had been previously gripping it, and without hesitation drew a diagonal slice down the chest and abdomen of the second campus-security official, who watched his intestines fall to the floor just seconds before he died. The first alien then lost his head with a swift backswing of the sword, while the second campus-security man had his spine exposed when he turned to run. He was blocked by the two astounded Auditors and fell facedown, his back split open like a canteloupe. Blood carpeted the ShipCom Arena and the stench of alien air leaked from the suits of the dead Accusers.

The two Auditors dropped their swords and stood against the nearest wall, faces the color of chalk. One had done something nasty in his pants.

"Ixion!" one Auditor said.

"Please!" begged the other.

Rausch lowered his sword, breathing hard. "Nothing would give me greater pleasure than killing both of you, *especially* when I have good reason to do so."

"We . . . we were only to secure ShipCom," the man said desperately. "We didn't plan . . . we never meant to hurt you!"

"You might not have," Rausch said. "But *they* were planning on it."

The second man fainted away.

"What a way to run a ship," Rausch said. He turned to Lisa Benn. "Our security cameras get any of this?"

Lisa Benn rushed back to her console and checked if their security equipment had been running.

It hadn't.

Lisa Benn looked up. "Recording systems are all shut down. That can only be done from campus security."

The one standing Auditor looked as if he were standing before a firing squad.

Rausch glared at the last man. "Lisa, get the Rights Advocacy people up here. Tell them to bring an Inquisitor machine." He stood just inches from the Auditor left standing. "Because when this is over, I'm going to nail every one of you motherfuckers to the wall."

The Auditor trembled. "Look, you don't understand! This was for the good of everyone! We're just trying to secure the ship!"

"Since when do Ainge Auditors tell *anyone* on the ship what to do?" Rausch demanded.

"And with swords!" one of Rausch's crew added.

The Auditor left standing said, "The Kuulo told us that—"

Lisa Benn jumped.

"Cutter!" she said. "I'm getting an outside hailing signal."

"Who is it?" Rausch asked.

Lisa Benn looked at Cutter. "Sir, it's a signal from an *Enamorati* ship."

"Bring it up on screen one," Rausch said.

The scene was a field of stars. Caught in the starlight coming from Kiilmist was a covey of ships newly emerged from transspace. The readout at the bottom of the screen indicated that the ships bringing the new Engine were about two thousand miles away and were now decelerating to an orbital velocity to match that of Eos University.

Rausch stepped close to the screen. "Magnify this, Lisa."

His second-in-command did so.

Rausch yanked the one Auditor over to where he could get a good view of the image on the screen. "This small ship here pulling the large one is the tug and its Engine. But these four ships. Do they look like your usual tug convoy?"

The Auditor stared at the screen. Lisa Benn raised the magnification once more. The Auditor's jaw hung slack.

Rausch said, "I don't know whose side you're on, pal. But *those* are warships. See the flanges? See those blisters underneath them? Those are cannons. And since when do Enamorati ships have cannons?"

The other man said nothing, having apparently just had a major revelation.

"They have swords and swordsmen," Rausch said. "And they now have battleships. And what do we have?" Rausch put an arm around the Auditor's shoulders as if he were a coach and the Auditor a star quarterback. "*We* have a group of humans who've apparently picked the wrong side."

The Auditor looked as if he was going to faint. But Rausch wouldn't let him. Rausch said, "Lisa, see if you can get Mr. Cleddman out of early retirement."

"Yes, sir," Benn said.

40

As soon as the lifepod's surviving engine shut down, George Clock got on the horn to let the nearest gondola know of their situation. To everyone's relief, the atmospheric chemistry gondola was about 160 miles to the north and was now changing its course to rendezvous with them since the archaeology gondola had been destroyed by the bizarre storm and the lifepod was too small to get every one of the students back to the university.

However, it would take the AtChem gondola a while to reach them.

Ben and Tommy pulled the Avatka out of the lifepod. The remaining engine was smoldering and Ben didn't want to take any chances that it might blow up on them. They moved a safe distance away, and just to be even safer, Tommy and George sprayed the engine with foam from the fire extinguishers.

Viroo had managed to regain consciousness upon landing and did seem able to walk, but only because his suit came equipped with sturdy servomechanisms in the legs and hips. Ben and Tommy had to hold the alien up; otherwise, he would have fallen to the leafy roof of the plaza.

"Ben!" someone shouted.

The students parted and Ben's group saw Julia standing at the ivy-curtained opening of the Mound.

"We saw your gondola to the east," Ben said. "It crashed. What happened to it?"

"The storm knocked it out of the sky," Julia said, pushing a strand of hair away from her face. "We had to hide inside the Mound."

Ben looked around. "Where's Dr. Holcombe?"

"He's back inside the Mound," she said somberly. "Ben, I think something's wrong with him."

"What?"

"I'm not sure."

The storm that had just passed seemed to fill the sky to the south and the west and looked as if it could come back at any moment. Ben considered the Mound.

"Let's get everyone back in there and wait for the atmospheric chemistry group to pick us up," he said. "I don't like it out here."

Julia led the group into the tunnel. Ben and Tommy supported the Avatka Viroo as George and Jim walked ahead of the remaining archaeology students.

At the entrance to the main chamber, Ben noticed the dried-out body. "Is this guy an Enamorati?"

Julia nodded. "And he's been here a very long time."

"The Enamorati live on this planet?" he asked.

"Oh, no," Julia said. "There was a totally different race of beings here. The continent seems covered by their bones and the bones of their higher animals. This Mound sits on a graveyard that goes on for miles. It's all covered by the ivy."

"But what's this guy doing here?" Tommy asked, pointing to the shriveled Enamorati miner.

"We don't know yet," Julia said. "But Professor Holcombe said the strangest thing. He said that *you'd* know."

"Me?"

Julia nodded, then stepped into the main chamber. Ben and Tommy, holding the alien between them, followed.

Benjamin then received the shock of his life: The hovering lanterns on the ledge and a dozen flashlights illuminated the hulk of a massive Onesci Engine.

"What is . . . what is *this* doing here?" Ben asked. "What *is* this place?"

Julia looked at him curiously. "You know what this thing is?"

Professor Holcombe, on his feet now, stood off to one side with two students close by.

"Sure," Ben said. "It's an Enamorati Engine."

"How do you know?" Marji Koczan asked, stepping forward.

Ben had everyone's attention . . . and he was about to incriminate himself. It was now impossible to estimate just how much trouble he was in. He swallowed. "Jim and Tommy and George and I . . . we saw the Enamorati remove *our* Engine just the other day. It was their *Makajaa* ceremony. They took out the Engine and sent it into the sun. It looked just like *that*."

He pointed to the artifact.

"That's impossible," Marji Koczan said. "This thing was organic at one time. It's a fossil now. No way was it a machine."

Jim Vees was standing at the very lip of the ledge. He said, "It looked just like this. It was *this* thing's brother."

"Or cousin," said the Avatka Viroo.

The Avatka was being supported by Tommy Rosales, the strongest of the Eos Bombardiers, but had found the strength to stand on his own. His eyes were barely open . . . he was barely alive.

In his hand he held one of the small globes that had been attached to his belt. "They are the greatest enemy your race—my race—has ever known. I killed the Eos's Engine with one of these."

Weakly, he went on. "I turned loose a very small *vehenta* because you . . . because *somebody* needed to see what we . . . what we let happen to this planet, Kiilmist, this poor world. I had . . . to bring you here."

The Avatka's legs gave out and Tommy Rosales gently lowered him to the ledge. The students gathered around and the cavern filled with only the sound of the Avatka's voice.

"I have waited decades for this moment," Viroo said. He looked back at the tunnel's mouth where the dried-up Enamorati miner lay. "I have so long wanted to do what *he* tried to do and failed."

"What are you talking about?" Julia asked.

But Ben was beginning to fit it all together in his mind. And by the expression Ben saw on Professor Holcombe's face, the old archaeologist had it pieced together as well.

Dr. Holcombe said, "Children, what the Avatka is suggesting is that we've been at war for as long as we have known the Enamorati. The enemy, however, has been *these* things."

"What?" Marji Koczan asked.

"The Engines which push our ships through trans-space are not mechanical at all. I didn't know that until we found this one here," Holcombe said. "The Engines, in actuality, are a race of highly organic, highly developed beings who can travel in and out of trans-space without mechanical means. They aren't machines, they're *living* beings, given to us by the Enamorati."

Julia pointed at the artifact. "Are you saying this is a creature that flies through trans-space?"

"Not this one. It's dead," Holcombe said. "It died when all the life had been sucked out from miles around."

"These Mounds cover this part of the continent," Bobby Gessner said. "Our landsats picked up hundreds of them. Are you saying that there's one of *these* things in every Mound?"

"Yes," the Avatka Viroo said. "They draw life toward them, then they feed. Only the *vehenta* can stop them."

"*Vehenta?*" young Gessner asked.

Here, Holcombe responded. "I believe that the 'cobblestones' that compose this Mound are *vehenta*, or their dead bodies. They are living energy organisms that travel in clouds, like the storm that attacked us . . . like the storm that chased my clone-son on Kissoi 3. My guess is that if found in their cocoon stage, they can be carried in pouches—"

"And used as hand grenades," Ben said.

"They accreted around this *creature* long after it had fed and started to die a natural death," Holcombe said. "But some of its feeding force lingered and those Kiilmistians who had survived, and perhaps a few Enamorati who came after them, tried to get in here and kill it off. Like our man right there." He indicated the dead Enamorati miner.

The Avatka said, "Thousands of years ago, just as my people had begun to travel between the stars in our sublight ships, we were beset by . . . the Onesci." The Avatka swallowed with some difficulty. "They come from a world deep in the Perseus Alley. They heard us through our early trans-space communication system, much the same way we had heard your Ixion Smith with his probing signals. The Onesci are terrible eaters of life, creatures of a profound body design, the product of millions of years of sophisticated evolution on their own planet, the first planet formed, we think, when the galaxy was very young. Over the millennia, they consumed all life in the Inner Perseus Alley. That was when they moved into the Sagittarius Alley and found us. And they would have consumed us had we not bargained with them."

"You bargained with them?" asked Ben.

The Avatka said, "We are . . . we *were* a race of traders. We told them that if they would spare us, we would find other life-forms upon which they could feed. We would put them in our sublight ships and use them as Engines."

"The destruction of the *Annette Haven*," Professor Holcombe said. "That was a *feeding*. Wasn't it."

"That, and all of the other ship disasters," the Avatka said. "The Onesci eat slowly, molecule by molecule, with every trans-space transit. But some become impatient over time and will swallow a ship whole, killing themselves in the process."

Ben had been standing very close to Julia, not wanting ever to leave her side.

Julia asked, "What happened to my little bear?"

The Avatka said, "You have an expression, 'miner's canary.' Your people used canaries a long time ago to warn coal miners of dangerous gases. I had been watching your bear for some time. It was weakening. The Engine that powered our vessel was about to gorge itself. I recognized the Ennui in the little bear."

"I thought so!" Ben said. "It *is* real!"

"The Ennui's real?" George Clock asked.

"Oh, yes," the Avatka said. "We have no word in our lexicon for it, but you do. A century and a half ago your people had sensed that the spirit was draining from humanity, but didn't know why."

Here, Albert Holcombe spoke. "But it only happened to that part of the Human Community who had frequently traveled to other star systems in ships powered by these . . . *engines*."

"The Ennui," the Avatka said, "is the cumulative effect in your population of the feeding Onesci."

"What about *this* world?" Bobby Gessner asked.

The Avatka said, "The Onesci, on their own, had found this world centuries ago. They settled here to feed. The *vehenta*, their only natural enemy, came later. They are beings, parasites, really, who follow the Onesci wherever they go. They breed in the wake trails the Onesci leave."

"Wakesprites?" Jim Vees said. "*Vehenta* are the wakesprites?"

"Yes," the Avatka said. "Some planets still have surviving *vehenta* who prowl the skies for Onesci. But they will feed on any advanced life-form. They can live for hundreds of years."

Bobby Gessner came over and said, "We made a map of several nearby star systems that have these '*vehenta*' moving about in their atmosphere. It looked as if they were part of a 'wave' coming from the inner part of the galaxy."

"That was the path the Onesci were taking when we met, when we were able to stop them, reason with them," the Avatka said.

"So you killed *our* Engine, on Eos," Julia said.

"My colleagues and I, the other Avatkas, decided that the Onesci as a race had to be stopped. Too many beings have been consumed and you were about to join their ranks."

"Then what was Ixion Smith listening to?" Bobby Gessner asked. "In trans-space, I mean."

"The feeding songs of Onesci as they moved through the Alley," the Avatka said. "The songs are very pleasurable. Hypnotic. They lure you in subtly."

The students who belonged to the Ainge Church would have heard those songs. In the Ainge Church, baptism, confirmation, and marriage all come with the privilege of putting on an Auditor's helmet and sitting at an Auditor's station, just like the one Ixion Smith himself devised.

"Trans-space is just an energy matrix," the Avatka said. "It's not God—not my God, not your God. Your man Smith brought down monsters upon your kind by accidentally hailing one of our ships." The Avatka had to gasp for air and his one lung could be heard bubbling: he was drowning from his internal injuries. "You helped us postpone our own demise. We fed you to them and let your Ainge lead the way."

"But why are you doing this now?" Ben asked. "Why us?"

"Because of the thirty-eight civilizations we have fed to the Onesci, only yours has had the intellectual ability to challenge their rule. But to do that, you needed to develop your own stardrive engines and you needed to be rid of the Ennui—your slow death at their hands. Once you become yourselves again, you will be unstoppable, if what I've read from your histories is correct. But first you have to stop *them*."

With that the Avatka fell silent. A moment later he was dead.

41

Cutter Rausch lost track of the charges he and the rest of the crew of Eos University would face when they returned to the worlds of the Human Community, to say nothing of the charges they would face if they made the long journey to Wolfe-Langaard 4 to stand before the Enamorati court. Either way, their careers, if not their very lives, were at an end.

Rausch therefore decided that Cleddman needed to be at the helm if they were to survive the threat of the warships escorting the new Engine into orbit above Kiilmist 5. Only he could get them out of this. Toward that end, Rausch faked an emergency call to the guard watching over Cleddman's apartment and immediately summoned the captain to ShipCom.

Rausch apologized for the blood and dead bodies in the Arena, and for the bound and gagged Auditors against a far wall.

"I had to take some rather drastic action to secure ShipCom," Rausch said. "It involved swords and these . . . people."

"So I see," Cleddman said, lifting his boot up and inspecting the goo the blood had become.

The main wall of ShipCom was active with its many screens. Cleddman considered these. One held a magnified view of the Engine escort, which was still several thousand miles behind them.

"The escort will match our orbit in less than three hours," Rausch told the captain. "But that's assuming they will still want to perform their insertion ceremony."

"I don't recall them ever using warships in their *Sada-vaaka* ceremonies," Cleddman said. "Where are our planetside people?"

"Four gondolas are nearly in orbit now," Rausch said. "But we've lost contact with archaeology. There's a hell of a storm down there blocking radio transmission. The sixth gondola is going to try to make contact with them, to see what the story is."

"Good," Cleddman said. "Now, where is Fontenot?"

"Campus security have turned off their com/pagers," Rausch informed the captain. "But we have been tracking them visually through the ship with transit-portal video cameras."

"Fontenot's smart enough not to use the transit portals to take over the ship."

"He isn't. But portals are on every floor and we've trained the cameras to scan for any sign of their movement."

"Very good."

"Fontenot's people are physically securing the ship, closing off the student commons, isolating the dorms and faculty apartments. Mr. Arendall, though, has so far kept Fontenot's people away from the physical plant."

Cleddman nodded at the report. "If I know Lewis Arendall, he'll keep the ship's systems on-line for as long as possible."

Rausch nodded. "If Fontenot's going to take over the ship, he'll have to do it floor by floor by hand using his own lock-code overrides. It will take him a while, but when he's done, he'll be the only man able to open them when all this is over."

"Where's Fontenot himself?"

Lisa Benn said, "We think he's with the Auditors. There's a lot of coded radio traffic going back and forth from there."

"So you're keeping the com lines open," Cleddman said.

"Have to," Rausch told him flatly. "We don't know if any of our friends, whoever they may be, would need to use the system. Unfortunately, Fontenot has as much access to it as anyone."

"I see." Cleddman pondered the screens before them.

Rausch said, "Captain, there's one other thing. The Hollingsdale deck is apparently abandoned. We've recorded no traffic from that location in the last two hours. Didn't you say that Fontenot was going to use it to take control of the ship?"

Cleddman thought about this. He then pondered the gagged Auditors and the four sliced-up bodies underfoot. "For all we don't know about the Enamorati compound on every Engine-run vessel, we also don't know about the Auditor facilities. We've historically granted them the same privacy as the Enamorati. It's possible they might be able to run the ship from there. A new Engine, after all, will only be a few yards away."

Lisa Benn bent over her board. "Captain, Mr. Rausch," she said. "I'm picking up a coded message sequence. It's being sent to us from the pilot vessel in the Enamorati escort fleet."

"Coded?" Rausch said, looking at Captain Cleddman. "Why would they send a message to us coded?"

"Because it's not meant for us," the captain said.

Lisa Benn nodded. "They're trying to send it in a tightbeam either to the Enamorati chambers or to the Auditors. The signal keeps wavering and they can't get a lock onto it."

TeeCee Spooner, sitting at her station, perked up. "Sir! I've got Lewis Arendall on the line. It's a priority call."

Arendall's visage appeared on one of the side screens on the monitoring wall. He'd apparently been roused from sleep. *"Captain, we're showing a diversion of power from the main electrical grid. The tap had your release codes. My people and I were wondering if you knew anything about this."*

"Where's it coming from?" Cleddman asked.

Arendall reported, *"Amidships. It's then dispersed along secondary lines to six areas, all amidships."*

Cleddman gave Rausch a worried look. The people who ran the ship's physical plant were supposed to be politically neutral. They were never to take sides in university affairs. Their calling was to keep the ship's functions going, no matter what.

"Lewis, we've got a situation," Cleddman said. "The taps are coming from Eve Silbarton and a number of engineers who are installing an experimental stardrive which has to be anchored to the ship's structural core. Eve says that the power use will take about ten percent from your system. That's probably what your instruments are showing."

Arendall stared. *"We've heard rumors,"* he said.

"Rumors," Cleddman said.

"That we've been handed over to the Enamorati for trial and that we'll be heading to the Enamorati home worlds as soon as the Engine is installed."

"That's true," Cleddman said. "Mr. Fontenot is acting on orders from President Porter and is in the process of taking over the ship.

Porter was given authority to do this by the H.C. Council and
Mason Hildebrandt himself."

Rausch added, "But the authorization letter was bogus. No such
letter arrived because no such request went out undamaged. All of
our messages have been going out damaged since we emerged
from trans-space. It's a ploy by Porter and campus security to remain on the Enamorati's good side."

Cleddman had to use the right words if they were going to include Mr. Arendall among their allies on board the ship. He said,
"Lewis, President Porter believes that some of our students *may*
have violated the Enamorati Compact, and he wants to put us before an Enamorati court, as a show of good faith. We are to head
to Wolfe-Langaard 4 as soon as the new Engine is in place."

Mr. Arendall, large and perhaps overly muscular, looked as if
there was no room in his body for an original thought. But he had
one of the most practical brains on the ship. He said, *"I take it that
you don't want to do this thing that President Porter wants."*

The Cloudman took a deep breath. "Not by a long shot. Eve Silbarton and her team performed several field tests of her new
stardrive at our last port of call. Remember those gravity perturba-
tions you registered? They were from one of those engines being
tested on the far side of the beta moon of Ala Tule 4. But I knew
nothing about her work until she told me the other day."

"Captain," Arendall said, *"I can't produce the power to run a
stardrive engine. We don't even know how the Enamorati do it."*

"These new units work on entirely different principles. Eve's assured me that you can easily provide enough energy for her drive
systems. And if you want to know the truth, my goal in all this is
to get Eve's systems on-line and get us the hell away from the Enamorati escort now approaching us."

"Which appears to be an *armed* escort," Cutter Rausch added.
"Take a look."

Rausch immediately transferred the screen with the approaching
warships to Mr. Arendall's board.

"Ix," Arendall said, passing a hand over his burr-cut hair.

Rausch then said, "I'm sure you've noticed that for the last several hours we've been using our rail gun. We've been sending out
bullets informing the H.C. about what has been happening to us

out here. Whatever happens to us, the rest of the Alley is going to know at the very least that Enamorati have warships."

Cleddman added, "Lewis, I believe that we are soon to be taken captive. We have proof the Enamorati have been lying to us. They have soldiers, they have swords, and they have warships. I'm sorry, but you're going to have to take sides on this one. I've got forty-five hundred people to think of. I need to know. Are you in or out?"

Arendall had apparently been thinking the matter through as they were talking. *"I'm in. But you'd better find Fontenot and his people. They've got guns."*

"I know," Cleddman said. "Meanwhile, I want you to block yourselves off. If he gets into the physical plant, it's all over."

"Don't worry about me. Just find Fontenot."

"We'll do our best," Cleddman said.

The image of Lewis Arendall faded from the screen, and Cleddman turned to Cutter Rausch. "Get word to all the gondolas. I want them to get back to Eos as soon as they can. When that happens, notify me. I'm keeping my com/pager open, just in case."

"What about Fontenot?" Rausch asked.

"He's the wild card," Cleddman admitted. "But if he hasn't taken the physical plant, we're still in the game."

"How are we going to fight the Enamorati, Captain?" Lisa Benn asked. The other ShipCom personnel looked on.

"We're not going to," he said. "We're going to run like hell and fight them later."

"Where are we going to run *to*?" Benn asked worriedly.

"Straight to Earth," Cleddman told them. "The Grays have no political clout in the Earth system. Not even the Auditors. Tau Ceti 4 and Ross 244, yes. But not Earth. They'll be the ones standing trial, not us."

"We have to get there first," Rausch said.

"Yes," Cleddman admitted. "That seems to be the next order of business."

42

Julia Waxwing was furious—furious as a Native American, furious as a human being. It seemed that there had never been a time when her people—once the Zunis but now the entire race of *Homo sapiens sapiens*—weren't being subjugated by one party or another. This time, however, there was something she could do about it. She could fight back.

"They killed my bear," Julia said to Ben as the AtChem gondola rose steeply and swiftly from the continent dolloped with the Mounds of the deceased Onesci.

"Not just your bear," Ben said. *"Us."*

They managed to get everyone on board the gondola with the exception of the Avatka. Professor Holcombe said he'd take full responsibility for leaving him behind, but no one now believed that relations with the Enamorati would ever be normal again. Not returning with the body of the Avatka was the least of their worries now.

"Vampires," Jim Vees said, sitting beside Jeannie Borland. She happened to be on board the gondola with the rest of the AtChem students. She had seen Ben with Julia and so had decided to sit beside Jim. "That's what those motherfuckers are."

"Which motherfuckers are you talking about?" George Clock asked. "You've got the Ainge motherfuckers; you've got the Enamorati motherfuckers; and you've got those really big Engine motherfuckers. Which ones?"

"All of them," Jim said.

The AtChem students, when they heard of the archaeology team's discoveries, sat in stunned silence. But once identified, the depredations of the Onesci on Kiilmist 5 had been confirmed by the AtChem team. They, too, had seen the Mounds and the grisly accretions of bones surrounding them.

"They're all dead men," Julia said. "This stops *now*."

Ben gave her a sly smile. "You sound like Jack Killian. Throw the bomb first; make accusations later."

"That's what Cleddman would do," Tommy Rosales said.

But as the gondola rose, much of the anger and vengefulness had seemingly gone out of them. At first Julia thought it was merely her concern for Professor Holcombe. They had gotten the elderly scholar onto the gondola, but he had remained strangely quiet as they shot into the sky. But now everybody seemed afflicted with it. As the gondola rose into orbit, everyone became silent.

Professor Holcombe suddenly lurched forward. "No!" he burst out. "It's happening again!"

That startled everybody.

"Professor Holcombe?" Julia said. "What's . . ."

Holcombe gripped the armrests of his seat and his knuckles went white. "They're doing it to us again! Can't you feel it? Can't you *feel* it?"

His outburst had been like a brick through a window.

"He's right," Ben said. "*I* feel it, too. It just started. Maybe ten minutes ago."

"He's right," George Clock said.

The head of the AtChem department, Dr. Reg Chassin, had been monitoring the flight from his seat, following the same readings as their deadman pilot. He said, "Eos is reporting that the Engine has arrived. There's the tug and four support vessels moving into orbit. I'm putting them on your seat screens."

The screens showed merely a cluster of bright objects suspended in the distance, perhaps a thousand miles away. But in Julia's imagination, she envisioned the very stars warping around the fleet . . . as if the new Engine was sucking in the very light of the cosmos around the vessels.

Holcombe struggling with his seat restraints. "The new Engine," he said, "is already starting to feed—"

Dr. Chassin, a man half Holcombe's age, called out, "There's nothing we can do until we dock. Everybody stay seated!"

Julia didn't like the wide-eyed expression on the professor's face. She had never seen it before.

"Motherfuckers," he said. "They've sucked the life out of us for years. . . . "

The minutes passed as the gondola finally entered the bay and locked itself into place.

"Call for assistance!" Julia shouted out to their deadman pilot. "Professor Holcombe needs—"

Holcombe was out of his seat as soon as the bay doors had sealed themselves.

The main exit hatch opened and Professor Holcombe led the students out into the bay itself. Jim, Tommy Rosales, and George Clock were right behind him. The Bombardiers entered with clenched fists, doing everything they could to fight the somatic call of the new Engine now approaching Eos.

Waiting for them in the gondola bay was Lieutenant Fontenot and as many of his men as he could muster. They wore riot gear and held stunners, the only guns on the ship. In the rear, Julia noted, were about a dozen of the Ainge Auditors, led by Orem Rood. They, too, were armed with crowd-control devices.

And behind *them* stood the Kuulo Kuumottoomaa and two of his aides, also in body armor.

"What is this, Ted?" Holcombe demanded.

"Stand aside, Holcombe," Lieutenant Fontenot barked, waving his stunner. "Bennett! Vees! Step forward right now!"

Professor Holcombe, a big man, walked right up to Fontenot, in full face of the riot guns. Julia followed behind him. Benjamin, though, had moved off to another part of the crowd.

"I have arrest warrants for Benjamin Bennett and James Vees issued by the H.C. High Council and signed by Nelson Porter himself. The rest of you will be detained for questioning."

"You'll have to get through me first, Ted," Holcombe said, apoplectic, his right hand forming into a fist. "And I'm not handing over *anybody* to *those* motherfuckers—" He pointed at Kuumottoomaa and two armored Accusers standing beside him. "Or *those* motherfuckers—" He pointed to Auditor Orem Rood and his junior partners.

Rood stepped forward. "We can have you on charges of blasphemy as well as for harboring fugitives, Brother Holcombe. Do you want to disgrace your family yet again?"

"What I want," Holcombe said, "is for little shits like you to die forever."

Auditor Rood's righteous smirk suddenly collapsed, as did his jaw. Professor Holcombe broke the man's jaw with a haymaker backed by the full strength of his body. Rood lifted off the ground and fell backward, knocked into blissful oblivion.

Holcombe turned to face Lieutenant Fontenot, both fists clenched, grim and determined. "What are you going to do now, you worthless piece of—"

Fontenot raised his stunner and fired it point-blank at him. Almost immediately, the rest of the security force brought their guns to bear on the aged professor and balls of powerful lightning pummeled the old man with a thousand explosions of spectacular light. Julia screamed terribly as Holcombe bounced once off a nearby wall, hair flying wild. He struck the floor with electrified violence.

He was dead before his body quit shaking.

This proved to be a tactical error for campus security. They had emptied their weapons on Professor Holcombe and had nothing left for the tide of students that came at them. Led by the Bombardiers, the once-obedient Ainge students set upon Lieutenant Fontenot and his men for the crime they had just committed against Professor Holcombe.

And Julia Waxwing, shrilling the way her grandmother did on wild horse rides across Hart Prairie in the moonlight, dove into the fray in what became the historic opening moment in Eos University's first fully-fledged and properly executed student riot.

Ben had never played rugby with Bobby Gessner. He had never even known the boy existed before that day. So he had no idea of the boy's physical gifts for the quick moves necessary in sports. But the Ainge youngster had executed one of the most efficient handoffs Ben had ever seen: to him.

Ben had been pushed to the rear by George Clock when Clock saw the searching look on Fontenot's face. At the same time, Bobby Gessner spun around and passed a shouldercam video cartridge into Ben's hands. It was the cartridge from Gessner's shouldercam, the one that had caught the Avatka's dying words.

Ben took the cartridge and spun around just as Fontenot had called his name, then whipped under the gondola's flanges and made for the nearest exit.

Behind him came the explosions of crowd-control stunners, and that was all the diversion Ben needed to make his escape.

Ben shot down the nearest corridor, cartridge in hand, and ran to the nearest transit portal. To his relief, no campus guard stood sentinel before it. Fontenot must have used all of his people in his attempt to corral the disobedient students.

"Command deck," he said to the portal's computer.

However, the portal did not power up. Instead, a mechanical voice, somewhat female, said, "Security override. Transmission to command deck prohibited."

"Well, shit." He then turned on his com/pager and called out. "Com, open. Benjamin Bennett calling Captain Cleddman."

Cleddman's voice returned almost immediately. *"Where are you?"*

"I'm standing before transit portal seventy-two, which isn't working," he said. "Lieutenant Fontenot has just killed Professor Holcombe in the gondola bay and now they're killing the rest of everybody else."

"The portal is now activated," Cleddman said. *"Get to ShipCom immediately."*

The transit portal flashed, sent a euphoric jolt through his body, and moved Ben instantly to the transit portal closest to ShipCom. No guards blocked him; no armor-suited Enamorati waited with their deadly swords.

Ben stepped through the gash in ShipCom's door to find bodies on the floor and a lot of blood to go with them.

Captain Cleddman was apparently controlling the ship from ShipCom.

"Bennett," Cleddman said.

"Listen," Ben said, holding out the cartridge from Bobby Gessner's shoulder camera. "You guys absolutely have to see this."

However, the entire ShipCom crew had patched into a visual and audio scan of the gondola bay, where students were fighting

Fontenot's men as well as the Enamorati Accusers. Fists flew, noses flattened, teeth exploded. The Kuulo Kuumottoomaa wobbled around the room, swordless, and with his helmet completely fractured. Somebody had put a fist through it, and most of the Kuulo's face.

"I think," said Cutter Rausch, "that the whole university needs to see our campus-security team hard at work. Ms. Benn?"

Lisa Benn touched a button. Since the university was in the middle of the third shift, almost everyone was asleep. But gentle alarms were now going off and every screen was now coming alive with the riot. Cutter Rausch specifically activated the screens in the dorms and the student commons, making sure that all transit portals led, by default, to the gondola bays where anyone who wanted to could respond to Mr. Fontenot's violence against students. Many did.

While this was being done, Ben told the entire ShipCom staff what had happened down upon the planet, especially the discovery of the fossilized Onesci creature inside the Mound and the Avatka Viroo's confession. Ben then told them the full story of their violation of the Enamorati's *Makajaa* ceremony, concurring with what Professor Holcombe had seen as a young man when he had witnessed an insertion ceremony.

"Every one of their ceremonies has been designed to prevent us from seeing that the Engines are actually newly born *creatures*," Ben said, "and not mechanical engines."

"Sir," Lisa Benn said, "I'm now showing the Engine escort fleet accelerating toward us. They're closing at twelve thousand miles an hour. Is there something we should do?"

"That all depends," Cleddman said.

"On what?" Benn asked.

"On whether or not Eve Silbarton's ready to try out her new stardrive," Cleddman said.

43

In Ben's mind, the greatest mistake the Ainge Church ever made was its indolence. For them to have had—or to imagine that they had—a direct ear to God, through the use of a sophisticated machine, created in the Auditors a misplaced belief that assumed that every human in the H.C. would, in time, come around to their way of thinking. They were the truth and the way, after all. Had more students traveling with Eos University been of the Ainge Church, had more members of the staff and especially the physical plant been Ainge brethren, the Eos riots might not have broken out and Lieutenant Fontenot's forces overcome.

As students rioted and faculty protested, Cutter Rausch activated every screen in the university and ran the confession of the Avatka Viroo, as taped by Bobby Gessner, over and over and over again. Mareé Zolezzi and Lisa Benn, meanwhile, began compressing the Gessner video into data bullets. The enormous amount of visual data would take several hours to be compressed before they could start sending it.

The problem they had now was time.

The approaching Enamorati convoy—the tug with the Engine, and four warships—was already making its presence felt. The Engine was young and the Ennui quickly started manifesting. As Ben rejoined Eve Silbarton's team, the rioting students were already calming down. He just hoped that the rioters would fight the Ennui as boldly as they had fought the Grays in the gondola bay. The physics team needed time.

Ben got to work, finding himself crawling down a maintenance tunnel somewhere near the ship's core. There were no temperature controls in the bulkhead compartments, and Ben was wearing only his regular tunic. It was colder in there than he thought possible for a ship. But he had to get to his station as fast as possible. Eve Silbarton was going to need all the help she could get, and the only option left to the dissidents now—besides not responding to the calls of the approaching Enamorati fleet—was to get Eve's engines up and running.

Ben's com/pager was open and he listened to the traffic between Captain Cleddman in ShipCom with Eve and her team strung along the ship's inner core.

The captain asked, *"How much time until you're ready?"*

"Twenty, thirty minutes, tops," Eve said.

"We may not have that kind of time," responded the captain.

Even deep inside a four-thousand-foot-long ship, Ben could feel the new Engine's pull. The convoy was closing into a matching orbit at eight hundred miles out.

Halfway along the beta spine of Eos, Ben found one of the drive units, manned by a grimy and greasy Cale Murphy. The unit had been molecularly welded to the spine shaft, and next to it was a small computer and communications unit all aglow.

"Glad you could make it, Dr. Bennett," Murphy said. "We need you four doors down. That way. The shaft is unsealed. When you get inside, lock yourself in. You'll find the unit on-line and the computer set, but we have to coordinate your unit and mine with Eve's. Wait for Eve's signal. Do you understand?"

There was a look of undisguised desperation in the young physics professor's eyes.

"Right," Ben said.

Ben scrambled back the way he came and found the correct shaft seal. Inside was a unit, already attached to the massive alloyed bulkhead but waiting for the proper synchronization commands from Eve's station about a half mile out ahead of him.

Ben put on earphones and got Eve Silbarton on the line.

"Jesus Christ, it's cold in here!" Ben said as soon as he was plugged in.

"Good," Eve returned. *"It'll keep you alert. On your screen, Ben, should be a graph with the bar heading to the yellow area."*

"I see it," Ben responded, shivering.

"Adjust the calibration carefully until the bar hits the yellow and make sure it doesn't go further than that. My computer can't hold the position and factor in the power exponentials at the same time. You will have to make the adjustments on your own, manually. But that's all you have to do. The program I've just installed should keep us from flying into a thousand pieces."

Ben heard the voices of several of the other members of Eve's team as they worked feverishly to calibrate their units with Eve's station. Some were disgruntled; some were downright scared. Some were even for giving up.

Alone in his tunnel, sitting down against the cold steel of the shaft, Ben knew what was going on and he shouted into his mike: "It's the Ennui! It's the new Engine coming!"

But nobody on Eve's team knew about the treacherous Engines and their effects on the human mind. So Ben told them what he and his friends had learned, telling them not to give in. "We can do this," he said. "We can do it."

Cleddman came on-line. *"We're showing the Enamorati escort at seven thousand eighty-two miles. What's your status?"*

"We need more time!" Eve called out. *"We're processing the trans-space tunnel to the C-graviton separation point and we can't leap across it until the computers match our present real-space location to the transfer's nexus-destination point. And for that, we need much more time."*

Dr. Israel Harlin came on-line and said, *"What we really need is a few weapons. Something we can throw at them, keep them at bay—"*

Ben watched his monitor as the calibration graph kept readjusting itself to the calculations Eve was programming into her unit. Pushing a ship nearly a mile long through a nonexistent transspatial tube to a theoretical destination point on the other side of the star-sun Kiilmist was going to be *very* tricky. . . .

Then suddenly a new voice came over the com. *"This is the Very High Auditor Joseph Nethercott. In the absence of Lieutenant Theodore Fontenot, I am asking that all students, faculty, staff, and ship's crew stand down immediately. We will be docking with the new Engine in sixty-five minutes and I want this time spent constructively in preparing for Engine insertion.*

There is no need to panic. We are still governed by the rule of law."

"Nethercott, you boob," Captain Cleddman snarled at his end of the com. *"Haven't you been watching your screens? The Enamorati are out to kill us! They've been feeding us to their god-damned Engines. The Engines are alien beings, you son of a bitch!"*

"What?" came from Nethercott.

Ben said, "They hypnotize us, robbing our brains one molecule at a time! It's the Ennui! You're probably experiencing it yourself right now."

The Very High Auditor said, *"My children. The day will come when you will see—"*

Nethercott's voice ceased in midsentence. Cutter Rausch or Captain Cleddman—Ben didn't know which—had cut him off.

"Not enough time—" Eve Silbarton continued to mumble from deep in the bowels of the ship.

And Cleddman asked, *"A question: Will we be able to move if the Engine docks with us?"*

"If it is attached, yes," Eve said. *"Except that the added mass will throw off our settings and shorten the trans-space leap."*

Ben quickly checked to see Eve's primary target. She was shooting for the same orbital position, but on the opposite side of the sun. It didn't take a genius to figure out that with the new Engine attached they would emerge somewhere inside the sun or very close to it. POOF!

Cale Murphy added: *"And we could never outrun an Onesci Engine with the Hollingsdale. Our acceleration would be too slow and if those are warships, they'd shoot us out of the sky like we were ducks or geese."*

Ben sat up. "That's it. That's our weapon."

"What?" someone asked.

And Ben said, "What if we use the Hollingsdale to project a discontinuity point somewhere *behind* the approaching Enamorati convoy? If we can project a microparticle somewhere in space behind the fleet, it just might slow them down with its gravity well or destroy them outright. If the gamma radiation doesn't kill them, it just might suck them in."

"You can't be serious," Cale Murphy said, aghast.

"Now *that* I like," came Captain Cleddman's voice.

Then Eve Silbarton came on-line. *"But who's going to operate the Hollingsdale breeder? All qualified personnel are down here—"*

Captain Cleddman said, *"I'll handle it. But I want you to get us out of here the minute your system is ready. Don't wait for my signal. Once you're ready, go. Got that?"*

"Yes," Eve Silbarton said. *"Got it. Gentlemen, let's get this thing configured so we can go home."*

Julia had never been in a riot before.

And it probably could have been fun if so many people hadn't been hurt or killed. The screaming and the punching and the pounding managed to convince campus security that fighting the students wasn't a good idea—particularly when the dorms emptied themselves of students who came into the gondola bay with baseball bats and enough rope to tie their aggressors up.

The Enamorati, however, had taken the worst of it. The Kuulo Kuumottoomaa and his companions were confused—and not a little bit frightened—by the rampaging human beings, and they were set upon before they could raise their deadly swords. The Kuulo died almost instantly when his face was punched in; the other aliens perished when their fragile bones broke under a rugby scrum started by Tommy Rosales. A dozen human males piling onto each of the Enamorati didn't leave much left, other than flexible insectlike armor, which remained intact. Everything inside became mush.

Also among the human casualties was Orem Rood, who had jumped into the fray thinking that his college-days boxing skills would serve him well. They didn't. Somebody put an elbow into Rood's face and the man fell backward, landing on the sword that the Kuulo Kuumottoomaa clutched in a death grip where he lay on the floor.

Julia stood beside George Clock, who had a black eye; Tommy Rosales, who had a torn tunic; and Jim Vees, who seemed unharmed but was bathed in a bright sheen of sweat. She herself had a fistful of hair and part of the scalp taken from Mr. Fontenot's head. But Fontenot himself was nowhere to be seen among the subdued campus-security people. Apparently, he and a number of others had managed to retreat back to the Auditor compound, where, Julia presumed, the Very High Auditor Joseph Nethercott waited to pronounce judgment on them all.

Suddenly, overhead came an authoritative voice. *"This is Ship-Com Chief Cutter Rausch. We are preparing to leave orbit and we need everyone in their rooms and at their transit couches, now. Captain Cleddman has evoked the Aniara Charter, taking back control of the ship, and will retain control of the ship until it returns to the H.C., at which time it will be turned over to the regents of the university in Earth orbit. Get to your transit couches now!"*

Then the hall screens changed. They had been showing Bobby Gessner's video cartridge results, but now these were taken over with exterior shots of the approaching Enamorati convoy, magnified in the distance.

Marji Koczan, who had a bruised lip, pointed to the screen. "Look!" she said.

The Enamorati had released the new Onesci Engine from its confines inside the tug vessel. The Engine was a bluish gray creature shaped like a giant almond—a *creature*, not a piece of advanced technology—edging toward the ship. It was streamlined, its "legs" trailing from beneath it, waiting for their anchoring posts. And its mouth was an oval almost a hundred feet wide, utterly dark inside, a vacuity whose purpose was only to drain life for miles and miles in all directions around it.

The escort vessels were now backing off.

"I don't think it has any plans on docking with us," George Clock said.

"The thing's going to feed," Tommy Rosales whispered. "Just like the *Annette Haven*."

It moved slowly, as if savoring the moment, getting nearer, nearer, nearer. . . .

Then the lights dimmed in the hallway . . . as if the ship had just lost about two-thirds of its power.

"What's that on the screen?" someone else then asked.

The hall screens ran riot with static, but then came back on-line showing the giant Onesci creature moving through orbital space toward them.

But *behind* the creature and its convoy a wavering whirlpool of distorted light seemed to appear—it was a rend, a *vacuity*, appearing at some distance behind the Enamorati vessels. The phenomenon was only visible by the swirling distortion of the stars behind it.

"I think," Jim Vees said, squinting at the screen, for it was difficult to make out, "that someone's thrown a black hole somewhere behind the fleet. Look!"

The Enamorati fleet seemed to waver in the distorted light of the discontinuity. One by one, the ships started to break up and elongate as the discontinuity's powerful event horizon sucked them in. They exploded violently even before a single molecule was consumed by the black hole. Even then, the gamma radiation of the discontinuity would have fried the Enamorati crew in their ships.

The entire convoy disappeared into the speck of darkly compressed matter.

The Onesci creature began to slow in its advance. It had been too far out ahead of the discontinuity to be pulled apart by its gravity well, but it *was* slowing down. Had the juvenile creature *known* that it was now alone? Had it known for the first time in millions of years another intelligent race had found a way to hold off its kind?

There was no way for the humans to know because the screen suddenly burned white and everyone was knocked to the floor. A massive wave of euphoria swept through the students—a wave similar to that of a transit-portal hop, but magnified a thousand-fold.

"Whoa!" Julia said. "What the hell was that?"

The screen came on with the answer: the planet of Kiilmist 5 was gone from view. So was the Onesci. Eos had shifted its position in space by a hundred and eighty million miles—to the other side of the sun.

Quiet Jim Vees found himself lying upon a heavily breathing Jeannie Borland who, looking deep into Vees's dark eyes, said, "Boy, we've got to do that again *real* soon."

"I'd say so," Jim Vees said.

The transit jump Eos University just made had awakened, and magnified, long-lost sensations in all of them. Big time.

The students looked at one another—as undoubtedly everyone else on the ship was doing as well—and quickly began dispersing, by twos, male to female, heading back to the dorms as fast as they could.

And Julia went looking for Ben. The new Silbarton drive, it seemed, had an unusual, unexpected, and *very* delightful side effect.

Epilogue

Ben and Julia did not surface for three days. Nor did most of the students and faculty, and many of the staff. Eos just sat in space until everyone could catch their collective breath. Which was probably a good thing as far as the captain and piloting crew were concerned.

They didn't need anyone underfoot in those historic first hours of the Silbarton drive. Their main interest was to determine how well Eos had made its jaunt to the opposite end of the Kiilmistian system and if the Onesci creature had been able to follow them.

Which, apparently, it hadn't. Whether it had been fried by the radiation of the dissolving black hole or not, they didn't know. When later they crept back to Kiilmist 5, the creature's body could not be found.

What also couldn't be found were the Enamorati of Eos University. Most had apparently fled into space just as the Silbarton drive pushed Eos across the solar system. They were undoubtedly consumed by the young Onesci. But the ranks of the Auditors were decimated by the rioting and, much to his surprise, Lieutenant Fontenot was demoted and put in detention when his apartment was found to be full of boxes and boxes of the illegal Red Apple cigarettes as well as jars containing several thousand wayhighs. Messrs. Wangberg and Sammons saw to that.

Ben had kept in touch with Eve and Captain Cleddman, but only when Julia was napping. When she awoke, Ben turned his attentions to more important matters: Julia. Then, after a while, he slept, too. This happened every time the captain engaged the Silbarton drive. Adults over the age of fifty did appear to have some resis-

tance to the drive. But when their shifts ended, they hurried home
to play catch-up. Everyone had it; no one was immune.

Curiously, the stock of prophylactics and birth-control devices
were lying about unused in the student health center. The student
health center, in fact, was empty.

On the third day, Ben woke somewhere around noon with Julia
entangled in bedsheets, one arm and one leg flung over him, holding him prisoner in her sleep. He decided not to move from where
he was.

Instead, he turned on his room's main screen to see the news of
the day. Students of the new student newspaper, *The Molotov
Cocktail*, were sending out bullets by the hour. New to the staff of
The Molotov Cocktail was young Bobby Gessner, whose personal
mission now was to tell the entire H.C. that organized religion was
the bane of humankind, and that humans really had a treat in store
for them when they traveled on ships with the new Silbarton drive.
He didn't elucidate.

Cleddman had a part in this: he made sure that the captains of
every Onesci-powered vessel—many of whom belonged, as did
Cleddman, to the KMA—got word as to the nature of their giant
Engines. They were to get to nonaligned worlds as soon as possible and abandon their vessels. Help would arrive soon.

But at least the truth was out . . . and so were the schematics for
the Silbarton drive, fully patented by patent attorneys Wangberg
and Sammons, formerly of the Eos University Rights Advocacy
Office. Every ship in the H.C. would soon have its own stardrive,
and the Enamorati would either be put out of business or, as Ben
thought more likely, be consumed by the Onesci in a final act of
gluttony.

And hopefully before the humans showed up. In large numbers.
With weapons.

Julia rolled over and blinked sleepily at Ben, who switched the
wall screen off.

"Mmm," she whispered. "What time is it?"

"Time to eat. Lunch, I think," Ben said. "Maybe dinner."

Julia sat up and crossed her legs, pulling back her hair. Ben had
been surprised at the fullness of Julia's breasts. The Ennui had pre-
vented him from noticing—*appreciating*—them, even from the

moment he had first met her. He began to get aroused just thinking about them.

Julia saw what was happening and leaned toward him on the bed, grasping the "little rascal," as she called it.

"I was wondering," she said, then kissed him.

"Wondering what?"

"What, exactly, does KMA stand for?"

"Cleddman said—" He kissed her.

"Mmm?"

"The captain said—"

"What did the captain say?"

" . . . means 'kiss my ass,' " he said. "But we're not supposed to tell anyone."

"Well, *I* won't tell if you won't."

Summer vacation had just begun.